St. Martin's Paperbacks Titles By

Susan Squires

One with the Night
The Burning
The Hunger
The Companion

ACKNOWLEDGMENTS

I'd like to thank Lisa Rowen for her expertise in tarot reading in the early nineteenth century. I borrowed her knowledge and even some of her words. If I've gotten anything wrong, the fault was entirely my translation of her facts into my fiction.

One
WITH THE
SHADOWS

One

Rome, the Eternal City, 1822

As Kate moved past the footmen into the glittering salon, conversation hushed. The heavy veil she wore gave her an air of mystery, but it did not prevent her from picking out her potential marks. A young man lounged by the window, his cravat tied much too carelessly. His coat, though of a noxious green, had been cut by an excellent tailor, and his watch fob sparked with diamonds. His weak chin was merely icing on the cake. And over by the ornate table laid with sweetmeats and small cakes, a beefy woman was practically wringing her hands in anticipation. A plump pigeon ready for the plucking.

Kate strolled into the center of the room. It smelled of human bodies, not all of which had bathed in the last few days, various clashing perfumes, and the pungent earthiness of snuff. Tonight she was Kathleen Mulroney, descended from all-seeing Druids. She had been called Katerina Petrova, Catherine von Duesing, and a hundred other names, but underneath she was Kate, just Kate, because that was the only name she'd had growing up on the streets of London.

Now that she'd riveted the attention of the room upon her, she made her curtsy to the delicate woman who was the hostess of this gathering. "Mi buona amica, Marquesa Trasemeno, I have come to reveal the secrets of the future to your guests." Her Italian was nearly flawless. Kate had an ear for languages. She spoke six or seven. There had been no choice but to learn languages after she and Matthew had fled his gambling debts in England to earn their livelihood wandering across the Continent. She had never called him "Father" or "Papa," even when he pretended that was what he was. To her, he was always just Matthew. But Matthew was dead and the obligation of earning her living now fell to her alone.

The room hummed again with conversation, much of it concerning her. She stood, a still center to the activity, in shimmering gray, her veil hanging from a silver Spanish comb pushed into the knot of hair at her crown. She let the tension build while she studied her surroundings. The house was Baroque, like much of Rome, its ceiling made of carved and gilded wood which framed oil paintings darkened with age. Tapestries depicting armies frozen in some grand victory lined the walls, and Aubusson carpets softened the marble floor. The whole was lit by candles set in chandeliers and sconces. Ornately carved chairs of heavy wood placed around the room looked so uncomfortable everyone elected to stand as they laughed and gossiped. The Romans were a voluble and silly race, easy to dupe.

And that was a good thing. Much depended upon tonight. It had taken her three weeks to worm her way into this invitation. She was running low on funds after her sudden, necessary exit from Vienna. If tonight was successful she would have perhaps a month of fleecing the fools lured into dependency on her predictions and advice with expensive private readings. If she was careful, Rome would add a pretty penny to the fund that would one day let her escape this life.

Best she get on with it. This was the part she hated

most. She picked out a chair that looked almost like a throne at the head of the room. It commanded a view of the salon. There was plenty of room to allow people to cluster round her.

She straightened. "Signore and signori." Her soprano cut through the chatter.

She turned and faced the room. *What are you afraid of?* she chided herself. *You've faced their surprise and pity a thousand times before, and at this rate, you'll do it a thousand times more. Best get used to it.* She had been trying to get used to it for seven years now.

"I shall connect with the Unseen," Kate continued, "that you may see your future in my cards." She performed a mental drum roll as they gathered around her, those in the back straining to see. Well, see they would. She closed her eyes and lifted her veil.

At first they clapped. But then they would look closer. She waited. She didn't even flinch at the little gasp one woman gave. Her mirror showed her every day what they were seeing. Her complexion was fair in contrast to her dark hair, her face heart-shaped, her mouth a bow that lied about her innocence. But it was the delicate white net of scars that snaked over her temple and spread out over her left cheekbone like a fractured spiderweb that made them gasp.

"I have been marked by the forces of the universe, even as they granted me sight into matters beyond the pale." Or marked by Matthew. She opened her eyes and another gasp went round the circle. The lenses she had ground in Zurich gave her eyes a pearly opalescence. At least they could be removed, unlike the scar, though she couldn't be seen outside her rooms without them.

She sat on the huge throne of a chair, dwarfed by its carved gargoyles. "Who would like to see their future?" No one stepped forward. She expected that. "Do none of you wish advice on matters of finance, matters of love? My cards see all." Of course they wanted to see their futures, the silly geese. But in front of everyone? Ahhh, now that was a different question. The weak young fop pulled at his cravat. He would be the first to book a private session, but he had not the courage for a public reading. At least these days she kept her clothes on in the private readings.

She turned her eyes to the heavyset woman who wore an unfortunate cherry satin dress. Eagerness and uncertainty warred across the woman's face. She was past her prime. But her cheekbones and her well-opened eyes said she would have been a beauty once. Jewels dripped from her bosom, heaving just now in expectation. Expensive ostrich feathers nodded from her tiara. Overdressed. She would not be here if she were not respectable, but Kate was willing to wager some impoverished aristocrat had saved his estates with a wealthy merchant's daughter.

Kate tilted her head and smiled. "Signora? Yes?"

The war was over. Uncertainty lost out. The woman beamed, looked self-consciously around, and stepped forward. "If you insist," she murmured.

"Draw the signora up a chair," Kate commanded. She opened her reticule of gray velvet embroidered with swirls of silver. An elderly gentleman provided a chair. She felt the crowd's attention, which had shifted to her cherry satin mark, snap back to her. The foppish young man placed an ornate table in front of her. The back of her cards showed black with a spray of gilt stars. It was a beautiful deck. She had had it made to her own specifications in Prague during a time when she and Matthew were flush. Her mark settled herself with much rustling of skirts.

"Signora, may I ask your name?" Kate began sweetly.

"Baronessa Luchina di Martigana."

"Baronessa." Kate nodded her respect for the title and offered her deck. "Will you shuffle? The cards must feel your destiny." The baronessa's eyes had a subtle puffiness, her nose, under its powder, was a little red. She had been crying. She didn't wear black, not even an armband. Difficult. She studied the baronessa's face. Deep sadness. Deeper than warranted by the death of a beloved pet, or losing too much at cards. And then there was the arranged marriage. How did that fit in? But there . . . she wore a simple ring—too simple for her normal taste. It was one of those grisly mementos intricately braided from human hair. Ahhhh. Good thing Kate had spotted it. Bereavement did not end with the wearing of black.

Kate took the pack and fanned it, face down across the table. "Take a card." The crowd of glittering Romans grew silent. "This card will be your past." The baronessa took a card after much hesitation and laid it down. The queen of swords. Excellent. "It has been more than a year, yet still you grieve," she said quietly, and watched the baronessa's tears well as the crowd murmured their surprise.

"How could an English woman newly arrived in Rome know that?" The older man dressed in chocolate brown was plaintive.

"Hush, Horatio, the cards know, that is enough." His wife's expression was rapt.

The baronessa couldn't speak, but only nodded.

Kate nodded to her and the baronessa chose again. The king of cups. "He was the love of your life," Kate continued. "People thought the match convenient on both sides, but they did not reckon with Aphrodite. She blessed you both." She paused for effect as the baronessa collected herself. "But let us turn to your future." She nodded and the baronessa chose again. *Let it be one I can weave into a story she wants to hear.* The card she drew was the tower struck by lightning. *Drat. What can I make of this?* A hiss of dread went around the room. No one could miss that the card was ominous.

"That seems bad," the baronness said, her expression worried.

Better play for time. "Our first trump card. They signify the large, moral questions, the life-or-death questions, the Destiny questions." The crowd always liked lore they didn't understand. Kate smiled. "This one is a sign of change. There will be an upheaval in your life." That was a safe prediction. She could use it later in many ways. She wouldn't say what the card really meant. And she wouldn't think about the uneasy feeling in her stomach. It almost felt as though someone would die. "We will get clarity from the next cards." *What does this woman want to hear?* She could fit almost any card to the story, once she got the story right. The conflict between their social mores and their most secret desires rendered people vulnerable to suggestion. Of course the woman would want to find love again, even if she couldn't admit it to herself yet. They all wanted to find love. And Kate, who didn't believe in love at all, always predicted it for them. But that was too easy. She wanted to amaze the crowd with her first reading. A thought struck her. She knew what this woman wanted to hear.

The baronessa chose a card with trembling fingers. It almost didn't matter what it was. The four of wands. Perfect. "This is a card of family. See the manor house?" She touched her temple, the one with the scar. "I think . . . I think that in conjunction with the tower, this means that your heritage is not what you thought." She rubbed the scar. "You will find you are of birth more noble than you suspected . . . and an uncle lost will be found."

The crowd gasped. The baronessa's eyes grew big. Kate would be long gone before they realized that the prediction wasn't going to come true.

The crowd stirred. A murmur started somewhere in the back. Did someone dare to distract her audience? She hadn't yet promised the baronessa love. Kate felt an energy in the air, vibrating almost at the edge of consciousness. Something trembled inside Kate in response.

"Urbano, you dog, I heard you were back in town."

"You look haggard, man. Hard living?"

Kate heard the hostess of tonight's soirée say, "Gian, it has been too long."

The crowd parted as though it were being cut by a knife.

Kate blinked. The man who strolled to the center was . . . was quite literally the most beautiful man Kate had ever seen. His skin was palest olive and flawless, his hair a cascade of dark curls around his head and down over his neck, his features in perfect proportion. But it was his eyes that riveted one. They were light, a kind of green she had not seen in Italy and intense as she had never encountered. He was big. His black coat was cut to fit his broad shoulders exactly, and his trousers could not conceal the muscle in his thighs. He had a weary grace about him. And in spite of the fact that he pretended to lounge in front of her, one hand in his trouser pocket, he was clearly the source of that electric feeling in the air. It was almost as though he vibrated with . . . maleness. And Kate felt something stir in her she had not felt in a long time.

He examined the crowd for a moment as though looking for someone before he turned his attention to her. "What have we here?" he asked as he flicked his glance over her. He didn't bat one of his long, dark eyelashes at her appearance.

"She's the evening's entertainment. Most amusing," someone said.

That's all you aspire to be, Kate reminded herself as she controlled her frown. *You entertain them right out of their gold. Large batches of it.*

"She's telling my future, Urbano," the baronessa simpered.

"I doubt that," the man drawled. How dare he? And really, his whole manner was arrogant. The creature was used to being so attractive to women he didn't even have to be civil. Apparently his name was Gian Urbano. The marquesa had pronounced Gian like John, but with a lilt. He was going to spoil her game tonight if she wasn't careful.

Kate lifted her chin. "Don't disparage what you can't know, signore."

"Oh, I know all right." He smirked as his gaze passed over her lenses. It was as though he knew her ruse. He examined her scar quite openly. He probably expected that was fake as well. His brows drew together. She flushed. "No," she wanted to say, "that is quite genuine." Then he cocked his head. "Would you care to read my cards?"

Kate wanted more than anything to refuse. But to refuse a challenge would be to lose the interest she'd created with her last reading. She inclined her head. "At your command," she said, putting all the sarcasm she could muster into it. She did not want him closer. Was it that energy about him that made her almost shiver in response?

The baronessa vacated her chair and Urbano eased into it, his knees nearly touching hers. Kate swallowed. Too close. Bloody hell. He was trying to put her off balance when all depended on remaining calm. She didn't like men, she reminded herself. Actually she didn't particularly like anyone. The life of a charlatan was necessarily a lonely one. But this someone in front of her thought everyone was in love with him, and he'd probably been right so far. He also thought a woman like her, scarred as she was, was depressed and nervous in his presence, knowing he could never find her attractive. Well, she was going to teach him a lesson, right here and now.

"Shuffle the cards," she said, holding them out. She resolved to ignore her body and his. He smelled like cinnamon and something else. It was seductive. He interwove the corners of the cards and arced them from hand to hand. The man had spent his share of time in card rooms. Several young men tried to push forward and were roundly repulsed by the elbows of ladies in the front.

Urbano handed the deck back to her. This close, his eyes were hard. She fanned the deck on the table. Hard, but cov-

ering something. One of the men greeting him had said he
looked haggard. True, upon close examination, but it wasn't
the smudge of shadow under his eyes. No, it was an expression that the hardness tried to cover—a disgust, a horror. Or
maybe pain. That did not square with his arrogant manner
and his languid certainty. Underneath the façade he was not
sure of himself at all. She had made her living for more than
seventeen years reading people, and this was one of the most
complex, most disturbing impressions she had ever gotten of
a man. Who was he, beneath that arrogant and beautiful exterior?

Nonsense. All she wanted to know was the answer she always needed from a mark: what story did he want to hear
from a reading? But that was a problem. If she judged only by
his surface, she would tell a story of triumph and adulation—
something superficial. But those eyes contradicted everything. He would despise such a tale. And she wanted to make
him eat his disdain. She pressed her lips together as his knees
touched hers and jerked away. She was actually getting wet
between her legs. *Get hold of yourself,* she admonished.

"The first card is your past." He picked a card. The devil.
A gasp went round the room from the women. Not bad for
her purposes. The men murmured, "better ask the women,"
or "evil is as evil does," or "no, Urbano the devil? Surely
you jest."

The straight reading would do. "Ravage," she whispered,
for effect. "A choice forced upon you, debauchery, abase-
ment, illicit lovers, slavery . . . even impotence." The crowd
tittered to cover their shock. *That* would teach him to challenge her. "It could also indicate a tendency to those elements in your present and your future."

He looked as though he had been struck.

"Not able to rise to the occasion, Urbano?" one of the
young men taunted into the din.

Anger roared into his eyes. She watched him master it.

His mask of nonchalance came down. "So, I am evil. Not something you would have had to go far to learn." A small smile played about his lips. She thought it was forced. He didn't address the impotence. "Ask anyone."

"I didn't say you were evil." She smiled. Let him realize who was in charge here. She shrugged. "But he who draws the devil plays close to the fire and must expect to be singed . . ."

His brows drew together. His drawl was forced as he said, "Excellent. Go on."

"This next card is who you are." He picked a card from near the bottom of the deck. "Strength—another trump. This card speaks of great force of will and personal energy, but always combined with the danger of beastly aggression." Personal energy? Did the cards know he fairly hummed with vitality? And what about aggression? Wasn't that the ultimate arrogance? That fit. She nodded to him and he picked again. Best be careful around him.

Kate took a breath as he drew another card. "The hanged man."

"I always knew you'd end on the gallows, Urbano."

"It isn't that," Kate said, almost against her will. "It is the card of trial, heedless sacrifice and surrender, even imprisonment from which only the offering of death can free you, often leading to rebirth." Her head began to ache. "A man must atone for his sins . . ."

She seemed to be growing more confused, not clearer. What would he want to hear? Did she want to tell this man what he wanted to hear? Her success demanded it.

What he wanted to know was that she was a charlatan. Which was true. But she couldn't admit that. Not and get the money she needed. *Or enough that I can stop displaying my scars, physical and emotional.*

Where had that thought come from? She didn't have any emotional scars. She was hard as nails and proud of it. In fact, she was doing just fine, thank you very much. *I'm smarter than anyone here, including this tulip.* And intelligence was what mattered in the end. Not beauty.

I'll talk about his fate being predestined. That's always popular. But, unaccountably, she didn't. "You have experienced much violence, caused through your own extraordinary efforts, and these events have taken their toll on you." Where had that come from? Maybe the violence was why he had such pain behind his eyes. But what violence could this sprig of fashion have known? No doubt some husband had called him out.

She could feel Urbano's stare. His knee grazed hers under the table again, sending a flood of sensation through her. He drew another card. "The lovers." She swallowed and managed a smile. "Do you draw nothing but trumps?"

"Apparently not."

Enough. She was going to skew a reading here. She wouldn't give him what the lovers traditionally indicated. He didn't deserve it.

She *meant* to say he would be crossed in love. But what she *did* say was, "Still, love comes. This card tells of attraction, possibly even true love, but with a trial of choice still to be overcome." Had her skill at weaving stories deserted her? And yet . . . the cards seemed to be telling their own story. *Nonsense. They don't tell the stories, I do.*

"But he's impotent, remember?" a young male voice called. "That doesn't make sense."

She closed the deck. "Impotent or not, he will find love." She had a feeling if she continued, something dreadful would be revealed, not about him but about her. Or about him, too. She couldn't tell. She blinked against the churning in her stomach. What was happening here?

"I want another card," he said roughly.

The blood drained from her face but she spread the deck again. He picked a card.

"What is it?" a woman in the second row of the circle asked.

He laid it down. "The star," she practically whispered. The crowd hung on her every word. "There is hope for redemption—perhaps through the intervention of a woman. The fates have not done with you." Perhaps he would overcome whatever had given him so much pain that he had to paper it over with that smirk and that drawl. That was something she could work with.

"Many words, my little card turner. What do they mean?" His voice was a deep baritone of course, an insanely attractive voice even though it was hoarse just now. "I'd like specifics."

He was challenging her to make the story that had eluded her thus far. She looked up. The eyes that could not hide the pain and doubt bored into her. Everyone else in the room hung on her words, the men wanting something they could use to jibe him, the women hoping for something that said he would be theirs. But she didn't have any words, only an ache in her head and a feeling of . . . dislocation, as though she were looking at herself from far away. *I don't know the story!* Panic churned inside her.

Yet words came.

"You have seen blood, rivers of it, in a desert." She blinked. The room began to swirl, the colors of the crowd melting together. "Blood you brought forth through extraordinary heroism in a cause you believed was just." She stood. The table toppled. Surprised, she glanced down to see the cards scattering very slowly to the floor. But the crowd behind them was spinning faster. "It has left you wandering in your soul, impotent. Evil is around you even now, and may still win out." Her voice did not seem to be her own. "Many trials are ahead. Thievery will be involved. I see a stone, an emerald. Your arrogance has still a chance to be tempered into wisdom by your trials." She had a sensation of falling, and yet she knew she stood, looking up at him. He too stood, staring in fascinated horror. "There is hope for you to understand true beauty and win love. You can be transformed." She gazed up into those green eyes and the room receded entirely. She couldn't even find herself, she had drifted so far away.

The green of his eyes turned into the green of a stone.

It was an emerald, as big as half her fist. It glowed in darkness. A woman's hand with long nails held it with a pair of silver tongs. The glow of the emerald cast refracted green light on the rough stone walls and floor of a cramped room. He was there: the arrogant, beautiful one. He was naked and chained to the wall. His pale skin stood out against the dark stone of the floor. "You are mine," the woman said. "The jewel will give you to me." Fear shone in the man's eyes. The woman came closer, touched the flesh of his chest with the stone. He arched and groaned. The glow brightened until it lit the cell with a blinding green light. The woman's laughter echoed crazily back from the rock walls.

And then nothing. The stone cell vanished. Kate took one breath, and collapsed.

Two

Kate struggled up on one elbow, disoriented, afraid. The marquesa hung over her with a vinaigrette in her hand. The acrid smell of ammonia burned her nostrils. She was arrayed on a chaise longue in a tiny anteroom of some kind. Behind the marquesa the tall figure of the arrogant man stood, with a frown so forbidding he looked about to strangle her. What was he doing here? She blinked, remembering. Her brows drew together.

"What . . . happened in there?"

"You fainted," he said. His tone was damping.

"I mean before the fainting part," she snapped. Her eyes opened wide as she stared at him. It all came back. "I had a vision. I saw you."

He snorted in derision. "A vision? No doubt."

"You were naked, and a woman had a giant emerald. She touched it to you and I knew it was going to hurt you . . ."

The man whose name was, she remembered, Gian Urbano, frowned.

"You shouldn't be upset, my dear," the marquesa interrupted. "Everyone has visions of Gian naked. The women at least. Well, actually, I'm sure some men do too, now that I think on it. I have them often." Here the marquesa glanced over to Urbano seductively. The woman thought there was something between them or would like there to be. "It means nothing."

He stood abruptly and loomed over Kate. He looked like he was about to shake her silly.

She cringed at the expression on his face, then mustered a defiant look.

"Now, Gian, don't glower at her." The marquesa fluttered between them and made sweeping motions with her hands at Urbano. "Out, out. Leave her to recover."

She saw him think about standing his ground. Then he thought better of it and bowed crisply. "I shall wait outside to arrange a more private conversation." He turned on his heel.

Kate watched her nemesis retreat. Had he carried her into this little room? She seemed to feel his body against hers, a tingling sensation of remaining . . . lust—there was really no other word for it. When she'd told him about her vision he'd looked exactly like the devil card . . .

Vision! What the bloody hell was she doing having visions? One couldn't see the future.

True. She took a breath. She had an active imagination. That was what made her good at her job, that and her knowledge of people. And the room had been hot. And Gian Urbano was attractive. The image of his naked body filled her mind. She'd never seen anything so beautiful, so masculine. Hard planes, articulated muscles, and then there was his . . . But it was all ruined by what the woman had been doing to him. She shook her head to banish the image. She had imagined him naked and the fainting spell had made it seem real. That was all.

Still it was bad. She was losing her touch. She was always the one who controlled the room, wove the story. She was the talent, Matthew had been the agent who turned her talent into gold. Now that he was gone she had to fend for herself. If she started losing control, she'd never earn enough to buy her way to her small, domestic dream. She didn't like her life, but there were no alternatives but the brothel with which Matthew had always threatened her, unless she had money. She had always lived her life by choosing the lesser of two evils. And between charlatan and whore, charlatan was easily the winner.

"Do you feel well enough to sit up, my dear?" the marquesa asked. Her breast was awash with diamonds, cascading in a net of gold filigree. Stones as big as the end of Kate's little finger dangled from her ears. A diminutive maid who had not escaped the nose of her home city came hurrying in with a salver holding a cut-glass decanter and a glass. "Have some Madeira. I must see to my guests." Kate sat up, and the marquesa patted her hand. "That's a good girl."

The older woman rose gracefully, started for the door, and then turned back, a wistful look on her face. "You're really very lucky. He wants a private conversation. I shouldn't have thought it . . . what with your . . . Well, it doesn't matter. Enjoy yourself. I did once. But the experience was expensive. His heart is untouchable. Don't let your own be broken." With that, she swept through the door, head held high.

Heart broken? Kate chuffed a laugh. Not likely. Whatever il Signor Bel Fisico wanted with her, it wasn't what the marquesa thought. He knew she was a fake. He'd taken some additional dislike to her, no doubt because of her appearance. Those who were beautiful thought it their right to be so, and seeing someone like her was a reminder, like a glimpse of mortality, that beauty could be marred. He probably meant to cut off her chance to get a bit of the "soft" Rome had to offer and stash it away. Well, she wasn't going to give him a chance to betray her.

"I'll take some of that Madeira," she said. The maid

poured her out a glass. She gulped it, much to the girl's surprise. Kate had cut her teeth on Blue Ruin. But if Madeira was all she had to fortify her, so be it. Now to be off. "I simply can't face the crowd out there, after fainting. So embarrassing. I'm sure you understand."

The maid nodded, eyes big.

"Can you retrieve my cloak and my cards and show me to the lane behind the house?"

She trudged up to the rooms she had procured on the Via Poli. Hardly as fashionable as the area around the Piazza Navona that the marquesa's townhouse occupied, but she had no wish to spend her earnings on luxury when she was saving for escape. It had taken her a while to walk here. She'd left the mantilla that hid her face in the marquesa's salon. That meant she must keep to the shadows, lest she have to face jeering rogues or shrinking ladies. Rome had back alleys and dark passages just like London did when she was living on the streets. But these days, being alone without protection brought back memories of the night she was attacked. Fear must be conquered, that was all, or soon one would be too afraid to leave one's rooms at all.

She opened the door, trying not to think about her strange lapse tonight. But she couldn't help it. She could practically hear Matthew threatening to abandon her for her failure.

"Don't ye dismiss me!" he'd say when she tried to ignore his drunken meanderings. He always lost his flash accent when he drank. "Gels like ye are mine for a song. Ten pound, no more. Younger and pretty and willin' ta please inta the bargain. And if I throw ye out, ye'll end in a . . ."

"I know," she'd always interrupted. "The only life other than this for one like me is the brothel, and a cheap one at that, where the men don't care what the women look like."

"And where a beatin' is part o' th' price o' admission. Ye'll end dyin' o' syphilis ye sucked from some lecher's cock if one of 'em don't beat ye ta death, or if ye don't bleed inside, slow, from a cock up yer arse too big fer ye."

That was usually when he turned violent. She'd spent many a night wandering the streets after he'd hit her and then fallen into a stupor. She took a breath. She was glad he was gone.

He did abandon her in a way. He'd died in a drunken stupor in Barcelona, choking on his own vomit. And at first she had panicked. He was the one who arranged the entertainments, dropping the right names at the gaming hells, hinting that his daughter could read the future. He was the one who got them invited to the soirées where they made their living. He'd arranged for young men to get more than a private reading from her, at least before the attack left her scarred.

She let herself into the little sitting room. But she'd hit upon another way to arrange the soirées. She loitered about in libraries, perusing the latest novels, until she struck up conversations with ladies or their maids. She took her cue from Matthew, blending in with her surroundings, appearing genteel, almost embarrassed, when she mentioned her "gift," reluctant when they suggested she entertain. One night, that's all she needed in a city, and if the hostess was well placed, she was all the rage, her calendar full.

It wasn't *that* hard. It just felt precarious. One step away from Matthew's threat of the brothel. She slipped out her lenses and laid them in a glass on the scarred table. Her life had always felt precarious . . .

Her head hurt. She rolled over and heard a whimper somewhere. The smell of spoiled cabbage and molding rags and old urine assaulted her. And something else she couldn't name.

"Get out o' 'ere," a deep voice growled.

She opened her eyes. It was night. And cold. She looked around, dazed. A flea-bitten cat slunk away from the heap she lay on. There were other, more subtle slitherings behind her.

"Ye're not wanted. Go on."

A huge man with black whiskers hauled her up by her arm. He smelled like ale. Her head hurt so badly it made her stomach turn. "Please, sir . . ." she choked out.

He shoved her down the dark alley. She stumbled and scraped her knee. On hands and knees she vomited onto the dirt. That was the other smell she couldn't name.

He dragged her up. "Ye can't stay here. We're not that kind o' public 'ouse."

She saw some kind of pity in his eyes. But then he hardened. "Get along now."

She glanced fearfully behind her. There was the garbage heap on which she had been lying. She had no memory of anything else. Nothing. Where had she come from? Where would she go? She turned into the cold and darkness. Looking down, she saw that she was dressed in a gray woolen frock. It wasn't ragged. She had shoes. But she had no idea where she had gotten them. And she had no cloak to guard against the cold.

He was watching her. Making sure she went away. Where did she belong? I'm little, she thought. I must belong to someone. She took a step into the darkness and another. Her name was Kate. She knew that much. Somewhere the cat yowled.

Kate found herself crouched on the floor of her tiny sitting room. She sucked in a breath and blinked. The memory of that night hadn't been so strong in a long while.

"I'm Kate," she whispered to herself. "And I belong wherever I want." She forced her mind to the future she was building for herself. She'd think about the little cottage she was going to buy someday. She could hoard enough to escape both the life of a charlatan and the brothel if she lived simply. Someplace out of the way in England where she could be alone, where she didn't have to face unfamiliar people who looked away or pitied her. Enough to live on—that was all she needed and enough to buy the cottage. It seemed so far away, that dream.

Matthew had gambled away whatever they earned even up to the moment he died. Getting to her feet, shaky, she made her way into her room and took the simple wooden box that held her dreams from the drawer in her nightstand. The equivalent of more than two hundred pounds in several currencies lay inside. The rooms pressed in on her as they often did. She couldn't stay here tonight. She needed the freedom of the streets. That was where she belonged.

On her way out the door, she took her cards and stuffed them back inside her reticule. She needed them by her tonight. Kate Mulroney, Kate Sheridan, or the hundred names . . . they weren't her. The box that held her dreams . . . the box and the cards were her. She grabbed up a mantilla from the drawer and wafted it over her head, sighing.

By morning she would be back in the cage, chained to the wheel of soirées and readings. But tonight she needed the illusion of freedom.

Kate had no idea where she was going. She looked up at the night sky, where clouds chased a gibbous moon. It would rain again. Running away from oneself was easier when one was dry. Her head ached. She stumbled and leaned against the wall of some public monument to right herself. She wanted to be where ancient stones poked up through the modern city, speaking of glories and tragedies that now slumbered in the earth, more tragic than her own small life, more glorious. She walked down to the great circular carriageway. Beyond lay the crumbled walls, the old broken temples, and finally in the distance, the arches of the Coliseum.

She didn't believe in God. She didn't believe in redemption. She didn't believe in goodness or love. She certainly didn't have faith in her fellow man. But the passage of time was comforting in some strange way. The world went on, in spite of petty sorrows, little sufferings, religion, war, individual death. That arc of time might be the only thing one could count on, even if one's own life was short. What would it be like to live forever? Would that make the little pains of every day dim, or would it magnify them?

She was walking around the great circle when she felt it.

Vibrating energy.

She jerked around and slid into the shadows under an arching tree she couldn't name.

She knew that feeling. She had experienced it tonight just before her nemesis appeared in the marquesa's grand salon. Was he following her? A thrill of fear wound around her spine.

But this energy was different. Less intense. She scanned the great open circle.

There! A shadow slipped down a side street. His silhouette looked . . . guilty, the way he crept against the wall, the way he glanced behind him. But, was it he? The figure seemed smaller, thinner, than Gian Urbano. She couldn't imagine her nemesis crouching.

She slid along her own wall, toward the figure, curious. It wasn't Urbano but someone who also had some of that vibrating energy. She put away her headache and concentrated on silent smoothness. There he was, slinking into a doorway halfway down the little street. A lamp flickered on in the first-floor flat. The man definitely wasn't her beautiful nemesis. His features were sharp, his eyes narrow, his nose

prominent as was his Adam's apple. He bent down and
came up with a very ornate silver box and put it in his
pocket. Then he blew out the lamp.

Whatever he kept in such an ornately wrought, expensive box must be very valuable . . .

She blinked. Here was a chance to kick her small store of
dream money into another category altogether. Perhaps her
cottage was closer than she thought. The door opened and her
quarry stepped out into the shadowed lane. She slipped into
the shadows of a hibiscus bush. He started off slowly, his
hand on his pocket. *Wait for just the right moment.* She strode
out of the shadows just as he was coming into them. Her
shoulder jostled him. His hands went up in defense. She
gasped as they bounced apart. It was done and he didn't even
know it.

"Signore!" she exclaimed in breathless fear. Her right
hand was already hidden in her swirling skirts. Her left
hand went up to ward him off, drawing his eyes in that direction.

"Pardonnez-moi." He bowed. "I did not mean to startle
you, mademoiselle."

She put her left hand to her breast, to draw attention now
to its heaving. She shook her head and hurried away. He
would not wonder that she was veiled. A woman out so late
alone could only be bent on an assignation. So he would
never be able to identify the one who had jostled him, even if
he did understand, when he finally missed the box, what had
happened. When she had dashed around a bend, she slipped
into a doorway and peered back. Even as she watched, he
shrugged and turned back down the street. She breathed
again and hurried down the alley past the chaotic outlines of
the Forum. She slid between the ancient stone ruins and
round into the circle once again. Her mark was just disappearing into the Via del Corso. She crossed diagonally in the
opposite direction.

Almost before she had left the circle she felt those vibrations again. And this time she knew just to whom they belonged. She had no desire to meet her nemesis, doubly so because she had just picked the pocket of someone who must be one of his acquaintances, if not family. She made a dash for the narrow street that ran along the Palazzo Venezia. It was dark here. Surely he couldn't see her. She backed against a wall, breast heaving. She sensed him pause. Then his vibrations receded as he moved on. She sucked in a breath and let it out to gain back her composure before she whirled and took her prize back to her lodgings. Excitement thrilled through her. She could hardly wait to see what her treasure box contained.

Kate turned up the lamp at the scarred writing table with shaking hands. She threw back her veil. It was all she could do not to rip the box open. Instead, she brought the box up where she could examine it. It was made of ornate silver, about three inches square. The chased filigree had an Oriental flavor to it, with crescent moons (or were they scimitars?) and what looked like ornate writing. Perhaps Arabic? The box itself was worth at least a hundred pounds. Not enough to escape her life, but then again, she hadn't even looked inside yet. What might such a box hold?

Holding her breath, she pressed the simple catch. She raised the lid, fingers quivering.

What first appeared was black velvet, scrunched into a nest. She opened the lid wide. In the nest lay an emerald.

Dear God in heaven. It was the emerald from her vision tonight. Had she really foreseen it? Impossible. As impossible as the stone before her. The thing was two inches across. It was cut, not in the fashionable square, but cabochon, smooth and elliptical on one side, flat on the other. But there must be facets somewhere, for the thing glinted and flickered.

It was almost . . . hypnotizing.

Her fingers seemed to reach for it of their own accord. She touched it gingerly, as though it might spark green lightning from its core and stun her. She lifted it from its bed and held it to the light, fascinated. Inside the great stone, light flashed in ripples. How could the light . . . move? It was as if a great snake was uncoiling, its scales catching the light and sparkling as it rolled. The stone seemed alive— alive with possibilities, if only one could read them. She gazed, unblinking, as the coils moved and flickered. They seemed to whisper to her, and what they whispered made her shudder, even though she couldn't understand the words. She looked closer, peering into the depths. On each glinting scale was writ . . . What were those? Tiny moving pictures? She couldn't make them out. They flashed like cards being shuffled, so quickly. She had an impression that each was a variation on the last. It made her queasy. She couldn't think.

And then the impression drained away. Her stomach settled.

She shook her head. How long had she been staring here? Light was leaking in around her curtains. Carefully she put the emerald back in its nest and closed the box.

There. She felt lighter.

Still, this was a pretty problem. All the answers to her prayers were here inside this box. This stone was worth enough to buy a cottage and keep her solvent even if she lived a hundred years. Escape, fulfillment, peace, lay right in her hands.

But not in its current form. To fuel her future, she must sell it. But who would buy such a unique stone without provenance or receipt? No one would believe she could own a stone like this. Whoever bought it would know that the true owner would come looking for it.

One man might come looking for it very soon. How long

before he realized that a casual bump in the street had cost him his most precious possession? Could he track her down? Did they cut off hands for stealing in Italy?

The gem had to be cut. And she must do it today.

Her mind began to race. Jewelers would know who could cut a jewel. Dialogue began racing through her head. *I have a necklace, from my mother. Much too large for current fashions, more's the pity. I want only the best to cut it, you know.* Her cache of money must be sacrificed to pay for the work. The cutter might also try to blackmail her for a share of the resulting stones.

So be it. Even part of the proceeds would make her dream a reality.

She should be exhausted, but a strange exhilaration rolled through her. Today, this very day, she might escape this public display of her scars, and her precarious existence one step away from a brothel. She packed the stone into its box and took it into the sitting room. She glanced around as a prickle ran down her neck. A strange dislocation settled on her.

The lightening room was replaced by a view of the square below her rooms in a single, shuddering motion. It was dark. People were running every which way. The night was lit by flames snapping against the night sky, and there was the arrogant Gian Urbano, vibrating with energy. Horror lit his eyes. Someone had just said something that shook him to his soul. The words almost trembled in the air, but she couldn't quite discern them. He turned slowly and looked at a building behind him fully engulfed in flame. His emotion hung in the air. He was appalled at some realization and that turned into determination even as she watched his back straighten. He struck off for the building. He charged inside and was obscured by a curtain of flame. He was running to his death.

And then the room around her reappeared. She felt herself

thunk back into place. Kate put her hand to her mouth. What was *that*? She shook her head as though to clear it. But it was perfectly clear. She looked around, wary. Would the room change again? But it didn't. The morning light, channeled through a wide crack in the draperies, made the room look shabby.

She shook her head again. She wasn't getting enough sleep. And the excitement of finding the stone was making her imagine things. Was she so struck by this Gian Urbano she couldn't help imagining him in circumstances that seemed so real they felt like visions? And how had she seen an emerald in her vision earlier tonight which had only come into her life for the first time hours later?

Never mind. The stone changed everything. She might escape this life and all the marquesas and Gian Urbanos. No wonder she was overexcited. She had escaped Matthew, through his death. But she had not escaped his legacy. He had given her a livelihood, and left her scarred. Was it right to hate him? He was the nearest thing she had to a father, though the relationship had turned out not to be biological. She hated the life he had left her. That was the next closest thing to hating him. So be it. If one couldn't hate one's father, who could?

And now she hated all of them, all the marks she had duped, and the ones who thought she was worth no more than an evening's entertainment. She hated the Gian Urbanos of the world who despised her for what she did. She would escape them too.

Three

Kate glanced around her to be sure the clerk with the limp had closed the door behind him. The room was dark except for the blinding circle of light cast by one of the new gas lamps on the scratched worktable. It crackled and fizzed as its shade glowed incandescent. The light revealed two hands set calmly on the table, fine hands with delicate, long fingers and carefully pared nails. Those hands did not fit with their surroundings. Equipment loomed in the darkness, though she could make out few details through her veil. The place smelled of oil and dust. An array of tools, tiny chisels, wooden mallets, polishing cloths, lay on the table just outside the circle of light. Sitting behind the table was a tall, wizened presence possessing a prominent nose with spectacles that occasionally caught the light, making them opaque.

"Jacob said you had something worthy of my talents." The voice was flat and nasal. He pronounced the name of the jeweler who had given her his name "Ya-cobe." Dutch. That was good. Amsterdam was the diamond capital of the world. All the best cutters were Dutch.

"Yes," she said. She didn't bother with her lie. This man would know this was no simple heirloom the moment he

28 *Susan Squires*

saw the stone. "And I must know that you have the skill to cut it."

The opaque spectacles revealed nothing.

Kate willed her exterior to calmness, though her insides boiled with anticipation. And dread. She sensed dread. But it wasn't her dread. She glanced to her reticule. The dread seemed to be coming from . . . the stone? How could that be? Jewels didn't dread things.

"Did not Jacob tell you I was the best?"

He had. So she had come to this winding street so narrow the houses nearly touched overhead in the warren of streets known as the Jewish Ghetto. The fact that the man had fled Amsterdam and set up shop in Rome meant he had probably engaged in cutting items with the same lack of provenance as her emerald. "And how good is that?" she asked, her voice polite.

The mouth went grim. But he wouldn't order her away for her impudence. A man who spent his life cutting stones would be waiting for the ultimate stone. He wouldn't chance missing it. Was it the stones themselves or the creation of beauty that fascinated him? Or was it the opportunity to prove his skill? It didn't matter. She had him. He knew she had him.

"I cut stones even for Urbano, and he uses only the best."

She set her lips. This Urbano creature seemed to haunt her. "That means nothing to me."

The jeweler found a small velvet pouch and upended it. Five or six stones rolled into the light. Two were perfectly faceted diamonds as big as the end of her little finger. The others were . . . rocks. Opaque whitish lumps of irregular stone. "My current project. I am an alchemist." Pride colored his voice. "I turn these lumps into perfection." His fingertip touched one of the diamonds, caressing it as though it were a lover. "Or perhaps I only reveal the perfection God created inside them." He handed her a diamond. She stepped into the light to take it.

It winked in her palm in cascades of color, a little pyramid that mimicked the sun.

"Would you like a glass?" He took a jeweler's loupe from the shadows.

She shook her head. She would not know what to look for. Where else would she find someone to cut the emerald? Who better did she know? She laid out the money that represented all her progress toward her dreams. The jeweler's graceful hands scraped it into a drawer. Then she set her box on the worktable. She thought she saw it slide back half an inch. The dread turned into a silent shout of accusation. It was as though the stone didn't want to be cut.

Ridiculous.

The jeweler's hands were perfectly steady as he opened the lid. Still, he gasped when he saw it. Then he smiled. He reached for his jeweler's loupe without taking his eyes from the stone. His brows drew together. Was he seeing that coruscating light she found so strange in a cabochon? He ripped off his spectacles and screwed the strange magnifier into his right eye.

"My God," he murmured. "I see . . ." His breath was coming faster. "My grandson . . . a man. My wife . . ." Now another sharp intake of breath. "No!" The only eye she could see blinked. "But yes, another view!" What was he talking about? Now he was blinking faster, breathing faster. "Too many! I can't see!" Then his eyes just went wide. In horror? She wasn't sure.

"Sir!" she exclaimed. "What is it?" Tears leaked from his eyes.

The man began to shake his head, ever so slightly. He sputtered incoherently. This was bad. She went round the worktable and shook his shoulders. He pushed her away and began to laugh, a high, trembling laugh, all the time keeping his gaze fixed upon the stone. Kate glanced toward it and saw the glinting scales of light moving inside.

"Sir!" she shouted, not caring if it would bring the clerk running. She pulled the jeweler's loupe from his eye. But it didn't make any difference. He stared at the stone, laughing hysterically and crying all at once.

And then he slumped in his chair, shoulders still shaking.

Kate lunged for the box and snapped the lid closed just as the door to the outer shop opened, casting dim light over the jeweler's workroom. She slipped the box into her reticule.

"Master, what is wrong?" The young clerk with the prominent Adam's apple glanced to his master, and then accusingly to her.

"He seemed to have a fit," Kate stammered.

The clerk came over and pulled him upright. His pale blue eyes were wide, unseeing. A manic light gleamed in them. Spittle foamed at his mouth and leaked over his chin.

"Master," the clerk called. "Master."

Kate would wager that man would never answer again in his life. What had happened here? She backed slowly out of the room into the front of the shop. A customer came in the front door. She whirled and pushed past the man, through the door, into the street, the frantic calls of the clerk still ringing in her ears.

Kate stared at the ornate silver box, as it sat in smug malevolence upon her writing desk. What in God's name had happened at the jewel cutter's studio? Looking at the stone had driven him mad. She was sure of it. But things like that didn't happen. That would border on the supernatural, and she of all people knew there was no such thing.

The world was formed of what you could see, and touch and taste and feel.

Well, the stone cutter had seen *something* in that stone. It must be something quite different from what she had seen. A few unusual facets within the stone had seemed to move. The illusion that they held actual pictures of events was in the beholder's imagination, nothing more.

And the impressions she had that the stone was . . . aware? True nonsense. That the stone seemed smug and satisfied to be in the box on her table was only a measure of her agitation.

She wrapped the box in a chemise and put it in the drawer with her other underthings. What was happening to her? Next she would believe in fairies or angels, or that tarot cards really did read a person's future. Maybe she was coming down with the influenza. That was why she had imagined seeing Urbano running into a burning building. She had had that dreadful waking dream and fainting spell at the marquesa's salon, too. She felt herself flushing at the memory of Urbano's naked body. She really *was* overwrought.

But how could she have known about the stone before she even saw it? Was it connected to Urbano in some way?

Just stop. This is profitless.

She sat with clasped hands and waited. She had three appointments tonight for private consultations. She needed the money from those readings or she would starve. But until it was time to go, she had no obligations. That left her alone with the box.

What was she going to do if she couldn't get the stone cut? Dared she try another jeweler? She couldn't risk driving anyone else to madness.

But she *must* cut that stone. *Even if it didn't want to be cut.*

She had to stop thinking things like that. She thrust herself out of her chair and lighted a lamp, leaving it low so shadows still hung in the corners of the room. Outside, the dusk was deepening into night.

The hair on the back of her neck stood to attention. She took a breath. Was that a presence behind her? Afraid to turn, she glanced to the mirror. It showed nothing behind her but the chest of drawers and her bed under the window.

And yet . . . She felt the throb of vibrating energy just at the edge of her consciousness. Could it be? She swallowed, pressed her lips together, and slowly turned. Just darkness. She sighed. But wait. What was that scent? Cinnamon! Cinnamon and something else . . .

Out of the darkness stepped Gian Urbano.

She gasped. Her hand instinctively went to cover her scar. Then she recollected herself. She wouldn't let this man intimidate her. She lowered her hand and suppressed her desire to ask him what he was doing here. What *was* he doing here? And how did he get in without her noticing? Instead she lifted her chin. "Well, speak of the devil."

He looked taken aback before he set his features in a hard line. "You were speaking of me?" he asked. His voice was hard, but he couldn't mask its resonance.

"More like thinking of you." Oh, dear. That was unfortunate. She didn't want him to imagine she was one of the stupid women who mooned over him.

A smug smile played across his lips. How she would love to wipe that smile away! "Understandable, but I must disappoint. I've come only for what you stole from LaRoque."

She kept her mask on, even as dismay caught at her. "I have no idea what you mean."

He advanced on her. His hands kept clenching and unclenching. He was trying to frighten her, and doing a fair job of it. "I think you do."

The vibrations of energy emanating from him cycled up

the scale until they were hardly detectable except as a hum of life. Then his eyes went red. They glowed as no eyes could glow. It was hypnotic. She felt herself drifting . . .

Nonsense! What was he trying to do?

"Where is the stone?" he whispered.

"Whatever are you talking about?" she choked out.

He frowned. His eyes went redder still. But now she was prepared.

She mastered her breathing. "Out of curiosity," she remarked, hoping to sound nonchalant, "do you get your lenses ground in Zurich? I admit they far outdo my own."

Now she had startled him. She could not help a smile. "Never try to dupe a charlatan, signore. Isn't that what you called me? We know the tricks of the trade. You're quite a decent hypnotist. Now what I would really like to know is how you get that sense of vibrating energy about you. I expect it is one of Signore Volta's electrical cells strapped to your body. And the exotic scent you wear is a nice touch. You create an air of mystery. I'm sure it is quite alluring to a certain type of rich woman who likes to flirt with a 'dangerous man.' " Well, at least she knew his game. The reason he had tried to catch her out last night was that she was competition. She remembered the marquesa's wistful statements and that the jewel cutter had said he worked for Urbano. No doubt Urbano brought the jewels he stole or was given as payment for his "services" to be recut. He pretended to be more than human to attract women. He earned his livelihood from them.

Gian Urbano was a gigolo of the first order.

He stared at her as though she had grown a third eye. Then he frowned.

"I wear no scent," he said through gritted teeth.

"Oh, I'm sure you'll say it is some essence of your elemental being, quite different from the humans all around you." She managed a laugh.

"Something like that." Anger seemed to war with disbelief in his eyes.

"Oh, do stop." She cocked her head. "You are quite good. I didn't even see you come in."

"You wouldn't." His voice hardened. "I'll take that stone. You stole it from the creature who lies dead in a house that burned to the ground in Via Alexandria. He lost his head trying to keep it from me."

Lost his head? What could Urbano mean? The possibilities reverberated in her mind. "And what would I know of this creature?"

"I saw you near there. He said he'd lost it, just before he died. I believed him. He had that look of desperation, as though he might see it anywhere he looked. But he didn't lose it at all."

"An illusion, signore. A figment of your imagination."

"Then let us have no illusions between us, and be frank about your situation. You have the stone. I plan on leaving here with it. You will give it to me."

"And if I don't?" She put on a brave face. Let him not see the fear in her eyes. He was an imposing figure, much stronger than she was. And even Matthew, old and drunk, had been able to beat her into submission when her tart tongue could no longer defend her.

He examined her, his expression fierce. But that expression turned to disgust. He clenched his fists, but it was more in frustration than anger.

Then he seemed to make a decision. He closed the distance between them in one stride and put his hand around her throat, lightly. It was all Kate could do to stand her ground. But she knew from living with Matthew that one couldn't let a bully know one was frightened. It was like blood in a sea of sharks. Her heart thumped in her chest. Was that fear? Or the fact that the feel of the flesh of his hand on her throat was . . . shocking. She swallowed, and watched his eyes get big. Did he feel it too? His grip did not tighten on her throat, as she expected. His fingers ran up the artery under her jaw, feeling her pulse. She had never felt so vulnerable.

"Throttling me is hardly effective. How can I tell you if you're choking me?"

He whirled away. What? Had she won him over so easily? He paced the room, apparently thinking. "I'll . . . unmask you for the charlatan you are."

He was looking for some other threat against her than violence. Fear washed out of her. She chuckled. "You already tried that. And now my appointments are booked for a fortnight. If you say I'm a charlatan, people will just think you're trying to belie what I said about you." Especially about the impotence. That must have hurt a man like him.

"Laughing either at your situation or at me would be unwise," he growled. He was still angry at her. He just wasn't willing to use violence against her. He began heaving up her mattress, pulling back her bedclothes. She watched him vent his frustration for a few moments.

"I wouldn't be fool enough to keep it by me," she remarked.

He chewed his lips. "What do you want with a stone like that anyway?"

She went still. Maybe the stone could still achieve her dream. "I want what it can buy."

"You can't sell it like it is."

"I know."

"You can't have it cut down either."

She took a breath. "So I discovered today."

He took two strides in her direction. "What did you do?" His tone and expression turned fierce and he loomed over her. She almost cowered before she recovered herself.

"I took it to a jeweler." She swallowed and her eyes filled.

Dismay swept across his features. "He went mad . . ." His shoulders sagged.

"How could you know?"

"I know the stone." He did not elaborate. But he looked down at her, calculating. "If you want what it can buy, I'll pay you for it."

She lifted her chin. She wouldn't let him fob her off, no matter that the emerald would not have any other willing buyers. "It would bring a very large amount."

"About fifteen thousand after you pay the cutter and commissions on the sale."

Fifteen thousand. Was one such as he so rich? "You have so much?"

"Money is never my problem."

"Then twenty thousand it is," she agreed, blithely upping the amount, and held out her hand to shake on the agreement. "Pounds sterling, not lire." But then she snatched her hand back. "I won't give it up until I have the whole amount, in cash."

"Agreed." He shrugged. "I shall visit my bankers tonight. It will take them a few days to gather such an amount in pounds sterling."

"Your bankers keep evening hours for you?" she asked, wary.

"With that kind of an account, they meet at midnight if I choose."

She chuffed a laugh. "You *are* arrogant, aren't you?"

"No more than you. Let us hope we both get our way from this transaction." She held out her hand again to seal the bargain. He took it. What the touch of her fingers to his palm did to her was more than surprising. A jolt of . . . of something tingled between her legs.

He snatched back his hand. Had he felt it too? He whirled to the door. But then he turned back, speculating. What did he want? "I wouldn't chance looking at the stone, if you want to keep your sanity long enough to spend the money." He despised her for wanting money.

Well, let him. Those who had money always despised those who didn't. "A pretty threat. What a gentlemanly gesture."

He did not rise to the bait, but slipped out the door.

Four

Kate trudged up to her rooms. She'd done five private readings. They would tell their friends. This engagement would be lucrative. But it had been exhausting when her mind had been on the strange and fascinating Gian Urbano. He had picked such an odd way to try to frighten her. Who would believe he was some kind of a supernatural being? And then, when he could have choked the location out of her, he'd lost his nerve. What kind of a villain was that?

But the night had been disturbing in other ways as well. First, word had come that the baronessa's sister had died. Kate shook her head. Coincidence. It had nothing to do with the feeling she'd gotten about the tower struck by lightning card the other night.

But what about the reading she'd given for that absurdly young man with the wispy mustache? She'd had another . . . well, whatever they were. She wasn't going to call them visions. She'd just blurted out that he needed to avoid carriages at all costs on Thursday next. What happened to "love lost and found"? Well, it wasn't as if she'd had any choice about whether to tell him or not. She had to make a push to avoid him losing his leg. And she'd seen it so clearly. Dear God, what was she thinking? It wasn't real. It wouldn't happen because she couldn't possibly know what would happen on Thursday next.

"No matter," she muttered, taking out her key. "When he avoids carriages and nothing happens to him on Thursday, people will be standing in line for readings. It's a ploy, that's all." She pushed the door open. She only wished she had more control over her strategies.

It was then that she smelled it. Cinnamon. But this time, sweeter, lighter. Not like the man from whom she'd stolen the stone. Or Gian Urbano.

She peered into the darkened room. A beautiful woman dressed in shades of plum strolled out of the shadows. Her black eyes snapped with an energy that hung around her in the same way Kate felt it around Urbano and the one whose pocket she had picked.

Kate froze. "What do you want?" How had she gotten in? Had she found the stone?

"Oh, I think you know that." The woman's eyes glittered like black diamonds.

To protect herself, Kate took charge. "I have no idea what you're talking about, and since I don't entertain mad-women, I think you'd better leave." She went to light the lamp. She'd feel better when she could see this woman more clearly. Still she didn't turn her back. This woman radiated danger, even though she was petite. She couldn't hurt Kate, could she?

"I'm hardly likely to leave," the woman snapped without ever removing her gaze from Kate's face. The light came up. The woman exuded sexuality, a ripe flower in full bloom. "The trail always leads to you. First LaRoque loses it on the way to our rendezvous. Then he turns up dead in a burning building, which leads me to Urbano, since who else could kill one of us? I thought Urbano was still fighting in Algiers, or we would have used another city. But when I accosted Urbano, he didn't have it yet. He had met his banker to arrange transference of a large sum, suggesting that he was going to buy it. He was always softer than he let on.

"And you . . ." she continued. "You, my dear, gave a very public tarot reading about the emerald, no doubt to signal Urbano you had it and wished to sell. Foolish, really. What can I conclude but that you stole the stone from LaRoque and have it still?" The woman gave a throaty chuckle. Kate was sure she'd heard that chuckle before.

"I have no stone. Is it a necklace? Perhaps antique?"

The woman rose, and her eyes went red just like Urbano's, even as the energy in the room ramped up almost past Kate's ability to discern it. "Where is it?" the woman hissed.

Kate had an almost overwhelming urge to tell her. She bit her lip and tasted blood. "Where . . . where you will never find it," she managed.

The woman looked shocked. Her eyes turned an even deeper shade of carmine. She must not know Urbano had tried to frighten Kate in just the same way. Kate peered at her. How did she do that? Even with lenses, there had to be a reflected light source to make them glow like that. The fire? But there was no fire now. Had Urbano had a source of light for his lenses? There had been a fire in the sitting room. But they had been in her bedroom . . .

"I . . . want . . . the . . . stone," the woman said.

Kate took a breath. "As do, apparently, quite a lot of people. I may have undercharged for it." Kate had her balance now. This woman had an extraordinary force of will and some experience with hypnosis, like Urbano. That was all.

The woman's mouth opened in a little O of surprise, before she set her jaw and glared at Kate. She began to pace back and forth, tapping one long-nailed finger against her lips.

"I have no intention of giving you the stone, so you might as well leave."

"I have a better idea," the woman said. She whirled so fast, Kate hardly saw her. She took Kate by the throat. "Tell me where it is, or you are going to die."

Kate looked up into those implacable eyes, coughing. She scrabbled at the hands that had locked around her neck. How could a woman of her size be so strong? Urbano's threat had been almost a caress by comparison. But the same ploy might work.

"I . . . I took it to a bank," she choked.

In the corner of the room, a whirling darkness seemed to gather behind the beautiful woman. It must be the onset of unconsciousness.

Urbano stepped into the lamplight. "Let her go, Elyta."

Kate had never been so glad to see anyone.

The woman he had called Elyta turned and straightened, but she didn't let Kate go.

"You dare interfere with a mission given me by Rubius himself, in *my* city?" Urbano growled. He was anything but nonchalant.

"You didn't seem to be getting very far with your 'mission,'" Elyta snapped.

Kate sputtered and gasped.

"I revoke your welcome. Leave my city this instant." Kate registered Urbano's determination from far away. "Now let her go."

Kate's vision began to darken at the edges.

"Do you really want to do this?" he growled. "What will you tell Rubius?"

The woman let Kate slump to the floor. It was as if Kate had forgotten how to breathe.

"That LaRoque killed you and I finished your mission." The woman called Elyta laughed. Her eyes went from burgundy to carmine.

"Who would believe that?" Urbano trembled with some unseen effort.

"You'd be surprised what an old, old man believes of a beautiful woman," Elyta hissed. "He appreciates me, even if you do not."

The power in the room seemed to batter Kate. She touched her bruised throat, willing herself to breathe.

Urbano began to tremble. A slow smile spread over the woman's face.

"I'm older than you, my pretty man, and so much stronger." The power in the room felt like a weight on Kate's chest. A sparkling blackness danced at the edge of Kate's field of vision. She sucked in a breath. It was almost painful.

A popping, fizzing sound reached through the haze in her brain. The draperies burst into flame. Urbano narrowed his eyes. Breath hissed in and out of Kate's lungs. It seemed enough. The upholstered wing chair near the cold grate to her right sprouted flickering tongues of flame. Urbano glanced to the flame, shock and dismay registering on his face.

"I want that stone!" Elyta shouted.

"By all means stay and look for it." Urbano too was gasping. The room was almost fully engulfed. "Are you ready to face the flames?"

"I'll heal."

"Ahhh, but the pain . . ."

Elyta hesitated. Then she decided. "This isn't the last," she hissed. "And when I return, I will bring friends."

The words came from a distance. The pain of being burned alive. That would be Kate's fate as well. She should crawl toward the door. But the sparkling blackness ate at her field of vision. And she couldn't crawl. She couldn't see. She . . .

Kate coughed and sputtered back into consciousness. Her cheek was pressed against woolen fabric. Cinnamon and something else, something sweet but quintessentially masculine, assailed her nostrils.

"Quiet. You're well." The voice was baritone.

She looked around. Gian Urbano was holding her against his chest and hurrying across the piazza in front of her lodgings toward the fountain. People were scurrying about the piazza, shouting. Behind Urbano, a building was engulfed in flames. That seemed familiar. She stretched up against his shoulder. It was her building! The stone was in there.

Urbano looked over his shoulder and cursed under his breath. A man came tottering out of the building in his nightshirt. Urbano put her down, and grabbed a man with luxuriant mustachios just coming up to gawk. "Watch over her," he commanded. He looked back at the fire. That seemed familiar somehow. "There are still people in there."

"Are you going for the stone?"

He swiveled his head and stared at her. "I thought you took it to a bank."

She looked up at him, still dazed, and shook her head. "In a drawer of the dresser, wrapped in my chemise."

He stared at her for one long moment. Realization struck him. She could feel his dismay, and then his resolution. He swallowed. Then he faced the burning building again, straightened, and struck off at a lope across the square.

Kate sat up, ignoring the protest of her guardian. He'd be burned alive. And what she had just witnessed was exactly what she had seen in her premonition.

Everything she'd ever had was in that building. She looked down. Her reticule still hung from her wrist. That meant she had her cards at least. But that was all. Oh, she had the money from her readings tonight, enough for a few nights' lodging, no more. She'd spent her dream money and never even gotten the stone cut. The stone was her only hope . . .

Urbano was up there getting the emerald for himself. Why, for God's sake, had she told him where it was? Either he retrieved it for himself or it was cracked or spoiled by the heat. Then no one would have it. At least if he got it out, she'd have a chance to purloin it from him.

Long minutes passed. People ran from the building, coughing. She thought she saw Urbano escorting them through the blaze to the front door, but she could not be sure because he always disappeared back into the smoke and flame. Kate pushed herself to her knees. The wait was unbearable. Where was he? No one could survive the inferno the building had become.

Behind her, she heard a great splash. She turned. People with buckets were taking water from the fountain to throw on the building. Useless.

Gian Urbano staggered up out of the fountain. People jumped back, shouting in surprise.

His coat was shredded on his back, his breeches burned away from his thighs, revealing skin red and bubbling everywhere it was not black with smoke or, worse, charred. She felt her stomach turn and scrambled to her feet, a little shaky. Dripping, he climbed with effort over the stone lip of the fountain. How had he gotten by her without her noticing?

There! He put something in the pocket of his tattered coat. It had to be the jewel.

She hurried over, resisting the urge to ask if he was all right. "Well, that was foolish." Her voice sounded tremulous. She cleared her throat. "Did you get it?" That was better.

He bent over, choking. He smelled like a doused fire, which she suspected he was. But finally he nodded. Well, then . . .

She put her arm around him, as though she was assisting him. It was the work of a moment to slip the stone out of its box in his pocket and into her reticule as he caught his breath. He'd never know it was no longer his until he opened the box and found it gone.

He coughed again, then stood upright. "If it makes you feel better, by all means keep it."

She was taken aback. No one had ever caught her out. Ever. She was the best at what she did. She wanted to protest, but she, for once, was at a loss for words.

"And now," he gasped, sounding stronger. "Let us away before we run into our friend Elyta once again."

"She'll be back?"

"I expect so."

He took Kate's elbow firmly. A sense of his electric aliveness ran through her, making her shudder. Sensation pooled between her legs. What a fool she was, to react so to a man! He seemed to have that effect on her, regardless of the circumstance. That was dangerous. He pulled her along. She squirmed, but couldn't wrench herself from his grip.

"Where are you taking me?" she protested as he guided her out of the square.

"To my mother."

Whatever answer she expected, it certainly wasn't that one. To his mother? It left her speechless for the second time tonight.

For one thing, it seemed so . . . unthreatening. And all he had done was threaten her since the moment she met him. She had no illusion she could keep the stone if he wanted to wrest it from her. His grip on her elbow told its tale of strength, despite his being burned.

At first he walked slowly and painfully, but soon she had to skip to keep up with him. In truth, she felt dazed by all that had happened. Red eyes, her vision of what had happened here tonight, a woman who nearly killed her, then waking up in the square with fire eating up all her hopes and Urbano rushing inside a burning building after the stone . . . She was numb.

She recognized the Piazza Navona as they hurried past Bernini's three fountains. Then, across from a park filled with ancient plane trees that lined the river Tiber, they came to a façade of old stone and arched windows. The door was opened by a very discreet servant, dressed in black, who gasped at the sight of Urbano.

"It isn't as bad as it looks, Paolo," Urbano murmured.

"May I attend you, signore?" the servant asked, concerned. Then his gaze found Kate.

"No. But your wife will attend to Miss . . . Mulroney." She had never told him her name, so he must have asked after her. "She has lost everything in a fire, but I'm sure there are . . . things enough somewhere . . . to provide . . ." He trailed off, looking around. Perhaps he was dazed too.

Kate examined him more closely in the light of the well-lit foyer. His burns weren't as bad as she'd first thought. She had imagined charred flesh beneath the holes in his clothes, but now it was really only reddened, blistered skin and soot. But he was still burned. How was he even standing? How had he hurried her across the entire Centro Storico of Rome?

A huge standing clock against the wall struck one A.M. Urbano blinked. "Have my carriage ready at five, and Piccolo. Pack a trunk."

"Do you . . . travel during daylight?" Paolo asked. He was hovering anxiously now.

"I'll ride inside the carriage during the day." Urbano staggered toward an elegant curved staircase with a carved wooden balustrade. They both stared as he trudged up the stairs. At the top he turned. "Oh, and did I say you should prepare a trunk for Miss Mulroney as well?"

Paolo nodded, though Urbano had done no such thing. Even trusted servants didn't dare contradict him. What must it be like to work for a man so arrogant and unfeeling? She looked around. The house was furnished with taste and elegance. That painting there . . . was it . . . was it a da Vinci?

It had all the humanity of the master shining from the face of the middle-aged portrait subject. And there, the one that hung at the landing of the staircase . . . surely the pastels of a Botticelli. How did even a first-rate gigolo afford such luxury?

She didn't care. She would be gone soon. These servants didn't seem too formidable. She need only wait until Urbano was asleep.

Paolo rang the bellpull at one end of the foyer. He was a compact man with snapping brown eyes and a fringe of longish hair around a bald pate. If he was nonplussed by his master bringing home an unescorted female at one in the morning, he gave no sign. It probably happened frequently, Kate thought grimly.

"Are you injured, signorina?" he asked, though he kept glancing up to where his master had disappeared.

Kate put her hands to her throat. Bruises must be forming even now. What must he think? "A bit knocked about. I . . . I hope your master is well." He had, after all saved her life tonight.

The thought struck her forcibly. She should be grateful to him. How dreadful.

But he had done it only because he thought she had the stone in some bank and he would need her to retrieve it. That thought made her relax. She didn't owe him anything.

"He is very . . . resilient," Paolo observed. "Still, I should go to him."

A woman appeared whose hair was just going gray under her cap and whose figure indicated a sincere and lasting love of pasta. She was fully dressed, even at this hour. Urbano no doubt kept them up to attend his every need no matter how late he returned.

"Sophia, just see to Miss Mulroney while I go up to the master," Paolo said. "She's lost everything in a fire, and we're to provide. A trunk must be packed and ready by five."

"He goes just before dawn?" Sophia asked, incredulous.

"Apparently there is no time to be lost." He bowed to Kate and trotted up the stairs.

Sophia surveyed Kate and threw up her hands. "My poor child!" she clucked. "Whatever has happened to you?"

Kate looked down at her dress, its ethereal gray now streaked with real smoke, and its hem tattered in one place by . . . by flames? Had the fire been that close? Thank goodness for Urbano's lust after the stone, or she would have burned to death. She looked a sight . . .

Her scar! She raised her hand to her cheek to hide it. She hadn't noticed Sophia looking at it, and so had forgotten for a moment.

"Now, now, let's just take that nasty dress off and get you a bath." Sophia put her arm around Kate.

Perhaps a bath would be good. And Kate couldn't escape looking like this with no money, and no clothes and no . . . anything. The enormity of her situation struck her. The stone couldn't be cut. It was no good to her even if she did escape. Urbano could take it back any time as long as she was almost a captive in his house. She felt her eyes fill. She sniffed. She couldn't be weak. Weakness attracted predators.

"Things will look better after a bath. And perhaps a few hours' rest."

Kate let the chattering woman lead her up the stairs. What else could she do?

"It must be difficult working for such a master," Kate observed to Sophia, as she stepped into the steaming bath the servant girls had brought.

"In what way?" Sophia asked, handing her the soap.

"Well, he is so . . . arrogant . . . his callous disregard of your comfort . . ." She sank down into the water and let its warmth seep into her bones.

"Arrogant, yes, sometimes." Sophia chuckled. "I think he has not heard the word 'no' enough in his life. But he never disregards our comfort."

"But . . . keeping you up so late, just to attend to him at this odd hour . . ."

"Oh, we sleep in the day as he does." Sophia bustled about. She had procured a night rail from somewhere, made of very delicate linen covered with fine white embroidery. It did *not* belong to a servant girl. Sophia laid it out on the bed. Perhaps it was part of the services provided by a first-rate gigolo. "He pays us most generously to keep his backward hours," Sophia continued. "He has bought Paolo and me a house in my village, so we may have a place when we are old. My mother lives there now, and he pays her as caretaker."

This was surprising. But no, he would have to buy their silence. His clients must be able to count on his discretion and that of his servants. Kate soaped her body, grateful to be clean again. "Does he stay up all night every night?" Such decadence!

"The poor man. He has an affliction. The sun burns his skin and hurts his eyes." Sophia sighed. "The Lord has made him pay a terrible price for his beauty. He has only the night."

That explained why he met his banker at midnight.

Kate stood and Sophia wrapped a towel around her. "Now just you stand in front of the fire to keep warm. You've had a shock tonight."

Yes, she had. Now she was in the power of a man who had threatened her at every turn. She was trapped in his power by her circumstances. She cast a glance over to where her reticule, lumpy with its precious burdens of the

stone that would save her and her tarot cards, sat upon the
dresser. The stone was useless to her without him. Who else
would pay her for it, when it drove men mad? She looked
around, feeling trapped.

Sophia must have seen her look. "Now, now, child, the
master will take care of you. You needn't worry. He is the
kindest, most generous man. I know he seems arrogant. But
put your trust in him. He will not fail you."

Kate was about to protest that he was the last man she
would ever trust, when Sophia put a finger to Kate's lips. "I
know what you are thinking, that he is taking you in a carriage all alone, but you need not fear for your virtue. He is a
gentleman of honor."

Kate could not help be feel bewildered. His servants'
high opinion of the man seemed senseless in view of what
they must know about his source of income. Paolo had been
positively anxious for his welfare, and this woman doted on
him. Perhaps they didn't know him well. "How long have
you been with him?"

"Twenty years and more." Sophia smiled, slipping the
night rail over her head. "Now, you just tuck into bed here for
a few hours." Sophia held back the richly embroidered linens
and Kate crawled up into a bed layered with feather com-
forters. "I'll come to wake and dress you. Don't worry your
head about packing." Sophia scooped up her burned dress,
and turned down the lamps before she let herself out the door.

Well, that finished Kate's chance to escape for the moment. She couldn't go out in a night rail. She had very little
money. She was so confused she didn't know if she should
escape or be carried along by Urbano's plans. Which was
the lesser of two evils? In Rome, a woman wanted to kill her
for the stone. If she could keep the stone from Urbano, get it
cut . . . perhaps his mother would even be her ally. A mother
must know what he was. Her thoughts were becoming muddled. Jealousy that he knew his mother and felt he could

depend on her wafted through Kate. Oh, well. She'd puzzle it out after she closed her eyes for just a moment . . .

" 'Ey! You there!"

Kate looked up from a garbage heap not so different from the one where she had awakened three nights ago. She wiped her mouth, ready to dart away. Too bad. This had been a good one. She stuffed the gristle left from someone's beefsteak into the pocket of her dirty pinafore and scrambled out of the moonlight.

"No, wait!"

She crouched behind the barrel set to catch rainwater by the tavern owner. The figure that accosted her was much smaller than those who had chased her off in the last days, its voice higher. It came into the moonlight now, approaching slowly. A boy. A ragged boy.

"I won't 'urt ye," he said, holding out a hand.

Kate said nothing. She knew she should try to make it down the alleyway. She had bruises over her back and shoulders for tarrying once too long. But this was the first child she had seen. Well, he was bigger and older than she was. But he wasn't a grown-up.

"Ye're 'ungry, ain't ye?" He fished in his pocket. "D'ye like a bit o' sweet?"

He held out a misshapen and half-melted lump. "A little 'ore'ound?"

She shook her head, though she could smell the sugar of it from the shadows where she lurked quite clearly. It made her mouth water.

"I bet ye'd like some mutton and gravy and roasted nips," the boy went on, approaching.

Nothing had ever sounded so good. Kate's stomach rumbled. The rain began again. Just when she'd been drying out.

"I knows a place where a nimble little one like ye, if

ye're quick ta learn and eager ta please, could get a roof over yer 'ead and a warm blanket and three squares."

"Where is that?" Kate asked in a small voice.

"Sir'll take ye in."

The man they all called "Sir" was impossibly tall and gaunt. His nose had a funny hook in it, but it wasn't that that made her afraid. Just now he stood in front of a coal fire that lit the cellar with flickering light. Children huddled in the corners under blankets, their stomachs full of the stew that still wafted its smell over the dank scent of brick walls underground.

But Kate's stomach wasn't full.

"Ye cain't eat till ye get me purse off me, gel."

Kate wanted to cry. She was so hungry she couldn't think. And he always caught her. She'd sidled up to him a dozen times and slipped her hand in the capacious pocket of his coat.

"If ye don't get it this time, it's out in the cold fer ye," he threatened.

Tears welled. She'd spent last night in the cold, hovering outside the door, wet and shivering. She couldn't do that again. She couldn't. She wanted whatever was left of that stew, and this dreadful man wouldn't give it to her, and she didn't even know who she was, or who might want her, so this man was her last hope. The other children wouldn't help her.

The boy who found her—his name was Ralph—was the only one who would speak to her at all. Today he told her about something called "hit 'n' go." She'd like to hit something. Sobs choked her. The man didn't understand that she couldn't get his purse if she couldn't think, and she couldn't think when she hadn't eaten in so long. The tears turned angry. Why didn't he just tell her how to do it? Maybe he was keeping the secret from her on purpose.

But maybe Ralph had told her how to do it. She thought back to this afternoon.

And launched herself at the man. She just ran smack into him, even as she reached for his pocket. He lifted his hands. She slipped inside the pocket and spun away.

The purse was somehow, miraculously, in her hand. She looked up, still heaving breath.

"Well, it's about time, I'd say," the man called Sir said. "Let me get ye some stew."

Kate opened her eyes on darkness. Sir had indeed taken her in. Maybe her anger had saved her. She ran her hand over the embroidered bed linens, as her surroundings thunked back into place. She was in a bedchamber belonging to a rich gigolo in Rome, not in the squalid streets of London. Twenty-three years had passed since she'd gained entrance to that strange society of thieves, one of several times her life had taken a dramatic turn. Thank God for Sir. An irrational drunk, given to beatings when one didn't bring back the fancy, but without him she'd have starved on the street.

The door cracked open and Sophia poked her head in, holding a lamp.

"I'm awake," Kate said. She had a feeling her life was about to take another turn.

Five

The carriage stopped on the outskirts of Rome as the sun was coming up. What was toward? Kate didn't peer out the window. She didn't want to look like she cared. She pulled the light cloak of fine merino wool in a very becoming wine color about her more tightly. The sable of the ruff around the hood was silky against her neck. The traveling dress Sophia had produced was likewise wine-colored, a sophisticated lustring with dyed Brussels lace lining its hem and its decidedly décolleté square neckline. It wasn't an appropriate color or design for a girl. But then, neither was her usual gray, which made her look as though she was a year into mourning or some kind of a ghost already. The hat Sophia provided was a confection of sophisticated feathers. Kate had firmly refused the garnet-encrusted crucifix and earring drops, but she would wager they were in that trunk the footmen had tied up at the back of the carriage. Sophia had produced a wide ribband to conceal the bruises on her neck.

Kate pressed her lips together grimly. She was no doubt wearing a dress of Urbano's latest mistress. How humiliating to take another's leavings. But beggars couldn't be choosers. And she was a beggar, surely.

The only thing Sophia had not managed to procure was a veil. No mantilla, no scrap of netting. Kate felt positively naked without something to cover her scar. At least she still carried her reticule with its precious cargo. What cared she that the gray velvet embroidered with silver did not match her fine new outfit? What counted was that the gleaming emerald still lay inside, tantalizing her, along with her cards. Her dreams were so close, yet so elusive. Urbano could take the stone without paying for it at any time. And if no one paid for it, it was useless to her.

She heard him shouting to the driver. Urbano made her uneasy in ways she couldn't explain. His red eyes were only lenses. There must have been a source for the reflected light. She still wasn't certain how he achieved that feeling of electric aliveness he shared with the woman called Elyta and the man from whom Kate had stolen the stone. And Urbano's disconcerting way of coming and going without one quite knowing how he got there . . . She set her lips. He must practice it carefully. He really had a most successful "man of mystery" act. No wonder women paid so much to keep him. She'd bet he had other services at which he was skilled . . . And that brought her to the other way he made her uneasy. She had not reacted to a man like she reacted to Urbano . . . ever, really. Even now, knowing he was just outside the carriage door made her conscious of her body in ways that she'd never been before.

She wouldn't think about that. Fruitless. He would never feel the same about her. She shook herself mentally. And what of Elyta? She shared Urbano's lenses and whatever he did to make himself seem so vibrant. But her strength . . . Kate shuddered. That had been real enough.

The door to the carriage opened abruptly and Urbano swung up into the coach. The small space immediately filled with the cinnamon scent he affected and that electric energy. Could he not leave off with his fraudulent ways, even when she was his only audience, and she'd already sniffed out his lay? He had been riding beside the carriage until now on a prancing dark bay stallion he called Piccolo. Piccolo was undoubtedly the finest piece of horseflesh Kate had ever seen, though altogether frightening to a city girl, and hardly deserving of a name that meant "little one." Urbano seemed recovered from his burns. How, even if she had been mistaken about the charred flesh she had first imagined? In the light of his foyer, the skin had definitely been red and blistered. He *had* been burned. She fidgeted in her seat.

"Excuse my intrusion," he murmured.

"The carriage is yours, sir, the intrusion mine." She made her voice frosty to discourage any intentions he might have of fraternizing. Sophia and her husband were obviously besotted with him. Therefore Sophia's opinion that he was a man of honor was worthless. How could a gigolo have honor? And if Gian Urbano had any thoughts of . . . seduction . . . or rape . . .

Nonsense! What man would seduce a woman as scarred as she was? None. Not ever. It was just as well she had no veil. Let him constantly be reminded that she was unattractive. That was her protection. It just didn't feel like a fortunate thing.

He reached across her to pull down the window shade on her side, jerked down the shade on his side, and wedged himself into the farthest corner from her. She suppressed a shudder as his elbow brushed her shoulder. It was not a shudder of revulsion. She truly hoped the man had no idea what effect he had on her. But she knew by his habitual arrogance that her hope was vain.

"I regret to impair your view of the passing countryside, but I am sensitive to the sun."

"As you wish," she said, and pointedly closed her eyes, as though she could sleep a wink with him in the carriage not three feet from her, exuding maleness and making her almost vibrate in sympathy in places she dared not name.

"I thought you would accost me immediately about the bargain between us," he remarked in that baritone that wound around her spine. "Or question my intent in taking you to Firenze."

She opened her eyes. So that was where they were headed. Now he would tell her his despicable plan. Best face it head-on. "You hadn't deigned to tell me our destination," she pointed out. "I assumed you had rethought your 'bargain.'" He was just going to take the stone and leave her somewhere on the road. She knew it.

He examined her, then turned abruptly away. "We could not tarry in Rome while Elyta Zaroff made new plans," he muttered. "Firenze serves two purposes. My mother will lend you her protection and her banker will arrange with mine the transfer you require."

Kate narrowed her eyes. If he could just take the stone, why wouldn't he? He must want something else. In her case it could not be that he wanted use of her body. "You could just take it." She wasn't telling him anything he didn't already know. "Yet you say you intend to pay me. What else do you want?"

He hesitated. "Do I have to want something?"

Kate racked her brain. Could he want her skills at deception? "People always do."

"Then perhaps I will surprise you."

This talk of paying her must be a ruse to keep her quiet on the journey. But why? Why didn't he just leave her in Rome? Even if he did have a mother in Florence, what mother would accept a light-skirt traveling alone in the company of a bachelor, even if that bachelor were her son? *Especially* if it were her son? If she didn't know about his profession, she would have aspirations for his marriage that did not include a penniless fake of no birth. If she did know, she certainly wouldn't want him to compromise his source of income by associating with a ne'er-do-well. No, Kate was the last thing Urbano's mother would welcome on her doorstep.

"I see you don't believe me." He changed to English from Italian. He spoke with barely an accent and what accent he had was, of course, incredibly attractive. "Perhaps I was mistaken and you have a husband or a father to whom I may deliver you?"

He wanted to remind her of her orphaned state to make her feel powerless. Well, she would just show him how much that mattered to her. "I have neither, and I have never given it a thought. I once traveled with a man I thought was my father. It turns out he was not," she said with almost complete composure. She kept to the Italian, lest his speaking English was a condescension. He must not think her weak or vulnerable. "He admitted as much to me in one of his drunken rages. He bought me from an orphanage and trained me to use in his schemes. Apparently he also hired thugs to attack me when I was seventeen and leave me with this . . ." She swallowed. "This scar, so I could not even escape him by entering into a liaison with some gullible but wealthy young man. He died." She realized she had switched to English. Damn it all, it seemed as though he had won something. "And I am doing just fine without him."

His eyes widened for a single instant. Then he looked down at his hands. "So you are glad to be rid of him." He kept to the English.

She'd already let him win, there was no use going back to Italian. "Absolutely," she said, with only an instant's hesitation. "I was the talent of the operation."

"It must be . . . hard, with no one to care about you," he said, after a moment.

He *pitied* her? Anger rose in her belly. She couldn't bear it if he pitied her. So she shrugged. "My real parents abandoned me when I was six. I made my way on the streets of London, so I am quite used to it."

"At six?" he asked, his brows drawing together.

"Oh, I found a place. A rather nefarious character provided food and a bed in return for picked pockets and robbed houses. No locksmith has made a device I cannot open." *That* would shock him. And she wanted to shock him with her hardness, her invulnerability.

"So how did you end in an orphanage?" Enough light leaked in around the shades to make his face dimly visible in the shadows.

"The Nefarious Character was clapped up in Newgate and that left us on our own." Those days had been hungry ones. She had been frightened. "The nuns finally came round to collect what was left of us in an act of charity and duty." She let her tone tell him how she despised their impulse. "I spent five years in the orphanage. Until I was fourteen."

"Better than the streets."

"Was it?" She leaned back against the black velvet squabs of the upholstery.

"Ahhh. Another version of indentured servitude."

He understood. That was odd. She pulled her chin up. "I was quite a trial for the sisters. They tried their best to beat the sin out of me. When Matthew claimed me, I wouldn't have cared whether he was my father or not. He was the one who trained me to act and talk flash."

"My congratulations. No one would think you were from any but the first of families."

Kate looked away. It had been nice in a way to think she had a father. It gave her a place. And she'd tried hard to please Matthew. The fact that he constantly threatened to abandon her again helped motivate her, though she had always told him she didn't care. That had been a lie, like so much else in her life. Well, he'd lied too. Everyone did. All

the time. Just like Gian Urbano was probably lying now
about paying her, about his mother. She glanced at him and
found him staring at her in a most disconcerting way.

"Well," he said slowly, as though considering his words.
"I see no event in your background which would have de-
veloped your 'powers.' Did you train to develop them?"

Now he *was* making game of her. He knew very well she
didn't have "powers." "Don't be rude. I learned the tarot because it can be bent to anything someone wants to hear. And
I'm very good at reading people." Except she couldn't read
him at all. The cards had seemed to take over and make
their own story when it came to him, and she had blurted
out some prediction over which she had no control. She
blinked at him, trying to master the fear that that brought up
inside her. She rushed into conversation so she didn't have to
think. "So you needn't take pity on me. I'm fully capable of
caring for myself. If you're going to take the stone, do it."

"Why don't you keep it for the nonce?" he remarked after a short silence. "It would spoil the cut of my coat if I
kept it in my pocket."

She narrowed her eyes. What kind of game *was* he
playing?

"So," he said, examining her as though he saw everything she wanted to hide from him. "What will you do with
the money?"

As if he would pay. She grimaced, seeing her dreams
slip away. Still, he could have stolen the stone last night. He
didn't have to take her with him. She searched his face. She
saw no answers. She looked away. "I am going to buy a
house, of course."

"After such a life of adventure, can one city amuse you?"
Was that a smirk?

"I'm not going to buy a house in a city," she retorted.
"I . . . I want to live somewhere out of the way." That was an
unfortunate way to put it. "I mean, somewhere quiet.

Twenty thousand will buy a cottage in England and keep me nicely."

"Quiet means no audience."

"Oh, and you think I love an audience!" He thought she *liked* to display herself for public pity? She turned away again, so he couldn't see the scar.

"I think you are very good at what you do," he said, clearing his throat. "I expect it would be hard to give that up."

"And you *so* respect what I do." She snorted. He, who had tried to unmask her . . .

He sat back, one leg lounging out before him. "I respect that you made your own way. You are intelligent, intuitive. I didn't say I respected the purpose to which you put your talents."

She snapped her head around to confront him. "Oh, you don't respect survival?"

"Honor is important. There were other ways to survive."

"Matthew always said my only choice was between chicanery and a brothel, since I had no money, no birth, and no looks. And a brothel of the lowest kind. Is there honor in that?"

The corner of the carriage was silent.

"And you know so much about honor anyway," she accused. "You who use your beauty to enthrall women. You take, but you never give, do you? Is there honor in that?"

He straightened, a little shocked. Good. "I . . . I never make promises I don't keep."

"Oh, you don't lie about loving them. How noble." She folded her arms across her chest.

His mouth gave something like a sneer. "They only want to say they've bedded me. I'm a trophy that gives them bragging rights. I see to their pleasure, but they deserve nothing more."

She felt her jaw drop. The . . . the *arrogance* of the man! He wanted them to give something of themselves, when he was already bleeding them for money? And he must be mad to think he didn't break hearts, if not the hearts of the rich women who kept him, then those of the ones who couldn't afford that luxury. "You can't tell me young girls have never pined after you until they fell into a decline. You're just the type to provoke that without any conscience."

"I don't seduce virgins." But he was looking guilty. He knew she was right.

"Just married women?" She snorted her contempt. "Now *that* is honorable."

He looked exasperated. "I *prefer* widows, but there are plenty of women coerced into marriage who manage to enjoy life by taking lovers. I've played my part in their charade."

"It's *their* charade, is it?" When his whole life was a charade?

"Yes." His eyes narrowed.

"Well, I'll tell you, Gian Urbano . . ." But he actually had her speechless. She folded her arms across her chest and closed her eyes. "I'm going to sleep." How would she bear being cooped up with this insufferable man all the way to Florence?

Kate woke with a start to find Urbano shaking her shoulder. "What?" she asked crabbily. The carriage was no longer rocking.

"Would you like to break your fast?" he asked, shrugging. "We are changing horses."

"Oh. Well, yes." Actually, she was famished. And the feel of Urbano's strong hand on her shoulder made her . . . irritable. She reached for the door handle. Urbano slid farther into the shadows in the corner. She glanced over at him. He looked very tired. That brought to mind the fact that he had been injured last night, though he showed little sign of it this morning. He was a puzzling creature. And he might be more than puzzling. He might be . . . whatever that woman, Elyta, had been. What was that?

Nonsense! She refused to think about the Elyta woman. Urbano was simply an arrogant charlatan. Not unlike herself. That thought hurt. She didn't want to have anything in common with this creature.

Yet she couldn't afford to make him angry. She was, at the moment, dependent upon him. She cleared her throat. "Will it cause you discomfort if I open the door?"

"It is nothing. Perhaps you should leave your reticule here for safekeeping."

"Perhaps I don't think that would be safe," she returned.

"As you wish, then. *Buon appetito*. Luigi will accompany you."

That was the coachman. She had heard Urbano call instructions to him. There was a postboy as well, Adolpho. She took her lip between her teeth. Urbano would have to stay inside. Which meant no breakfast for him, or luncheon, whatever time it was. She had no idea how long she'd slept. Well, then, she'd order him some food as well.

Except she didn't want to spend the little money she had feeding her nemesis.

"Luigi will pay the shot," he remarked from the shadows in the corner. He seemed to read her mind. How exasperating!

"You can deduct it from the payment for my stone." She opened the door. Luigi, once a large, athletic specimen now just going soft about the middle, hovered, waiting to help her down. She took his hand quickly, jumped into the yard, and slammed the door.

Then she turned, blinking, and looked up at him. She had an impression of a busy posting house yard bustling with horses and carriages, hostlers and passengers around her. The sun said it was late morning. The caramel light of Italy bathed everything in warmth.

A sense of distance from herself came over her. Her surroundings faded away, replaced by a dark room with a low ceiling. The room was filled with low moans. Luigi knelt by a narrow bed. She was certain it was him by the expressive brown eyes, though they sat in a face with jowls and under a mop of gray hair. Luigi was bent over a bed with a frail woman lying in it. The woman's skin was like yellowed paper in the light of the candles at the bedside table. Her eyes, a watery blue, searched Luigi's face.

"Mi amante," she murmured. "Don't mourn me."

"I cannot live without you," Luigi sobbed, holding her fragile hand to his lips.

"We will be together again soon . . ." The voice drifted farther away. The head turned away, as if answering some other bid for her attention, and stilled.

Luigi let out a shout of grief that collapsed into sobs as he laid his bulk over the small form in the bed.

Kate gasped as the vision faded and was replaced by the face of a much younger Luigi, looking concerned.

"Is the Signorina well?"

"Yes. Yes, of course," she stuttered, breathing hard.

It had happened again, just like her other visions. Had she seen this man's future, the moment when he would lose the wife he loved very much? Kate found herself shaking, both from the fact that she might be having visions and the emotion that had filled that room. She experienced the love, the hopeless anguish of Luigi. She even knew the feelings his wife—Maria? Yes, Maria—had of drifting toward some other destiny, the moorings loosening, the emotion of her husband growing distant.

"Perhaps some coffee?"

Kate swallowed. "Yes." She followed him into the busy tavern. She kept her head down, since she had no veil.

"A private room, man," Luigi called to the proprietor. He sat her at the table in the room the man indicated. "I must

go, Signorina, else they will fob off their worst slugs on
Adolpho and that the master would never tolerate. Order as
you will. But be quick. He wants haste."

Luigi was gone. What a terrible responsibility to know his
future sorrow. What could she say to him? She could not burden him with her knowledge. Yet, what if knowing he would
lose his wife could make him treasure each moment more?

But man was not meant to know his future. It was not her
place to tell him.

With a start she realized that she believed she could see
the future. How unlike her! She believed only in what she
could see and touch and taste and hear. And now she seemed
to have another sense. One that was disrupting her life.

The proprietor came in, pointedly avoiding looking at
her. He had seen her scar and didn't know where to cast his
eyes. She ordered breakfast for herself, an egg, some toast.
Her appetite was gone. The pudgy man turned to leave.

"Oh, signore," she called. "Could you also prepare a breakfast for my companion in the carriage?" The man looked
wary. He was no doubt imagining her companion even more
marked than she was, since he had not come in at all. That almost made Kate chuckle. And she needed to chuckle. "Two
rashers of Parma ham and four eggs, bread and cheese and
mushrooms grilled, with a flagon of good, strong coffee."

He looked surprised. Italians never ate so much in the
morning. But he nodded at her decisive order and withdrew.
As Kate was finishing, Luigi entered to escort her to the
carriage and took the basket exuding delightful smells the
landlord brought.

"Did you and the boy have time to eat as well?" she
asked Luigi.

He laughed, showing white, even teeth. "The master says
I always make time to eat. And I am training Adolpho well."

This time she held her chin up as she followed him. There
was no use doing anything else until she could procure a

veil. Let the surreptitious glances fall where they may. When she got to the carriage, she took the basket from Luigi.

"How does Maria do, Luigi?"

He looked surprised. "She has some small complaints. They worry me."

"Oh, I wouldn't worry. You'll have many happy years with her yet." She smiled as he frowned at her. "You don't have children." There had been only Luigi at Maria's bedside.

"The Lord has not blessed us," Luigi said, sorrow in his eyes.

"Oh, yes He has, Luigi." She opened the door and stepped up into the carriage with her basket, pulling it quickly shut after her. Had she just had a vision of true love?

"Here," she said unceremoniously, pushing the basket over the seat to Urbano in the dimness. She could hardly see at all after the bright yard. "I ordered you food. And not those paltry sweet breads Italians like, but a good English-style breakfast. You were looking peaked."

"Was I?" he rumbled. He pulled back the checked cloth even as the coach lurched forward. She watched him tuck into his breakfast single-mindedly. He was so . . . physical. The energy that always seemed to coil about him spoke of life and virility. She imagined his naked body moving inside his well-cut coat and clinging breeches. Her brows drew together. If she believed these visions she had were real depictions of the future, then someday he would be lying naked in chains while someone touched that stone to his body and gave him pain.

What nonsense! What one saw in the world was all there was. Physical substance and the venality of human nature— that was what you could count on. Everything else was wishful thinking. She was seeing what she wanted to see. And seeing Gian Urbano naked and forced to submit was but the unspoken fascination she had for his beauty and her desire to see him taken down a peg for his arrogance. She should be ashamed that her unacknowledged wishes were thus made corporeal in these "visions." The vision of Maria's death was really a wish that someone would love her. She hated to admit that desire, but it had been present ever since she'd been abandoned. It was her imagination that what happened with Urbano at the fountain in front of the burning building matched a vision she had had earlier. One always remade a supposed vision in the face of facts. Why had she seen a carriage accident? Perhaps all these imaginings just revealed how badly she wanted to be "special" now that she was alone in the world. She was making up supernatural powers for herself. Pathetic!

But Luigi had made no demur that his wife was named Maria. How had she known that?

"You were kind to ask after Maria," Urbano said, wiping his mouth with the napkin.

Kate realized he must have heard the whole conversation.

"Did Sophia tell you about her and Luigi?" he continued. "They are quite in love, even after so many years. I am never quite sure if that is a mark of the lower classes. Love seems to be in short supply among the aristocracy."

That was it. Sophia must have told her about Luigi and Maria. She had been so tired she had just forgotten. "In my opinion, love is an illusion altogether." She had imagined that Luigi and Maria loved each other because she was weak and that's what she wanted to believe. Ever since she was abandoned, even through the assignations Matthew had arranged for her and select "admirers" before the scar, she must have held on to a wish that there was such a thing as true love. There wasn't, and she should get over such weakness immediately.

"It does exist," he said, sipping his coffee, "though I have never felt it personally."

He was just being contrary. "You take it on faith? I don't mean infatuation," she warned.

He looked up at her. She could barely make out his features in the shadow of the swaying coach. "My mother loved my father, and I believe he returned her love." The pain that drenched his voice was palpable. Why would that give him pain? Unless he didn't believe it, and was just saying that to try to make it true. With his next words, he deliberately lightened his tone. "He died long ago, of course. She knew he would. She always says it gave their love poignancy." He snorted derisively. "No good came of it. Certainly not my birth. And it ruined her for anybody else. Personally, I think she would have been better off not loving him."

What could she say to that? He apparently shared her cynical view of the world at least. "Did your father tell you he loved her in return?"

"He was not the type."

"So you have only her word for it. People like to imagine themselves in love. Me, I never take anything on faith."

"No faith . . ." he murmured. "Unusual in one who was raised with nuns."

"Not as unusual as you would think," she said grimly.

"You are sure there is no God?"

She wasn't sure, and the question made her uncomfortable, so she deflected it. "And what do *you* believe in? Does it include God?"

He put aside his tray on the seat next to him and took a careful breath. When he let it out and leaned back into the corner, some of the arrogance seemed to be let out of him. "God? I'm not sure anymore. But I believe you must live as if God existed. I . . . believe in duty, I suppose . . . honor."

"So you've said." She let her voice reveal what she thought of that.

"I agree they're little enough," he said, voice tight. "Sometimes they're all that's left."

She realized she had touched some painful point. They were like two hedgehogs set in a tiny box. They'd prick each other bloody at this rate. But there was nothing else to do but talk to him or sleep. And she had slept her fill. She threw up her hands. "Couldn't you at least have provided some books to pass the time?" Of course she couldn't read in the dark. "And a candle or something?"

"I wouldn't have guessed you for a reader," he said dryly.

The man was astounding! "And why ever not?" she shot back.

"Well . . . your past . . ."

"And what do you think I did at the orphanage if not read?" Books took her away for a few hours from that stifling atmosphere.

"Ahhh, the nuns." She could hear the smile in his voice. "So you read the Bible."

"I liked the Old Testament," she said, just to shock him. "All that smiting and lying together. That seemed real. The New Testament was harder to take, requiring belief in the power of transformation and all." She cocked her head. "And what are *your* favorite books?"

"I like the Romans. Philosophers, but practical too."

"Cicero? Marcus Aurelius? Julius Augustus?"

"You pronounce Cicero correctly," he said, surprised. "Most English use the soft *s* sound and not the *ch* sound."

"Wonders never cease." *Just another sign of his arrogance.*

"You've read them, haven't you?" It was an accusation.

"*Rem acu tetigisti.* After reading the Bible in Latin, it was a natural progression."

"I can't believe the nuns kept copies of Roman writers."

"Oh, so I must have stopped reading after I left the orphanage?" She shook her head, disgusted. "I just *might* have read other books as well." She didn't say she read so much because after she'd been scarred, she stayed much in her rooms. She often borrowed books from her patrons. Since most of them didn't care for books, they often gave her free run of their libraries.

"I stand corrected. Forgive me."

She would have expected a mocking tone, but none was in evidence. His apology was straightforward. If it wasn't Gian Urbano, she would have thought it was sincere. "Apology accepted." She cleared her throat. "I suppose you like the Romans because of your heritage."

"One likes that with which one is familiar." He paused. "My father gave me Cicero's diatribe against slavery and what it did to the Roman psyche. Cicero loved freedom."

"All the time he kept slaves, as I recall."

Urbano obviously didn't want to recall that fact. "I also read the British. Fielding, Shakespeare, Marlowe. Though I can't say I found Richardson sympathetic."

"A heroine who fades away rather than make the least push to escape her fate? I should think not." She stopped for a moment. Would a Roman gigolo have read *Clarissa,* for heaven's sake? "And how are you familiar with British literature?"

She felt his smile as much as saw it.

"One likes that with which one is familiar. How do you think I got my green eyes?"

She sat up straighter. "Mother or father?"

"Father."

The one his mother loved. "A bored aristocrat making the grand tour?"

"Hardly." He chuckled. The sound was a warm rumble. It was the first humor she had heard from him.

"No doubt a soldier in one of the various armies that swept through here, a deluded idealistic aristocrat or a mercenary." She waved a hand, dismissing his father.

"Close enough. A soldier."

"But you knew him, so he must have deserted the army and stayed on to be with your mother. How romantic."

"Now you are being snide."

"Well, it is no wonder your English is so good," she said grudgingly. He was right. The snide comment had not been fair. Perhaps deserting the army wasn't the convenient or cowardly thing to do. Perhaps deserting had cost him something. In which case Urbano's father might really have loved his mother, or thought he did for a brief time.

"And the fact that you read Latin is probably why your Italian is so good."

"And my French and Spanish and my Romanian, since they share Latin roots. German was a little harder." There, let him take that. He was always so eager to dismiss her.

"Voi Vorbiti româneşte?" He spoke it with a strange, archaic lilt to his inflection.

"Destul de bine. Şunt puţin a-şi fi pierut obişnuinţa. Not a language commonly spoken in Rome." She lifted her brows in question, not sure if he could see her face in the darkness.

"My mother was born there."

"I thought she was Italian."

"Now she claims Italy as her own. But she comes from an . . . old family in Transylvania." He sat up. "Enough about my parentage. You will meet my mother and judge for yourself. At the next change of horses, I will provide you with a book from my trunk. You can hold the shade out to let in enough light to read by. I have Byron's poetry, I believe, and Cervantes . . . but it is not a translation."

She looked at him under her brows.

"My apologies, of course you would not mind that. I believe I have one also from a British female writer, Miss Austen. Have you read her comedies of manners?"

"But they are so much more!"

"She knows the human condition," he agreed. "Indeed,

my only reservation is that the principles of the French philosophers and the Revolution are nowhere in her works. Was she so cloistered that the most cataclysmic event of her time did not affect her?"

"You have obviously not read deeply enough . . ."

Six

Urbano closed the door on the cacophony of drinkers outside the parlor of the osteria in the hotel where they had stopped. Quiet descended on Kate. They were not to spend the night, but go straight through. Sleeping in a rocking carriage—ugh. His conversation had been surprisingly educated, even entertaining today, though he had grown increasingly fidgety throughout the afternoon. She hadn't had a conversation that challenged her intellectually since . . . well, since she'd argued with the visiting abbess about the concept of original sin when she was fourteen. She walked to the cheery fire burning in the grate and held out her hands to the heat. The evening was cool.

She felt his energy snake seductively along her skin. The vibrations weren't as strong as they had been, were they? It didn't matter. Even slow, they were a danger. Best she find some armor to protect against his effect on her. He came up behind her.

"I . . . I will return shortly," he said, his voice husky. "I've ordered refreshments."

She chanced a glance behind her. He did not meet her

gaze, but turned abruptly and strode to the door. "We stay an hour. Make what you will of it."

Was her company so odious to him? The door closed softly behind him. She frowned. Where was he going without even an explanation? That felt almost surreptitious. And hadn't he looked a little guilty? If he was going to see to the carriage he might have said so. He might be going to wipe off the dust of the road. Had he bespoken a room for himself? He hadn't ordered one for her. If one had a room, one could do many things.

What was he doing?

She slid over to the door and cracked it open. He was in the taproom beyond. She could feel him. Where . . . ? She opened the door a little wider.

There he was. Talking to a serving maid. Only this one was no maiden. Nor was she even comely. Her features were coarse, flat, and broad, with a nose too big and ears that departed from her skull at an alarming angle. There were no two ways about it. She was plain.

But Urbano was staring at her as if she were the only woman in the room. That caused a little frisson of annoyance to pull Kate's lips downward. And the girl was staring back, no doubt hypnotized by his beauty. Men who looked like Urbano did not smile at a girl like that one. As Kate scanned the room, in fact, she saw every other woman staring at Urbano openly. Urbano leaned in to whisper in the wench's ear. The eyes around the room grew hard with jealousy. Kate was ashamed that she could understand the sentiment. Abruptly, Urbano headed for the stairs. Kate hastily shut the door. She knew what was going to happen. And she could hardly credit it. She cracked the door open once more after she felt him pass.

The girl gave Urbano barely a minute before she set her tray on the bar and trotted up the stairs. Kate shut the door and turned to lean against it as though she was keeping something out.

Fool that she was, she was trying to keep herself in.

But she couldn't. She was going to see what he was doing with her own eyes and put the last nail in the coffin of her opinion of this arrogant creature. He didn't value women enough even to care what he did. A homely girl like that would do anything just to feel for a moment that he wanted her, even if she knew it was a lie. He would give her a quarter hour, spill his seed, and throw her away like yesterday's newspaper, leaving her surer than ever that she was nothing.

Bloody bastard.

Kate swung open the door, marched across the dining room and straight up the stairs. She didn't care if the people saw her scar. Let them look. She had no fear that she'd get the wrong room. She'd be able to feel where he was.

At the top of the stairs, she paused, though. She wanted to catch him in flagrante delicto. *In medias res,* as Cicero would say. She went still, going back in her mind to being nine, when she was sent to glide through the night, past locked doors into the bowels of a house that wanted plundering. She was air. She was shadow, silent shadow, sliding along the corridor. No one would know she had passed, except perhaps as a tickle of breeze along the nape of the neck.

She focused on the third door to the right. He was there. And she would catch him out. She reached for the knob. Would it be locked? That would delay her.

But it was not. He was that arrogant. She turned the knob slowly. Would he hear the click when it opened? Inside she heard a moan. She pushed the anger down. It was the girl's moan. Poor deluded thing. She had to give herself to any stranger who asked, no matter how cruel he might be, because that was her only chance to experience an illusion of fulfillment other than what she achieved by her own hand.

That hurt Kate. How different was she? She had been with men. Matthew had seen to that. But she had not known a man in, what, nearly eight years now? She didn't miss their sweat, their grunting efforts, their moist mouths. Yet, sometimes, with one of the younger ones, it had been at least . . . interesting. It had held the possibility of . . . something. Something this poor ugly servant wench was searching for as well.

Just concentrate on being still, she admonished herself. The familiar energy hummed in the air, cycling up until it seemed to throb in her brain. She waited for long minutes until she heard what she thought was a moan of ecstasy. Well, the brute didn't waste time. She'd give him that. She held her breath. Imagining what she was most likely to see turned into a full feeling in her core. Her blood seemed to pool between her legs. She was as misguided as the poor serving wench who would be naked inside the room. Would Urbano be naked too?

She cracked the door.

The tableau that met her eyes was not horizontal, but vertical. Fully clothed, he leaned over the girl, the muscles in his back flexing in a most provocative way under his coat as he held her in his arms. His dark curls fell forward over his ears and neck. The girl leaned back, arching her body into his in ecstasy. He was kissing her throat. The way he was fastened to it, he didn't care if he left a strawberry mark.

He pulled away. The vibrations that battered at Kate's psyche ramped down a notch. But he didn't let the barmaid go. She swooned in his arms, her eyelids fluttering.

"You have a secret charm every man values," he whispered. "Know that. Be sure of it. They will come to you because of it. And one day you will find one who worships you, in a place and time that will surprise you. Know this, and be sure of yourself."

What? Kate straightened, frowning.

He set the girl on her feet. She looked dazed, but happy. No. She looked . . . sure.

"Go," he whispered.

She turned to the door. Kate was about to step aside and run down the hall, when she saw it. Two tiny rivulets of blood trickled down side of the girl's neck from twin wounds. Bites?

"Wait!" he whispered. He took a handkerchief from his pocket, the embroidered initials clearly visible. *GVU*. He gently wiped her throat and then tied the snowy cloth around her neck. "A souvenir," he murmured. "Wear it for the next few days."

The smile that lit the girl's face was genuine. "When will I see you?"

His expression was wistful. "You will not, mi amante. I am only a passing shadow on your life. But a grateful one."

The barmaid came to herself. "I should think so," she said archly. "Perhaps we will play together again if you pass this way."

Kate was confused. What had just happened? She melted into the shadows of the doorway opposite as the girl exited the room. Kate followed her silently down before Urbano could appear. She had expected to see seduction, even a quasi-rape. Is that what she had seen? His tenderness with the girl . . . his gentle encouragement . . . That didn't seem like rape. And what, for God's sake, were those wounds on the girl's neck?

Had he . . . *bitten* her?

Of course not. A man's bite would be a semicircle of even marks. Bruises perhaps, but they wouldn't puncture the skin like that. To break the skin would require something sharp.

The girl must have been bitten by some insect or animal. His kisses had just opened the wounds.

Hadn't they?

Kate was even more tired than hungry. She meant to remain rigidly awake in case Urbano joined her in the carriage. She had questions. But did she? What would she ask?

Some things were niggling at her mind. The wounds in the girl's neck, the strength of Elyta, her red eyes, the way Urbano slipped up on one without anyone seeing him, the fact that Elyta, Urbano, and the man from whom she had stolen the stone all seemed to be related by their scent, their vibrating energy . . .

And there was something about the story of his mother . . .

But it wouldn't come together. If he joined her, she wouldn't know what to say to him. That she was uneasy? He wanted to have that effect on women. And she wasn't about to give him any kind of satisfaction.

But then, he did not join her. *That is a relief,* she told herself. And she was so tired. She'd slept only a few hours at his house in Rome. Fighting off Elyta unsuccessfully, the fire, the tension of the carriage ride with Urbano, all had taken their toll. Before she knew what she was doing, she laid herself out on the comfortable upholstery of the carriage.

What did Urbano want with a stone you couldn't cut down and sell? It must cost a pretty penny to keep that town house and staff, to buy his servants cottages for their retirement . . . Didn't men like him always need money? Perhaps he wanted to give it to a "patroness" to curry favor. Somewhere between fussing about Urbano's patroness and her general dislike of men like him, she slipped off into oblivion, dead to the world.

She only woke when the carriage door opened. She sat up, disoriented. Once again she hadn't even noticed when the rocking movement stopped. Urbano swung himself up and into the corner of the carriage, and peremptorily pulled the blinds.

"Am I not allowed a stop?" she asked, querulous with sleep.

"Soon," he said shortly. "There is no inn hereabouts."

"Where are we?" She felt rumpled. Her mouth was dry and coated with dust.

"Very near Montalcino. A mile or two. I can see the towers on the hill. We can stop there to break your fast and change your clothing, or you can wait for Siena."

"I can *not* wait for Siena."

He paused. "I can get out if you would like to use the chamber pot under the seat."

"No," she said shortly. She would not make him get out in the sunrise. The pale light was leaking in around the shades already. She could wait a mile or two. Wait! "Montalcino? But that isn't on the route to Florence." A little tendril of fear wound round her.

"No. But then, the direct route would be easier to follow."

"You think she might follow us?" She might be uneasy about Urbano, but she was actually frightened of Elyta.

He nodded. "She wants the stone."

Kate shook her head. "I wonder why she would be so persistent. I mean, it's beautiful, but really too big to wear, and of course it's hugely valuable, but one can't sell it as it is . . . oh." Kate felt stupid. "It isn't because it's beautiful or worth a lot of money, is it?"

"No."

"It's because it drives people mad?" She still could hardly credit that. It hadn't driven her mad. But the stone cutter . . . Perhaps it didn't affect the owner of the stone.

He nodded in the darkness.

What could one do with a stone like that? Have revenge on one's enemies, or on important people? "How . . . how does it do that?"

He paused as if considering what to tell her. "Some say it tells all possible futures. The human brain cannot accept the myriad possibilities, and just . . . shuts down."

That was actually very like her first experience with it. She remembered those flashing scales that grew into little scenes, going by so fast one couldn't quite comprehend them and then . . . then she might have had a vision of the future, where she saw Urbano run into a burning building. Had the stone provoked her vision? No. "Stones don't tell all possible futures," she managed to scoff. The carriage began to head up a long rise. "No one knows the future." Of that she was a little less certain these days. She hoped her voice didn't show it.

"Then what drove the jeweler mad?" he asked softly.

"I . . . I don't know," she admitted.

"Well, well. Then there are some things that cannot be explained, Lady Charlatan, by what one can see and what one can touch."

That had her.

"Montalcino, signore," Luigi called. "Shall I stop?"

"Si, Luigi. All'Osteria de Quattro Fiumi."

"Luigi must be terribly tired. Shouldn't he rest?"

"I drove through the night while he dozed beside me. Adolpho rode inside with you. And to answer your next question, we stopped three times last night to change horses, so they are not being mistreated either. I know that disappoints you. You like to think the worst."

"I'm a realist." Was all that true?

He seemed to guess her thoughts. "You slept through everything."

"I was . . . tired." The carriage now clattered through narrow cobbled streets.

"I should think you would be. Here we are. You may wish to freshen up." The carriage rolled to a stop. Adolpho opened the door. Urbano didn't even speak sharply to him for letting in light. He merely squinted painfully and thrust himself farther into his corner.

Very well, she thought crossly. *So he's considerate to his servants, to his horses, and to me. That doesn't mean there isn't something strange about him.*

The young postboy handed her down from the carriage with a bow.

"Take in her trunk," Urbano ordered. "Don't dawdle." He pulled the carriage door shut.

Kate stalked across the early-morning piazza. Women were already queued up at the well in its center to get their morning water. Around her were arched stone houses and shops. Several carriages lined the edges of the little piazza. Towers thrust up everywhere around the town. Eleven, fifteen—there were dozens of them.

"Signorina," Luigi called. He and Adolpho carried a leather-covered trunk between them. She hurried after them.

Luigi bespoke a room. He and the proprietor carried up the trunk and left her alone to her ablutions. Three maids soon arrived with buckets of water for a bath set near a coal fire. No matter how he got his money, she could not regret that Urbano was prone to spend it on luxury. She sank into the hot water gratefully. As the last maid went out the door, Kate glimpsed her lying in a bed, a bloody child in her arms. It was not dead though, thank God. It was screaming in protest. The maid was weeping and crooning to it. The moment was one of extreme joy. The maid had thought that she could never give her husband a child; but here was a boy, healthy and screaming in her arms. The girl felt fulfilled. She herself was in pain, but she didn't mind that. A man bent over her, murmuring endearments, and kissed her.

Bloody hell. Another of these blasted glimpses into . . . into nothing! This was *not* that girl's future. This was wishful thinking because Kate herself would never have a child. Enough. She was *not* going to have these daydreams anymore. She was exhausted, her thoughts muddled. What did she expect, with all that had been happening to her recently?

As she washed the grime of the journey from her body the gears of her brain got moving again. She could practically feel them chunk into place. Sleep and a bath worked wonders.

Her thoughts turned to Byron. She had read *Don Juan,* this afternoon, holding the book up to the channel of light made by raising the window shade an inch. *Something* was niggling at her. She just couldn't quite bring it out. Was it about Byron? She was amazed she had never read him before. How like Urbano to be enamored of his muscular, active poetry. Not unpleasing verse, though, on the whole. What was it she had heard about his secretary really writing one of his works? Polidori was the man's name. Which book? Oh, yes, the one about the vampire. There had been quite a flap because it was quite clearly about Byron himself . . .

She froze, the sponge in mid-sweep down her soapy arm. Vampires.

Who couldn't stand the sun.

Who moved from place to place silently as they transformed into bats.

Who hypnotized their victims with red eyes. It was red, wasn't it?

Who sucked souls!

She found herself trembling as though with cold in the steamy room. All she had heard of vampires came crashing in on her. They drank blood from people's throats—my God! Just like the girl in the hotel. They couldn't stand crucifixes or . . . silver (or was that werewolves?) or garlic. They were dead; corpses come to life. And strong—horribly strong. They had no reflections in mirrors. Had she ever seen Urbano in a mirror? She dropped the sponge. Where had he said his mother came from?

Transylvania.

An old family, he said.

Two parts of her began to argue. *It makes such sense,* the first part shouted.

Are you mad? There are no such things as vampires, the second said, more reasonably.

You know it's true in your soul.

I believe in what I can see.

Like you believe you're having visions of the future, or that stones drive people mad?

But I don't believe those things!

Then how can you explain them?

"Stop this!" she whispered, shivering. She rinsed herself, stood, grabbed the towel and wrapped it around her torso. She believed in proof, not superstition. But what proof could there be that Urbano was or was not a vampire?

Dear Lord, she was going to have to dress herself and go down to that carriage or slip out the back way and set off on her own. He would come after her. She was sure of it. What she wasn't sure of was whether he would do it so that he could suck her blood and her soul, or to protect her from her own rash action. Because if she escaped with no money, no connections . . . she'd be back fending for herself on the streets. Or in a brothel. Oh, she didn't like that thought. At the very least, her dream of a cottage would be up in smoke. She raised the lid of the trunk with a shaking hand. What would she do? The next minutes held a decision that was . . . unthinkable. Her mortal soul was in danger, but something else was in danger too. She had to know whether the world held things like vampires or not, because if it did, then everything else that was happening to her might be true too, in which case the world was a very different place than she'd imagined.

Why hadn't he sucked her blood?

He'd sucked the blood of the tavern maid instead. Who hadn't seemed the worse for wear. Indeed, she had been given a new confidence and the joy of feeling valued. But vampires are monsters. How were they killed? A stake through the heart.

Dear me. I can't imagine stabbing anyone in the heart.

You who have lived on the streets by your wits? Is there anything you couldn't do?

Perhaps there was. She took a breath. She must know for certain what he was before she cast herself away from all chance of realizing her dream. Her eyes had been seeing nothing of the room around her. Now her glance fell to her trunk. There, on top of the folded dresses in tissue laid neatly inside, was the garnet crucifix she had refused. It was set in silver filigree.

At least she could know.

Seven

Gian tucked into a beefsteak in the little osteria that served the hotel, feeling better for a quick bath and a change of raiment. He should be thinking only of how he could get the emerald to Mirso Monastery where the world could be protected from it. That was his sworn duty. And he had always lived his life by duty and honor. Why else had he fought those damned wars in North Africa against appalling odds? He'd paid the price for that duty in nightmares and an ennui that left him uninterested in any aspect of life, including women. The girl had been right about the impotence just as she'd somehow guessed about the violence and the pain in his past. Perhaps LaRoque had told her when she had wormed her way into his confidence to steal the stone. Blast the girl. He should be concentrating on his mission. The Elders had sent him to find the stone. He had a purpose. That might be his only hope of finding a way back to what he had been.

But he just couldn't keep his mind on his work. His world had dissolved in chaos. The fires for instance. Were those really his doing? First the fires in Algiers, then LaRoque's lodgings, and finally the girl's . . . all started with spontaneous combustion and the only thing they had in common was . . . him. And the girl. She didn't even seem to realize how odd it was that she could resist his powers of suggestion. In fact, it always came back to the girl . . . She was an exact opposite of him, in every way. She had no honor at all. A thief, a charlatan who seemed to be able to ignore what she didn't believe in. But courageous, educated, thoughtful. He'd never encountered her like.

Well, speak of the devil. That's what she'd said to him that night in her rooms.

He rose as the waiter let her in. She was wearing red again. Emilia, the unconscious donor of the wardrobe, loved red. This dress was burgundy, like new wine, with soft, loose sleeves and a waist just below her ribs in the latest fashion. Gian had never liked those high waists that refused to reveal a woman's form. The bodice curved over the girl's breasts. She wore a thick black ribband around her neck to hide the fading bruises Elyta had left. That would become a fashion, if the women of Firenze had eyes. It made her neck look slender and elegant. She had knotted her hair up hastily, for tendrils wisped around her neck and ears, but the effect was . . . attractive. She was so stupidly conscious of that scar. One didn't even notice it after the first day or so. And except for that she was a diamond of the first water. He frowned. Something was bothering her. Her eyes glittered with fear and determination.

She stalked in and stood, rod-straight, in the center of the room. The door closed behind her and still she did not move.

He raised his brows. "Will you eat something?"

Her jaws clenched. "I . . . I wonder if you would assist me with this clasp?" She came forward, hesitant. Her hand was clenched around a delicate silver chain until her knuckles were white. She opened it slowly. The garnet crucifix.

Ahhhh. Gian could not help but smile. So, she was even more intelligent than he thought. She had put the clues together. Now she wanted to know for certain rather than run screaming away because she was courageous, and because she did not want to believe those clues, since that would mean that all things were possible whether you could see them and touch them or not.

All those hours in the carriage he had half wanted to tell her what he was, perhaps in recompense for her revealing her own past. Or perhaps because he had revealed himself to no one except his mother and at some point that didn't count. Or perhaps he had wanted to tell her because, in the telling, he might reveal his nature to himself. He knew little of himself these days, and what he knew appalled him. But now that the moment when he could reveal himself was on him, he knew he would hide the truth. Why spoil her certainty? Why burden her dreams with monsters? Why risk her revulsion? It was his job to tell her that monsters did not exist and keep her by him until he could see her safe.

He nodded. "Of course." She was actually holding her breath. He took the crucifix from her and undid the clasp. So many things people believed about his kind were myths, garlic and crucifixes among them. He'd never been dead. He was flesh and blood, as painful as that was at times. He glanced up. She was staring at him as though her life depended upon what she was seeing. "Will you turn round, or shall I clasp it behind your neck?"

She seemed incapable of moving. So he leaned in and reached around her neck. His lips were inches above her hair. He could feel her heaving breath. He was strangely touched. And excited. He eased closer. Her breasts brushed his waistcoat. His cock stirred as it had whenever he was near her. A false promise these days and a torture, knowing it was false.

He stepped back, feeling almost awkward, hoping she did not notice her effect on him. She looked up, her blue eyes big, searching his face. Just to be certain she understood what was happening, he reached out and lifted the cross as though to examine it. As his knuckles brushed across her breasts he noticed that his hand was trembling slightly. He cleared his throat lest his voice betray him. "A pretty bauble, and old." He let it drop to the cleft between her breasts. It nestled there, snug. He turned her to the great mirror that hung over the mantel, so she could see her reflection and, more important, his. She still did not say a word. She was thinking. He could see it in her eyes. He was not out of the woods yet. "Will you sit? I ordered you tea, since the British seem to like it so. And Luigi said you ate eggs for breakfast."

He pulled out a chair. She hesitated, and then sat. He poured her tea from the pot and returned to his seat.

"Tell me about this disease your servants say you have," she said, without preamble.

Good. She was already searching for other explanations for what she had seen and guessed. "An . . . infection in my blood. I was born with it." Well, not exactly an infection. An infestation more likely, though a glorious one. He must let her ask the questions. That would tell him exactly how much she had guessed. He wouldn't volunteer any more than he must. He laid a plate with eggs and bread and butter and passed it to her.

She took it absently. "Sophia said that is why you go about only at night."

"I am sensitive to the sun. It burns my skin quickly and hurts my eyes."

"Burns." She thought for a moment. She was thinking about how he had survived the burns she saw in the square outside her lodgings.

"It isn't all bad." He shrugged. "It also lends me a certain resilience. I heal quickly." Healed anything except decapitation.

She nodded, pensive. "You do not wear lenses, do you? Elyta had the same red eyes and they seemed to glow when there was no reflective light source."

Red eyes that should have made this little charlatan do

anything he wanted, but somehow didn't. He cut a bite of meat. "My condition affects the pigmentation of my irises."

"You share the disease with Elyta?"

"And LaRoque. The one from whom you stole the emerald."

"How was she so strong? Are you that strong?"

He managed a laugh. "I should hope I'm stronger than a woman. But still, who knows? She trained in the Orient. You have heard of the art of *jujitsu*?"

She shook her head.

"An old martial art. The fifteen hundreds, I think. It uses points of leverage and the enemy's weight against him. Elyta could throw a man twice her size across her hip."

The girl chewed her lip. He saw her gathering herself. This could be bad.

"You know hypnotism, do you not?"

That was one way to describe the power he had from the parasite in his blood. He called it compulsion. "Not a crime, surely." Neither of them was even pretending to eat at this point.

"You used it on . . . that girl in the tavern, didn't you? You don't need to deny it," she added. "I saw you."

Had she seen him with his fangs run out, taking that girl's blood? He answered warily. "Then you saw that I left her feeling better about herself than when she came in. As a woman should after an . . . intimate moment."

She gathered herself again. Would she ask about the blood? Then she closed her eyes and shook her head, half laughing under her breath. "It's none of my business who you like to kiss. How silly and rude all these questions are."

He relaxed. "We are always curious about that which is strange to us."

"You will never believe what I . . . well, never mind. You're right of course. I didn't understand about your disease. I was imagining all sorts of things." She looked stricken. "Oh, dear! I've been blurting out whatever comes into my head. How many times have people pointed at me and asked astounding questions? I of anyone should be sensitive to another's differences." She bit her lips. They were really quite lovely lips, pink without rouge, full. Made, in fact, for kissing. "I'm sorry if I gave you pain," she said.

She, who pretended to be so cynical, had a generous spirit underneath. An achievement, surely, with the life she had led. "I'm glad you asked." As long as the asking had resulted in her thinking she was imagining things, all had turned out for the best. He returned to his meal, and she to hers. A wall came up between them. He could feel her turning over his answers. It was in her nature not to believe what she had guessed. That would be his protection.

Yet a certain sadness came over him. She had just shown how appalled she would be if what she imagined were true. And it was true. Oh, she had the details wrong. But in her eyes he would be a monster. The word alone for his kind struck fear and loathing into human hearts. And that meant he could never share with her what he was. Or with any human. Paolo knew his healing, his long life. But not about the blood. Not about the strength or his more-than-human senses, or his ability to translocate from one place to another.

He could share what he truly was only with his kind.

But could he? They were allowed to live only one to a city to conceal their presence among the human population. The only one of his kind he knew well was his mother, a remarkable woman who made others pale by comparison. But even his mother wouldn't understand what the wars in North Africa had made him. Even the ones who had fought by his side there weren't as sickened by the experience as he was. Then there was the spontaneous combustion he could apparently cause. Not even he understood that.

He was alone.

So he would see his mother tomorrow. He would provide for the little charlatan. Then he would take the stone to Mirso Monastery. And his duty would be done.

He had always wondered why his kind retreated to Mirso and took the Vow, never to leave the confines of its walls again. They said it was because they had grown heartsick with age, ennui gouging out globules of sanity with its teeth. The rigor of the chants, the ascetic rituals that starved the Companion in their veins of its need for blood, gave a life one could understand, control. Perhaps not much of a life, but better than the alternative: drugging yourself into a stupor or going insane. Too bad vampires could not commit suicide. The Companion's urge to life was what incited it to rebuild its host forever, and its power over its host was absolute. It did not allow suicide. The mere thought of trying to put himself in a position to be decapitated generated a shuddering revulsion in his veins even now. That was why no vampire lived in France, what with Madame Guillotine on the rampage there these last years.

For the first time he could see that Mirso Monastery might be all that was left to him. When the duty of returning the stone was gone, when all he had were the memories of women he did not love, and of the vampires he had killed in the desert, some innocent, some not, when all he could remember were endless rounds of human venality and cruelty—what then?

Maybe if he lived an ascetic life at Mirso, his pyrotechnic abilities would disappear. If you had no strong emotions, then you couldn't bring forth flame. That sounded appealing.

He looked up and found the girl staring at him. She flushed and looked away.

Did she flush because she was thinking carnal thoughts about him, and he caught her out? That was usually the case

with women. Did she flush with embarrassment that she had
thought him a vampire? Or did she flush because she was
self-conscious about her scar? When she turned, she instinctively turned her marked cheek away.

She had not eaten, but pushed her plate away. "Let us
go," he said, rising. He left his own steak half finished.

He was sleeping in his corner of the coach. She could hear
his even breathing. That was a good thing. The man had
been sleeping far too little in the last days. And even if his
condition gave him healing properties, surely healing the
burns she had seen would have taken his strength. She wondered if the healing properties shortened his life span. She
couldn't ask him about that. She flushed again just to think
what she had already asked him.

How could she have believed he was a vampire? And
asked him to touch a crucifix as proof that he was not. She
cringed just to think about it. As though he was a risen
corpse. She knew from experience just how warm his touch
was. At that inn the first night she had seen him eat a pigeon
pie liberally laced with garlic. There was nary a glimpse of
fangs on his even white teeth. The poor man had a disease
and she had vilified him for it. How different was she from all
those ignorant creatures who blamed her for being scarred?
And that she could even consider there were such things as
vampires meant she was losing her grip on reality.

Dear Lord! What would the nuns think? What would
Matthew have thought?

And why should she care? Because she might be a crea-
ture of her upbringing, and for better or worse the nuns and
Matthew had formed her character: they and the streets of
London.

That depressed her.

She sighed. Thinking him a vampire was as stupid as

believing she saw the future. Best get her mind on what counted. Would he pay her for a stone he could just take? And if he did, was there something else he wanted of her? She still didn't see what he got out of the bargain.

More carriages were passing outside. They might be coming to a town. Florence? She peeked out behind the shade. The Tuscan hills rolled away into the distance. Some were covered in neat rows of vines, like a chenille bed coverlet. Some were crowned with square houses sporting tiled roofs, their plastered walls painted curious shades of brown and brick red and dusty gold. They looked sturdy, confident. The trees were cypress, standing upright in lines along the roads or clustered about the houses.

"Beautiful, isn't it?"

The deep rumble startled her. She let the flap down. "In a cultivated sort of way."

He chuckled. "You prefer the sublime of Turner, all wild chaos? Less comfortable, I assure you."

She had to smile. "I'm sure you're right."

"I am. I've been to Turner's Alps. But I grew up around here."

"In the countryside?"

"My mother's estates. When my father was alive we liked it better than Firenze."

"I think we are coming into the city."

He sat up, pulled the shade open a crack and squinted into the brightness. "Would you care to tell me your real name?" He let the shade slip back into place. "I hate to lie to my mother."

Kate sat up straighter, incensed. But after she had asked him all those impertinent questions about his disease, it might not seem unreasonable to him to ask her name.

She grimaced. "Kate. I always keep some version of Kate."

He raised his brows. "And the last name? Not Mulroney, surely. It hardly suits you."

"Why not?"

"Inelegant."

"One doesn't choose one's name."

"One always chooses who one is to some extent, in spite of one's background."

He was right about that too. The thought made her uncomfortable. She spent a fair amount of time around this man feeling uncomfortable.

"Names included," he continued. "I chose mine because I liked the Eternal City, and wanted to be called after it. Urbano means 'from the city.' "

"I know what it means," she snapped. "Were you rebelling against your family?"

He gave a small, rueful smile. "Hardly. My mother encouraged me to change it. What woman wants to acknowledge a grown son?"

Kate was appalled. What kind of a mother was that? "Your other names as well?"

"No. I always keep my given name. I think of myself as Gian. Currently Gian Vincenzo."

"I'm not sure of my real surname," she admitted, "since Matthew was not my father."

He nodded, silent, not pressing. So she went on. "Come to think on it, I'm not sure *his* real name was Sheridan, though that was what he claimed."

"Sheridan." He considered. "That fits. Shall you be called Miss Kate Sheridan?"

"I suppose so." It was a commitment, after all, only for a few days.

"Then that is how I shall introduce you."

Eight

Gian made certain to arrive when his mother was out. She might not be overjoyed to have the protection of a girl thrust upon her. Gian suspected she liked to think of herself as a girl in spite of her age. She had taken up residence in the Palazzo Vecchio on the central Piazza della Signoria of Firenze. Inconvenient. He had to bring Kate in the back entrance to avoid one particular piece of statuary in the piazza. He bribed his mother's majordomo liberally and installed Kate in a comfortable bedroom behind the map room until he could prepare the way.

He waited in his mother's apartments overlooking the piazza. The salon was lighted only by flickering sconces. The walls were covered with frescos now dark with age. It smelled of the oil and lemon used to polish the heavy furniture. The palazzo had not been modernized. His mother liked it for its location next to the former government offices, called, directly enough, Uffizi, now turned into an art museum. She also relished the fact that it had once been the town residence of Cosimo de' Medici before he moved to the Palazzo Pitti across the river. His mother always liked taking something from the Medicis, though they had now vanished and it was only from their ghosts that she took it.

A carriage clattered into the courtyard and servants began bustling about in preparation. His mother always seemed to move about like a brisk breeze whirling up leaves before it.

"Gian? Gian is here?" Her footsteps quickened up the grand staircase from the audience hall. "At last." The door burst open in a wash of cinnamon and ambergris.

"Gian!" She hurried to take his hands, laughing. "I thought you might be in the vicinity."

He smiled. How could one not? She was so alive! She, for all her years, had not grown bored with living. "You look well," he said. Her red and old gold brocade dress had full slashed sleeves and much Brussels lace, its waist lower than was the fashion at the moment. On her it looked timeless. She was a beautiful woman: dark hair, porcelain skin, and great, dark brown snapping eyes fringed with long lashes. No one would guess she was Gian's mother, not only because of his light eyes, but because she looked younger than he did. She would have to be moving on soon, or her claim that excellent skin creams and cosmetics kept her looking young would no longer fool her jealous rivals. How she would hate to leave Firenze, even for a time.

"Of course I look well," she said, laughing, "I always look well." A frown appeared as she examined him. "But you, my son, look . . . worn. Were the wars so terrible?"

He shrugged. "War is war." But he saw she would not be satisfied with that. "There were a lot of them. The killing was ugly."

"Khalenberg says you were quite the hero." She took off the tiny hat of old lace that nested in her upswept hair. "Algiers would have fallen without your leadership."

"Hardly."

"Why did you not have Bucarro send for me? I was

dallying at some state function most intolerable when I could have been here with you, hearing all about it."

"I . . . I'd rather not discuss it, if you don't mind." He paced to the balcony.

"As you wish." Her voice held concern.

In the piazza below, women clustered about one of the statues just in front of the Uffizi's main entrance in the May Tuscan evening. He sighed. Did they never tire of looking at it?

"When did Buonarroti finish that damn thing?" he growled.

"Oh, 1504 or 1505 I should think." His mother's voice drifted out from the darkness behind him, sounding fragile and feminine. That fragility was a lie.

He took a breath and leaned on the balustrade of the balcony. The air was scented with jasmine, warm with the promise of summer heat. Not so different from the heat and the jasmine in North Africa. He shook his head, lest the memories come and overwhelm him again. All this talk of the wars unnerved him. He tried to focus on the statue. "I don't see the attraction."

"Don't you?" He could hear the smile in her voice.

"The hands and feet are too big," he grumbled.

"They forgive Michelangelo that, my dear. It was meant to stand on the top of the Duomo. He wanted people to be able to see everything from the ground."

"Well, now it stands in the piazza." It was sixteen feet high. The pale marble gleamed in the moonlight through the patina of age. He couldn't deny the sculptor's genius. The contrapuntal stance of the body, the articulation of ligament and muscle—the damn thing looked like it would step off the pedestal at any moment. But the real artistry was in the expression. Buonarroti had captured young David in the moment after he had slain Goliath. Any other sculptor would have made the victor jubilant. But in Buonarroti's *David* there was no triumph. The figure's puckered brow showed only the realization that killing was not satisfying and the knowledge that, from this moment, everything had changed. It was a pensive look, disturbed and disturbing. Buonarroti had captured the instant in which the simple shepherd was transformed into an uneasy king. Where had Buonarroti seen that expression?

He didn't think the expression was why the women clustered, though.

"Why ever did you pose for it, if it upsets you so to have it on display?"

The point exactly. Buonarroti had seen him at the baths. The brute could be very persuasive. Everything for art and all. Gian never thought anyone would recognize him with the statue perched so high up on the Duomo. Who knew they would set it in the Piazza della Signoria where every woman in Tuscany could ogle his nude body at their whim? White marble couldn't render his coloring. But if women who met him didn't jump to the pertinent conclusion at once, he was soon treated to a gasp of recognition. Even when he was fully clothed.

He appeared in the piazza these days only when he wanted women in his bed, for love or for blood. He made up stories of an ancestor who had posed for the statue. They wanted to test how far the likeness went. He clenched his jaw. Buonarroti had not exaggerated. Gian had put on a little bulk of muscle since then, but the essentials from a female point of view were the same. These days they would be disappointed in the actual operation of those essentials, but he made sure they had their pleasure of him, took his blood from them, and left them with ecstatic memories.

He turned into the salon, trying to assume nonchalance. "I wonder you can stand to have your son's circumcision displayed beneath your window."

"The statue reminded me of you. Two years is a long time to be without a son."

Two years of killing. He blinked against the memories. An army of men who had been made vampires by an evil vampire woman called Asharti. She had thought to use that army to rule the world.

A pack of them descended on him, snarling like animals. His sword flashed but they came and came. Only a clean decapitation could kill them. Canvas flapped from the abandoned tents of the Kasbah. The night sky was black and moonless. He ducked under the blade of a scimitar. The aroma of unwashed bodies mixed with the scent of cinnamon and ambergris that marked their kind. His kind. And over all, the smell of blood. A blade found his side. One reached for his head ... Rage washed through him. A tent erupted in flames ...

He swallowed convulsively, blinking, and pushed down the memories. Strange, he had not had a single uncontrolled memory during the journey here. They had used to take him frequently at night, and haunt his dreams during the day ever since he'd returned. Perhaps his preoccupation with the stone was a good thing. Or was his real preoccupation with the girl? "I ... I'm glad the statue was a comfort."

His mother drew her brows together. Had she seen his lapse? "Come, sit." She motioned to a carved mahogany chair with a cushion. "The war is over. It is time to think of your future."

"Not yet. I have a final task to perform. A stone from the Temple of Waiting has surfaced. I must return it to Mirso." And then there would be nothing left to do.

She drew a breath and let it out.

"I stay only to ... make certain arrangements and I will go."

Again she pointed to the carved wooden chair. "Then what?"

Ahhhh. That was the question now, wasn't it? "I have no plans." He didn't want to reveal the turmoil inside him. But out of deference to her, he sat.

She simply waited, her snapping eyes filled with questions.

He shook his head. What could he tell her?

"Perhaps you could interest yourself in politics," she suggested. "All these warring city-states allow foreign powers to pick us off one by one. The Spanish are bad masters, the Hapsburgs no better. They bleed us dry. The best thing that happened to us was Napoleon. He set things to rights. But he is exiled to Elba. What we require is a united Italy. The Carbonari have started an underground movement to achieve that. But they need a leader."

He shrugged. "Some greedy new demagogues would just tear it all apart again."

"Then speak out against the Inquisition. The Church has suppressed all original thinking. You write persuasively, and you certainly have no fear. You could make a difference."

"The Renaissance is officially over, Mother, in case you haven't noticed. All society talks about is opera and the latest castrati. No one cares about original thinking."

His mother shook her head, exasperated. She picked up a parchment from her desk, but she only pretended to read it. She chewed her lip. Finally she looked up at him. "You know what you need?" Her tone was too casual for his liking.

"I have no idea." That at least was true.

"A woman."

He chuffed a bitter laugh. "I have plenty of women."

"That's not what I mean and you know it."

He looked away. "I won't get entangled with a human woman just to watch her age and die, Mother. Your own experience is a lesson to me."

Her eyes registered her hurt. He hadn't meant to hurt

her. But he wouldn't let her push him either. She took a breath and answered. She had always been courageous. "I loved your father well. The pain was worth it."

"You didn't take another lover for two hundred years after he died."

"I have had many lovers since."

He simply raised his brows.

She colored. "Very well. Not the same. But I keep looking. You never look at all."

He shrugged. "I decide quickly."

She frowned at him. "In one day?"

He rose, restless. "How am I to impose what I am on any human woman? Aside from the pain of watching her age, how do you tell her you are something she considers a monster?"

"Then one of our own kind."

"With only one to a city allowed? Short visits with permission. I've done that, Lord knows." He'd done it with Elyta, to disastrous effect. She was still angry that he'd left her. Not that her heart had been engaged. Elyta didn't have a heart. She was just used to being the one to leave. He wouldn't repeat that particular mistake. "It smacks of shopping at the Kasbah. 'May I stay in your city for a week to sample the goods?' And if by chance I did meet a female, and if by greater chance we suited, we could not live together. What life is that?"

"You always were one to obey the Elders' Rules." She sighed.

"I come by it honestly. You did not make Father vampire because it is against the Rules." He saw the pain in her eyes. Did she regret her choice? "I would call that honor, by the way." He tried to tell her she had done the right thing. He saw she didn't believe that anymore. "The Rules are the only thing between us and chaos. Look what happened when Asharti made a vampire army. It was almost the end of everything."

She looked away. She wouldn't be comforted even after a thousand years. "And anyway, I'm dry inside, just dust. I've nothing to give."

Her eyes softened. She smiled. That smile had always warmed him, inspired him. He wished it would do so now. He wanted to feel enthusiasm again, as she did. "You're wrong, *cara mia*," she whispered. "You have *so* much to give."

He couldn't smile in return. "You're my mother. Of course you think that."

She toyed with a quill on the desk. "Elyta Zaroff was here yesterday. She said she came to see you. I was glad of that at first." His mother tapped the quill's feather to her chin.

"Elyta was here? Why didn't you tell me immediately?" Elyta *had* guessed he would come to his mother. How glad he was he had taken a devious route.

"Because then your attention would have been only for the problem she creates for you, and I would not have been able to have my useless conversation about your future."

He ignored her barb. "What did you tell her?"

"The truth, of course, since I possess a cursed sense of honor. I said I hadn't seen you in two years. She seemed quite perturbed. Said I should give you a message when you arrived."

"And?"

His mother shrugged and looked away. "That it was a long way to Mirso."

Gian let his breath whoosh out. There it was. Elyta was probably somewhere near even now. She would dog him to Mirso as he tried to take the stone to Rubius and the Elders for safekeeping. She was stronger than he, and she had threatened to bring other vampires. What was she planning? He glanced to the night outside the balcony. "Were there others with her?"

His mother looked a little shocked that Elyta might have

gathered vampires to her cause. Now *that* was against the Rules. "Not to my knowledge."

"Do you know where she's staying?" He'd better confront Elyta and be done with it. If there were others he'd need his mother's help. He'd brought trouble to her door. That thought produced a surge of guilt. But where else could he have gone once Kate was involved?

"She isn't in Firenze. I revoked her welcome. I . . . I didn't like her tone."

"And you think Elyta would respect your wishes?"

"I think she fears me." His mother stood and drew up her diminutive frame. "I am old, Gian. I've seen the pyramids built and the Tower of Babel. I am strong. She will not dare attack me. Which is why I am going with you to Mirso with the stone."

"Out of the question."

"You defy me?"

"You should be used to it by now."

"But not in this matter, *cara mia*. You need me." She touched his sleeve.

That was true, though not in the manner his mother intended. And with Elyta out of the city, they had a little time. He could not leave Firenze without providing for Kate. She not only needed money, but also his mother's protection from Elyta Zaroff. Elyta would make sure Kate didn't have the stone. At the least she'd send one of her minions to torture Kate and kill her. The journey to the Carpathian Mountains with Elyta stalking him would wait a day or two to be sure Kate was protected. He would get the stone to Mirso somehow. Maybe he would take it by sea from Ravenna through the Strait of Bosporus, into the Black Sea, landing at Varna, and from there into the Carpathians. Elyta would never expect that.

When he got back, if he got back, Kate would be gone. The dust inside him rose again, threatening to choke him.

Maybe he would stay at Mirso Monastery. He'd take the Vow and lock himself into a narrow existence of chanting and abstinence. Maybe, if he were lucky, his spirit would find peace. It was not a course of action his mother would condone.

So she need not know. Not now. "There is one thing you can help me with." He cleared his throat. Suddenly this was difficult. "Well . . . the stone is in the possession of a young woman." He saw his mother's wary look. "She is asking . . . twenty thousand British pounds for it. And since I had to come away from Rome, I was unable to complete the transaction."

His mother went still. That didn't mean she wasn't thinking.

"She's here, isn't she?"

There was never any hiding from his mother. "She's sleeping in the Blue Room. I couldn't leave her in Rome. Elyta tried to kill her. I thought you could give her countenance, and . . . protection until she can get back to England." He saw his mother's expression soften. "It isn't what you think," he hastened to add. He began to pace the carpet. "She's an orphan of no birth, a trickster and a sham who bilks a gullible aristocracy for her living. She's hardened and cynical. Thinks the worst of everyone and . . . and she's disfigured by a scar." He must prepare his mother for Kate's appearance. He didn't want Kate hurt by his mother's pity. She obviously didn't tolerate pity. And he hoped to God that his mother never tried to compel Kate by using the power of her Companion. The fact that she couldn't might truly shock his mother.

"In short, not your type at all."

He stopped pacing and sighed, grateful for her understanding. "Exactly."

"And you want to pay the little mercenary off?"

"Well, I can't leave her destitute. She's alone in the world. The stone is her only future."

"I see. And how long am I to entertain this paragon of virtue you care nothing for?"

"Only until . . ." He cleared his throat again. "I wouldn't call it 'entertaining' precisely."

"You don't want me to introduce her to society, ensure an advantageous marriage of convenience so you can dally with her while we hold Elyta off at the gates of Firenze?" His mother was probing him somehow. And it had nothing to do with her words.

"Don't be sarcastic. Besides, she'd be charging your friends for tarot readings and visions if you did." He had to smile at that image. But he suppressed it almost immediately.

"Ahhhh . . ." His mother lapsed into silence as she studied him. Gian didn't like the thoughtful way she chewed her lip.

"What I want is for you to loan me the twenty thousand, and provide her an escort to London. If you could point out a dressmaker, that would be helpful."

His mother gave him a questioning look.

"Don't raise your brows at me. Everything she had burned in a fire." He wouldn't mention how that fire started. "I did what I could, but I could lend her only a few things."

His mother blinked, twice. "Well, then, you'd better bring her in and introduce her."

Gian sighed. The first hurdle was passed.

Kate smoothed the cherry-striped lustring morning dress over her breasts. A morning dress at night—not done of course. But it was the only dress she hadn't worn into a crumpled mess. She raised her chin. This was their morning, was it not? Well, afternoon if one was counting hours since dusk. It was almost two A.M. So it would have to do. She still carried her gray reticule with the silver beading, but that couldn't be helped. She was going to keep the stone with her at all costs and the trunk had contained no reticule, though every other article of female clothing, no matter how intimate, had been provided.

Now she sat in the elegant suite of rooms assigned to her, back stiff, waiting. She fingered her deck of tarot cards and the stone's box inside her reticule for comfort. Il signore Bucarro, an austere man with a pointed beard who was the majordomo of the place, had told her the mistress of the house wanted to see her and that a maid would lead her to the audience. Where was the maid? Kate wanted to get this interview over with.

One thing had her in a puzzle. This house was the richest she had ever set foot inside, its stately rooms filled with priceless statuary and medieval tapestries. Apparently they had estates all over Tuscany. With a mother who owned all this, why did Urbano need to live off women? Surely his mother didn't keep him in penury. He must be the heir. Unless he was a bastard? She chewed her lip. Or was it possible she'd been wrong? Maybe he wasn't a gigolo who lived off women. That would make him just as annoying, but a *little* less vile.

The servants, all dressed in scarlet livery, pointedly did not look at her face after the first surreptitious stare. She could practically feel them judging her unworthy to be anywhere near the opulence of her surroundings. That made her angry rather than intimidated.

But the incipient meeting with Urbano's mother was intimidating. The old harridan might just throw her out. At the very least she might refuse to front Urbano the money.

If he was going to pay her for something he could just take.

She still couldn't see his lay. And the fact that she

couldn't read him was entirely disconcerting. She had made her way across the Continent reading people, knowing what they wanted and showing them a future where they would get it. She was good—no, *very* good at it. So why couldn't she see what Urbano wanted from her?

A knock at the door was followed by a slip of a girl sliding though the opening. At last. She recognized the maid who had laid out her clothing. "Carina, isn't it?"

The girl nodded and made her bob, sniffing. She'd been crying. Something cutting had no doubt been said to her by Urbano or by his mother, if she was as arrogant as he was. Or perhaps Urbano had made advances to her. That would make anyone cry. Or perhaps he hadn't. That just might make one cry as well. She set her lips. Not her affair.

Kate gasped at a feeling of dislocation that was beginning to be familiar. In an instant the room washed away and was replaced by a tiny room up under the eaves. Kate knew it was under the eaves because of the drumming rain. Carina was crying. These were tears of joy, though. Emotion hung in the air. And there before her, kneeling, was a man, plain, but made appealing by his air of candid openness. His hair was wet, his hands roughened with work. He had on the livery of the household, but he was wearing riding boots from which the mud had been carelessly brushed, leaving tracks on the braided rag rug. A groom? And his eyes gleamed with tears in the wavering light of the single candle by the bed.

"I swear I never looked at her. 'Twas she who made eyes at me. It's you I'm askin' to marry me, Carina. If you have me, you'll find me true as tempered steel, and I'll wear as long."

Carina nodded. It was all she could do through the sobs.

The Palazzo Vecchio of the present settled in around Kate again.

"Signorina, are you well?" Concern had replaced misery on the girl's face.

"I'm fine." *If you call insane fine,* she thought. But she didn't feel insane at all. That was just the problem of the whole thing. Why in the hell was this happening to her? Maybe . . . Oh, it was useless to speculate. The visions in general were useless. She seemed to see moments of extreme emotion as though they hung around the principal actors like incipient shrouds.

But were they useless? Was there some purpose to her seeing them? Only in telling those she saw would she know. She never knew whether the young man had avoided being run down by a carriage on Thursday. Probably she would never know.

Carina looked about to collapse into tears again.

Kate sighed. "Don't worry, Carina. Your groom loves you and you alone." The girl looked shocked. "He will propose marriage to you in a room under the eaves on a night when it is raining hard."

"How can you know?" The hope in her voice would be ludicrous if it wasn't so pathetic.

Kate shook her head, disgusted with herself. "I know what I know." She pushed past before the girl could ask any more questions. Kate had a coming ordeal and she didn't want any more disconcerting incidents to unnerve her. She'd find her own way to Urbano's mother.

Urbano himself met her in the Map Room. This strange room was lined with twoscore paintings of maps of various parts of the world and littered with globes. But she had no eyes for them. Her preoccupation with the vision dropped away. Apprehension at meeting his mother likewise. She saw only Urbano, his black coat smooth across his shoulders, his trousers sleek over his thighs. He wore riding boots still, which only served to make his person seem even more masculine. The snowy cravat was tied simply and tucked into the gray figured waistcoat. But it was his eyes that captivated one. No wonder he was a consummate hypnotist. Who could resist staring into those eyes?

She came to herself and crossed the room. She was wet between her legs just looking at him. A terrible realization washed over her. She had always known she was attracted to him. What woman would not be? But the physical reaction he caused in her was not the worst of it. She *liked* the fact that she could not read him. She liked the fact that he could argue with her as only the abbess had before him, and that he had taken her to his mother. She was glad he probably was not a gigolo. In fact, she liked *him,* in spite of how annoying he was, in spite of the arrogance that made her want to shriek sometimes.

Dreadful.

Liking him, and being attracted to him so that it made her hurt inside, was a fatal combination for a woman who looked like she did, who came from nowhere, and whose only ambition was to return there. That way lay heartache, and she had steeled herself against heartache from the moment she found herself in the streets of London, alone and invisible.

She raised her chin. "Come to lead the prisoner to her judgment?"

"Can't you try to be nice?" he grumbled. "My mother may lend me the twenty thousand, if we're lucky. But it would help if you were on your best behavior." He took her arm.

Lord, but she wished he wouldn't do that! It only made her throb the more. He, too, seemed startled, for he looked down at her with something like distress in his eyes.

They proceeded in uneasy silence, up a small staircase. He released her and swung open a huge door. Really, the place was quite archaic and rough-hewn underneath the marble urns, the carpets and paintings. It must be at least five or six hundred years old. She took a breath and went to meet the harridan.

But the only person in the room was a petite and incredibly lovely woman dressed in red and black brocade. She couldn't be old enough to be Urbano's mother. But was there an echo of the set of Urbano's lips? Kate felt the same electric energy vibrating in the air around her, so fast it was merely a hum at the edge of consciousness. *So that's where he gets it,* she thought. Maybe this woman *was* his mother. The woman rose and stepped forward, holding out her hands. To her credit she didn't even blink when she saw Kate's face. That didn't stop Kate's flush.

"But welcome, dear Miss Sheridan. My Gian has told me much about you."

Kate cast an accusing look at Urbano. She'd wager he'd told his mother nothing of what she really was. The least he could have done was to tell Kate what lies he'd put about so she could go along with his ruse.

"My mother," he murmured, "Contessa Donnatella Margerhita Luchella di Poliziano."

Kate dipped her most graceful curtsy. "Contessa, I am honored." There was a lovely scent of cinnamon about her, like Urbano's but sweeter, more feminine.

"I know what you are thinking." The contessa laughed as she led Kate to a carved wooden chair with U-shaped arms and back. "I am much too young to have a grown son." The contessa sighed dramatically. "A pronouncement with which I myself agree. I find it very daunting. He reminds me that my beauty regimen will soon fail me. I *should* wish that he would stay away, and yet he gives me such joy that I cannot."

One whole wall of the room was open to a balcony that looked over lighted buildings around the huge central square of Florence. It was a beautiful view, but all Kate could think about was how alive the woman before her seemed. It was something more than the vibrations that emanated from her. This was a woman who embraced life. And that was a different feeling from Urbano's electric danger. Kate sat, careful to position herself so her right cheek was turned away from the chair in which the contessa arranged herself. Urbano stood looking out over the balcony at something below in the square.

Very well, so the woman wasn't a harridan. But she would still be protective of a beloved son if she thought Kate a fortune-grabbing female. And what else would she think when she discovered she was being asked to front twenty thousand pounds? If Urbano actually planned to ask her that. Kate couldn't quite see her way. All she knew for certain was that she had to display a total disinterest in Contessa di Poliziano's delectable son. And what woman, even a mother, would believe that?

She cleared her throat. "Does he give you joy? I am glad."

"Does he not give everyone joy?" the little woman asked.

"I personally find him exasperating," Kate said. That was very un-lover-like. And it had the virtue of being true.

The contessa gave a peal of laughter. "Well, that also."

"You are not alone in finding someone exasperating," he muttered, his back still turned.

"How very rude, Gian, to the delightful Miss Sheridan. Miss Sheridan, would you like some tea? I have some very fine oolong. I import it myself."

Kate smiled. "That would be very kind, thank you." She had been missing tea.

The woman clapped her hands and a servant appeared. The tea ordered, she continued. "Now, you were saying that you find my son exasperating. Do elaborate."

"Well, uh, he seems to enjoy bickering over nearly everything, and he belittles one."

Urbano turned from the view out the balcony, his eyes

narrowed. "*I* bicker? If I said Cicero was a lover of freedom, you had to point out that he owned slaves. If I ordered you a meal, you did not eat it. You certainly did not appreciate my exertions on your behalf."

"*You* did not believe I read books, let alone that I read Cicero in Latin. It's all part of your arrogance. Besides, I exerted myself for you as well, a fact you hardly noticed. If I had not brought you breakfast that first morning when you could not go out in the sunlight, you would have starved until evening."

"He is certainly arrogant. I shall give you that."

They both jerked toward the languid observation. Kate colored. How could she have forgotten herself so far as to argue with Urbano in front of his mother? And to point out his faults. No good would come from such poor manners. She bit her lip. At least it displayed how little Urbano cared for her, and how little she cared for that fact. "My apologies, Contessa, I—"

"No need." The contessa waved a hand. There was some expression in her eyes Kate couldn't quite describe. Amusement? "I know my Gian well. Arrogant, yes." She sighed. "It comes from having women throw themselves at him. And the fact that he is intelligent. Normally he also knows his own mind, which is rare in a man. It makes him a good leader. Though of late I think he questions himself, and all the while he misses the obvious."

"I had not noticed him questioning himself." Still, Kate thought of the pain she had seen cross his eyes at unexpected moments. That might be what the contessa was talking about. It was one of the things that drew her to him, in spite of his beauty. She found herself staring at the lamp glowing on the table, its shade casting an amber warmth around the room.

"I leave you two to your dissection of my character." Urbano stalked from the room.

"Oh, dear." Kate put her hand to her cheek. The fine web of her scar against her palm brought her own arrogance crashing down around her. Why had she worried? The contessa would never believe any designs Kate had on her son could possibly succeed. No wonder she was amused. No man so beautiful would ever be ensnared by a woman who looked like her.

She took a breath and steadied herself. Very well. That simply made her job easier.

She lifted her chin.

Before she could think what to say, the servant returned with a tea service. She gathered her thoughts as he set it out. They did the usual "Cream? Sugar?" exchange until the door shut.

Best just assault the citadel. "Has your son told you of our . . . bargain, Contessa?"

"He says you want twenty thousand for the stone."

Kate swallowed. "Yes. Do you object?"

"Why should I? It is his money. I only loan him the amount."

Kate blinked. No resistance? "How long will it take to get it?"

"I could give you a draft upon my bank immediately."

"I'll wait for cash, thank you. My bank is Drummonds. They have a branch in Zurich."

"A letter then to Drummonds from my banker. You don't want to be carrying so much cash the way you carry that emerald in your reticule."

Kate flushed. Of course she would know that. A woman like the contessa would assume that only the most dire need could make a woman carry a reticule that didn't match her dress. Kate looked up at her. The old puzzle revolved in her mind. Maybe this woman had the answer. "Why does he not just take it from me?"

"Can't you guess, my dear?" The contessa sipped her tea.

"Frankly, no. Anyone I've ever known would have taken it long ago. He tried to throttle it out of me once. And now he's willing to pay twenty thousand for it. I hardly credit that."

"How interesting. What did you do when he tried to throttle it out of you?"

"I said throttling me was not the way to get me to tell him since I couldn't breathe. And I lied to him and said I didn't have it by me."

The contessa blinked several times. "Did his eyes seem almost . . . red at the time?"

"Yes, as a matter of fact. I didn't understand then that red eyes were part of his condition. I thought he was wearing lenses, as I do sometimes to make myself seem exotic."

The contessa seemed taken much aback. "So he explained his . . . condition?"

"I'm sorry. I shouldn't have mentioned it. I know you must share it since you have a similar scent and the electric . . . vibrancy I feel in him. I . . . I was rude enough to ask him about it. I, who know how hurtful questions can be. And I'm even more embarrassed to say that I had some . . . wild ideas about what he was." She shook her head. "Unusual, because I'm really not romantical in the least. Anyway, he explained about the infection in your blood."

"Are those his marks on your neck there?"

Kate touched the ribband she had wound around her neck. "No, no. He left no marks at all. These are Elyta's. She nearly *did* strangle me before your son showed up so suddenly."

"Here, let me." The contessa leaned forward and untied the ribband, looked at both sides of her neck, and then retied it gently. "They look to be fading."

"I hope so. I am tired of this ribband."

"So, you lied to him when he had red eyes." She tapped her chin. "And the stone, what did you think of it?"

"Beautiful, of course. One wouldn't think that a cabochon cut could sparkle so. But . . ." She cleared her throat. "It seems to have some very unfortunate effects on anyone but its owner."

"That would be you?"

"Well, at the time I looked at it, yes."

"I see." The contessa was looking at her very strangely. "So you and Gian agreed on twenty thousand for it."

"What I don't understand is what he wants in return."

"In return for what?" The contessa looked confused.

"In return for not stealing it. He must want something."

"He values his honor. It is honorable to pay you for what is yours."

Kate thought about that. "But it isn't really mine. He knows I stole it, after all."

"Oh, really?" The contessa must only be pretending to be calm at *that* revelation.

"I picked the pocket of a friend of Elyta Zaroff's." There. The contessa knew exactly what she was now. Kate lifted her chin again. "I'm quite good at it."

"Well, then, if you won't believe it is his honor that demands he pay you, I'm afraid his motives will have to be a mystery, at least for a little while." The contessa set down her cup. "Now, you will also need clothes and an escort for your journey."

"No, no, I don't want to be more trouble. I can take care of myself. And I already have several fine dresses your son . . . loaned me. If I could keep those . . . perhaps have them cleaned?"

"You'll deny me the pleasure of dressing you, child?" The contessa's overpowering presence almost demanded acquiescence. And there was one thing Kate coveted.

She took a breath. "There is something . . . If you can put me in the way to buy a mantilla . . . I mean . . . I would need an advance from the twenty thousand . . ."

"Nonsense. You may have one from my wardrobe. But are you certain it is necessary?"

Kate looked down at her hands. "You see how necessary it is." She raised her head and managed a laugh. "I have already frightened your servants."

"Oh, I think they are not so easily frightened as that." The contessa rose and took Kate's arm confidingly. "But let us see what I have in my closets."

Nine

The next afternoon, Kate decided she would see something of Florence before she left. The contessa had talked her into many things from her closet in spite of Kate's best intentions. Indeed the contessa had been very kind. She was now well provisioned for her journey. She wore a mantilla even now and was feeling much more comfortable. The contessa had sent round for the draft on her bankers—Monte dei Paschi—the oldest bank in Europe, and some ready cash for Kate's journey. Even the bank's name had a nice, secure feeling to it. The servants had taken away her clothing for laundry and brushing. Now all that was left was to pack her trunk and arrange to hire a carriage on the morrow. One of the contessa's footmen trailed at her heels, insisting the mistress of the house would sack him if he let her go alone.

In truth, she was grateful for his direction. He took her to all the best works in the Uffizi, bequeathed fifty years ago by the last of the Medicis, Anna Maria Ludovica, to the public. They had walked out the back of the Uffizi over the Ponte Vecchio, lined with goldsmiths' shops, to the marvelous Pitti Palace. In the monastery of San Marco, she gazed in fascinated horror at the preserved cell of Savonarola, the monk who led Florence at the head of a mob-rule theocracy and burned priceless paintings and irreplaceable illuminated books. Then it was back to the Duomo to climb the 463 spiraling steps to view the city from the top of the cathedral dome. It felt good to walk in the sunshine after so many hours in the dim carriage.

She turned back toward the Piazza della Signoria, determined to cross it on her way back to get the full effect of the palazzo's tall campanile. The footman, for some reason, had led her out a side door from the palazzo to the Uffizi earlier.

The afternoon was winding down. She was about to get everything she wanted.

Why did that feel so depressing?

And now her feet hurt. These half-boots were not as comfortable as she first supposed. She should have realized she was getting blisters and skipped the Duomo altogether. So she really did not want to hear the footman's imprecations about going round back of Palazzo Vecchio. Through the piazza was the quickest way home. Besides, it was getting dark.

She took off across the vast expanse of cobblestones at a hobble in the twilight, the footman trailing in her wake, protesting. She passed Ammanati's Fountain of Neptune with barely a glance. On the far side an open-air market was just closing up for the day. Carriages crisscrossed the open space with chaotic abandon. Over to the right was a huge crowd, mainly composed of women. They gathered around a nude figure of a man.

Kate gasped and froze.

"Come, miss," the footman pleaded.

She had seen drawings of it, of course. But none did it justice. Michelangelo's *David*.

But it was more than that.

She started moving slowly toward it. Behind her, the footman sighed deeply. Her feet were not as important as they had been a moment ago.

Oh, my God.

It was Urbano! Of course she recognized the face. But she had also seen his naked body in a vision. And there was no question. The vision burned upon her brain had more muscle in the shoulder and thigh. But it was he, down to every other detail.

Her eyes drank in the marble rendering. Buonarroti had got his likeness perfectly, even to the expression that said he had seen the painful side of life, that his dreams had come true and turned out to be dust. But it was the worship of his masculinity that struck one. Michelangelo had been enthralled by him too. No wonder the women clustered and whispered.

And no wonder no one wanted her to go out through the piazza. She turned on the footman. "It's him."

"Of . . . of course not, miss." He gave a nervous laugh. "How could it be?"

Kate turned back to the statue. And that was just the issue, wasn't it? "You will say it is an ancestor."

"But of course. The statue, it was carved long ago."

"Fifteen hundred four, in fact." But Kate, in her heart, knew that didn't mean it wasn't him. He said his condition gave him properties of healing. Was not age a wound of the most insidious kind? And his mother . . . Kate shook her head, half laughing, half wanting to cry. Pretending that her youthful appearance was an aberration brought about by good face cream . . . That heartsickness she saw in his eyes, echoed in the statue's expression—was it age? Had he seen everything and now could find no joy? His mother still found joy. But perhaps she had not seen what he had.

Her thoughts careened around her head. He had explained away any supernatural elements about him through his disease. Could a disease make one live forever? He might not be eternal, but he had lived more than three hundred years and showed no trace of it. She believed her eyes, no matter any tales he might tell of ancestors who had posed for the *David*. He might not be supernatural, but he was certainly beyond her experience of natural.

In the twilight, she gazed up at the statue. She had imagined him looking just like this, in a stone prison, in chains, being tortured in a way she couldn't understand by the great, green stone that had come into her life shortly after he did.

She felt sandwiched between two unimaginable realities. Gian Urbano was, by any human standards, something beyond natural, regardless of his disease. And she was having visions about things she could not possibly know.

She pushed through the crowd, unseeing, as chaos trembled in the air around her.

"Gian, *cara,* you are up early. The sun isn't yet set."

Gian didn't look up as his mother entered the dim room. He had not even been to bed today. He was still in shirt-sleeves and trousers from last night. He ran a hand through his hair, knowing he looked haggard and disheveled. So much was eating at him: the things he had done in North Africa in the name of a cause, how to get the emerald back to Mirso, his strange pyrotechnic abilities. Everything was confusion. Then too, Kate was leaving soon, and he could not get her out of his mind. For an instant he had considered telling her what he was, asking her to stay. One should never trust anything considered in the small hours of the afternoon. In the twilight, they were revealed as ridiculous.

"I've been thinking about whether I should escort her to England before I embark for Mirso with the stone." He realized he hadn't used her name, but just referred to Kate as "her."

"Ahhhh." His mother sat, her dressing gown of rust-colored silk shushing softly around her. "And you have been considering this all day at the cost of your rest?"

He shrugged. A crack of light around the shutters let in one bar of light.

"But of course you can't do that. You must go to Mirso. Is that why you look so bleak?"

He rose, filled again with the restless energy that had made him pace all day. "No. I just don't see the point anymore, Mother. I mean, after I return the stone . . . it's done. The war is over. Mission completed. Then . . . what?"

"Find something that interests you and do it."

He chuffed a half-laugh and paced to the door and back to the shuttered windows. "What else is there? I've done it all. I built a shipping industry at Amalfi. I worked to establish the duchy here, I was a patron of the arts, but—"

"I never forgave Lorenzo for giving Firenze to his own wretched son when he knew you would have been a better leader. The Medicis." His mother was still bitter after more than three hundred years. "Dynasty over the public good."

"I even joined the Church. Venality, political machinations." He stopped. "I admit you were right about that."

"A miracle, your mother was right." She smiled up at him, her eyes soft. "So does nothing interest you? Not even women?"

He swallowed. "Not . . . not since I returned from Algiers." Her eyes narrowed and he turned away in order not to have to watch her speculate. She wouldn't stop until she knew the whole. So he might as well just tell her. "I can't believe I'm admitting this to my mother." He took a breath. "The man who made Casanova look constant can't . . . hold up his end of the bargain. Perhaps it's a sign that I'm ready for Mirso. I'm half an ascetic already."

"No, *cara mia.* Mirso is the absence of life, though the Elders won't admit it. The war was horrible. But these things pass. You have had no . . . stirrings at all?"

"Well, yes. Stirrings. Always stirrings. But that does not consummate the act." He happened to be standing in front of a heavy bench with an ornately carved back, dark with age. He collapsed onto it. "But I'd lost interest in life even before the war. People, events, places, all took on a dreadful repetition. I think the war actually gave me purpose, for a while." He closed his eyes. "What a purpose. Killing innocents."

"Innocents! Hardly."

"Some of them. Deluded but not evil."

"Delusions have their own evil." Now it was her turn to rise and pace in front of him, her hands stuffed into her rust-colored wrapper's pockets. It swirled around her delicate form. "There is much in the world to do. What one does doesn't always last. But the world inches along toward order and goodness. Sometimes it takes three steps back." She sighed. "All you can do is push the world forward as best you can."

Gian wondered what gave her the strength to find purpose. She had her fingers in a dozen pies. She financed building and improvements across Europe. She provided for artists exiled by the Church, so their work could continue abroad. It was she who encouraged the treaties with Napoleon and suggested his brother Joseph as the king of Napoli. Now she was looking for a way to oust the Spanish. She was indefatigable.

"You didn't seem so defeated yesterday." She stood, tapping her finger on her chin.

"It was you who started me thinking about my future. Or lack of it."

"Was it I?" Now her foot was tapping too. They both felt the sun go down. Their kind always knew where the sun was. She went to the window, throwing open the shutters. "I think perhaps it was the fact that the girl is leaving."

"Nonsense." There *was* something else he wanted of her. "Could you escort Miss Sheridan to England in my stead? Elyta might think she still has the stone." His mother did not move. "And she thinks to start life over in an English village. You must convince her not to do it. She would never listen to me. She doesn't understand the provincial mind. She would be dreadfully unhappy there. The local boys would taunt her. People would look away . . ."

"You told her about the Companion." His mother's voice drifted back into the room.

He shrugged. "She is not unintelligent. She guessed I was vampire. I had to give her some explanation for the traits she observed."

His mother turned into the room. "She knows about the blood?"

"No. Nor about translocation or compulsion. That would only frighten her."

"It is good to have one person who knows. Perhaps you should tell her the whole."

"And have her despise me for a monster? I have considered it carefully."

"In fact, you are preoccupied with this girl." She stared at him without seeing him as she speculated. "I think it is because she does not fawn over you. Indeed, she doesn't seem to even want you. It must be hard for you, who are used to every woman wanting you."

At that he turned, disgusted. "She wants me. I smell her woman's musk." Heightened senses were another gift from the Companion. It was one of the things that had preoccupied him so today. Her wanting him should have made her like all the other women he'd known. It didn't.

"Hmmm." His mother was a silhouette. "Then it shows strength of character in her not to fawn. She will never have anyone make love to her. She knows that."

"Nonsense, Mother. One gets used to her scar. Why, I hardly even see it when I look at her. She's a diamond of the first water, except for that. A man will love her one day." That was good, wasn't it? She deserved love after the indifference she had known in her life.

"You accept her because you were enclosed with her in a carriage for three days and got used to her scar. I doubt that will happen again. Especially in some remote English village."

"You will talk her out of that silly scheme."

"I have no faith in my ability to do so. She seems extremely strong-willed." His mother tapped her finger against her chin. "I would merely like to point out that you do seem to have an interest in life. It is this girl. You should either pursue that interest, or determine she is unimportant so you can move on." She came to stand over him. Now he could see her eyes plainly. "You take the time to find out. I'll bring the stone to Mirso."

He was about to protest when she put her fingers to his lips. "I must away to feed my Companion. Think about it. I will do this for you gladly, *cara mia*."

In a rush of copper-colored silk, she was gone.

His mother was right. Kate might never have a man make love to her again. That was bad. She deserved a full life. He was certain she wasn't a virgin. In a life like hers, what woman could be? That was good. He found virgins boring. But . . . but it must have been a long time since she'd made love. She'd been scarred for what, eight years? And her experience might not have been a good one. To the men who took her, she was no doubt just an object to be used.

As she had been all her life. The "nefarious character" used her to steal. The nuns used her as a good deed in the eyes of God. Matthew Sheridan used her talents. The people she duped used her as a conduit to their dreams. Had anyone ever valued her for herself? Probably not. And no one had ever cared for her comfort or her pleasure. She deserved more.

He wanted to give her more. And if he made love to her, he might just get her out of his system. His mother was no doubt right about that too. That Kate didn't fawn over him or treat him like an object to be acquired was what enthralled him. If he made love to her and she began to cling, well, then he'd know that she was just like all the other women. He'd be free of this strange obsession and be able to go on with life. He could ask the Elders at Mirso if they had any other tasks for him when he returned the stone. Maybe that wouldn't sound so pointless after he had freed himself of Kate Sheridan.

Could he complete the seduction? He couldn't compel her to have wonderful memories in order to erase his failure as he usually did. He swallowed. *Courage, Gian.* There were other ways of making love than with an erect cock. He'd show her the pleasure of mouth and hands. He'd go gently so she wouldn't be frightened, since he was willing to bet no one had cared enough to pleasure her in that way. Perhaps she would forgive his other failure.

He sniffed the air around himself. If he was going to engage in a seduction, he needed fresh clothes and a bath.

Kate marched into the grand Palazzo Vecchio's carriage-way, determined to confront Urbano with his crime of concealment. What else had he concealed from her besides the fact that he had a very, very long life span? It was his fault entirely that her world was infested with visions, and stones that drove one mad, and people with red eyes who smelled of cinnamon and something else, something sweet.

Footmen pulled open the great, carved door.

She had been a perfectly normal person who knew very well that cards didn't tell the future, and that people were out for what they could get, before she met him. And now it looked very like he was going to give her twenty thousand pounds instead of stealing the stone *she* had stolen, and nothing was normal at all.

She limped up the grand staircase, furious. First, she'd just get off these damned half-boots. A maid appeared at the door to her apartment, took one look at her countenance and went wide-eyed. It was Carina.

"Signorina?" Her voice held a tremor.

Kate felt ashamed. "Oh, please, Carina. Don't mind me. My feet hurt."

The girl looked much relieved. At least she wasn't crying. She seemed positively cheerful. "The pinched feet always make for the foul temper. Let me take them, signorina."

Kate collapsed on the dressing table chair and Carina knelt to unbutton the boots. "Joseph! Joseph, a bath," Carina called. "I have the salve, signorina, that will soothe your feet." Taking the offending boots, she pulled open a tiny drawer in the dresser and retrieved a green glass jar. The bath was poured in no time. Did they keep hot water boiling constantly in the kitchens? Kate was soon soaking in nirvana. Her feet felt slightly less like burning logs the size of those in the fireplace in the grand hall, but she was still fuming inside. She heard Carina moving about in the outer room, brushing and hanging her clothing.

The door to her apartments opened. "Signore!" she heard Carina gasp.

"That will be all," the familiar voice rumbled. "You can go."

"Si, signore."

The outer door closed. Kate went still. She wanted this confrontation, but not when she was in a bath. He would never dare enter. Would he? She sighed in relief. She'd locked the door.

The knob turned, stopped . . . and then clicked open with a snap. She gasped. Had she not locked it after all? She covered her breasts with her arms and sank into the water.

He strode into the dressing room and looked around at the shelves for shoes, and cupboards of mahogany imported from India to hold a lady's dresses as if he had never seen anything like them. She would wager he had, a thousand times.

All her planned remonstrations seemed to have dissolved in the steam from the bathwater. "Sir, what . . . what are you thinking?" was all she could say.

His gaze stopped its fluttering progress about the small room. Lord, but he filled it! His energy flapped at her psyche. His eyes came to rest on her. She flushed. They went liquid, hot and swirling in that sea of green. She had the sense of . . . secrets, glimpsed and concealed, almost like the emerald. They fascinated and frightened in equal measure, just like the stone.

"I . . . I came to ask . . ." He cleared his throat. "Do you plan to leave tomorrow?"

"Yes, if the draft came through today and if the carriage can be arranged."

"I am not sure the draft came through."

"Oh. Perhaps it will come in the morning." She frowned. He was in his shirtsleeves. His cravat had been tied in haste. His hair was wet, and . . . and now that she noted it, his shirt clung damply to his body, as though he had not fully dried himself after a bath.

She imagined him bathing, naked, the muscles in his back moving, like the statue in the piazza, but living and warm.

Oh, dear. She was naked in her own bath. Had she ever felt so vulnerable? "Sir, I beg you to retire. I will attend you in . . . in a room of your choice when I have dressed."

He seemed to come to himself. "Yes. Yes, of course." But his eyes never left her. And they had a look in them she was not used to seeing. It was the same look the young men who wanted private readings once had displayed—as if she was a chocolate torte. But that was before the scar. How could he look at her like that now? She turned her face full on him, so he could see her scar clearly. He didn't even flinch. The moment stretched. Finally he tore his gaze away and threw open one of the closets. He pulled out a wrapper and flung it over a stool.

"Don't stay to dress. This will suffice. We have important matters to discuss."

He was gone, the door slamming behind him. Important matters? She pushed herself out of the bath and was surprised to find herself shaking as she dripped. Well, she could hardly be blamed. It was not every day one saw a statue of male perfection come to life and enter one's dressing room while one was bathing.

Ten

He was still there. Kate peered out from the cracked door of her dressing room. She heard his restless pacing, and felt the energy humming along her spine at a rate even more unnerving than usual. He heard her too and turned, confronting her as though he was a Christian in the Colosseum and she an entire pack of lions. She took a breath. She had taken as long as she could to dry herself and put on the cerulean blue silk wrapper he'd chosen. But one couldn't stay locked in one's dressing room all day.

All her anger at him had disappeared. She should try to find it somehow. It might help the way she felt. And how was that? Unnerved by his presence. And why? She managed to hold her head up as she emerged. Because she wanted him, just like every other woman in the world. And she hated that. "You make very free with a lady's boudoir." No doubt he had experience with boudoirs.

He looked her up and down. She might be consumed by that gaze. Could she be mistaking what it meant? She must be. She turned her head, just slightly, to conceal her scar but still observe him. She didn't want to let him out of her sight for several reasons.

His gaze rested on her feet. She hadn't been able to bring herself to put on slippers.

"I . . . I walked too far today." An admission as lame as she was at the moment.

He glanced around and began to roll up his sleeves. "Sit on the bed," he ordered. His voice was hoarse and he cleared his throat. He took the green jar from her dressing table.

She should protest. She never took orders. But she didn't. Perhaps she was distracted by his forearms. They were strong-looking, with a light sprinkling of dark hair. She limped over to the huge bedstead and hoisted herself up on it. "You wanted to . . . to discuss my plans?"

"Yes. Yes, of course." As though he had forgotten.

"You can have the stone the instant I get my draft."

He was unstoppering the jar and . . . kneeling in front of her. She blinked, taken aback.

"That . . . that will be fine." He looked up at her, registered her shock, and . . . smiled at her. No man should have a smile like that. Was he laughing at her reaction to him? That would match his arrogance. But the smile didn't say that. She wasn't quite sure what it said, she who was normally so good at reading people. Maybe . . . reassurance? Hardly. Maybe. But mixed with . . . she didn't know. Wonder?

Without another word he took up a glob of cream and rubbed his hands with it.

And then he began to rub her foot with both hands. She shut her eyes against the tremor of feeling that went directly from her foot to her loins. He massaged the cooling cream deeply, daubing extra on the blisters that were forming on the ball of her foot and her heel.

"Better?" That rumble was quintessentially masculine. Her core turned liquid.

She opened her eyes. The muscles moved in his shoulders

under his shirt and in his forearms. The kneeling position made his thighs bulge. "Uh . . . Yes," she murmured.

He turned his attention to her other foot.

What was she doing here? She was allowing a man in her boudoir to rub her naked feet with his bare hands. And the man was Gian Vincenzo Urbano. The man who had whatever woman he wanted. The man who knew exactly what effect he had on them. And he was having that effect on her. He couldn't want her. He must just want to use her because there was no one else to hand. She shouldn't allow that.

The feel of his strong hands massaging her feet was making it difficult to think.

Then out of the muddle came a clear voice in her head. *Why not? Two can play that game. If you want him, you can have him, right here, right now. He's made that clear. So take what he offers, no matter why he offers it. You'll not get another chance to be bedded by a statue come to life. Or any man at all for that matter.*

He'll discard me after he's had his way.

What of it? You'll have at least one night you would never have had otherwise.

She'd had a dozen men before the last acted as if he might offer her carte blanche and an escape into another life. That had induced Matthew to make certain it could never happen and resulted in her scar. Dalliance with them had been mildly pleasurable. The act itself was merely a moment of grunting and sweating. She had never looked forward to it. But now she thought she might want to feel Gian Urbano grunting and sweating between her thighs. Even the thought of it made her shudder.

He looked up at her again. She turned her head slightly, lest the sight of her scar spoil everything. He rose and took her face between his hands and turned her head. He rubbed his hand over the white spiderweb that laced her cheek.

"Nothing I haven't seen before, Kate. It's been a long time since I even noticed it."

She felt the blood rush to her face. He looked so sincere. Oh, he was a devil, this one, a master in the art of making a woman feel she was the only one in the world, cherished, treasured.

It didn't matter. She wanted to bed him, devil or no. For the next hour, she would pretend he meant what he said. She'd manage her heart tomorrow.

The way she turned her head away nearly broke Gian's heart. She had been so hurt. No wonder she put on the cara-pace and pretended that she didn't care about anyone or anything.

Conflicting emotions churned inside his belly and made his head spin. If she did cling to him after he made love to her, demanding, had he the heart to spurn her? If she didn't, if she didn't care for him at all, and just wanted the use of his body like every other woman he had known, could he bear it?

Gian lifted her chin, expecting her to close her eyes. Her dark hair fell in a mass of waves down her back. But her blue eyes stared up at him, examining, expectant, but not of love. She didn't expect him to love her. Just make love to her. He could smell the musk of her need.

So he would, whether his cock would obey his com-mands or no. It was doing just fine right now. The damned thing was straining at his breeches. The mere feel of her small feet in his hands had sent a charge down his spine and fueled a full erection. But there was no guarantee it would stay the course. That sent a flutter of fear through him. But fear was a luxury he could not afford if he was to give her what she wanted. And right now, that was paramount. He put down his pride, and the part that was ashamed to let her see his failure. He was going to see this through to her end, whether he reached his own or not.

In some way that thought was freeing. He bent to brush her lips with his. Hers were open slightly. He felt her shiver. He pretended he thought she was cold, and took her full in his arms. Her knees opened and he stood between them. He opened his eyes and found her still looking full in his face. And then he bent again and kissed her, thoroughly, his tongue opening her lips and questing inside her mouth, then retreating in invitation. She took him up on his offer and thrust her own tongue inside his mouth to caress his tongue in turn. This was a bold miss, this one. She reached to hold his head, wanting more. So he gave her more. He crushed her breasts against his chest. His cock was throbbing now. She scooted to the edge of the bed to wrap her thighs around his hips. The silk of the wrapper that matched her eyes split apart. She must feel his cock. It pressed against her woman's parts, damp against his breeches. How long since he had wanted a woman like he wanted her now? Since long before the wars, he realized. Years? Decades? Centuries? He couldn't remember.

He pulled away. "This wrapper has more than served its purpose," he murmured.

She shook her head and clutched at the neckline, askew now, so that it revealed almost all of her ripe breasts. "You first."

"Very well." If those were her terms, he'd take them. He'd take almost any terms just now. He leaned against the high bedstead and pulled off his boots. Thank God for the strength of a vampire. He didn't struggle awkwardly with them as a human male would have. She watched him, knees drawn up under her wrapper again, and her lips pink and swelling with their kisses. He pulled at his cravat and tossed it aside and drew his shirt over his head. Her sharp intake of breath did not escape him.

Bells sounded in cascading ripples across the night as the city's churches marked nine o'clock. Good. They had the whole night ahead of them. He wondered how many times he could drive her over the edge to orgasm. And then there was the day. He imagined alternately dozing and making love to her inside the shuttered room, in the heat of Tuscan May. He fumbled at the buttons on his breeches. Leisurely pace was for later. Now, he wanted to make love to her. And "now" was the operative word.

"Damn these buttons." He gave up and ripped the flap of his breeches open. The remaining buttons on each side popped and clattered under the bed.

He stood before her, naked. His cock thrust out straight and bobbing slightly in anticipation. Some seducer. He wanted to thrust it between her delectable thighs and bury it to its hilt while it was still up to the task. That wasn't right, of course. Not what he intended at all. The opportunistic thing was just confusing him with its insistence.

He stood, hesitating. Her eyes were round. A small smile played over her lips as her gaze roved over his body. She raised her brows in a gesture of helplessness as she chuckled a little, and slid off the bed. She put out a hand. It trembled slightly. She wanted to touch him.

He took a breath. Very well. He was here to please her. He stilled himself. She ran her hands over his chest, her thumbs rubbing his nipples. Venus and Bacchus himself! The sensation made them clench and peak. Her hands moved over his shoulders, caressing the place between the muscles in his upper arm, then back up, over his shoulder blades and around to his belly, over the ridges there and down, down to his hips. His cock still bobbed between them. She hadn't touched it, though it was screaming to be touched. She stepped around behind him, the silk of her wrapper shushing against his thighs. She cupped his buttocks, slid one finger along between them, gently, then pressed herself against him and ran her hands back around his chest. Her breasts pressed against his back through the wrapper. He could feel their peaks. Now both her hands ran down his belly and through the hair at his groin and then, gently, lightly, over the length of his cock. He couldn't help the moan that escaped him. More. He wanted more of that.

"Your cock is beautiful," she murmured.

"Where . . . where did a girl like you learn that word?" It was shocking on her lips.

"The streets. It's an Anglo-Saxon word. I know them all. Do you want to hear them?"

He smiled. "Not unless you want to say them." She had known coarseness in her life, and yet she transformed that coarseness into some new substance that wasn't coarse at all through the alchemy of her strength and her resilience.

But she was cupping his stones, lifting them, though they were tight and high with need already. The sound he made this time was a growl, not a moan. Enough!

He turned into her and swept her up in his arms. He laid her on the bed and climbed up after her, breathing hard. He laid himself along her length. His cock throbbed against her thigh. There was time enough for mouth and tongue yet tonight. But first . . . "If you've no objection, I'd like to make use of this erection before it fails me."

"Fails you?" Her brows drew together.

Not what he'd wanted to admit, but he wasn't thinking clearly. "Your reading of the cards, remember? About that you were right. Impotence."

"A temporary condition, if I recall." She smiled in reassurance. "It seems to have passed." She had the strength of character to reassure him even when she was uncertain herself.

"All this dawdling might tempt fate." He was surprised to find he could hardly get the words out around the lump in his throat.

"By all means, then." She spread her knees. That made Gian stop and think, through the haze of lust that throbbed up from his groin. She had done this before all right, and she expected him to just thrust himself inside her and start pumping.

He did not want to give in to that expectation, no matter his need. He gritted his teeth and gently pulled at the tie that held her wrapper. The blue silk slid aside. She was as beautiful as he had known she would be. She had full breasts with rosy nipples, their peaks just now erect and sensitive. Her waist was slender. He had guessed as much. The full hips had been concealed by her dresses though. They were a delightful surprise. She was voluptuous without being coarse in the least. In fact, the fine texture of her skin cried out to be touched. He cupped a breast and bent his mouth to her nipple. She gasped in surprise, and then, as he dedicated himself to his task, she arched and moaned. That was better. That was what she deserved. He gave the other breast the same treatment. She was writhing under his mouth now.

"How . . . how do you do that?" she gasped.

He propped himself on his elbows. "Do what?"

"Cause all that . . . sensation?" She arched again, encouraging him.

Had the men who had bedded her been *that* paltry or inept? "Has no one ever done that to you before?"

She shook her head. Her hair was a dark fan on the midnight blue and gold brocade of the duvet cover. "But I . . . I'm not a virgin. Does that matter?"

Perhaps she was, in many ways having nothing to do with her hymen. "Virginity matters not in the least to me." He might have to revise his opinion that virgins were boring though. He was suddenly more excited to show her what it meant to really make love than to satisfy his own needs. Let his cock fail and be damned. "There are other sensations you'll like." He scooted down and set himself on his belly between her thighs. "Trust me now. I know women."

He saw a little frisson of doubt cross her eyes and be replaced by a determined look. "That's right." He smiled, then turned his attention to the thatch between her legs. He parted the curls, drinking in the scent of her musk. He bent and let his tongue part the lips beneath. She gasped in shock. He laid his hands on her thighs to keep her from instinctively closing them against the intensity of feeling, and lapped again. Her wetness was salty and clean, like the sea. After five or six gentle strokes she relaxed into the sensation. He then paid more attention to her nub of pleasure. He would have her moaning and lifting her hips for more in a moment.

He did. She did.

Her shriek, when it came, was followed immediately by a wrenching shudder and she collapsed in tears. He wiped his mouth and slid up beside her to cradle her in his arms as she sobbed. He knew full well they were sobs of release and amazement, not sorrow. His own release seemed unimportant at this point. That was not to say his interest had flagged. On the contrary, his erection lay along her hip even now. He could feel the wetness at the tip born of denial. Fine. Let it be denied. Kate needed something very different just now.

Kate shuddered and sobbed in his arms. She couldn't think why she was crying. It was the most wonderful sensation she had ever experienced. Though she'd thought she might be going mad, or maybe *had* gone mad when her world seemed to shatter into points of light. None of her other lovers had ever done *that* to her. It must be because no one had been brave enough to lick her . . . down there. She'd never even heard of that before and she thought she'd heard it all. How good of Gian to sacrifice himself in that way. It must have been a horrible task. And she would never experience it again.

That made her sobs subside into hiccups. He had been very good to her. Surely he deserved something in return. His arms around her felt more comforting than anything she had ever known. Had anyone ever just *held* her like that? She couldn't remember it. Her mother, unknown that she was, perhaps. But then perhaps not. Who could have held anyone like this and still abandoned them? Gian Urbano, she reminded herself. He had held many just like this, and abandoned them, just as he would her shortly.

It didn't matter. He still deserved something in return for what he had just done. Come to think of it, he undoubtedly expected it. No one performed such a generous act without expecting something in return. But what could she do to equal that?

"Is there some way I can give you that much pleasure? I will do it gladly." She didn't like that she sounded shy. Definitely not like a woman of the world.

He smiled down at her. Did he practice it to make it seem so . . . genuine? Of course he did. He'd done a good job. "Probably many ways. If you don't mind, I'd like to stay simple. When you are ready, of course."

"I'm ready now," she assured him.

"So soon?"

Was there something to be ready for besides his sweating weight on top of her while she spread her legs and lay there, trying to breathe? Oh, he wanted to know if she had caught her breath after sobbing. She nodded and turned in his arms so she could spread her knees again.

But all he did was kiss her neck. It made her suck in air as though the breath was her first. And then his lips came back to kiss her lips again. The urgency of the first time was gone. He bit at her lower lip gently and swabbed it with his tongue.

That marvelous tongue. It made her shudder just to think of what it had done to her. The prickle of his chest hair across her nipples sent sparks of sensation across her body. His hand on her waist made her acutely aware of how smooth his palm was. It moved to her hip, and then around it. He pulled her to him, and then he scooted around *under* her. Before she knew it, she was kneeling, straddling his hips, his cock lying between her legs with its leaking tip peeking out in front of her.

She smiled a question at him. What kind of a position was this? In truth it made her feel a little vulnerable, since her breasts and belly were so exposed. Even in the dim light, he would be able to see her clearly. Always before, the men wanted to spill their seed in her by crushing her underneath them where they couldn't even see her. This was in some ways much more intimate. He made no suggestion, though his eyes were burning with heat. He wanted something. She looked down. Maybe he wanted her to touch his cock. She placed her thumb on the vein of the shaft and ran it up to the tip. It was larger than those of the men she had known when it was fully erect. She wondered uneasily if it would tear her when he started thrusting. She put that thought aside. He expected. She owed. She concentrated on giving him sensation. The leaking fluid made it easier to rub. He was breathing hard. She liked that. When he ran out of moisture, she slid her hips up and back across it. Her slickness was good for something. His hands sought out her waist and helped her move. That started her own nether parts tingling again. The vulnerability of her body to his eyes seemed to matter less as the sensation ramped up.

"Now you're ready," he whispered as he half sat and put his arm around her bottom. He lifted her as though she weighed nothing, and angled his shaft with his other hand. He eased her down until she was kneeling upright, his cock rubbing at her entry. "You are in control now, Kate. Do as you will."

He meant to do it like this, with her sitting astride him? She set her lips. Well, if this would please him, she would do it. "Am I too heavy?"

A tiny smile played around the corners of his lips and lighted his eyes before he suppressed it. "No."

She eased herself lower, settling, and felt his cock enter her, just barely. This was really quite nice. She could decide exactly how fast she could accept it. That would eliminate that awful dry, skewered feeling she remembered. Though dry didn't seem to be a problem at all. It might even mean she could encompass all of him if she did it slowly enough. And she could decide just how she wanted to give him his pleasure. It was a peculiar feeling—being in control during the sexual act. Always before she had seemed . . . detached, a witness, a victim. But here he was, ceding her the direction of it. It was . . . equalizing.

She settled further. It felt quite satisfying to be filled. She wiggled her hips and pushed herself down. Ahhhh. That was nice. He sighed as she accepted him. And she wasn't torn at all. She pushed herself up, experimentally, and lowered. He lifted his hips to meet her. Yes, that was even better. She had all of him inside her now. His hands moved to her waist again. He lifted only when she began to raise herself. He assisted only. His hand went round to cup her buttocks. She began to move just as the men had moved on top of her, slowly at first and then a little faster. He arched to meet her and lifted at her cue. It was effortless, really. On a whim she stopped and just rocked a little as she sat. He groaned. She could feel his member pressing against the inside of her belly. He changed the angle just a little by shifting her weight, and . . . and the sensation inside her seemed to multiply. She tried rocking again. "Oh!"

"Does that feel good?"

"Oh, oh, yes." And what made it so special was that they

were both feeling it. The pleasure was shared, and seemed to multiply as they passed it back and forth between them.

It felt so good she . . . she thought the madness might come on again, what with her nether lips grinding against his groin and him filling her so fully, and the tip of his shaft rubbing against the inside of her belly. And now she was raising and lowering herself faster, but he was helping her, and her buttocks were slapping against the soft mounds of his stones and the clenching muscle of his thighs, and he was arching, a grimace on his face, of pleasure? Pain?

Impotence was not a problem. Gian was driven almost to madness by the sensation of Kate sliding up and down on his cock. And he was filled with satisfaction because he was a true man again, and he had given her a pleasure she had never known before, and he would give it to her again and again in short order, until she was sated and dazed. He lifted her as she moaned and grunted. His chest, his belly, his brain were all full to bursting with emotion.

Oh, God.

Wasn't high emotion just the trigger for things around him to burst into flame?

He stilled her movement. She pressed herself down on his cock until he gasped. *Banish emotion!* Maybe it was good he'd been denied orgasm since he got back. Maybe he would have set fire to anyone around him at the climax. He licked his lips and tried to quiet his breathing.

She opened her eyes. They had a question in them. "What's wrong?"

He managed a wobbly smile. "Nothing. It's just . . . just that I want to pay more particular attention to your pleasure." He lifted her off him. She knelt at his side.

Her brows knitted. "I was having quite a bit of pleasure there. You weren't?"

She knew very well he'd had. "Yes. Yes I was. But I'll . . . I'll just save myself for later." He got up on one elbow and reached for her to draw her into his body where he could kiss her. His cock was screaming its disappointment at him.

She stayed his hands, looking wary. "I don't want this to be one-sided. I've only just realized how . . . good it is when two share sensations . . ." She sat back and glanced to his cock, throbbing insistently against his belly. "If you're worried about . . . about faltering, that really doesn't seem to be a problem." She gave a roguish smile and reached for his erection.

That would be bad. He flinched away. And immediately saw the hurt in her eyes.

Her smile wavered and she turned her damaged cheek away. "If you'd rather not . . ."

"God, Kate, no . . . it's not that." He gathered her into his arms, though she had stiffened. She was trying to harden herself against the hurt. He swallowed. The only thing that might spare her pain was the truth. "I . . . I didn't tell you everything about my condition." He buried his head in her neck so he didn't have to look at her. Her soft scent assailed him. "I think I started the fire in your rooms. I was angry at Elyta. My anger expressed itself in . . . flame. It's happened before. What if, at the climax now, I did something like that again? What if I burned you?"

"What?" Kate couldn't believe her ears. He thought he started fires with just his anger? And if he spilled his seed he might burn her? This was too wild.

"I create spontaneous combustion at times of high emotion." His voice cracked.

She held him back from her. Even now the feel of his satin skin covering the hard muscles on his shoulders sent shrieks of sensation to her loins. She glanced to his en-gorged member. Even as he protested, he wanted to climax with her. He couldn't hide that. She examined his eyes. Pain, regret, determination. He believed what he said.

She didn't. No one could create flames from nothing. He was just nervous about ending a long bout of impotence. The pressure was too much . . . He was making excuses in order not to face it. There was no chance she'd let him give her pleasure without taking his own. That smacked of what she'd experienced with the marks so long ago. And she rather thought she'd been on the brink of some discovery when they'd stopped, some transformation that would change the rest of her life. "How many women have you burned at . . . intimate moments?"

"Well, none," he said as though that didn't matter. "But I haven't . . . carried through in more than two years."

"Oh. That's right. When you actually started fires, it oc-curred when you were angry."

"Don't make fun of this. I . . . I started the fire when Elyta and I were struggling, and I set LaRoque's lodgings on fire when he was trying to kill me. And now that I look back on it, I started fires in Algiers, when I was fighting a war there."

Kate suppressed a smile. The fires were all coincidence of course. Lamps overturned in struggles, coals from open fires in North Africa scattered. She'd never make him be-lieve that. So she took another tack. "Sounds to me like you start fires only when your life is in danger."

She saw him cataloging the incidents, behind his eyes. "It may be." His eyes focused on her. "But what if it's not?"

Now she let her smile show. "I promise I will sing out at the first sensation of burning."

"You don't know the danger . . ."

"I won't let you pleasure me if you won't join in." Ulti-matums were never fair, but really, he was being ridiculous.

A stubborn look came into his eyes. "Are you really going to let this come between us, when you aren't certain?" His resolve flickered. "You'll be a monk, and I . . ." She had to say it. "I'll never experience what it's like to share that sensation together."

"Don't say that." He sat up and took her in his arms. She softened into his embrace. She'd won. She knew it if he didn't. "Of course you will."

"I don't think so. Don't deprive me, Gian." It was his turn to hold her away from him. His eyes were filled and still uncertain. "It will be well. You'll see." She ran her hand along his jawline and he melted. He took her hand in both of his and kissed her palm. His lips were soft. It made her almost shudder with desire. She pressed her body into his, and rubbed her breasts across his chest. Her hand strayed to his cock and stroked it lightly. "Now where were we?"

He kissed her neck, gently, just as he had caressed her palm. The brink that she was sure he had been on seemed distant now. He'd try to hold himself back. Well, she wasn't going to let him. Her lips found his and she kissed him thoroughly. His cock was throbbing in her hand. Satisfaction warred with desire in her. She pushed him back firmly onto the tangled bedclothes and straddled him again. Now it was he who must feel vulnerable. She took his eager cock and tilted it up, then eased herself down over it. That made her breath come in hissing gasps. She reached around to caress his balls. She raised herself and lowered. He was beginning to breathe heavily. That was good.

"Can you help me find the proper angle?" His eyes closed once before he nodded and held her bottom with both hands to adjust her. God. There it was. Sensation ramped up. She pressed her hands against his chest, thumbing his peaked nipples, to push up and lower herself. Now he was helping her again. His chest heaved. Was that a low moan? He bit his lip, but he didn't stop. She felt as though she was swelling around his erection. Each trip up and down his cock increased her pleasure, but she kept careful track that he was coming along with her. She wouldn't let him hold back.

She knew he was near the edge when he tried to still her movement. "No, no you don't," she warned and pushed herself down again. She rocked against him and then thrust up. He groaned and sucked in breath. Sweat gleamed on his body in the lamplight. He was the most beautiful thing she had ever seen.

She couldn't hold it back anymore. Inevitability washed over her. The world exploded a second time. This time she saved enough of herself to know she was contracting around him in rhythm to her shock waves, squeezing him, until he arched and grunted. Inside, she felt him spurting. That was familiar, though nothing else about this whole experience had been. He was trembling, his hips making small, fierce thrusts even at the maximum arch against her. It went on and on, much longer than the brief spurts she'd experienced with her former partners.

When at last he was done, they both collapsed together. He settled her in against his side. She looked up at him. "Not a flame in sight."

He smiled. It was the most tender expression she'd ever seen. "Thank you for that."

"I acted only in self-interest." Not quite true, but near enough. "Dear me, but you were *très puissant*." His smile grew. It looked a little smug. That was very well. If he had been that long deprived, he had a right to be satisfied with himself. Kate was satisfied with herself as well. She had done that to him. Even when he had tried to hold back.

It occurred to her that in some ways he was the opposite of arrogant underneath the surface. He had been so unsure of himself tonight.

And what had happened to her? Had she tumbled over

that brink at last and been transformed? She couldn't remember quite what the brink had been. Her imagination most likely. Still she had never realized such incredible sensation could be part of having a man's cock inside you. Or maybe it was only Gian Vincenzo Urbano's cock. She was glad she'd done it, even if it was over and done with forever. Even if he was gone when she woke. She settled in closer against him, drinking in his scent, and closed her eyes.

Eleven

That was a disaster. Gian looked down on her where she slept in his arms. She'd hardly wakened when he'd lifted her and pulled back the covers to lay her on the sheets. Her dusky lashes swept her cheek, the one without the scar. Her black hair gleamed in the guttering candlelight. He pulled the coverlet up over her shoulders.

Two disasters were avoided. He hadn't set anything, including her, on fire. Or rather he'd set her ablaze only in the sexual sense. She certainly was a passionate little thing. And he had done his part from first to last. Even now his cock was willing. It rose where their thighs tangled wetly together. He was a man again, well and truly. That felt good.

The lazy smile rising to his lips turned sour. The true disaster was that he had not gotten her out of his system. Far from it. She had wound her way even more tightly into his psyche.

I . . . I think I'm in love with her.

The thought struck him like a blow. He had never allowed himself to fall in love in all his years. Was that why he hadn't recognized it? They bickered. She was impossible. She was a charlatan and a thief who had not the slightest conception of duty and honor. They had nothing in common but a certain distance from their fellow man, and a biting, cynical perspective on the world. Strange in one who had lived not a single lifetime. And intelligence. He had always been a snob about intelligence. Courage? He should have so much courage as she did.

Still, they were different species altogether. But pleasing her, protecting her from her own insecurities or anything else that threatened her, was the most important thing in the world to him. Was that . . . could that really be love? All he knew was that he couldn't imagine being without her. And that had never happened to him before. He wasn't quite sure how it had come about. Who knew that love could coexist— no, flourish—with exasperation and annoyance?

And by the way, how could any prick have made love to this woman and never given her an orgasm? He was fairly sure tonight was her first. And second. The smug smile rose to his lips again. He could not help it. There were advantages to having a carnal knowledge of thousands of women. He'd given her pleasure. He would give her more tonight, and later today.

And then what? That was the disadvantage to his centuries. He could not lie to himself. It was one hell of a disadvantage.

I am a vampire, just as you suspected, a monster who drinks blood, and I will live forever while you fade and age. Join me.

Hardly an alluring proposition for any woman. One he had vowed never to propose. If she somehow could manage to care for such a monster, the difference in life span stood between them and would ultimately break her heart as it had his father's. And if he didn't tell her and she accepted him . . . well, then he could conceal his failure to age for a few years. A dozen? Two? Such a short time in the span of things. And after that there was only telling her or desertion.

How could he abandon her, who was scarred by her parents abandoning her?

Perhaps there was no choice about that. Better early when she was not involved emotionally with him than after they had spent a dozen years together. That would be even more of a betrayal. A dozen years with Kate would be heaven. But he could not be so selfish. He must begin imagining life without her.

He settled her more securely in his arms and brushed his lips across her hair. The air around him felt thick, like a weight on his chest. The ache inside him couldn't decide whether to come to rest in his heart or his belly. He almost wished he hadn't realized he loved her. How would he bear giving her up? He had thought his life seemed bleak when he returned from Algiers. Now the landscape of his life was dry and featureless.

"Kate," he murmured. "Kate."

Rain began to hammer at the roof. Outside the open doors to the balcony, it came down like a curtain of tears. He looked down at her again, sleeping so securely in his arms. He must not let her become attached to him. That would be difficult. Women always seemed to fall in love with the first man who gave them an orgasm. Yet another reason for his rule against virgins. But was she attached? He wasn't sure. Maybe she had just wanted his body. If that was true, it was just as well. He would not let her see his sorrow. He would do his duty and send her on her way. No, better, he'd ask her to stay here with his mother while he went to Mirso with the stone, then he'd accompany her to London himself, see that she was settled. And then he'd have done his duty all around. Maybe he'd return to Mirso, for good this time, and take the Vow. He squeezed his eyes shut. All that was for later. For the next hours, he just wanted to take care of Kate.

He eased himself out of bed. He'd start by getting her

some food. She'd be hungry when she woke. Some wine from his vineyards at Montalcino, cheese, fresh tomatoes from the garden, olives, a little bread and olive oil . . .

He dressed hastily and slid out the door to find a servant. Or no . . . he'd go directly to the kitchens.

Kate rolled over and considered opening her eyes. The bed was empty. She could feel that. What had she expected?

What she had not expected was how much his leaving hurt.

You are in trouble, Kate, my girl. Best get out your suit of armor. Because if he ever knew how vulnerable your heart is, he would use it against you in a second.

She had taken him to bed for purely selfish reasons. And some deity or other had dispensed her comeuppance. Because she had lost her heart. Actually had probably lost it long before he ever stripped and made love to her so tenderly. How had this happened? She had never loved anyone before. Maybe she loved her parents, but she couldn't remember that. And it had turned out badly anyway.

This would turn out badly too. She had thought when she first met him that he was just a pretty face that turned her head. A pretty face and an exquisitely masculine body. But what she felt was more, much more than that. She liked him. And it was comforting that she was not the only one. His servants, his mother, even his horse Piccolo doted on him. But somewhere along the line in the last days he had wormed his way past liking.

Her mind returned to how generous he had been, how . . . sweet to her. Not a word she would have associated with Gian Urbano before this night. Why had he done it? Why had he bothered to give her so much pleasure? No other man had ever done so. And no one had ever had the

inclination to bed her at all since the scar. The way he had
lifted her face and looked full in her eyes without flinching
had been . . . unbelievable. What must it have cost him to
make love to a woman who looked like her? She had not expected such generosity. Even if he was lacking for other
partners (which he couldn't be, could he?) she would have
thought when he had been ready to get past his fear of being
impotent, he'd have chosen one of the servants, or . . . or
anyone besides her. And once she knew he was willing to
bed her, she would have been content to have him in the
same way she had accommodated Matthew's arranged partners, but he had given her so much more. And he seemed to
want so little in return.

His silly fear of starting fires—what was that about? No
matter that it was born of his fear of failing as a man, it was
real enough to him. She was glad she could help him get
past it. Perhaps that had been recompense at least in part for
the realization he had given her that pleasure could be
shared. Lord knows, he'd be back to arrogant again now.

She remembered how angry she had been at him about
the fact that he was centuries old and hadn't told her. He did
seem to be the nexus of all the chaos in her life. But she
couldn't be angry with him, not anymore. Indeed, what
point to accost him about it at all? Just to hear him lie? One
thing hadn't changed. He was a consummate liar. He'd
probably tell her he loved her, as he must have told a thousand other women, right up until the moment he paid her,
packed her off for England, and never thought of her again.

She sat up, sighing. Best she get her clothes on before
the servants saw them scattered all over the carpet. His own
clothes were already gone. He had exacted his price for the
lovemaking after all. Or soon would. He was about to break
her heart.

Nonsense, she told herself. *You had never known what*

making love was before tonight, and your life was poorer for it. Now you do. That was a generous gift. Don't be greedy.

Gian picked up the tray from the table in the hall where Kate's dresser had set it. The world looked . . . clean from the arches in the hallway that looked out over the Uffizi. He had put on a silk jacket over a pair of breeches he wore without the benefit of smalls and picked out several books from his mother's excellent library. For Kate a first edition of Dante's *Divina Commedia* to introduce her to Firenze's most famous literary son, and, since she seemed to like the Romantics, he brought his copy of *Don Quixote*. He'd also brought a very special book he had from India. He grinned. She might be offended by that one. Or she might just like it very much. He'd been surprised at how open and sensual she had been this night, for one who had never experienced a generous partner. It was bad that he loved her. But on the other hand, he hadn't set his lover on fire. And he was more than capable for the first time in more than two years of holding up his end of the sexual bargain. Which he intended to do repeatedly tonight and right through the day.

"Bring up some extra candles, Carina, if you would." The serving girl looked remarkably radiant, though her eyes were red. She had been moping about since the moment he first gave her orders for Kate's comfort after the journey. "You seem more cheerful."

"Giovanni proposed to me, just like the Signorina said he would, in my room with the rain coming down. I expect I has her to thank for it somehow."

Gian drew his brows together. "Miss Sheridan told you he would propose?"

"She saw my eyes last night, all red they was from cryin' over that fat girl that delivers the shellfish, because I thought he was making eyes at her, and the Signorina went all funny like for a minute, and then she comes to herself and says I wasn't to worry, that a groom would propose to me up under the eaves with the rain coming down. And he did, just now."

Gian managed a smile. "And you said yes, I presume."

The girl beamed. "I hope the mistress don't mind. I mean, I'd hate for one of us to have to find another situation."

"I'm sure she looks fondly on true love," Gian said. "My congratulations."

"Just call if there's anything you or the Signorina need. I expect you won't want to be coming out for a while just yet." Carina waved most improperly as she skipped toward the narrow servants' staircase.

Gian sighed. Well, he and Kate hadn't actually been quiet. It wasn't surprising that the whole household knew. They would also shortly know that Kate had "predicted" the proposal of the feckless Giovanni. Had she? If she had just been playing at her chicanery and she'd been wrong, the girl would have been devastated. Kate wasn't that cruel, was she? She pretended to be hard and uncaring, but he had seen beneath that. She might have guessed the girl was crying over a man. But the detail of the rain and the fact that he was a groom?

Everything he'd heard said about her fortunes indicated they were humdrum predictions about whatever her victim wanted to hear. Except that very pointed warning to the conte about staying home on Thursday and avoiding coaches. He wished he knew exactly what had happened to the conte on Thursday, but they had left Rome by then.

And then there was his own reading. He hadn't minded all the foolishness about being the devil. He was used to that. But the impotence? A lucky guess? Something she'd heard? He'd taken pains to conceal it, else the supply of bedmates to give him blood would have dried up.

And the part about the stone? He'd always believed she got that information from LaRoque. But then, why alert Gian to her knowledge? She should have wanted to keep their association secret. As for this latest "vision," maybe she had seen or heard Giovanni do something that indicated he would propose. But again, how could she know about the rain?

Hmmm. Interesting. When had he not known everything about a woman? He should mistrust her. But on some visceral level, he trusted her more than he had ever trusted anyone in his life. It had to do with the vulnerability he saw beneath the hard exterior. She only pretended to be heartless and amoral. Didn't she?

He knocked at the door with the corner of the tray.

"Come in." Kate's voice drifted out. It had a somber tone to it.

"My hands are full. You'll have to let me in."

Hesitant steps. The door cracked open, hardly an inch, and Kate peered out.

"I thought you might be hungry."

"Oh."

"Well, aren't you?"

"Yes. Yes, I'm hungry."

"Well, then, you might want to let me in."

"Oh." This time the door opened wide. She was dressed in that beautiful blue wrapper that matched her eyes again, and she smelled of what they had done together. He smiled. How could he not? Like Vulcan drawn to Aphrodite, he was lost, no matter who she was.

What was he doing back? And bringing her food, and . . . were those books under his arm? And . . . he had on a man's dressing gown. Kate's mind fluttered around what that might mean.

Then he smiled. Kate stepped back and swung the door

wide under the blast from that smile. Perhaps she would get used to it, but at present, it devastated her every time he did it. But then, she would not have time to get used to it. She was leaving today, if the draft arrived. She glanced to the doors open onto the balcony and saw the first hint of lightening in the sky.

He set the tray down on the bed, closed the shutters to the balcony tightly, and pulled the heavy velvet draperies across their rod. In order not to be caught staring at the body she knew moved beneath the silk of his dressing gown, she sat cross-legged and busied herself with the tray. He had brought quite a repast. She popped an olive into her mouth. They were green, pungent. They seemed to hold the summer sun. "This is good."

He opened the bottle and poured her some wine. "My own vintage," he murmured. He unveiled the cheese and the tomatoes, sprinkled them with basil and drizzled oil over them.

Kate took a bite. "Lovely. The oil tastes fruity."

She looked up to find he was watching her as she ate. He made no move to eat himself. He was going to tell her he was leaving. He had come back only for that.

"Your maid may be preoccupied today. One of my mother's grooms proposed to her last night during the rainstorm."

Kate felt the blood drain from her face. The fork she held clattered to the tray as the room began to spin. "So . . . so soon? I . . . I wasn't sure just when . . ."

Somehow he was holding her. He'd swept the tray to the other side of the bed and she was shaking as he held her to his chest. "Oh, God, Gian." The sobs took her. "I wasn't . . . sure, not . . . not until now."

"It's all right." He stroked her hair. "It's all right."

She wanted him to hold her forever. And that was exactly why she couldn't let him continue. She sat up and tried to get her breath. "I'm fine. Just startled, that's all."

He handed her the glass of wine. "I take it this is a recent development?"

"Since . . . that night at the marquesa's little gathering. That was the first time. The one with the stone." And the one with him in it. Dear God, he was going to be tortured! She had to prevent that somehow. Could it be prevented? She grabbed his biceps. "Gian, I saw you, chained to a stone wall. Like it was a dungeon. And someone was . . . hurting you with that stone."

His face turned grim, but his tone was light. "Did you happen to see who it was?"

"A woman's hand, no more."

He lifted his brows, thinking. "Probably Elyta. I have not . . . endeared myself to her."

"What is this stone that it can hurt you and drive the jeweler mad?"

He frowned. He was thinking how to lie to her. "It is a . . . a relic if you will, from the first of those with the Companion in their blood."

"The Companion?"

"The parasite that shares our veins."

"I thought you said it was an infection. Gian, you have got to tell me the truth about you at least, because so many strange things have been happening to me, I just don't think I can bear it if I don't understand at least in part." Still she saw him hesitate. "I know, for instance that you are very, very old. Don't even bother to tell me that Michelangelo sculpted some ancestor." That closed his mouth before he could even speak. "And I've been having visions about people's moments of intense emotion in the future. I could have been mistaken about the others. But one has just come true. Not to mention the emerald that drives people mad. It's all too much."

He started to speak, then pressed his lips together and looked away.

"Very well," she said, rushing on. "So you won't tell me. Probably out of some mistaken sense of duty to somebody or other, or honor or something. You have to tell me what the stone can do. Why do I see it hurting you? I have to know that."

He looked down at the brocade bedcover, obviously disgusted with himself. "It takes energy from those who have the Companion."

"I've felt your vibrations. Is that your . . . Companion doing that?"

"Yes. The Companion provides energy to us. The stone saps it and leaves us weak. I think it can kill us. But only if it touches our flesh."

She realized that he'd never touched it. No wonder he'd let her keep it after she'd removed it from its box. "And we . . . others?" She couldn't say "humans."

"It drives you mad when you look into it."

She knew that first hand. But it was hard to hear it confirmed so calmly. "How?"

"It is said that you see all possible futures in it."

"But it didn't drive me mad, and I looked at it."

He looked up at her under his brows. "Yes. That has me puzzled. There are many puzzling things about you."

She sighed. "Why does Elyta want it?"

"I don't know the particulars. But think what she could do with it." His voice was grim. "She could kill the Elders of our kind. She could drive the men who direct history mad, bring down governments . . ."

"I see what you mean." But Kate really didn't care much about all those theoretical possibilities. "We must prevent this . . . this thing from happening to you." She had always thought he wanted the stone to give to some woman, if she considered it at all. But he couldn't, not if it drove people mad. "What do you mean to do with the emerald?"

"Take it to Mirso Monastery, a refuge for those who are

infected as I am. The monks there will keep it from doing harm to anyone."

"Just throw it in the nearest lake. That's the way to keep out of anyone's dungeon."

He let out a breath, as though he had been holding it. "I can't do that."

"Why not?"

"Because I'm honor-bound to return it to Mirso."

She could hardly believe what she was hearing. "With Elyta waiting to kill you for it, and my vision of you being tortured, you're still considering going on some insane journey to . . . where is this Mirso Monastery?"

"The Carpathian Mountains."

"Transylvania." She frowned. "Does it have dungeons?"

"I expect so." He dismissed that. "I'll make arrangements tonight and go tomorrow."

"So that's it. You're going to just throw yourself in the way of being tortured for some stupid promise you made to some monks."

"We live by our promises. They are the only compass we have." His voice went distant.

"Well, I don't have that compass. If you made a mistake promising, just don't do it."

"That's not who I am." His brows drew together.

"Well, maybe you ought to change that."

He took a breath. She felt him recede again. He was shocked at her. But then he reengaged. "We don't know that your visions all come true. Only the one about Carina has for certain." He took her shoulders. "Even if it is true, for all we know, if I don't go, Elyta will storm Firenze and imprison me in the dungeons of this palazzo."

She gasped. "This house has dungeons?"

"We use ours for wine." He shrugged. "We cannot know how to avoid your vision, if it is true, or if it could be avoided."

"God, this is awful."

He touched her cheek, the one without the scar. She had almost forgotten about the scar. "Perhaps that is why one shouldn't take too much stock in visions." His voice rumbled even when it was almost a whisper. "Perhaps the visions are only a possible future. And anyway, we can do nothing today except worry, and that seems a waste of precious time." He took a larger book from the stack he'd brought. "Let me distract you." He opened it to a random page. Figures entwined together. They had slanting, dark-lined eyes, and they were . . .

Kate peered closer. Oh, my dear Lord in heaven. That was a phallus, and another there, and there. And the people were . . . copulating? It was a little hard to tell.

"It's called the *Kama Sutra*. It's Indian."

Kate drew the book closer. "Can people *do* that?"

"Oh, yes. Though I must admit some positions are not entirely comfortable." He lifted her chin. "But there are one or two I can personally recommend."

She looked into those green eyes. If there was only to be one more day together, she knew how she wanted to spend it. She clutched him to her. "I am afraid."

"So am I," he murmured into her hair. "So to hell with fear. Let's make love."

How could he sleep like that when tonight or tomorrow night he was going to leave the sanctuary of Florence and take the bloody emerald halfway across Europe with Elyta and Kate's own vision waiting to waylay him? Kate took a curl of dark hair and pushed it behind his ear. He didn't stir. Not that today had not been wonderful. She smiled when she remembered how she'd surprised him by licking him in return. She'd seen a picture of a woman doing that in the book, and after some initial hesitation, she'd gone about it quite enthusiastically. How she liked to make him moan. It hadn't been distasteful at all. A little salty, perhaps, along with the cinnamon.

But now the light leaking around the shutters was copper red and fading. Soon it would be evening. He would take the emerald and go to some god-awful place in the mountains, if Elyta didn't catch him first. What to do? She felt sure his impulse to follow his duty at any cost was wrong. The man seemed to have a thousand bloody internal rules about how he should act. And he was stubborn to a fault. She sat up and hugged her knees to her chest beneath the brocade bedcover. The wardrobe loomed in the corner. In the lower right-hand drawer, the stone sat inside her reticule. She could practically feel its presence. It was as though it was . . . brooding. Or threatening. It was a threat, all right, to Gian more than anyone.

Why didn't she go mad when she looked at it? She chewed one nail.

Perhaps it was because while it showed all possible futures, she saw the real future and she was immune to the chaos of possibilities. And hadn't all her visions started when the stone had come into her life? Maybe it was the reason she was having visions. Maybe the stone was the answer to all her questions.

She eased herself out of bed, so as not to wake Gian. Books were scattered on the floor, along with two large silver trays, assorted china, three wine bottles, and the remains of their meals. And their dressing gowns. Gian's was nearest, black silk embroidered in red to highlight some kind of Oriental writing. She slipped it on, reveling in the scent of him that clung to it, and went to kneel in front of the wardrobe door.

A certain satisfaction hovered in the air. Did she imagine that it was the stone that called her, and that now hummed with satisfaction? She opened the drawer and rummaged to the bottom, pulling out her silver-embroidered reticule. The stone was heavy inside it. She swallowed. *I'm immune, for better or for worse,* she told herself. *Stop delaying and just open it.*

Still, it took her several moments to pull open the drawstring and fish around for the stone. Its cool, smooth surface in her palm promised, threatened. She opened her hand. At first she saw only the green cabochon mound, perfect, without the little clouds of imperfection most emeralds contained. Then, deep inside, the lazy coils rolled with their glinting scales. She tried to breathe, but it was hard. The scales flashed, coruscating. She couldn't quite make out . . .

A feeling of dislocation from herself descended.

No! But it was too late. The room disappeared abruptly and was replaced by a desert landscape. A few gigantic hewn building stones littered the sand. A red and gold striped tent was pitched among them and five camels knelt in its shade. She sensed a yearning in the air almost painful in its intensity. Then the sand began to whirl, and she whirled with it. And she was home. *Home!* She was shouting. It was the most joyful moment she had ever experienced. She wanted to cry and laugh and scream and tear at her hair. *Home!* She caught a glimpse of many other giant gemstones, blue and red and green and clear white, gleaming and whirling in a tower of light. And over all poured water, precious water. Around the fountain, huge stone statues of some unknown gods loomed up into the darkness. It was a frightening place. But she wasn't frightened. Peace filled her.

The room wavered back into view around her. The feeling of peace still enveloped her. She looked down at the stone, cupped in her hands.

"Gian," she called softly.

"What, my love?" His voice was sleepy.

She rose, cradling the stone. He sat up, alarmed now. "What is it, Kate?"

"The stone doesn't want to go to Transylvania. It wants to go back to the desert."

He frowned. But he didn't say that stones don't want things. He didn't ask which desert.

"Not just the desert, though. There were other jewels there. Together they seemed . . . alive. And it was . . . a temple? Maybe. Dark and underground. That's where you must take it."

"I can't." His voice was flat.

"What, you don't have boats?" He was just being contrary. The stone *had* to get back to the desert. She could feel its need even now.

"Of course I have ships. I still keep a small fleet at Amalfi."

How wrong she had been to think him a struggling gigolo. "Well, then. It's settled."

"I promised I'd take it to Mirso."

Now he was just being difficult. "Take it to the desert, Gian. Avoid the dungeon."

"Or maybe the dungeon you saw is in the desert. I'm won't play that game." He got out of bed and pulled on his breeches. His expression said he was struggling with something. Then it hardened. "I must make arrangements to go."

She felt herself shut down. "I must as well. I'm sure the draft on your mother's bank is ready. I'm not giving you the stone until I have it in my hand." Why had she said something like that? She hadn't even been thinking about going yet. She'd forgotten all about England. Maybe because he was leaving her just like he'd left every other woman in his life. Just like she'd been left so long ago. She didn't want to be like all the other women in his life and she didn't want to be the one who was abandoned. The best way to do that was to let him know it was really she who was leaving. She wouldn't wait and wonder if he was in some dungeon somewhere . . .

"Stay with my mother until I get back. I'll escort you wherever you want to go myself."

"Who knows if you'll *be* back?" she said, taking the stone and putting it back in her reticule, just to escape the need she felt emanating from it. It didn't work.

He set his lips together. "Then my mother will escort you."

She raised her brows. "I hardly think so."

"You don't understand." He pulled on his shirt hastily. "If Elyta thinks you might have the stone, you are not safe outside our protection."

She wanted more than anything else to shout, "Then stay and protect me." But she didn't. His bloody honor wouldn't let him. And she didn't want to be just an . . . an obligation. He was so bound to his horrible compass they would never suit. Suit? They had no future together. She was weak enough to imagine he might care enough to stay with her. Not likely. So he might as well go and be done with it. "Very well. Your mother will escort me." She had *no* intention of waiting around for his mother to pack what would no doubt be enormous trunks and muster an entourage for a stately journey back to England. But he need not know that.

His shoulders relaxed visibly. He looked at her, once, with such tristesse in his eyes it startled her. And then he smiled. "Thank you. Thank you for that."

She looked away.

He hopped on one foot and then the other as he pulled on his boots. "I'll see if Mother has received the draft." And he was gone.

She found herself somehow sitting on the carpet just where she'd been standing, as though she'd been deflated.

That was it, then.

Twelve

His mother was sitting at her writing table when Gian burst into her apartments. The deep rose satin of her dress spread out around her in lustrous folds.

"Did you get the draft?"

Her quill scratched across the heavy paper for almost a minute before she deigned to answer. Gian had a premonition of trouble.

"Yes," she said finally, sitting back. "As you would know if you were not locked up day and night in our young guest's room doing who knows what." She frowned at him. Then she sighed. "Or I suppose everyone does know what."

Gian flushed. "I did not mean to make trouble for you."

"You never do, *cara mia*."

He took a breath. He must go carefully here. She wanted to take the stone to Mirso for him. He couldn't allow that. "I crave a boon, Mother."

"I suspected as much." She looked him square in the face. "You intend to go to Mirso and you want me to take care of your lady love."

"Yes."

"You are an honorable man. I'm proud of that. But in this

case I must insist that I go with you." Her eyes turned pleading. "You are my son, Gian. Precious to me and made more precious by the fact that children are so rare for us. So I will see you through this mission of yours. Your paramour can stay here until we return. Elyta won't pursue a mere human."

"Kate won't stay without one of us to keep her here." He ran his hands through his hair. "Don't you understand? If anything happens to her, my life will mean nothing to me."

"If something happens to you, I would be the same." Her voice was adamant.

He chewed his lip. Should he tell her? How could he not? It might be the only way to get her to stay with Kate. "I'll be safe from Elyta."

"And why is that? She's older."

"I . . . I have been exhibiting some unusual . . . abilities under duress."

His mother frowned. Then she sighed. "Fires?"

Gian's mouth actually fell open. "You knew?"

"You are what they call a 'firebrand.' That's why Rubius sent you to North Africa."

"But . . . but I only began starting fires in Algiers. How did you know?"

"Actually," she said, putting down her quill, "you didn't realize it, but you started fires the moment you came into your powers at puberty. That's why I had you train with that Zen master. To gain control."

"Why didn't you tell me?" He felt betrayed.

"The first flush of hormones always brings it on in a powerful one. We thought it would pass. Rubius warned me that in your case it might return."

Warned. That was an ominous word. "So I gather it isn't the best news to have your only son declared a firebrand. Are there many of us?"

"I have known of only one. And that was long ago. He . . . died."

"How?"

His mother cleared her throat and looked away. "His moods began to be . . . unpredictable. He started fires everywhere, anytime . . ." She trailed off. The vampire had gone insane.

"They killed him, didn't they? The Elders?" Of course they did. He didn't fit the Rules.

She nodded. "But it doesn't have to be like that. I told Rubius that even if we couldn't suppress it, you could learn to control it. It . . . it could be useful even." She didn't believe that. He could see the worry in her eyes. Maybe that was why she didn't want him going to Mirso alone. Maybe Rubius and the Elders would kill him too. And if they did not? Was he doomed to sink into insanity, starting fires everywhere he went? It occurred to him that he had lived his life for the Rules, when by his very nature he was outside them.

"At any rate," he said, "I can keep Elyta at bay. Keep Miss Sheridan safe until I return."

She rose and gripped his arms. "I can't let you go alone. You know that. Elyta will bring others. Even your abilities as a firebrand will not save you. How can I stand by and risk the stone falling into her hands?" She shook her head. "No. You will thank me for this in the end. And when it is over, your light o' love will be waiting for you."

He stared into her liquid brown eyes. She meant what she said. He bowed his head. "Then be ready to leave tomorrow night, Mother. We travel light and fast. No carriages. You'll have to ride astride if you're to keep up with me."

"I can ride you into the ground." She smiled.

"And the draft?"

She opened the drawer to her desk and took out an envelope. "Perhaps you should wait to give it to her until we return. That will keep her here."

He set his lips. "I gave my word."

"Oh, well then, that's it." His mother laughed. "Your honor is a little too precious to you, sometimes." She handed him the envelope with the draft.

He smiled tightly and turned on his heel. Not too precious. He'd just lied to his mother. He stalked out of the room and shut the doors carefully behind him. He handed the draft to the first footman he saw. "Give this to Miss Sheridan, with my compliments. And you," he called to another, "order my horse up from the stables."

He was for Ravenna tonight, now, before his mother expected him to go. Only then could he leave without her. He'd take the jewel to Mirso by sea. He tried to keep his mind on his plans, but they kept darting to the fact that Rubius, the Eldest, had killed the other firebrand. Maybe Rubius had hoped Gian would be killed in Algiers. Was that why he had sent so few to defend it against Asharti's hordes? Mirso did have dungeons. Plenty of them. And Elyta might well be in league with Rubius. Everyone knew he was besotted with her. Who said Rubius would keep the stone from doing damage? Might he not want it for himself? It would make a powerful weapon against other vampires. God, but he was getting as cynical as Kate.

Kate thought the stone wanted to return to the desert. Stranger things had happened lately than stones wanting things. And if anyone would know what the stone wanted, it would be Kate. She seemed incredibly sensitive to forces unseen.

Well, that would fool Elyta. She'd think he was going north, either overland through Bologna or to Ravenna harbor on his way to Mirso. He'd go south, to Amalfi and the Sahara.

It was full-on night. Kate couldn't make arrangements for carriages or outriders until tomorrow, her acquaintance in

Florence not extending to stables that would take night-time orders. And she couldn't depend on the contessa, who would no doubt tell her son every detail of Kate's plans. But first thing in the morning she'd be off. She rang for a bath.

She thought the discreet knock on the door was Carina. But it was a footman with an envelope on a silver salver. "With il signore Urbano's compliments, signorina." He bowed.

The moment he was gone she tore open the envelope to find the draft. She clenched her eyes shut. Twenty thousand pounds sterling and another thousand in hard currency for her immediate use. He'd more than kept his word. Her dream had come true. Only that wasn't her dream anymore. All the draft did was make her feel small. He wouldn't be back to her room tonight. She knew that. By this draft he had fulfilled his obligation. He was now free of her.

But no . . . she still had the stone.

The scent of cinnamon and something else wafted over her, and she felt the electric energy outside the door. There was another knock.

"Come in." Her voice was steady. She was proud of that.

He stepped into the room. He was crisply dressed now, his unruly hair brushed back from his face severely. He hesitated, then bowed.

"You're here for the stone." She tried not to make it sound like an accusation.

He nodded. He had a pained expression. Was he so anxious to go?

She went to get her reticule.

When she returned, he had the little silver box out, and opened. That was right—he couldn't touch it. She dropped the emerald into the black velvet lining. The emerald was practically screaming "desert." He appeared to be oblivious.

He nodded once. "Thank you," he said, voice hoarse.

"For . . . everything. I hope you enjoy your village in England. If . . . if ever you require . . . anything, don't hesitate to write to me."

Oh, that was rich. "I will certainly do so." He must realize that was a lie.

But he only nodded once, and let himself out.

She wouldn't wait for his mother to escort her home. She didn't want an escort. She didn't want a single reminder of Gian Vincenzo Urbano, ever.

Damn him.

Kate sat in the carriage as it creaked and rocked, fuming. It was evening. In spite of her best intentions, it had taken her almost all day to hire a carriage and outriders on her own, to bribe a servant to carry her trunk quietly down to the small side door where the carriage waited, and to finally set off. It was fifty miles to the sea and Livorno, a small port city on the west coast where she might find a ship to England. She clutched her reticule with the draft, the money and her cards in it tightly.

And now she was having second thoughts. It was all his fault.

It was his fault because, as she thought about their time together, she realized he was the only person who had ever been generous to her without wanting something in return. Oh, he wanted the stone. He had made no bones about that, but he had paid her fairly for it. He had wanted to bed her, but she had gotten the better of *that* bargain without doubt. He had thought of her welfare by trying to get her to stay with his mother, and when she rejected that offer, he had offered to coerce his mother into escorting her. She opened her reticule and ran her fingers over the tarot deck. They represented who she was. A predator, a charlatan, self-contained and self-sufficient.

The shadowy hills of Tuscany rolled by, the red poppies that blanketed the fields now closing in the fading light. The perfume of star jasmine was heavy and sweet in the air. She couldn't decide *what* to think now. True, he had left her. But maybe that was only because his overdeveloped sense of honor demanded he discharge the duty he had promised. Was such steadfastness something to be despised?

And he told her he would return. If anyone kept his word, it was Gian Urbano. But she had been so afraid of being abandoned yet again, she had taken fright. She was abandoning him first, without giving him a chance to prove constant.

So who was she hurting by refusing to wait for him?

He had never said he loved her. How could he ever love someone like her?

But he had said he would return for her.

What should she make of that? It occurred to her that she had not given him time enough to . . . to what? Grow attached? Ridiculous. One look at him and anyone could see why he would never be attached to her. But didn't she hate the way people judged her just by her appearance? Was she any different in the way she judged him?

Oh, this was just dreadful. He might be killed by Elyta. The final abandonment. He couldn't . . . feel about her the way she felt about him. The most he wanted was a frolic in bed. She couldn't imagine going back to tell his mother she was going to wait until he returned.

But she couldn't run away from the one man she had ever cared for either. Maybe the one person. Even if he wanted only sex, and did abandon her in the end, she might have a small amount (A week? Could she hope for a month?) of precious time with him.

All right. Then there was only one thing to do, no matter how it frightened her.

She didn't have to stay at the Palazzo Vecchio. She could

stay somewhere else in Firenze. She leaned forward and opened the small door in the opposite side of the carriage that gave on the box where the driver sat. "Return to Firenze," she called in Italian.

Kate ran up the shallow stairs from the courtyard to the great doors of the Palazzo Vecchio. She'd changed her mind about that too. It was full night now. There was just a chance he hadn't left. She wanted to tell him she'd wait for him. She wanted to see him one more time before he left, just in case . . . in case the worst happened and Elyta waylaid him. Or in case he ended up in a dungeon, tortured to death. She wouldn't think about that. She only knew she had to see him. What else could possibly bring her to confront his mother when she had left in such a surreptitious manner without even thanking her for her hospitality?

The driver and the outrider set her trunk down with a disgusted thud. She paid them as though she had actually taken the entire journey, with a generous *doucement* into the bargain, and turned back to the imposing doors. The huge brass knocker was almost too heavy to lift. Did no servant hear the clatter of the carriage and come to see what was about?

As the knocker hit its strike plate, one of the doors swung slowly open.

Kate stood there, wary. Inside the house was only silence. This was not good.

She pushed the door open. The tiled foyer was empty. Wait. No it wasn't. The twisted body of a footman, his throat slashed, lay by the heavy chest that supported an epergne filled with flowers. Blood leaked onto the tiled floor in a pool. Oh, dear . . . Elyta.

Stand or run? Every instinct told her to run.

But if Gian was here he might be hurt . . . or worse. She

swallowed once and tiptoed across the tile so that her heels would not click. *Silent,* she told herself. *Be as silent as you were as a child thief and pickpocket.*

The house was still. She glided toward the back and the kitchens. That's where the servants would be, and she could use some help before she went upstairs alone.

A voice. It was coming from the kitchens, just across the yard in the outbuildings. Was it a servant, or an intruder? She kept to the shadows of the trees that clustered in the tiny yard. Water trickled over chubby cupids in a small fountain set in the center. What was the voice saying? She drew closer to an open window that cast a channel of light through the foliage.

That was when she felt it—a burst of cinnamon scent and a feeling of vibrating energy. The contessa? Gian? She slid up under the window and peered in.

What she saw was most puzzling. A crowd of servants stood, glassy-eyed and still in the middle of the kitchen. She recognized Carina, and her groom. There were housemaids and cook's helpers, the cook herself, the contessa's major-domo, Bucarro. They stared at a man whose back was toward her. He was the one vibrating with intensity. It wasn't Gian. It wasn't LaRoque, but it was one who shared their condition.

"You will obey my commands," he muttered. "And you will remember nothing."

Kate stood there, shocked. What, for God's sake, was going on here? Were they in some kind of a trance? Kate backed away from the window. She had to get help.

Then she heard a moaning that cycled up into a muffled shriek. She looked around wildly. It was a woman's voice. Thank God for that. It wasn't Gian. Then guilt flashed through her. No one should suffer. And whoever had made that sound was suffering. A door of old and heavy wood, braced across with iron straps and bolts, stood open at the corner of the yard.

Stone steps led down into darkness. She hardly needed the next shriek to tell her that the sufferer was down those stairs. She was fairly certain that female voice would be the contessa. Gian must not be here. Or else he was already dead. He would never allow his mother to suffer so.

Kate stood, rooted in the middle of the yard. Her heart thundered in her chest. She could feel its throb in her throat. The moan died away and she heard other voices. She clenched her eyes shut. She wanted to run away more than anything. But she couldn't. If Gian wasn't here to go to his mother's aid, she had to do it for him. Somehow.

Her decision surprised her almost as much as it would have surprised Matthew.

Kate took a breath and glided to the doorway. The voices echoed up out of the dark. The palazzo had dungeons, Gian had said.

"Where is your precious boy-child?" Elyta's hiss did not surprise Kate. Who else could it have been? "And don't try telling me he went to Mirso. My spies told me he took a horse out last night. We transported to the road north and waited. Going either by land or by sea, he must take that road. But he did not come that way, Contessa. Therefore, he did not go to Mirso."

Transported. What an odd turn of phrase. Gian had left last night while she was sleeping fitfully, waiting, all packed, until the dawn?

"I do not know where he went, if not to Mirso." The contessa's voice was gasping, but there was still a note of iron in it. "You can feel the truth of that, since together you are strong enough to compel me."

What did they mean, "compel"?

"We must make certain."

Another shriek ensued. She put her hands over her ears. Whatever was Elyta *doing* to the contessa? Kate couldn't bear it.

A male voice, cracked with hard use. "We are compelling her. She doesn't know."

"We'll be certain our compulsion is enough when we've sucked out all her power."

Gasping, and another long shriek.

Kate had to stop this. She slid down the stairs. Her hand, steadying herself against the stone wall, expected to encounter damp. But the stones were only cool and rough-hewn. Now as she descended into the stairwell, she could see a glow emanating from below where the stairs turned. The cinnamon and something else that marked one of Gian's kind overlaid the dank smell of basements everywhere. She peeked around the corner.

The room was large, its edges lost in darkness and its stone walls and packed-earth floor revealed in flickering light from a lamp set upon a small, crude table. Wine bottles, thousands of them, stood in racks off to her left. Three silhouetted figures crouched around the contessa, who was recumbent on a rough bench. The scene looked like a painting of the death of Mary Magdalene. Two were holding her down, and clearly male. Their eyes glowed red as though they were released straight from hell. The third was Elyta, her back toward Kate, holding a cabochon ruby half the size of her fist in a small pair of silver tongs that looked like they should be set at the dinner table with a butter dish. The light from the lamp made the ruby glow like translucent blood. Even from here, Kate could see the rolling coils of the serpent inside it.

The emerald had a mate.

As she watched in horror, Elyta held the ruby to the contessa's breast. The contessa arched and shrieked again, a sound even more wrenching at close quarters. A visible aura glowed around the contessa, a corona of red light that swirled and then whisked itself into the ruby and seemed to be absorbed. It was just like her vision of Gian being tortured, except that the tongs had held the emerald and the light had been green. The contessa collapsed as Elyta withdrew the stone, light still trailing from it. Kate covered her mouth with her hand to keep from shrieking herself. She couldn't bear seeing someone hurt so.

"What . . . what do you want with the emerald when you have another stone from the temple?" the contessa gasped. Her voice was visibly weaker. A red weal stood out against her pale skin where the stone had pressed. It was one of several.

"I must control all the refugee stones if I'm to challenge Rubius." Elyta said it almost conversationally. "It wouldn't do for the Elders to have reciprocal power."

"But you were well on your way to becoming a member of the Council yourself." The contessa was trying to keep Elyta talking.

"A member only." Elyta snorted. "Of a body that wants to rule a mountain and a monastery. They have no idea of what we could do with these stones. No, that would not have suited me. I have more vision than any of them. I should have been acknowledged as a leader."

"They . . . they will hunt you down."

"By the time they realize what has happened, it will be too late to stop me. Even if my little escapades come to Rubius's ears, he will not want to believe ill of me. Old men can be quite foolish." As she turned Kate could see that her eyes, too, were red. They seemed to toss glittering color back and forth with the ruby. She was dressed, as seemed to be her wont, in purple. This time it was a riding habit of palest lilac. It did not make her look delicate or fragile though. Her face was hard. Kate wondered how old she was.

And let's not forget strong. Kate felt so helpless. She was glad Gian wasn't here. But he would not want to see his mother hurt. And who was there to help her? There was no way Kate could overpower three of them. She looked around. Stone pillars with Romanesque arches held up the ceiling of the room. No weapon she could see. Not even any torches.

"Stop, Elyta. There is no point," one of the men said.

"Oh, but there is. Urbano is so smug. He betrayed me once. And now he deserves to be hurt in return. What better way than through his treasured mother? She who so dotes on him. She'll live forever, her powers crippled, her pain permanent." Elyta laughed. "The gift of eternity might not be so precious after all."

Eternity? They could live *forever*? Kate locked that thought behind a door in her mind. The important part was that the contessa would be maimed, and she had to stop it, for Gian's sake if not for the contessa's. How? *How?*

Then it came to her. She stood slowly as the implications washed over her.

She knew where Gian was.

And that was the only way she might be able to stop this thing happening to his mother.

Betrayal. There could be no other word for it.

Elyta held the stone to the contessa's welted breast. The woman screamed and arched. Again the corona of red light spread and was sucked into the stone. It seemed fainter this time.

Kate's mind raced. By what she was about to do she was ensuring that the vision of his torture would come true. They might kill him. Or they might not. She hadn't seen him actually die. And there was time before Gian was hurt. It might still be prevented. They might kill this woman no matter what Kate did. But she would be killed or harmed permanently from what Kate could gather, tonight, here and now, if Kate did nothing.

That made betrayal the lesser of two evils. Had she not always lived her life by choosing? Nothing was truly good, truly evil. There was only the choice.

She stepped down the half-flight of stairs and into the room.

"I know where Urbano has gone."

Everyone in the tableau did an about-face and focused on her.

"Well, my disfigured thief, are you here?"

"Let her go." Kate pushed her fear into some cellar of her soul. "She doesn't know."

Elyta drew herself up to her full height. She was an inch shorter than Kate. "We can compel you to tell me."

Again the mention of this "compulsion." Kate thought back. She was willing to wager it had something to do with the red eyes. She swallowed, trying not to be frightened. "No need. As for the contessa, you have done your damage to her, and through her to Urbano." Kate hoped it hadn't gone too far. The contessa seemed to have swooned.

Elyta smiled. "True. Release her." That didn't mean the contessa was saved.

The two men stepped back, looking relieved. But the contessa did not move.

Kate took a breath. "He's gone to Amalfi."

Elyta frowned. "Why Amalfi?"

"Because he has ships there, and the emerald wants to go home to the desert." She glanced to the ruby, and saw it shimmer in excitement. "Your stone does too."

"Nonsense. Stones don't *want* anything. But Urbano is stupid enough to fall for your chicanery. That would explain why he was not on the road to Bologna. He headed south. But how do I know you tell the truth?"

"Compel me," Kate said.

Elyta's eyes went carmine. "I will need your help," she commanded the two men. "This one has a strong will." The others turned to stare at her. Their eyes, too, went red. Kate felt their hypnotic influence. Something wafted at the corner of her brain and beckoned her to unbar the door. She had felt that before, when Gian had first asked her for the stone and, again, when Elyta wanted to know where it was. And in both instances, it had been a fleeting illusion that could be easily broken. She suspected she could break even this stronger demand. But she did not. She let the three invade her mind.

"Where has he gone?" The question echoed in Kate's mind as though Elyta were the only patron in a concert hall with excellent acoustics.

She wanted to answer for several reasons. "To Amalfi."

The need to answer waned. Elyta chuckled. "Very well." She turned to the contessa, thoughtful.

Damn her. "Do you stay to amuse yourself when your real target is getting farther away every moment?" Kate asked. She hoped her voice didn't sound desperate. "You've done your damage here."

Elyta decided and whirled on the men. "Away, my friends. Illya, get Sergei. He can leave the servants now. Transport to the Villa Dovari. We start from there within the hour."

Kate sighed her relief. One of the men pushed by Kate and took the stairs two at a time. Elyta and the other one stood in the center of the room. Their eyes went from red to carmine. The energy in the room ramped up until it was almost unbearable. A whirling black mist tangled round their feet, obscuring them, and began to make its way up to their hips. Kate felt her mouth drop open. What was happening here? She had never seen anything like it. In no time at all the blackness engulfed them. And they were gone. As though they had never been.

My God. What was *that*? Where had they gone, and how? That couldn't be the result of any disease. Was that what Elyta meant by "transporting"? Her mind raced. Whatever it was, Gian probably could do it too. He had neglected to mention that. And also about this "compulsion." And eternal life. What else had he neglected to mention?

Then the contessa moaned.

No time for speculation now. Kate hurried to the contessa and knelt beside her. She lifted the contessa's head into her lap. "Are you all right, signora?" The contessa's eyelids fluttered. She opened them and tried to speak, but couldn't. Her face was deathly pale. The red marks stood out over her breasts. *I hope you have your son's power of healing.* "I'll get help."

The contessa's eyes pleaded with her for something. But she could not stay to find out what. She laid the contessa down gently and scrambled for the stairs.

In the yard she found the servants milling about. Confusion hung in the air. "What happened, Luciano?" "How did I get here?" "One moment I was polishing the silver . . ."

"Your mistress needs help," she cried. Several stopped milling, but still seemed too confused to be of any service. "She's in the . . . the wine cellar." This elicited no purposeful action. Kate looked around wildly. The contessa's majordomo, Bucarro, sat on the rim of the fountain, his head in his hands. "You, you there." She hurried over to him. "Get two strong men and follow me. Your mistress needs you."

He blinked, and shook his head. Then he stood, as purpose banished whatever cobwebs clouded his thought. "Guiseppe, Pietro, get your wits about you." He was a small, active man with drooping mustaches. He herded the larger footmen toward the door in a determined manner.

"She is near the wine racks," Kate called as she hurried after them.

They trotted down the stairs. "Mater de Deus!" he exclaimed, rushing over to his mistress. Under his muttering guidance the two footmen carried the contessa up the stairs and into the house. Her dresser tut-tutted and ran ahead to prepare her bedchamber.

Kate was left behind at the top of the grand staircase feeling lost.

What had she done? Sent the vile Elyta and her cohorts after Gian. And his mother might well die anyway.

Kate had betrayed the man she loved.

Thirteen

Kate knocked on the door and entered the contessa's bed-chamber without waiting for permission. There was no time for courtesy. She had been pacing her own room for nearly an hour trying to find some way around it and she couldn't. There was likely nothing to be done. It was too late. But someone had to do it anyway.

The contessa lay in a great four-posted bed hung with red and gold brocade and covered in red velvet embroidered in gold. Her dark hair spread out around her in a halo over her white pillows and her white embroidered nightdress. She was as pale as her sheets. The smell of cinnamon and that elusive something else still hung in the air, but all the contessa's electric feeling of life had drained away to a steady, small tapping. A maid fussed with a vinaigrette at a small table under the window. At Kate's hurried footsteps, the contessa opened her eyes.

"Contessa." Kate sighed, relieved. "I must speak with you."

"You leave her ladyship alone," the maid scolded. She was an angular woman with her hair drawn back at the nape of her neck in a severe style that only made her cheekbones seem to jut the more.

"No, let her stay." The contessa's voice was a frail whisper. "You may leave us."

Kate approached the bed. "Will . . . Will you be all right?" she asked. She couldn't remember when she had felt so timid. How could she ask a woman this ill to rescue her son? And come to think of it, the contessa had fainted before Kate had told Elyta where to find Gian. Oh, that was bad. Kate tried to imagine telling the woman she had betrayed her son.

"Perhaps. Eventually," the contessa replied. "Bucarro brought me a restorative."

"Eventually" would not help Gian. Kate smelled something more than cinnamon in the room. It smelled like . . . Was the contessa wounded? It didn't seem to be coming from the contessa. Kate glanced around and spotted a pewter flagon on the bedside table. She sidled over to it. The scent of blood was overwhelming. Kate froze. It was all true! All this talk of a disease was very well, but the disease was vampirism. Elyta and her cohorts hadn't turned into bats, but they had been eaten up by a whirling blackness and disappeared. That was the next best thing.

"We don't kill for it," the contessa breathed. She must have seen Kate's horror. "Bucarro bought this from a strong young man."

Kate could only blink at her, her brain struggling to function. Gian was a vampire . . .

"Don't hate him for it."

"Hate . . . has nothing to do with it." Suddenly she was angry. "He might have told me."

"Forgive his cowardice." She looked up at Kate with a distant curiosity in her eyes. "You were there, weren't you? Why did they not finish me?"

"Because I told them where Gian had gone." There. She'd said it. And her voice was calm if the emotions in her breast were not.

The contessa's eyes narrowed in shock. "You *what*?"

"It was the only way to save you. I got the impression you could be damaged for life with that stone. In spite of the healing properties of your condition."

"Ayyyy," she moaned, then caught herself. "But, did you tell the truth?"

"Yes. I think they would have known if I had not."

Despair washed through her eyes. "But Gian said we could not compel you."

"I don't think you can. But when Gian and Elyta tried, they both knew they'd failed. I needed her to believe what I said. So I let her compel me."

"You have condemned my Gian to torture and death." She clenched her eyes shut.

"All isn't lost," Kate continued. She had to believe that. "Someone must warn him."

Gian dismounted from his horse on the waterfront in Amalfi, aching and tired. The lights of the town were inviting on his right, but he had no intention of availing himself of their hospitality. It was about eleven in the evening. He patted the lump that was the small silver box he'd stuffed into his breeches pocket, comforted. The fecund scent of the sea and the gentle slapping of the water against the wooden piles of the pier reminded him of peaceful times past. Small fishing boats were tied up along the length of the quay. Out in the harbor he could just make out the silhouettes of the ships rocking. He hoped his harbormaster was about. He needed his tender *Reteif* prepared and a crew assembled. They might make the evening tide tomorrow.

"Pescaro," he called. "Where are you, you old ruffian?" His hired horse trudged behind him, its vigor spent. Once he had made it out of Firenze without encountering Elyta, there had been no need to rush. No one even knew his destination.

He'd taken the journey in easy stages, riding at night and spending the daylight hours at inns along the way. Piccolo was now stabled at a comfortable posting house a little northeast of Rome stuffing himself with oats. His journey had lasted a week thus far, but there was still a long way to go. He must brave the deserts of North Africa to take the stone home. He had no idea exactly where that home was, but he had two friends who did. He'd stop in Algiers and look in on Ian Rufford and his new wife. They knew exactly where to find the Temple of Waiting.

A large, florid man with a sandy beard stepped out from the forest of masts along the pier. "That you, Master Urbano?" His voice was a booming baritone that could be heard over the wind and the creak of wood.

"None other. I'll want the *Reteif*. I'm taking her down to Algiers. She's to wait for me there. Two or three days there and the same back, at least two weeks at anchor. I'm guessing three weeks. Can you provision her and set her to rights for tomorrow's evening tide?"

Pescaro made a mental list. "She'll need some new ratlines and provisioning . . . Gaetjens will get the crew . . . I expect it can be done."

"Eight of the clock sharp, then." Gian was glad Gaetjens was there to captain her. The man was a French wizard on the sea. Now for a hot meal and refuge from the daylight. The servants at Villa Rufolo were in for a surprise. He glanced to the horse, drooping beside him. Best stop at a stable to get a beast that could climb the Valle del Dragone tonight.

Gian led the horse in through the lush front gardens of the Villa Rufolo toward the Moorish arches of the colonnade. Where was Ponciano? He kept a minimum staff at the villa when he was not in residence, but surely Rudolpho would have hired a boy to watch the front gate when Ponciano was at dinner. He patted the small box stuffed into his breeches pocket. That had become a habit in the last days.

"Ponciano! Rudolpho! Where are you, you old reprobates?" He tied the reins of the horse to one of the slender columns of the colonnade. He'd send someone to take it round to the stables as soon as he roused the house . . . He looked up at the lighted rooms on the first floor. That part of the house had been built in the seventeenth century. Most of the house was far older. He'd started building it in the twelfth century when he'd gone by the name Gian Vincenzo Rufolo, and enlarged it every time he spent twenty or thirty years or so in the vicinity. He saw no moving figures. The rest of the house was dark.

Well, Signora Ponciano would certainly be in the kitchens off to his right past the courtyard. This is what he got for coming unannounced.

But the kitchens were dark, their cheerful fires cold. Anyone in the house should have heard his hail. But no one appeared. He frowned.

He strode around to the back gardens, feeling strangely reluctant to simply bang on the front entrance. The gardens of Villa Rufolo were famous up and down the west coast of Campania. The pergolas were hung with honeysuckle vines, the tidy flower beds filled with cheerful annuals. He made out the yellow of marigolds and the red of salvia clearly in the night. Gardenia bushes lined the walkways. The air was heavy with scent. And on beyond the lower-level stone balustrade the rugged Amalfi coastline plunged to the night-black sea.

He stood for a moment, his back to the sea, looking up at those lighted windows where no shadows moved. This was not right.

Then he felt it. The air began to hum with energy. Four black vortexes appeared against the shadows of the garden, surrounding him. *Companion!* He called for power. A shock ran up his veins as it answered him. His field of vision went red. *More!* The black melted away, revealing Elyta Zaroff and three others. Their eyes were already red. A pool of black whirled around his ankles. But it was too late. Their combined will shushed over him, powered by their Companions' energy. He was riveted where he stood. His breath hissed in his lungs as he drew more power. His body throbbed with effort. The pool of black rose to his knees.

And then subsided. He was caught like a butterfly in a net. With their combined power, he was helpless. He might flutter against it, but he could not escape.

"Gian," Elyta cooed. "How nice of you to come. You look well. Better than Donatella. I'm afraid that is a hopeless cause."

Gian's stomach heaved. He bit his lip to stop himself from saying something that would give the bitch satisfaction. "What have you done with my mother?" Anger boiled in his belly.

Elyta ran her palm along his jaw, feeling the muscles that clenched there. Her burgundy gaze caressed his face. "Don't look so dismayed. Her suffering served a purpose." Gian smelled smoke. God, maybe his mother had been right, his talent for setting things ablaze might come in handy. "I needed someone powerful on whom I could test the stone."

"What stone?" He had the emerald. Though she might well have it soon enough. That made him even angrier. He saw a wooden bench begin to smolder.

Elyta laughed. She was dressed, absurdly enough, in an evening cape of darkest aubergine clasped at her neck, and underneath some loose linen shift of a lighter shade. He could see her breasts move under it, unrestrained. "Yours was not the only stone that escaped the temple. Apparently

Asharti took them from the fountain. They were left adrift in Casablanca when she died. One of her lieutenants thought to follow in her footsteps, but alas, it didn't work out." He fanned the anger in his breast as she talked. Fire might be his only hope. "The stones kept changing hands." Here she glanced to the other vampires. "Sergei found the ruby in Athens. Now I have both of them."

She looked around. "This is quite a lovely villa. I have been exploring today. I found, for instance, a perfect room for trysting. Just you and me and the stones." She turned on her heel. Gian felt the clamps of steel power that held him go weaker as her attention turned elsewhere. He struggled against his remaining adversaries, but it was no use. Three of them were still stronger than he was. "Bring him."

Two gripped his arms and dragged him toward the old part of the building. The old stone rooms had tiny barred windows in the fashion of the eleventh century when every house was required to be a fortress too. They might well be mistaken for a dungeon.

Another of Kate's visions was about to come true.

Elyta's voice floated back on air scented with honeysuckle and jasmine. "We need some time to make our plans down to the last detail, decide when and how to make sure I have all the influence I deserve." She looked back over her shoulder, smiling seductively. "You, dear Gian, will be recreation. One can't work all the time. I'll have you on my terms now though."

He gritted his teeth and held on to his anger. He had no desire for Elyta to have him on her terms. There—a pile of leaves rotting into compost began to put up swirls of smoke. The pergola sprouted tiny fingers of flame. Satisfaction bloomed inside him.

Elyta turned. She hadn't noticed the fire yet. "You may want to know how I found you."

Gian stared at her. Right. How *had* she found him?

"Your little scarred friend said you would arrive here sooner or later."

Kate? Kate had betrayed his destination? She would not. And yet, she was the only one who might have guessed he had not gone to Mirso. She would *not* have betrayed him to Elyta . . . unless . . . "What have you done with her?" They were allowing him to speak.

"Your concern is touching, considering she betrayed you without an instant's hesitation. But I did not have time to take your revenge for you. I should think living, looking like she does, would be better punishment than killing her."

Gian felt his stomach go hollow. He thought he might vomit. Kate. Kate had betrayed him to Elyta? He'd thought, even though she cheated people, stole things, she still had some moral center that wouldn't allow betrayal. He felt his knees go weak. The flames at the base of the pergola flickered and died. The compost heap stopped smoking.

They pushed him with their will onto his knees just outside the heavy wooden door, barred and riveted with iron, to the tiny chapel. Elyta stood over him.

"Look at me, pretty, pretty man." She added her will to the curtain that shrouded him. He fought, fought to keep his chin down. But he couldn't. Slowly, he raised his eyes to hers.

"Once you left me after only one night. No other man has done that." She ripped his shirt and waistcoat open, baring his chest. "But now you are mine for as long as I care to use you." From a pocket in her skirts she took a box and a small pair of silver tongs. The box was carved mahogany. It didn't matter. He knew what was in it. She opened it, smug satisfaction writ across her features. "Not only did you leave me in Capri with hardly a backward glance, but when next we met, you tried to burn me. Gian, Gian, whatever will I do with you?"

He didn't bother to deny it, or tell her the fire had been accidental. He'd burn her on purpose this instant if he could. But fire was far away. Kate's betrayal had robbed him of his fury. He felt only empty. Kate had brought her own vision to life.

With the tongs Elyta picked up the stone, quiescent now in darkness, but still deadly. She held it up and smiled, bursting with the need for revenge.

He held his breath. She touched the stone to his breast, almost lovingly. A searing fire shot through him that grew and grew. He gasped and then a scream tore itself out from his belly up through his lungs and his throat. His Companion was screaming too. His body arched as the pain went on. It felt as though his soul was being sucked out through the stone. A luminous red fog clouded about his body and then was drawn into the ruby. It glowed now, even in the dark.

The pain stopped. He collapsed to the paving tiles of the garden.

"Take him inside." The voice echoed from far away. Hands under his armpits dragged him up. He tried to make his muscles move, but he couldn't. Weak. He'd never felt so weak. Head hanging, legs limp, he was dragged into the tiny chapel, now empty, but with four stout stone walls and that great heavy door. The two who held him dropped him at the far wall.

"Strip him," Elyta said. Her voice grew clearer. He felt the clothes being ripped from his body. The stone floor was cold on his flanks even in the warm May night. He *wouldn't* lie supine before her. He grunted with effort as he pushed himself up on his elbows. Two of her vampires grabbed his wrists and pulled him up to sit. They locked him into heavy shackles. He raised his head. The chapel didn't have shackles. But there they were, mortared into the wall with a huge iron bolt. No problem to pull them out if he was at full strength. But somehow he didn't think she would let him get back to full strength soon. That meant translocation was beyond him too. A chill gripped him. Had he ever been helpless before?

He lifted his head. She was going through his breeches pockets. She had the box. The look of triumph on her face was painful. "Now I have both of them," she whispered.

He tried to think of something defiant to say, but everything that occurred rang melodramatic or patently untrue. He hadn't been able to use his powers as a firebrand to stop her. What good were they to him? What good was he?

"Leave us," she said to the others. Two, as they left, looked resentful, and one looked positively murderous. Was that . . . jealousy?

"You . . . have a quite the harem here," he choked out. "You always did need adulation."

She opened the silver box and took out the emerald with her tongs. She held it up where she could look at it. "I deserve it, Urbano. I'm more intelligent than they are, stronger, more focused on my goals." Here her eyes snapped to his. "Altogether a better specimen. What a waste that the Elders do not recognize it." She came and knelt beside him. "Just because I'm a woman doesn't mean I was not meant to rule. I should be the matriarch of dynasties." A shadow passed across her face. "But you know how hard it is for us to have children. I almost envy humans that, to see yourself replicated, spread out not only vertically through the ages, but horizontally, through wider and wider ripples in the pool of life."

She pressed the emerald to his naked hip. He tried to jerk away, but she pushed it into his flesh. He smelled the sizzle of meat before he screamed. It wasn't just a burn. It felt like his veins were being stripped from his body. This time the pain was briefer.

"Just testing this stone. I'll keep you too weak to escape, but not too weak for my other purposes." She put the stone back in its silver box as Gian lay gasping. But she left the box open and the little tongs laid across it, within her reach. "I think the stones can kill you. Perhaps we shall find out, if I tire of you. But not yet." She unfastened the clasp of the cloak she wore. "You know, I gave myself to you so generously. I didn't use my will on you at all that time in Capri. But I did expect you to acknowledge me, my abilities, my life force, as superior."

"You wanted submission," he gasped. "Like those poor bastards in your harem."

"They do their best. But after a while, one needs new earth to turn." Her eyes went red.

Companion! he called silently. But there was no answering buzz of life along his veins. The world did not go red. Fear made his mouth dry. He had never felt powerless before. She could do what she wanted with him. He wasn't surprised to feel the throbbing in his loins. She could compel arousal, and that's exactly what she was doing. His cock responded, swelling. "You can't attract a man, so you resort to rape?"

She laughed and leaned over him. "I attract all men, my dear Gian. They are drawn by my beauty and personality. I am larger than they are, in every way. That's why it is my destiny to rule. Even you are not immune. You're just willful. We can't have that." His cock was rock-hard along his belly. His stomach churned. "So I will do what men have done for millennia, I will *make* you acknowledge me."

It wasn't about sex for her. It was about power. She straddled his loins and lifted his member, then settled onto it. She was wet and ready. She'd been stimulated by his pain or his forced submission. "You're twisted," he managed to gasp.

She moaned in satisfaction and slid up and down. "I am a force of nature, Gian dear, and like a great wind, all in my path bow to me, even you. Now, you will move as I direct."

Fourteen

"What is the fastest way to Ravello?" Kate asked the hostler at the posting house yard in Castellammare di Stabia. "My map shows a line going over the mountains. Is it a road?"

The hostler pulled his forelock in apology. Kate was glad she had the veil, or he probably would not have been able to take his eyes off her scar. "Not for a carriage," he said. "Touch-and-go with a horse. Donkey or a goat'd be best."

Not for the first time, or the fiftieth, she wished she knew how to ride a horse. "How long will it take to go round the coast?" They'd lost so much time already with the broken axle.

"Well." He scratched his head. The hairline low over his forehead made him seem a little dim. "Two and a half days, maybe. Three. Very twisty round the coast. And narrow."

She wanted to scream at him.

But she couldn't. The feeling of dislocation that was becoming so familiar washed over her. A vision took her and shook her. This man would see his child die of smallpox, and it would change him forever. She shook the vision off. They were happening so frequently these days, they had started to seem almost normal. And that wasn't normal at all.

But she'd have to think about that later. So she didn't scream at him. How could she, when she understood his coming trial? "And how long to ride over the mountains direct to Ravello?"

"Day and a half," he drawled.

If Gian had gone across the mountain and they had to go round the coast it might be only a day's difference. But she had been eight days on the road, and she started two days behind Gian. She gave the hostler a gold coin and strode into the inn, ordered some sandwiches, and watched the horses being changed out.

This was senseless. What could she do for Gian if Elyta had him? What kept her at this maddening journey? She was a girl who could pick pockets and read tarot cards. She had visions of the future, but she never saw herself, so they didn't tell her what to do.

She loved him. She remembered a Kate who would have suppressed that feeling and just . . . moved on. She'd have built scar tissue around the wound and done what she must to survive. Survival was *always* the lesser of two evils. Yet here she was, ready to sacrifice everything, including likely her life, on some quest for which she was totally unprepared. She couldn't even ride a horse, for pity's sake.

But she was all he had. So she must do what she could. Was that a sense of duty? She was beginning to sound like Gian. She shook herself. It wasn't duty. It was just that the lesser of two evils had changed if surviving meant suffering your whole life knowing you hadn't tried to help Gian. Proceeding, even though she might be killed, was now the lesser of two evils.

She handed Luigi and the groom their sandwiches and got into the carriage, waving away the groom's efforts to hand her in. There was no time for courtesies.

She'd just have to use what she was and what she had to hand. Improvise. That was what you did on the streets of

London to survive. That's what you bloody well did in the salons of Europe or any night in your lodgings with Matthew.

The carriage lurched off. So she'd improvise.

Elyta shuddered and grunted with her orgasm. But she
didn't let that distract her from controlling Gian. She kept
his mouth and tongue at their job and his cock erect. It had
been a long night. The woman was insatiable and she loved
gloating.

At last she raised herself from where she had knelt over
him. She pulled him up and locked his wrists back in the
manacles, then curled on the thick fur she had laid beside
him. The control that commanded him washed away, leaving him hollow. Despair slunk round him like a wolf waiting to lunge in and rip out his heart. He was helpless. And
Kate had put him here.

"Very skilled." She sighed. She ran her hands over his
body. "And very, very pretty." She stroked his cock. "I think
you deserve release after that."

"I don't want release," he said through gritted teeth.

"When I've kept you erect for three nights without ejac-
ulation? Of course you want to come. You're crazy for it."
She rubbed her thumb over the head of his cock and made
his breath hiss in his throat. He would *not* give her the satisfaction.

But she was relentless. Soon he was breathing hard. He
tried to think of other things. The vampire wars in Africa,
blood spurting from a young boy's headless corpse, even
Kate's betrayal—anything he thought might soften him. It
didn't work. She sank her teeth into his throat and sucked in
rhythm to her strokes. Even that didn't dampen the urge. He
was on a path of no return. He grunted with the first spurts
of semen, and hated himself for his weakness.

Elyta pulled away. Her mouth was smeared with his

blood. He felt it drooling down his neck. The twin wounds did not heal immediately as they once would have. Elyta took up a cloth and a small knife with which he was only too familiar. She wiped his belly.

"Your blood is sweet." She licked her lips. "I worried about the danger of ingesting your Companion. But it's so weak I can hardly even taste it." She took the knife and made a neat incision just in from his hipbone. There were cuts all over his body now, as well as the burns from the stones, in various states of healing. She leaned down and licked at the welling blood. Her tongue worked the wound. It would not even begin to heal until her saliva dried. By continuing to lick it, she could keep it open for hours. And he was healing slowly these days. It had taken all he had to heal the burns from the sunbeams coming in through the little round window yesterday. What would happen today?

She made another slice in his chest over his nipple. She liked to cuddle and talk and sip his blood after using him. "I think I'll base in Paris, since no vampires live in France. And France is influential." She bent and licked the wound at his chest. "Asharti was wrong to make a vampire army. Why create competition for blood? That woman was a lunatic."

As if Elyta wasn't mad?

"Made vampires are an abomination. It's almost the only thing the Elders have right. And you needn't make vampires. Just supplant the key ministers of a human government with our own born vampires, and you can rule a human population for generations. I could rule all of Europe with the French army at my service."

Gian felt the blood at his hip begin to congeal. She noticed that and leaned down to lick it. "Is that what you want, to rule a human country?" Gian tried to distract her.

"I want to be valued for what I am," she snapped, looking up.

"I thought you planned to use Rubius's influence to get yourself a seat on the Council."

"Just like a man." Her voice dripped scorn. "Why must I have influence only through Rubius? Rubius sent me to Scotland to retrieve some formula he thought was a cure for vampirism as though I was a pet dog. He was so blind he didn't see that I would take the formula myself. What could one not do if one controlled a cure?" She laughed, then sobered. "It all came to nothing. There was no cure." She bent and lapped at his chest. Then she sat upright, licking her lips. "And who would want to rule in Mirso anyway? A hundred ascetics, denying their passions. The Elders are dried-out old men who suffer women only when women pretend to be exactly like them. Well, I am a living, breathing woman, more intelligent and more alive than they are. They should beg me to join their ranks, bow to my intuition." She was hanging above him, almost hissing in his face. A bit of spittle hung at the corner of her mouth. "They don't value women for what they are. Mothers abandon their daughters, instead of coddling them and cooing over them like your mother dotes on you."

So, her mother had abandoned her. She had been a disappointment, whether because she was a girl child, or she had demonstrated her instability at an early age, it was impossible to tell. She wanted to be a man. And she hated everyone for the fact that she hated herself. She didn't know what femininity was, or how to be comfortable with it.

"They won't like you controlling a human government," he observed.

She grinned. "The stones will take care of anyone they send after me."

She really was insane if she thought Rubius and the other vampire Elders would tolerate her rebellion.

"Don't look at me like that!" she shouted.

Definitely insane. And he lay weak and bleeding in

shackles at her mercy. He gathered enough courage to ignore those facts. "Being head of a government is so public. There are other ways to influence."

"Like your mother?" she scoffed. "I want people to know who pulls the strings."

He changed tactics. "Are you sure the path to power is not more attractive to you than actually getting it? Wielding power is rather dreary work."

"*You* are advising me to be satisfied with what I am?"

"I'm telling you you'll never be satisfied with what you are."

"You arrogant bastard." She reached for the tongs. "You think you're better than I am?"

The stone sizzled into the wound still open on his hip. He bit his lip and twisted away, trying not to cry out, but she held it there until he couldn't suppress the scream. When she finally took it away, he collapsed.

How long can she keep me here? How long can I take this?

Elyta stood. Her figure swam before his eyes. "I'll teach you some respect before I go. Or maybe I'll take you with me. You're no threat, now." She turned on her heel and let herself out through the door to the chapel. The bolt clunked into place on the outside. They'd put in a bolt and lock, just as they'd put these shackles in the chapel's walls.

Time passed. He might have lost consciousness.

The sun rose over the mountain that loomed behind the villa in the east. Gian blinked. He still knew where the sun was. That might be the only thing left of being vampire. That and the need for blood. His Companion was screaming inside his veins for it, longing for the strength it would give to speed his recovery. But there was no blood.

Sweat had dried on his body. His erection had subsided. He buried his face in the crook of his arm. The shackles held his wrists just above his head. So this was what rape felt like. This was why women feared men. Maybe they hated them, somewhere deep down inside. He hated Elyta. But he had to admit he understood her too. She *was* brilliant. She was beautiful. She was passionate and intuitive and alive. And no one valued her. Her mother had abandoned her. And that had festered in her until the canker had swallowed her heart.

He didn't have the strength to hate right now. Soon the room would be bathed in light. Painful. But in the afternoon, the sun would shine through the aureole window above the door. Elyta had chosen well the location of his chains. Would the healing stop altogether if enough of his power was siphoned away? Maybe the stones would kill his Companion. Death was better than her keeping him for recreational rape and torture. Once he thought eternity had grown boring. Now he longed for ennui, and failing that, death.

Perhaps his mother was dead even now. He didn't want to think about that, or the way she would have ended.

And Kate. He didn't want to think about the fact that she had betrayed him to this fate. He took a labored breath. She had many things in common with Elyta. Both had been abandoned, never valued. Kate had been even more a victim than Elyta. He understood being a victim as he had never understood that before. That was why Kate built up the carapace of cynicism. So she couldn't be hurt. Maybe their experiences had had a similar effect on the two women. They'd been twisted like the little trees the Japanese made to grow in dishes.

He just had realized what they were too late. And his mistakes had put the emerald in Elyta's hands. She had two stones now. He wouldn't say she couldn't rule France. Paris was in for a shock. And Europe for that matter. And his mistake had cost him his pride and his life. Let it end soon.

Kate opened the door to her room above the tavern on the piazza of the tiny village of Ravello. The sun was rising.

She had sent Luigi out to gather intelligence last night while she tried vainly to sleep as she waited for the right time. As if she could sleep knowing what might be happening to Gian even now at the Villa Rufolo. That was his home according to his mother. The image from her vision of Elyta torturing him floated before her eyes, waking or dozing. But she had to wait until daylight. She wanted the vampires asleep and Gian alone. She was no match for Elyta and her crew. The problem was Gian. How would he escape in the sun?

She carefully folded a blanket from the narrow bed in her room and tucked it under her arm. She could only hope that wrapping him up would let him make it to the shelter of the carriage where Luigi could take them away. The room lightened. She tiptoed down the stairs and out into the stable yard behind the little hotel. Luigi was waiting with the carriage.

"Well? Are they there?" she whispered.

He nodded. "Four visitors. They arrived four days ago."

Four days. She wouldn't think about that.

"No one has seen the servants lately. Provisions are being delivered and left in the kitchens. They say the owner hasn't been about for years."

But he was there all right. She swallowed. "This is dangerous, Luigi. These people will kill you and the groom if they find you. So you mustn't take any chances."

He nodded, nervous but determined. He, like everyone else, was devoted to Gian.

"Wait at the gates to the villa. They open off the west end of the piazza. Be ready to leave at a gallop. If I'm not back in an hour, I'm . . . I'm not coming. In that case, get yourself and the boy out of danger. Return to Firenze and give the contessa the news."

"And what would I tell her, Signorina Sheridan?"

"Tell her I'm dead, and that when she is better, she must

track down Elyta Zaroff in case her son is still alive." If she never recovered, at least she could send her vampire friends.

He reached out and touched her shoulder. "Don't go, signorina." His brow was puckered with worry. "There is nothing a girl like you can do to help him. He is strong and wily. He has been in scrapes before and come out whole."

"Not like this one." She took a breath and mustered a smile. "Don't worry. I'm wily myself. Now promise me you'll leave in one hour."

"Oh, I promise, signorina. I am wiser than you are."

She gave a nervous laugh. "I should hope so." She took off her veil. She'd need all her vision. Then she hurried across the empty piazza in the graying light to the gates of the Villa Rufolo. She removed a pin from her hair and turned to lean on the gates, trying to look as though she was waiting for someone. Her heart was thudding in her chest. She felt for the tumblers in the huge old padlock. They were almost too heavy for her hairpin. They slipped.

Focus, you bloody little fool, she thought, and closed her eyes.

The next hour was the most important of her life. She could hardly believe she was going to try to best four vampires and steal Gian out from under their noses.

The tumblers clicked into place.

She pulled open the lock. It might be ancient, but it was kept well oiled like the gates themselves when she pushed them apart to slip inside. She shut them behind her, left the hasp through the handles to keep the gates shut, and picked up the blanket she'd brought. The wide graveled carriageway was overhung with trees and lined with ferns and flowers. Kate kept to the shadows along the edge as she stuck her precious hairpin back into her knot of hair. The house loomed behind plane trees, pines, and cypresses in the early light. It was wide, with a tile roof and thick, whitewashed walls. The architecture went from very old on the left, perhaps twelfth century, to more modern on the right. On what looked to be the first story of the more modern part, the lights still shone in several rooms, revealing they had been decorated in the Baroque style. That part was perhaps sixteenth century. A silhouette crossed the room and then another. Men. Or more accurately, vampires. They had not retired yet. She waited behind the bole of a large tree. The day grew brighter as the minutes jerked slowly by. She stole glances up at the rooms until finally she saw only a single silhouette closing up the shutters. Better.

She darted across the open drive for an archway over a walkway. Off to her left squatted a square stone tower. The bottom was covered in vines. A heavy door stood half open. A tower might seem like the ideal place to hold a captive, but peering round it she saw no aureole window. Her vision said that Gian would be held in a room with an aureole window.

She headed around the end of the twelfth-century part of the house. Stone walls had pointed arches on the windows that pierced them. She came to a door under a portico. This had probably been the main entrance at one time. She stopped and sniffed the air. No cinnamon here. She stepped off the walk into the flower beds. She had worn soft slippers, the better to be stealthy. The last thing she wanted was gravel crunching under her weight. Now she was round to the back. Through the huge trees she could see a long terraced garden with columns and pergolas, and beyond that the sea. Waves crashed against cliffs somewhere below. The whole place was scented with flowers, and under that, the fecund brine of the Mediterranean. The line of the house stretched away. She craned her neck to see through the foliage.

There! An aureole window.

She hurried ahead. A narrow wooden door under the window, all iron straps, had a heavy padlock very like the one at the gate. She dropped the blanket, took her trusty hairpin and bent over it, listening to the mechanism. This lock was not as well cared for as the one at the front gate though. The tumblers were stiff as well as heavy.

Strange that she didn't smell cinnamon. She couldn't feel Gian's electric hum of energy either. It didn't matter. This was her best chance. One tumbler. Bloody hell. The second one was bending her pin. She held it with one hand and pulled out a second pin. A loop of hair escaped with it. Inserting the second hairpin, she worked with both hands now.

She wanted to scream in frustration. An agonizing moment—lifting with one pin, catching with the other . . . The tumblers slipped. She let out a breath and jerked on the lock. It opened with a clunk. She threw the bolt with another clunk and pushed on the door. It creaked. Did everything have to make a racket? She opened it only wide enough to slip through. The place was cast in shadow. Only a dim glow of the dawn from the round window and the door ajar broke the darkness. But she could hear breath rasping in and out of lungs.

"Gian?" she whispered.

"Kate!" The baritone was his, but its usual air of command and arrogance was gone. Now she could make out his form in the shadows. He was chained to the wall, naked.

God in heaven, it was her vision.

"Is there a light?" She set down the blanket again and looked around.

"Why are you here?" His voice was hard, but without its usual force.

"To get help you escape, of course." Why else would she have come three hundred miles, and risked being caught by Elyta?

"Had second thoughts about betraying me?"

Oh. That was what made his voice hard. Well. She'd made the decision, and now she had to face the consequences. "No second thoughts. The way I saw it, your mother was going to die immediately if she didn't tell Elyta where you were, whereas your death was not yet a certainty. Telling Elyta about you to save your mother seemed the lesser of two evils."

"She's alive?" He still had control of his voice, but she could hear the hope there.

"When I left her. But weak."

"Thank God," he breathed.

"Now, stop jumping to conclusions for a minute." She peered around. "Is there a light?"

"A candelabrum to . . . to your right on the bench . . . in the arch."

She had never heard his voice tremble. Feeling her way along the wall, she came to the arch, bent to the bench. Candelabrum. Striker? Yes. She flipped it twice and the flint caught. She lit the candles and turned.

She almost gasped. Even in the flickering light, Gian looked horrible. In the vision he hadn't had all those burned places on his body. Those must be where Elyta had set the stones against him. Or the cuts, half-healed, the jagged tears. Why hadn't he healed?

"Oh, Gian." She hurried over and knelt beside him, touching his belly, his chest lightly, not knowing how to help him. His cinnamon scent was very faint, just sensed beneath the blood and the sweat. There was no feeling of electric energy about him at all. He shoved himself up with effort. He had a three-day growth of beard and there were dark circles under his eyes. She must get him out of here immediately.

"Luigi has the carriage at the gates. Will you burn if I cover you in this blanket?" She fished in her hair for the hairpin yet again and pulled the heavy shackles toward her. His wrists were chafed bloody.

"I might burn, I don't know, but it will heal."

She glanced up at him. "That doesn't seem to be going so well right now."

"Get out, Kate. This is too dangerous."

"They've retired for the day. Be quiet." She twisted her hairpin in the lock. These were quite simple locks because they were so old. Not a great deal of demand for iron shackles these days. It clicked open and she grabbed the other one.

Electric energy. Cinnamon. Kate turned.

A vampire pushed in through the open door, wearing a hooded cloak. "What do you think you're doing?" he growled. "Elyta!" This was shouted. He shut the thick wooden door with a bang and stood in front of it.

Kate leaped up. She gave him a shove. He stumbled back. Kate lunged for the door.

Vibrating energy washed over the room. By the time she turned, the other vampires had already materialized into the shadowed corner of the chapel. Elyta was dressed in a wrapper of purple so dark it was almost black. Her hair was down about her shoulders, as though she had been interrupted at undressing.

"Well, well," Elyta cooed. "How touching. The tragically scarred thief has fallen in love with you, Gian, and has gallantly come to save you. But then, everyone does fall in love with you. You count on that. Everyone except me." She motioned to the two vampires who stood beside her. They stepped forward and grabbed Kate. "How good, Frederico, that you made one final check before we retired."

Elyta knelt beside Gian and held out the shackle.

"Let her go, Elyta," he rasped. "She is nothing to you." Elyta raised her brows. He put his raw wrist back inside the shackle and she snapped it shut.

"Let her go? When she obviously cares so much for you? I think not. Perhaps she'd like to stay and watch us frolic tonight. She would love to see your cock stand to attention, eager to service me. I know Sergei and Illya have been pestering me to watch."

Gian jerked against his chains. Kate heard the threat to herself, but all she could think about was that he had . . . had made love to Elyta, after what she had done to him.

Elyta laughed. She looked at Kate, much struck. "But no, why should they not play too? You can have her, lads, before we suck her dry."

The image of vampires sucking all her blood out danced before Kate's eyes.

"I wouldn't want the likes of her," one of the pair spat.

Kate flushed. Ahhhh. The scar. Perhaps it had its uses.

"Take her from behind, you'll never know the difference, Sergei," Elyta advised. They both laughed this time. Kate felt her stomach roll and wasn't sure whether it was from the thought of Sergei and Illya, or the thought of Gian with Elyta. She glanced to the vampires.

The melting of her surroundings that presaged a vision clamped down and held her rigid.

She saw the vampire named Illya falling overboard in the dark of a storm at sea. A great wave scraped him from the deck of a ship like he was nothing, and she *was* him and he was rolling over and over, water filling his lungs. Panic seized him. But then she felt the realization that he couldn't drown. Relief washed through him. His Companion sent a surge of power up through his veins and he thought of the ship. There was a sear of pain, but he was used to that. Then he was standing on the deck again. He scrambled to the hatch and threw himself down into the relative safety of the hold as the deck rolled and pitched.

The vision faded.

"What's wrong with her?" Elyta was barking. "Are you having some kind of a fit?"

"No," Kate said as calmly as she could. Could she turn her vision to advantage? "I saw his future." She nodded toward Illya. "You were swept off the deck of a ship. But don't worry." She made her voice kind. "You are frightened, but of course you can't drown. You survive."

"Nonsense." Elyta snorted. "Don't try your flummery on us."

"I'm not. I had a vision of you touching Gian with the stone. That's how I knew where to find him." She pointed to the window. "I looked for the window I saw in my vision."

"I don't believe in supernatural powers," Elyta said.

"Strange for a vampire. But neither did I. There you have it though." Kate shrugged.

"She's valuable to you," Gian croaked. "Think what you could do if you knew the future." He was trying to protect her.

"These are easy things to say."

"There is proof." Was Gian daft? There was no proof at all until something she saw came true, and who knew how long that might be? "The stones don't drive her mad."

Brilliant. She could use that. "The reason they don't affect me is that I already know the future. My brain sorts out the true line of events." It might not be true, but it was a good story. "As a matter of fact," she said, pretending to be much struck, "I didn't actually have a vision until after I saw the stone. Perhaps it triggered something in me."

Kate could see Elyta sorting through the possibilities.

Elyta put a finger to her lips. "I wonder—would you dare to lie when proving the assertion is easy and lying would be so deadly?"

"Give me one of the stones." Kate held out her hand.

Elyta fished in her own reticule, and came out with the

silver box. She handed it to Kate. Her eyes were steely hard, but they glittered with avarice.

Kate opened the box and took out the great emerald. She walked over to the candelabrum Sergei held and raised the stone to the light. Immediately the rolling coils appeared in the depths of the stone, glittering with scales. The scales grew larger, flashed into pictures, each a scene, flipping ever more rapidly as the serpent within coiled itself. And then they flickered more slowly and finally resolved themselves into a stream of pictures. She watched Elyta, standing in a desert, triumph writ large upon her face. Kate wanted to see what was happening more than anything else in the world. But she couldn't lose focus now.

She ripped her eyes away and managed a smile. "Uncomfortable. But the futures do resolve themselves after a moment." And then another possibility occurred to her. She fingered the jewel. It wouldn't work. But she had to try.

Kate lunged at Elyta with the stone. But fast as she was, the vampires beside Elyta were faster. They moved in a blur. One grabbed Kate's wrist. She screamed and struggled. The creature banged her hand against his knee. The stone clattered to the marble floor.

Elyta drew herself up, breathing hard. One of the vampires scooped up the stone with the edge of his coat and deposited it in the silver box.

"You'll be punished for that." Elyta grew thoughtful. "But not killed. You will have your uses."

Kate knelt, panting, and looked at Gian. He was straining against his shackles. She'd failed. The only sliver of hope was that Elyta intended to keep her alive. Of course, neither she nor Gian had told Elyta that she could not control when the visions came or what she saw. That disappointment could come later.

"Doesn't mean she can't serve two purposes," Illya pouted.

"Yes it does," Gian said. His voice had grown rather stronger. Now that she looked at him more carefully, some of his wounds had closed a little. His healing was slow but not gone. "Haven't you heard that only virgins can peer beneath the veil of time?"

Elyta raised her brows and chuckled. "And you're telling me she's a virgin?"

"Look at her." Gian's voice was flat.

Kate swallowed and flushed to the roots of her hair. She knew they would believe the lie, humiliating as that fact was.

"Do you want to take the chance, just to serve these three a night of fun?"

"The day progresses." The room had indeed lightened. Elyta turned to Gian and Kate. "We'll just lock you in here with your friend today while we rest."

"Locks don't seem to hinder her," Sergei muttered.

"She can't pick a padlock on the outside of the door from the inside." Elyta examined Kate and held out her hand. "Still we want Gian locked in place right where he is today. Hairpins please." Kate pulled the pins from her hair. "Really, Gian, how could you even associate with one straight from the gutter? Picking locks." She snorted in derision.

Kate tossed the pins to the floor. Elyta frowned and motioned Illya to pick them up. While they were distracted, Kate slipped the one pin still in her hand down the back of her collar and shook out her hair over it.

"Your reticule and your cloak?"

Kate slipped it off her wrist and whirled her cloak off her back. Elyta took them both. Her tarot deck was now lost. Her former identity was slipping away.

Sergei picked up the candelabrum and the blanket. Frederico, swathed in his cloak, braved the sunlight to lock the door from the outside. Blackness whirled around Elyta and the other two. "Stay away from him. He's dangerous to you today," Elyta warned.

And they were gone.

What did Elyta mean, dangerous?

Fifteen

Kate turned to Gian, blinking as she thought about what to do next.

"I'm sorry you came." His voice was barely a whisper, his eyes sad. All the strength he had mustered to face Elyta was gone.

"I am too." She was, now she knew he had made love to Elyta, even though she was torturing him. Was he *that* besotted? That was twisted in ways that shocked her, hardened as she was. And what he and Kate had done together meant nothing to him. She took a breath. "But I promised myself I'd get you out. That is, if you are sure you want to leave her."

He looked incredulous before realization hit him. "You don't think I . . . I . . . serviced her of my own free will, do you?"

"Men can't be coerced into sex."

He swallowed. "Look, there is a quality about vampires . . . it's called . . . compulsion."

"I know about that. Like hypnotism. You tried it on me once, and so did Elyta. I actually let her and the others compel me, so they would believe me about your destination."

"Well, it . . . works on . . . arousal as well. Now that I'm weak, she can compel me to do anything." He paused and looked away. "Even have sex." The words were a hoarse whisper.

"That's rape." The true horror of his experience over these days began to sink in.

"Yes." His tone was flat. It covered pain.

All right. She accepted that vampires could compel. Then she could accept that he'd been raped by a female vampire.

"We must find some way for you to escape." He squinted around without much hope.

"Don't look so glum. We're not beaten yet." The room was growing brighter still.

"I'm too weak to translocate." He meant that whirling darkness, and he was ashamed.

She raised her brows. "And who said I was depending on you to get us out of this?" Bravery she didn't feel. She turned and peered up at the small round window. "Won't the light make you uncomfortable?"

He chuffed a weak laugh that turned to choking. "Yes," he gasped. "And from about two to three in the afternoon, it won't be a pretty sight."

"Well, you're not a very pretty sight now anyway." She could release him from the shackles to avoid being in direct sunlight, but still there would be plenty of light in the room as the day wore on. If only they hadn't taken the blanket and her cloak. She glanced around. A fur on the floor, no doubt designed for Elyta's comfort. It wasn't big enough to shelter him, even if he crouched. Still . . . She studied the window. It was small. Too small for her shoulders? No time like the present to find out. How good that she had worn these little slippers with the suede soles. She grabbed her skirts and knotted them around her knees.

"What . . . what are you about?" he asked.

She untied the fabric belt at the waist of her dress and

knotted it around the fur. The stone of the walls was old, the mortar worn away. The deep grooves it left between the stones would give her good purchase. She reached for a stone above her head and pulled herself up. A perfect hand-hold. She placed her right foot on another protruding stone. Almost easy. Like a spider she climbed the wall until she reached the little window and peered out. Eighteen inches, twenty at the most. Enough, perhaps, though she was no longer nine. Clinging with one hand, she shoved the fur into the wide curved bottom of the window created by the thick walls and balled it up. Not perfect, but better.

She dropped to the floor and brushed her hands. "There." She unknotted her skirts in the dim light. When she looked up, he had managed a smile.

"I've never seen a girl do that."

"I expect not, with the insipid kind of girls you probably fancy." The bulge of muscle at his biceps, the hard planes of his chest and the ribbed abdomen were hypnotizing. Maybe he *could* compel her, in some ways. She wouldn't look lower. But she couldn't escape the impression of a dark nest of hair at his groin to match the hair in his armpits and the light spray across his chest. God, what was she that she could so desire a man who was injured? Taking herself firmly in hand, she removed the hairpin from her collar at the nape of her neck, and held it aloft. "And now for these shackles."

Elyta's words came back to her. Should she release him?

She shook herself mentally. He was Gian. And if she was anything, she was an excellent judge of character. He was arrogant and intelligent and maddening. But he was not violent toward women. Indeed, he had been kinder to her than anyone in her life. She descended upon him, determined to ignore the throbbing inside her that he evoked.

"I never knew what accomplishments I should . . . desire in a woman."

"I'll wager sleight of hand or breaking and entering were

not at the top of your list." She worked the lock until the mechanism clicked. "Now you can move around our little cell to escape whatever sun gets past that fur."

"It won't matter. She'll be back tonight." Despair lurked in his eyes.

There were things she had to know, since he was so weak. He was too big for her to carry or drag. "What effect would going out now have on you?"

He took a breath. "I'd burn in seconds." He shook his head. "Normally I'm old enough to go out in the sun briefly. We toughen with age. But right now I'm . . . I'm fairly weak."

That was an understatement. "With clothes?"

"Noticeably absent."

"With clothes?" she insisted.

He closed his eyes as though he didn't care to argue anymore. "I'd burn less."

She wasn't going to subject him to any more torture than she must. How much was that? "If we wait until late afternoon?"

"Kate, we're not going anywhere." He looked at her expression and relented. "But late afternoon is better."

All right. Late afternoon. The later, the better. But not too late. When would Elyta rise and come for him? Kate's mind was racing. Luigi would be gone. Either he had returned to Firenze, or he and the groom were dead. She and Gian were alone against Elyta and her crew. She was only human, and Gian hardly more and maybe less right now. She took his hand and felt the thrill of touching him. But his flesh was cold even though the early mornings of May were warm. It was a mark of his poor condition. How could she give him strength?

She sucked in a breath as she remembered the contessa's restorative. Kate knew what would help Gian. Human blood. And they had some of that. It was running in her veins.

That's why Elyta said he was dangerous to her. He needed blood. She found herself blinking rapidly as the voices inside her argued back and forth.

You can't be thinking of giving him your blood!

And how else is he going to be strong enough to escape by this afternoon?

Maybe he just needs rest.

She looked at him, haggard and shivering. *You know that's not enough.*

But what if he sucks you dry?

You got yourself into this mess, Katie my girl, and now you'd better have the courage to get out of it. Giving him your blood is better than failing both of you entirely. She wasn't going to admit failure. She'd come for Gian, and she was going to leave with him.

No matter what that took. Giving him blood was the lesser of two evils.

She chewed her lip. Could she just . . . offer that? *Here, have some of my blood.* And how would he get it? She had no knife to slit her wrist.

Oh, God. He didn't take it like the contessa from a German pewter tankard. She had seen him getting his blood in a tavern from that serving girl. He bit her neck. And vampires had fangs. He didn't have fangs now, but somehow he got them. That's how that serving girl got twin puncture wounds just over the artery in her neck.

Very well. Pressing her lips together in determination, she curled beside his naked body.

"No," he protested. "No."

"You're cold. I can warm you."

"I'm not . . . safe." His hot breath hissed in and out. It bathed her neck in his scent, more man now than cinnamon and that something else that was sweet. "You don't know . . ."

"But I do." She slid her arm under his neck and pulled

him to her. "Your mother took blood when she was weakened by the stone to help her recover. Wouldn't it help you?"

He didn't answer. "I'm depleted. I might take too much."

"Let me worry about that." Fear wound round her spine. She remembered his strength when he hurried her across town to his house in Rome even when he was horribly burned. Still, what other way was there? "You need strength if we're to get out of here." She lifted her chin.

But wait, didn't the children's stories say that you became a vampire yourself if a vampire bit you? Or was that a werewolf? Maybe that was the danger Elyta meant. She didn't want to become something that needed human blood to survive. She could ask him, but did she really want to know? Because she was going to do this anyway, no matter if she became a monster or not. She was going to do it for Gian, who was not a monster, even though he needed human blood. She steeled herself and drew him closer.

His breath was hot on her throat as he struggled with himself. He gave a low moan, and she felt the vibrations that had been quiescent now throb slowly in the air. They were not as electric as they once had been, but they were there. "Yes," she breathed, though inside she was trembling. She stroked his hair and eased him even closer to her throat.

His lips brushed the flesh of her neck and sent gooseflesh down her right side. But she did not draw back. The fear, his nearness, his scent, all combined into a brew of anticipation, and . . . sensuality. Her blood began to pool in her center, leaving her almost light-headed.

The twin pains were not unexpected, but she jerked a little in reaction. His arms came round and held her to his body. He began to suck. Horror drained away. All that mattered was the feel of his body moving against hers in matching rhythm to his sucking.

"Kate," he murmured against her neck. "Kate." And the word was not a paean to hunger, but a caress. She arched into him, and the feel of her blood pounding inside her matched the rhythm of his lips, sucking, caressing her neck. That vibrating, electric feeling in him ramped up. She could feel his ecstasy and it was infectious. His hold grew stronger on her and she held him tightly in return. Their breath, matched now in some urgent pull toward life, pressed her breasts against his chest. She could not help but thrust her hips against him, and in doing so she found something quite unexpected. Oh, her blood was giving him strength all right. He had an erection. How she longed to make love to him, with him sucking at her neck. The sensuality of this most intimate exchange of fluids, him to her, and her to him in return, would be . . . paradise.

Abruptly, he pulled away, with a moan of frustration.

Kate felt . . . bereft.

He was gasping for air. "Did I . . . did I take too much? Are you all right?"

"A little . . . disoriented." As though she had been pulled from ultimate intimacy back to an everyday world. Yet she still throbbed inside. Her heart pumped. Her breathing pushed her breasts against his bare chest. And she still felt his erection against her thigh.

"I can't erase the memory of this unpleasantness with compulsion as normally I would." He was looking at her so . . . tenderly. "I'm sorry."

"It wasn't unpleasant." She realized he was still holding her against him, and she was still holding him. "Do you feel . . . better?"

He smiled. There was no trace of fangs. "Yes. My Companion is stronger. Thank you."

"It was nothing," she lied. "Tell me more about your Companion. It seems more to you than just a parasite."

"It makes us who we are. We have a symbiotic relationship. It gives us strength, and more acute senses, and allows us to draw on its power."

"It makes you hum like that?"

He nodded, but he looked surprised. "I've never met anyone who could sense our vibrations. They experience them as an attraction, or a feeling that we are very alive."

"Vibrant in fact?" She had to smile.

"My Companion wants survival. Enough to rebuild its host constantly."

"That's why you live so long and heal so well."

He nodded.

"It gives you red eyes?"

"The red eyes are a symptom of the Companion's power coming up." It all sounded so reasonable in that sensual rumble. "Bringing the power up enough causes that black vortex you saw around Elyta and her friends, and when the field of energy grows so intense that it collapses in on itself, we pop out of where we are and into another space. With practice we can direct where we reappear. We call it translocation."

She couldn't think what to say. She had seen it herself a number of times at this point, and yet in some ways it was the most astounding trait of all. That and the healing, and the age, the blood and the energy, the strength.

"Quite convenient, really," he remarked.

That was one way to put it. And he made it sound so . . . prosaic. "And . . . and what else is there?" She steeled herself to know it all.

He pulled back a little and smiled at her, those green eyes crinkling. God, but she loved that smile. "Most of the rest is myth. I didn't lie about that. Garlic doesn't repel us. Or crosses, as you know. I was once a cardinal, and cardinals really spend an inordinate amount of time around crosses. I happen to like garlic on my pasta. The only time we cast no reflection in mirrors is when we are about to translocate. Then even light does not escape the field of power our Companion creates."

"What . . . what do you call yourselves?" There must be some other name besides the one she knew. Perhaps using it would be some sort of slur.

"Vampire."

She sucked in a breath. The word was ugly. There was no getting around it. And maybe she was vampire now too. "Am I now like you?"

He shook his head and held her close to him. The faint cinnamon and man scent rose from his chest. He breathed the words into her hair. "No, Kate. That's another myth. Vampires can be made, Lord knows. But my blood would have to infect yours . . . Oh, God." He held her away from him abruptly. "Do you have any scrapes or cuts? I've been bleeding." He took her hands frantically and examined them.

She too felt panicked as he turned them first one way then another. "I . . . I don't think so." Then he swept his gaze over her face, her neck and breast. "No . . ." He began to breathe again and so did she. "No, you're fine." He clutched her to him. "I thought for a moment . . ."

"That was close." She had very nearly been made a monster, if Gian was a monster.

He held her away again. "You must never touch me if you are bleeding. Even from the tiniest scratch. Do you understand?" His voice was fierce with either anger or . . . or pain.

"I understand," she snapped. What he was stood between them.

He squeezed his eyes shut. She hadn't meant to give him pain. Her hand reached out and caressed his jawline of its own accord. That made his eyes open, at least.

"I'm sorry to have dragged you into all of this." He took her hand and kissed her palm. That sent shivers down her body to the place between her legs.

"I stole the emerald." She sighed. "I got myself into it." She realized that through all this conversation, she had been lying in his arms, that he was naked. She must distract herself from the feel of his lips on her palm. "I . . . I am glad your . . . your Companion is better."

He ran his hand up her arm to where the sleeves of her traveling dress left the inside of her elbow bare. His thumb moved over the pulse there. Dear Lord. "The Companion loves living more than anything," he murmured, bending to kiss the place he had been rubbing. "The truest affirmation of life is . . ."—here his tiny smile appeared—"the sexual act."

"You can't be thinking of sex right now when you're injured and you've been . . . abused by Elyta, and we're locked up waiting for her to kill us, or worse?" Her outrage was dutiful, if not wholehearted.

He looked half apologetic, half wicked. "A Companion is always eager to affirm life. It gives vampires a heightened sexuality." He sobered. "It might be the last time."

She didn't want to think about that. "I can't make love to an injured man. It isn't right."

He lifted a curl of hair from her shoulder and smoothed it back behind her ear. "Sweet Kate. There are many kinds of healing. I need to feel good and true right now, as well as stronger. Not . . . defiled. Not a victim. And only you can make me feel that way, after . . . her."

Oh, he was good. How could one resist the expression in his eyes, the soft caring in his voice? He had probably practiced that expression. But she didn't care. "Let me see if your wounds are healing now that you've had a 'restorative.'" The cuts on his chest were now no more than pink lines of new skin. The circular burns had disappeared entirely.

He pulled her in to him again. He was decidedly warmer now. Hot even. "You see? I'm fine." He leaned in to her, and this time his lips just brushed hers.

Their touch made her shiver. Arrogance be damned. Monster? She didn't care. The fact that they were essentially two different species? That was going to bring tragedy, since she had lost her heart to him so thoroughly. Perhaps Elyta would bring tragedy first. So all they had was this moment. And she knew what she wanted to do with it. She swallowed around the lump in her throat. She mustn't let him see into her heart right now. "Does that mean I needn't feel guilty about taking advantage of you?"

She felt his smile as he kissed his way down her jawline. "Yes." The word was a caress.

She lifted her chin once more, wondering if he would take her blood again, and not unwilling for him to do so. But he only made his way down her throat. The feel of his kisses was so delightful she hardly realized he was untying and unbuttoning, and soon he was pulling at the bodice of her dress until her breasts were revealed. She became so intent upon what his mouth was doing to each nipple in turn, she lost track of exactly how she became naked.

"Kate," he murmured as he changed nipples. "Kate."

She ran her hands over the muscles in his back and down over those lovely buttocks she had first seen in the piazza in Firenze. Really, Michelangelo was an incredible sculptor. Women had been worshipping that statue for three hundred years, and she, Kate, had the real, live version here, its warm, living flesh pressed against her. She giggled.

He drew back, affronted. "What?"

"I was just wondering what would have happened if Michelangelo had sculpted you erect. I expect there would have been female riots in the piazza."

His expression softened. "That would have been bad."

"Yes. And it would have gotten worse, because all the men who weren't so well endowed would have gotten together with chisels to remove the comparison."

"Ouch." He kissed her mouth. "As long as you like it, I am satisfied."

"I like it." She wanted to say she liked him. Actually, she half wanted to say she loved him. But that would be useless.

He had said himself his sexual appetites were more than any human's because of his Companion. She was just another in a long line of women whom he used to satisfy those appetites. So she said only, "And I would like to know it more intimately now, if you please." She scooted onto her back.

"Happy to oblige." He hung over her, braced on one elbow.

This time when she spread her knees, he did not demur or find a new position. He angled his member at her entrance and lifted her hips slightly. Three careful thrusts, each deeper, and she was filled. Their satisfaction was sighed in unison. He moved inside her, adjusted the angle so that his member pressed against the secret spot that washed sensation over her. Perfect.

And yet she wanted more. She reached up and pulled him toward her. "I want to feel your body on mine," she breathed. And in truth his warm flesh on her belly and breasts even as he thrust inside her was fulfilling. Still . . . was there not one more intimacy they could share? She wanted . . . everything—all the experience she could have of him. "Now," she whispered into his ear, "take my blood."

He pushed himself up on his elbows and blinked at her in disbelief.

Did she have to explain? "It was so intimate . . . I want to feel you sucking at my throat even as you release your seed inside me."

His breath was coming fast. "I . . . I just took blood from you."

"I'm as healthy as the proverbial horse. I want this."

He swallowed once and nodded. He let himself down, but left his weight still supported on his elbows. Slowly and deliberately, he thrust into her. She turned her head to the side, exposing the twin wounds that must still be there. She felt his growl of desire rumble in his chest as much as heard it. Out of the corner of her eyes, she saw his eyes turn red. And there, sliding out of half-open lips panting with desire, were his canines, elongated. But she wasn't afraid. She knew what would happen, what it felt like. She trusted Gian not to take too much. After all, hadn't he stopped in time even when he was starved for blood?

He bent to her throat. Again the small sear of pain—like being pricked by thorns, no more. He withdrew his teeth immediately. And then he began to lick softly, in time to this thrusting inside her. He was consciously taking less blood this time. She moaned in pleasure. It was as though she was giving herself in every way to him. His desire was palpable in the air around them. He began to thrust more forcefully inside her, faster, and then to suck in rhythm with his thrusts. Her heart beat in syncopation. She hung suspended between his cock and his lips, a vessel filled and flowing. Satisfaction filled her.

And then he couldn't hold back. He stilled and trembled as he exploded inside her. He stopped his sucking and let his tiny grunts of orgasm be breathed against her neck. And that was even more satisfying, that she could make him almost insensible with pleasure.

He collapsed against her, nuzzling and kissing her neck. "So generous. So generous, Kate," he murmured.

"Nonsense," she breathed in return. "I just wanted it all." She had experienced all of who he was and it was devastating. Her feeling for him was a gushing fountain. It would flow long after she had gotten him out of here and he had moved on to pleasure other women.

"But you haven't had it all." He slipped out of her and slid to her right side, cradling her against his body. She curled there, contentment washing over her. But he parted her thighs with his right hand, and two fingers glided inside her. She was very wet. She opened her hips to him and he slid his fingers out and over that spot she never knew she had before those nights at the Palazzo Vecchio. Oh! That was perhaps the most intense sensation yet. She touched his bearded cheek as he moved his fingers over her moist flesh. She had a hard time breathing calmly. He surprised her by taking her fingers into his mouth. The moist flesh she felt there seemed to mirror her own. He sucked gently on her first two fingers as he rubbed her. She had been lusting for him for so long at this point that she was teetering on some edge. But just as she seemed about to leap over that edge he would pause with his fingers and just suck on hers for a moment. And when she was just about to beg him to begin again, he did, and off and on until she couldn't think about anything but his fingers and her fingers and moist flesh.

Her world squinched shut and then thrust wide. He didn't stop rubbing her and that was good because she never wanted him to stop. She was just about to scream when he kissed her quiet. She yipped into his mouth as her orgasm rocked her in wave upon wave. It seemed to go on forever, until she had to wrench away from his hand or lose sanity entirely.

Sixteen

Gian looked down at her sleeping form. Her scarred cheek was laid against his chest. She was beautiful, scar or no. Generous and fearless too. His love for her was doomed to tear at his intestines like the wolf cub at the legendary Spartan boy. But at least it made him feel alive. He was not bored. And the wars seemed far behind him.

He had to get her out of here. The sense of urgency brought him fully awake. Her blood had given him enough strength for healing, but he could feel the need for more itching in his veins even now. She could give no more. He didn't have power enough to translocate, let alone take her with him. Jupiter and Hera, how were they going to get out of here? As if she sensed his fear, she stirred and opened sleepy eyes.

When she looked up at him, his heart almost gave out. There was a warmth, a vulnerability, in those blue eyes that made him want to crush her to his chest. He drew his brows together. What was he seeing there?

She glanced up to where light leaked in around the fur she'd stuffed in the window. A mote of light was creeping across the floor toward them. He'd have to move soon, but that meant he had to let her out of his arms, and he wasn't ready for that yet.

"What time is it?" she asked.

"Getting on toward one." She turned in his arms and her breasts brushed his chest. He felt himself rising. *Down, boy,* he thought. *You'd better save your strength.*

She smiled at him, a knowing smile. She'd felt his response to her. But then she frowned, and glanced back to the window. She sat up abruptly. "I must go."

"And how will you manage that?"

She glanced up at the window, then back at him. She examined his face as though she could read the future in it. "I'm going out that window."

She was leaving him. Well, that was what he wanted. She at least should survive. She nodded once and stood. He watched her dress, knowing he would never see those perfect limbs, those delightful breasts again. He rose and helped her lace her half-corset, tie on her bodice. Really, female clothing was so complicated these days. He preferred the stolas of ancient Rome. He tried to keep his mind on those small tasks instead of on the fact that Kate was about to climb out of his life through that window.

When she had put on her slippers, she tossed her hair behind her back and strode to the wall. "Let me toss you up," he offered.

Again, she only nodded. He cupped his hands, and she put one dainty foot in them. "Ready? One, two," he counted. "Three." She jumped and he lifted. He still wasn't strong. She barely reached the window. But she grabbed hold of the deep embrasure and pulled herself up to crouch in the opening. She tossed the fur back into the chapel.

"Cover yourself as much as you can," she said. "I'm sorry this will be uncomfortable. I'll be back before two."

He squinted at the blaze of light. "I'll stay out of the direct rays." Indeed, he was burning even now. He strode over to the most shadowed corner.

They stared at each other for a long moment. And then she put her arms through to the outside, slid her hips into the room, turned and pulled her shoulders through the opening, angling them. She was really quite clever about it. She twisted, so she was on her back. He watched as she squeezed through. He thought her hips might get stuck, but soon she was sitting in the embrasure from the other side. Then her feet slithered through the opening.

She was gone.

She'd left him. He wanted that. But it did not make him feel less bleak. He slid down the stone wall and huddled under the fur, his head on his knees to keep the light out of his eyes.

Now he was alone. Elyta had the stones. And she had him. He wondered idly how long she would keep him alive. He hoped it wasn't long.

Kate slipped through the lush gardens, drowsy with sunlight, and out the gates into the piazza. She had a plan, such as it was. She had thought briefly of trying to muster help from the villagers. But who would believe her when she said the owner was held hostage in his own house when they hadn't seen him for a score of years?

So, her first stop was a clothesline or a laundry. A girl was much too conspicuous. She slipped into a narrow corridor off the little square and picked her way down an alley behind the whitewashed buildings with tile roofs. Cats slunk among the barrels of refuse that smelled like rotting vegetables and scraps of meat past their prime. Those smells were a part of her now, ever since she'd awakened on a trash heap when she was six.

But this smell emanated from a butcher shop whose

discards attracted flies. On a line in the butcher's back garden fluttered coarse white shirts and aprons. Excellent. She let herself in by the gate. Through the open doorway, beyond a storeroom, she could see a clerk shooing the last customers out so he could close the shop for the traditional midday dinner break. She pulled down what looked like a boy's shirt, an apron. None were big enough for Gian. Sergei was probably her best bet for clothes for Gian. Which meant she'd better make this quick. If only there had been breeches. So she'd need a boy . . .

"Buon giorno," she called, and smiled as the young man ducked under the foliage of the lemon grove that clung to the side of the hill to see who hailed him.

His features slowly cracked into a grin. "Buon giorno, signorina." He pulled his forelock. He did not yet shave. He was probably, what, twelve? Then he looked closer. "Wot's wrong with your face?" Not a bright light.

"Never mind that. I want to make a trade," she said.

He looked puzzled. She unveiled two very large sausages. His eyes grew round. "For wot?" he asked suspiciously.

"Your breeches and shoes." She held her breath. "And stockings and cap," she added, thinking about how uncomfortable those shoes were going to be. She had a flash of this boy, now with a grown beard, proposing to an unassuming girl with dark hair on her upper lip. When she said "Si, signore," a flood of happiness washed over him. Kate pushed the vision down.

"These is only my work shoes, and the breeches is torn," he said.

"And these are only two of the butcher's best sausages," she said mournfully.

His expression grew sly. "Well, I guess I could trade."

Hooked. She turned around. "Then give them to me now."

She could hear him stripping, muttering gleefully to himself. "By the way, signore, did . . . did you hear of a murder hereabouts this morning?"

"Murder! No."

"Ahhhh." Maybe Luigi and the groom had made it away. God, but she hoped so. She hated to think they had lost their lives for her. "Just wondering."

"Here. Now trade fair and square."

She turned to find the boy in his flaxen smalls, holding out his articles of clothing. She gave him the sausages, and he took off running toward the village, apparently unconcerned at his near nakedness. So, using the cover of the lemon grove, she struggled out of her dress and half-corset, put the lad's stockings over her own, pulled on the breeches and shirt, and slipped her feet into the stiff leather shoes. They were still too big. It didn't matter. She tied the apron about her neck and waist, and twisted her hair up in her cap. There.

But who would not recognize her scar? She took some damp earth and rubbed it over her cheek and her temple. Maybe. Now where on earth was she going to get a cart? Back to the butcher . . .

By the time she was through the gates of the villa she was breathing hard just from willing the horse to move faster. She pulled him round to the old part of the building near the chapel, the cart wheels creaking, and asked him to halt, a command he was most eager to obey.

She dashed back to the newer wing, painted palest pink, and looked up to where the lights had been on last night. Everything was shuttered. The sun was just past its zenith. It beat down, hot on her face, and reflected off the walls of the villa in that brilliant Mediterranean light that drove artists to their canvases in a frenzy. Insects buzzed in the garden, but all else was silent. Surely, the vampires would be fast asleep at this sunniest of times. She took slow breaths and closed her eyes. Calm. Silent. That was what she was.

She found a passageway into a shadowed cloister that gave onto a huge room with pointed stone arches that held up the newer part of the building. The moist stone reeked of the thirteenth or fourteenth century. And there at the far side was a stairway leading upward. She hurried up the stairs to a stout wooden door. She tried the latch. Of course it was unlocked. Who would dare to steal from the Villa Rufolo? She took off the boy's clunky shoes, and let herself in. The room beyond was one of the salons she had seen this morning from the garden. She recognized the chandelier. But she wanted bedrooms. She stole along the Turkish carpets to a door at the other side of the room. Yes. A corridor. The bedrooms would be off a corridor.

The doorknobs were almost at her shoulder height, and made of the finest porcelain. As a matter of fact, the entire villa was furnished in the first style, Baroque and Rococo veneered sideboards, chandeliers dripping with Venetian crystal, silver epergnes as big as she was. Once she would have been looking for plate and silver and jewels in a house like this. Something about jewels niggled in her brain.

She checked each dim room until she came to the one that held Sergei. His snoring filled the hall. She slipped inside. *Control your breathing. You are air. You are vapor wafting over the carpet.* Sergei's massive form under the coverlet was still except for the rise and fall of his chest. She slid over to the wardrobe, timing her movement to the snorts. The wardrobe door clicked, once, as she opened it. She froze. But Sergei sawed on. Boots, shirt, coat, and a cloak. She pulled open a drawer on Sergei's buzzing intake of breath and grabbed stockings, smalls, cravat. Holding her breath entirely, she crept out of the room.

In the dim tiled hall she exhaled. Now for Gian. Would he not be amazed and relieved to find she had engineered the whole? She had a solution for his nakedness, a cart to get them down to Amalfi, and a disguise for herself. They could get a better carriage in Amalfi. Surely his credit was good in these parts. Someone at the shipyard must know him. And then they would go back to Firenze and . . .

Bloody hell.

She could see it now. He wouldn't go back to Firenze. He wouldn't be happy with her arrangements at all. The damned fool.

He wouldn't leave the stones to Elyta. His bloody inconvenient sense of duty would demand he try to complete his stupid mission. She could just see him blundering around the villa making who knew what noise as he tried to steal the jewels back. She stood in the salon staring, unseeing, at the unfamiliar ragged boy in the great, gilt-framed mirror over the mantel of the fireplace. Damn the man to hell and back.

She retraced her steps. The stones would be in Elyta's room.

Gian crouched in the corner, as much of himself covered with the fur as possible, not moving. A sense of failure pervaded him, along with the itching burn of light along his skin even under the fur, worse where his feet and shoulders were exposed. In a few moments, the sun would be at the right angle to shine directly through the little rose window above the door and fill the room with direct sunlight. It wouldn't be as bad as the bubbling flesh he'd experienced when Elyta had chained him naked in its channel of radiance, but it would be no evening picnic.

He lifted his head only at the sound of the lock being opened. It could not be much past two. Elyta would have to transport inside the room. She wouldn't come through the sunlight outside. A flicker of hope sprang up and was ruth-lessly suppressed. He stood. If it was she, he didn't want her to see him crouching. He vowed that he would curse her, at least inside his mind, with his last breath.

The door swung wide. A figure was silhouetted against a blinding light. A man. Gian covered his eyes. It wasn't any-one he knew. The figure was short, and . . . lumpy. He hissed in a breath and turned away.

"Sorry about the light." The door swung shut with a thunk.

Kate! He squinted against the light that remained in the chamber. He couldn't quite see. It didn't look like Kate. The figure moved into the shadow and bent over him. It was Kate all right. She was dressed in rough peasant's clothing, an apron, and stocking feet, her hair tucked up under a cap with a short brim and her face muddied.

"Are you all right?" she asked.

She had come back for him. He was touched. And angry. Nothing had changed. "You were going to get out of here, remember?"

"We're both getting out of here." She tumbled some clothes at his feet. He stared at them. Men's clothes. Boots. Even smalls and a cravat. They smelled faintly of cinna-mon. He looked a question at her. "Sergei. He was the only one whose coat might remotely fit your shoulders. Now could we have a little haste, please?" She raised her brows, exasperated.

He stood and threw off the cloak. Immediately, the dis-comfort of the buzzing burn along his skin ramped up. He pulled on the shirt first. "You stole these from the house while they were sleeping?" By Jupiter, the girl was brazen. She shrugged, and motioned him for haste.

Everywhere his skin was bare the light scraped at him. "Even with clothes I won't make it far." He didn't mean to growl at her. "Leave now, Kate."

"I brought a cart. It has a tarpaulin. Between the clothing and the tarpaulin I thought you might survive the sun."

He paused to look up at her. She was frowning, anxious. He shrugged a grudging assent and she relaxed. "You acquired clothing for yourself, clothes for me, and a cart all in . . . in about ninety minutes?" Astounding.

"It will all come to naught unless you *hurry*. The cart will be missed soon."

"Yes, yes," he muttered, pulling on the breeches. She was tapping her foot. For heaven's sake, she'd brought boot pulls. He slipped them into the tabs at the insides of a boot and pulled it on. She threw the cravat around his neck.

"Don't bother to tie this now. We must be off."

He straightened, as realization came crashing in on him. "I must do one thing first."

She sighed. "You are so predictable."

He drew himself up even taller and looked down at her. "I have my—"

"Yes, yes, your duty." She fished in the pocket of the trousers that were loose around her waist and a little tight over her hips. She held up her reticule, the silver one with beading she always carried. It was full and lumpy. She pulled open its drawstrings and took out a little silver box. "There." She snapped it open. Inside nestled the great emerald. "I have the ruby too. I knew you wouldn't leave without them."

"You stole them from under Elyta's nose?"

Kate shrugged. "They were asleep. I'm very quiet." She raised her brows again and pointed to the coat. "I got my reticule back too. The money and my tarot deck were still inside."

He grabbed the coat and shrugged into it. Not hard, since it was a little big across the middle. Sergei had something of a paunch. He took the two boxes and put them into the coat pockets. He nodded, steeling himself for the coming ordeal in the sun. "Let's go."

"Wait." She threw the cloak over his head before she opened the door. The rays felt like a rasp against even the skin that was covered. He was damnably weak. Light blinded him where it bounced off the rock of the walk and up under his shroud. If only he had his spectacles of dark blue glass, he might be able to see. "Go," he said through gritted teeth. "I'll follow."

"Nonsense." She put her arms around his shoulders to guide him. He stumbled beside her, trying to breathe, nearly blind. They reached the shade of the cypress grove at the end of the house. He smelled horse, recognized the wheel of a cart. She pulled at ropes that tied down the tarpaulin. He crawled up under it and was surrounded by the smell of cheese and raw meat and sausages, fresh-baked bread and the yeasty smell of a cask of wine. He pushed everything aside and crouched next to the cask. The pain of the sun eased and he heaved a breath. He heard the hiss of hemp as she tied the tarp down.

Relief shot through him. Then a nasty thought intruded.

"Can you drive a cart?"

There was a pause. "I drove it here from the square, didn't I?"

An image of the treacherous road down to the sea from Ravello rose in his mind.

Oh, excellent. Just excellent.

Seventeen

Kate took a breath and willed her heart to stop pounding. The vampires could not be a threat to them in daylight. With any luck the villagers would still be drowsing. She had the money from her reticule. She was only nervous because Gian was so helpless in the sun, and that meant everything was up to her. Was she up to it?

She took up the reins and clucked to the horse. No danger of this beast careering through the piazza and attracting attention. She willed herself to patience. The cart creaked as it turned. Gravel crunched under the wheels. Did the damned thing have to make so much noise? The horse plodded down the drive and out the open gates. The piazza was quiet. A man dozing on a bench looked up, frowning as they passed. Did he recognize the cart?

Just walk on. Clip-clop. The pace was like to drive her mad.

Out of the little town, now. The road turned steeply down in a hairpin curve. She urged the horse into a trot. The cart jolted along between the lemon grove terraces, empty now of workers.

"Be careful." She jumped at Gian's voice. "This road is treacherous."

He was right about that. The narrow road wound at the edge of a deep ravine. The stream was lost in the green gorge below. She heard a commotion behind her over the rumble of the cart. She glanced back. A horse was coming around the last bend. And it was coming fast.

Bloody hell! She slapped the reins over her horse's rump as hard as she could. The beast lurched into a canter. She jerked it up short to take the next curve, and the cartwheels slid toward the verge. The cart rocked, then righted itself and careened on. Kate's cap fluttered over the edge and her hair fell down her back. She imagined the shattered cart and their broken bodies in the stream far below. Three riders galloped into the turn above her.

"Slow down, you fool, you'll ruin my cart!" one shouted.

"Look, Giuseppe, it's a girl."

Kate slapped the reins over the horse again.

Another turn, barely negotiated. She glanced up. Her only comfort was that the horses chasing her were anything but speedy. They were probably farm horses, big and heavy-boned. Her pursuers hadn't taken time to saddle them, if these horses had ever even known a saddle. The men were not handy riders either. She had a chance.

"Hah, horse, hah," she yelled. Another turn, and another. They were only a hundred feet or so above the stream now. The road suddenly forgot how to be a tangled ball of brown string upon a green carpet. It sloped gently downward as the valley widened. The cart went faster, but so did the horses behind her. She could smell the sea now. The stream widened into an estuary.

What was that mewling sound?

A flock of sheep milled out from behind some cypress. She glanced behind. The horses, their riders bouncing uncomfortably on their backs, were only fifty feet behind her.

She set her lips. "Hah, horse, hah!" She slapped the reins. The cart bounded ahead. A grunt behind her told her Gian was still alive. The horse veered to the left, trying to miss the sheep. Baaing distress boiled up from the right. The horse was through. The cartwheel grazed the leader of the flock who wore the bell. A man with a crook swore at her.

And they were clear. Kate glanced behind. Sheep jostled the pursuing horses. There must be fifty of the wooly beasts. The horses' alarmed whinnies alternated with snorts of dismay. Two began plunging and rearing. Their riders slid off and disappeared among the sheep. Kate couldn't help but grin. A tidy piece of work, that. She turned onto the coast road, north toward Amalfi. "Are you all right back there?"

"You do *not* . . . I repeat, you do *not* know how to drive a cart." The words were muffled by the tarpaulin.

Well! "You'll be glad to know we lost them at the sheep."

"I'll be glad when we get to the harbor, if I've any senses left at that point."

What a curmudgeon. Didn't he appreciate that she had driven a cart for the very first time in her life down the Valle del Dragone at breakneck speed and brought them home safely?

They were just clopping into the outskirts of Amalfi when she heard horses approaching behind her again. She turned, shocked. Were they so determined? She got the horse back into a reluctant canter, but he had spent his strength. Ahead the town marched up the hill to the right, the quays poked into the aquamarine water, and a small forest of masts nodded to each other on the swell. A wide flagstone piazza lay on either side of the road between the harbor and the town.

Was there refuge here? Perhaps not. The three horses caught up to her as the cart edged into the piazza.

"Thief! Help!" the butcher shouted to the men unloading provisions from small boats tied at the quay. "This woman stole my horse and cart."

The horse stopped in the middle of a gathering crowd.

Wild thoughts of how to explain her actions careened through Kate's head. "We're running from vampires" didn't have a successful ring to it.

People gathered round the cart. Murmurs of "she's dressed like a man," and "look at that scar," ran round the crowd.

"Ask for the harbormaster," Gian suggested sotto voce from the back.

"What can he do?" she shot back, annoyed. He was no help. It was up to her. "Signori, I had to borrow the cart. But I always meant to pay for it."

The loud guffaws were led by the butcher. "Get a magistrate. Gaol is the place for her."

Kate felt for her reticule. "I'll buy the cart and contents. You can have the horse."

"And what would the likes of you pay with?" More loud laughter. "No coin I would take."

She peeled off what she thought was the equivalent of thirty pounds sterling, three or four times what the whole was worth. "Good, because I have soft money. Will that do?"

Silence fell.

"Here, let me see that," the butcher said, grabbing the money. "Probably counterfeit."

"Looks real enough to me," one of his compatriots observed, sidling closer.

"She still stole the cart and horse. Paying now don't mean she shouldn't go to gaol."

"Well, then take it back, and I'll keep my money," Kate said calmly.

"If I got anything ye might want ta steal, gel, let me know," a seaman said. This provoked laughter from the crowd. The butcher blustered.

A man in a blue uniform sauntered up to the edge of the crowd, looking naval and official. He examined the money. "It's genuine. Make your choice," he said to the butcher.

The butcher opened his mouth, closed it, and pocketed the money.

"The harbormaster," Gian whispered. "Say you want passage on the *Reteif*."

To where, for God's sake? "Thank you, kind sir. Now if you two will unhitch this gentleman's horse from my cart, I have business with the harbormaster." She stepped down from the cart. Her legs would barely hold her, as though she had been long at sea. She was still in her stocking feet. Two men stepped up to help, and she peeled off another bill and gave it to the nearest. The crowd parted before her as she strode toward the harbormaster. He was a big man. She felt uncomfortably small.

Well, she was used to that. "I'd like to ship this . . . this cargo on the *Reteif*."

The man's face was weathered by years of wind and sun. He narrowed his eyes. "The *Reteif*, you say?"

"Yes." Nothing for it but to brazen it out. "When could the boat be ready to sail?"

"*Reteif*'s a tender, signorina, a sloop. She's been ready these four days."

"Good. Have the cart pulled on to the quay. And I'll tell you my plans."

But of course she didn't have any. She hoped Gian did. But she had to make it to darkness to get his help.

"Will you hurry?" she demanded, watching Gian climb out of the cart. They had pulled it behind a stack of barrels. The sun was about to set like a red ball into the Mediterranean. That meant Elyta and the others would be up. They'd find their prey gone and come looking. And the first place they'd look would be the harbor, since she'd told them Gian came to Amalfi for a ship.

She'd changed into fresh clothes she'd bought in town,

boy's clothes, in view of what most likely lay ahead. But at least her breeches were clean, her face was washed, and her boots fit. She'd bought a change of clothing for Gian too, if she'd sized the articles of clothing right.

Gian brushed himself off, looking disgusted. "I didn't know you had money."

"Your mother gave me a thousand in notes in addition to the draft that was in my reticule."

"You *could* have bought the cart in Ravello and spared us almost breaking our necks."

Ungrateful man! "Well, I didn't think of that at the time. I had other things on my mind, like Elyta and her crew. And I *did* get us down the mountain and onto your precious boat—"

"A tender, *Reteif* is a tender."

"Which is a kind of *boat* according to the harbormaster. And you *might* show a little appreciation." She was working herself up now. "You *could* still be in the chapel with Elyta."

He looked self-conscious. "Let's get going. She will have discovered we're gone."

"*Now* you're in a hurry." Now that it was his idea.

He took her arm and helped her onto the narrow plank that teetered between the rocking little ship and the quay. A sailor who wore a horizontally striped shirt and long, braided hair let go a flapping sail. Four others on the deck let go their sails too and began tying down the bottoms. They moved as in a precisely figured dance. A small, wiry man barked orders, none of which made the least sense to her. Everyone was very busy. But when they saw her, all movement stopped. A sail flapped free where slack hands had let go the rope. After an uncomfortable silence, everyone started talking at once. What with their various nationalities and accents, she could hardly make them out. She didn't need to. The tones were of protest, and the object of their distress was obvious. The captain tried to quell them with threats and a raised voice.

Gian stepped forward. "Gentlemen." He didn't shout, but she could feel him call what power he had and put it all into that one word. The protests died.

"I am Gian Urbano." At the name, their eyes went wide. "*Reteif* is my tender." He glanced around at the other ships floating in the harbor. "So are most others in port. I go to Algiers, with my guest. If you do not choose to take us, do not expect employment from me again."

Two or three swallowed visibly. Several others looked down at their hands.

"Then we are clear. I would say also that common courtesy will be expected." His voice was hard, but he ramped the power down.

They cast off from the quay, but she heard murmurs of "bad luck" "devil woman," and "what woman dresses as a man?"

"Here, sit on this coil of rope," Gian said, "where you are out of the way."

She rolled her eyes in protest, but she sat. She was not wanted here. Was it that she was a woman, or because of her scar? The little ship pushed off the quay and turned into the harbor. Memories of a dreadful Channel passage one stormy night with Matthew were already affecting her stomach. The crew would really warm to her when she vomited all over this tidy little ship. Gian stood above her, hanging on the web of ropes. The wind rose. The sails belled out and the little ship picked up speed. In no time they were skimming over the water.

"Where are we taking the stones?" she asked to distract her thoughts from her stomach.

"You mean me—where am I taking the stones? *You* will stay with my friends in Algiers."

"I'll bet I know what kind of friends those are." If he

thought she was going to be fobbed off on some vampires she didn't even know, no doubt as vicious as Elyta, he was very wrong. She'd find a way to thwart him when he tried to leave her behind. He would say it was for her own protection. She was getting to know him well.

"They are good people. Ian Rufford and his wife, Elizabeth. They helped me fight a . . . war in North Africa." His face closed down. He looked forlorn.

She couldn't ask what kind of war or what role he'd played in the face of that expression. "I'm not sure I'm up to any more vampires."

"They were just like you five years ago, before they were infected. You'll like them."

They were made monsters? Now they lived forever and had to drink blood. How tragic.

"So, where are *you* taking the stones?" she said, to change the melancholy subject.

He let out a breath. "I . . . don't know."

"What?" This was too much. "I thought you said they were from some temple."

"Rufford knows the general location, but it was buried under tons of sand. I'm not sure anyone knows exactly where it is." He sounded thoughtful, but not defeated. Was he a lunatic?

"So . . . Your plan was to wander the desert until . . . what? Hell freezes?"

"No."

"Then what?"

"Come inside the cabin." He glanced about pointedly. Seamen scurried about, trimming sails or whatever. The cabin was not appealing. But he was right. There was no privacy here.

He held her elbow as she rose. Did he have to do that? The thrill of touching shot through her. He had to duck his head to get into the cabin. It was tiny. Several hammocks hung in tiers against the wall. The legs of a rough wooden table were securely fastened to the floor. Above the table a swinging lamp cast careening light around the room. He set her securely in a chair. The rolling floor of the cabin reminded her of the hold on that Channel crossing.

"Give me the stones."

She fished in her reticule. What was he about? He took the mahogany inlaid box and flipped it open. First he stared at the winking ruby within, then closed his eyes for a long moment. Kate began tapping her foot.

His eyes snapped open. "Must you break my concentration?"

"Whatever do you think you're doing?"

He cleared his throat. "You . . . you said the stones wanted to go back to the desert. I thought . . ." He shrugged, looking like he felt foolish. "I thought they might tell us where."

Her laugh died in her throat. Actually, not a bad idea. "Let me."

She took the stone from its box. He practically shuddered as she touched it. But of course it had no effect on her. She held it to the swinging light. The blood-red scales glittered inside it, rolling, hypnotizing. The scales expanded, wanting to show her all possible futures, but she squinted her eyes and thought hard about a single thing. The temple.

A sense of dislocation overcame her. She was looking up at sheer sandstone walls rising above the dunes of the desert floor. She got a sense of eons of running water cutting deep chasms all along its perimeter. But this chasm had been filled. Sand and scree ran out into the desert floor in a huge alluvial fan. The scene held no human figures. But just as in her other visions, she was filled with emotion. This was an overwhelming jubilation. Was she seeing the future of the stone at the moment when it realized that it was home?

She opened her eyes. Gian stared at her with a worried frown. She had risen from the chair and was holding the box out toward one corner of the little cabin. There was a palpable tug from the box, as if it *longed* in that direction.

She heaved a breath. "I saw where the temple is. Or was. And I think you're right. The stones will tell us how to find it."

His tiny smile was satisfied, determined. He nodded.

Kate glanced around the lurching cabin. Her stomach heaved. She stared at Gian, wide-eyed for a single instant, before she whirled and dashed for the door.

Kate leaned over the side in the rising wind and vomited. She had barely had enough time to make it to the leeward side. The sailors gave her a wide berth.

Gian came up behind her and hovered. "Are you all right?" He pulled a handkerchief from the stolen coat's breast pocket and held it out to her.

"Jolly. Just jolly." She tried to get her breath. Still she was grateful for the handkerchief.

"Normally I could help that with a little compulsion. Works wonders."

"I've always been seasick." She held the kerchief to her mouth at another wave of nausea.

"We're heading into a nasty blow." He pressed his lips together. "Let me try."

"It doesn't work on me, remember?"

"You said you let Elyta compel you. That was a conscious act. Could you do it with me?"

She looked up at him. "I don't think so." She had no wish to give in to anyone else's will. That time with Elyta had been *in extremis*. But then she had to lean over the side again abruptly. Bloody hell. How long was the trip to Algiers? Two days? As she raised herself, shaking, he took her shoulders and turned her to him. Then he pressed her body against the rail with his to steady her. A tremor ran all up and down her frame. But she had no time even to regret her reaction because his eyes just . . . went red. Not the deep red she knew, but a pale wash of rose.

"Think about letting go, Kate. I promise, I'll only quiet your stomach." She felt his words as much as heard them in the rising wind.

Nothing happened.

"Relax." His voice reverberated in her chest. "I can't overwhelm you. I only have a little bit of power." Did he know her every thought? He rubbed her shoulders and neck with those strong hands . . . "Think about yielding."

When had she yielded to another? *She* was the predator. But two days of vomiting? *He's trying to help,* she told herself. *It's still Gian.* She held to that and thought about . . . opening. Some iron rod inside her back crumbled and with it some lock on a part of her brain.

In came a wonderful feeling. Calm. Sure. She hadn't even known what that felt like. Until now. She smiled. She couldn't *not* smile. A sense of well-being came from that place in her back where she'd been so stiff and the locked part of her brain that had opened. She seemed to hang suspended in that green-red gaze, and it was a very good place to be.

His eyes went back to green. He smiled in return. "Feel better?"

She blinked in surprise. Her rebellious stomach was quiet. Yet the little ship was pitching at ever greater angles. Seamen scurried about the tiny deck. But she was calm. "I do."

"Good, then go below where it's safer. This storm will get worse before it gets better." He led her to the cabin, a firm grip on her elbow.

As they passed a sailor, she heard him say to his fellow seaman, "Her fault, this blow."

So many things were her fault. But not this. Wait! She had seen the vampire Illya pitched from the deck of a ship in a storm. She turned on Gian. "They will come after us, won't they?"

"I expect so." He continued to move her toward the little cabin door. "But Elyta will think a bigger ship is faster. She'll likely hire that xebec that was anchored in the harbor."

"And . . . and she's wrong?"

He smiled. "Very wrong. That's why *Reteif* is used to tend one of the behemoths. It carries messages, brings supplies, that sort of thing. Goes back and forth in half the time. We'll be in Algiers long before Elyta."

Gian stood barefoot, in shirtsleeves and wet to the skin, hauling on the lines to the mainsail as Captain Gaetjens shouted for the change in tack. His strength was hardly more than human at the moment, but it was needed. The wind and rain slashed in on him as the tender headed into the trough of another wave. Water would cascade in over the prow again in another moment, and the deck would be awash.

They'd be lucky to clear this storm. It was one of the worst he'd seen, and he had seen a thousand storms. He wouldn't regret sending the stones to the bottom of the sea. And he'd survive. But what if he couldn't save Kate? He tied off the line and held fast to it as he scraped the wet hair plastered to his face out of his eyes. He'd brought her into terrible danger. Even if they survived, they might fail. And if he reached Algiers, there was always the threat that he would succumb again to the nightmares that had plagued him so when he was back in the land of their genesis.

Dawn was probably just ahead. The sky roiled charcoal instead of pitch-black, but there wasn't much difference. The storm could go on for days. Could the tender hold out against it? He staggered along the rope they'd strung from fore to aft, up to the quarterdeck above the little cabin. Gaetjens stood, feet apart, grappling with the wheel.

"We must run before the wind," Gaetjens yelled. "She won't tack in this blow."

That meant they wouldn't beat the xebec to Algiers. "Do what you must, Captain."

"Take in the mainsail," Gaetjens shouted.

A shriek of wood split the storm. Gian and the Captain turned as one to the mainmast. It was bending in the gale at an unnatural angle. The sound of canvas ripping and the protesting whine of rope stretched taut rose over the howl of the wind. A monumental crack sounded and the mast toppled slowly over in a billow of wet canvas. A man's scream of pain came from the tangle. Gian bent into the wind and fought his way through the slashing rain to the deck below. The tender listed dangerously, unbalanced under the weight of the broken mast. Already sailors hacked at the ropes. The wreckage would carry them all to the bottom if they couldn't cut it loose.

"Jenkins!" one of the sailors called. "It's Jenkins."

One of their number was trapped under the mast. A bloom of blood on the canvas marked the spot. Gian waded into the melee of activity and pulled the canvas free. The sailors hauled at it. He knelt, knees wide for balance, and held to the carcass of the mast to avoid sliding down the steep slope of the deck. The man was alive. Gian waited for the roll and stood. He bent, got his knees under him, and heaved on the mast. Two sailors dragged Jenkins from under it.

Gian staggered several steps toward the rail. Four others joined him. They clung to the wreckage of the mast on the windward roll and shoved it toward the sea on the leeward. The balance tipped. The waves tore at the end of the mast and snapped it free. Another shove and the bulk of the remaining stump slid over the side in a tangle of rope and splintered wood.

Gian heaved the unconscious Jenkins up and pulled him into the relative calm of the cabin. Kate stood, clinging to a rope handle on the wall, her eyes wide. When she saw the injured man, she pointed to a hammock. Gian laid the injured man down, and one of the other sailors bound him into the swinging cocoon.

"Go on," Kate yelled over the creaking and the wind. "I'll take care of him."

Gian nodded. The other sailor pulled his forelock, and together he and Gian staggered out into dawn that looked like wet charcoal. At least there would be no sun today.

In the morning of the third day Kate woke to the cry of birds and a softly rocking ship. It was over. Gian and two sailors hung in the hammocks, dead asleep. The sailors were snoring. The injured one would make it. He had a concussion and broken ribs. After he had wakened she'd felt safe in giving him some laudanum she'd found in a little cupboard. It was actually good to hear him snore. Just to keep the little ship afloat had been all the sailors could do. She had provided food and tended the injured man. It didn't seem like very much.

There was a sense of unreality about her situation. She couldn't see a future she could even recognize. What was she doing going to North Africa with a vampire, with vampires chasing them, and dangerous jewels any one of the crew would probably kill them to obtain?

If only the stones would tell her own future.

She frowned. But they never had. She had not once seen herself in any of her visions. That was odd. Her two visions of Gian had both come to pass, and now there was nothing to say what his future would be either. How much she would give to see either of their futures at this moment.

Bloody hell, she thought. *You're turning into one of those weak minds made to become marks for people just like you.*

The cry of gulls interrupted her morbid thoughts. Surely that meant they were near shore. She slipped out of her hammock and let herself out into the blinding sunlight. The captain stood at the wheel, looking exhausted. On the left about a mile away, dry hills loomed above a beach with huge surf crashing on the sand. One sailor moved about the deck coiling ropes and another sat on one of the same mending a sail with even stitches.

She smiled at the captain. "Well done, Monsieur le Capitaine. We made it."

He gave her a grimace. "We did indeed, if you call Cagliari on Sardinia our destination."

"We're not in Algiers?"

"The shore's on the north," he said in disbelief.

"Oh." She'd never been much on direction. But now that she looked at the sun behind her, it was coming up directly in back of the boat. "How far is Cagliari from Algiers?"

"About three hundred sea miles."

That would not please Gian. The cabin door cracked open. Gian squinted against the light. "Good job, Gaetjens."

"I'm not sure we could have done it without you, signore."

"Come. Let's draw a new course." He shut the door abruptly. Kate knew why. The captain gave the wheel to a sailor and ducked into the cabin. She followed. Gian had a parchment spread out on the table and weighted with the heavy tankards they used for ale.

The captain thrust an index finger at the map. "We must stand in to Barcelona or back to Rome for repairs and supplies. Shouldn't take above a week to get a new mast."

Gian shook his head. "No time, my friend. Can she limp into Algiers?"

The captain frowned. "Maybe. If the weather holds."

"I think the weather has done its worst." Gian moved his hand over the map, looking for a route, then pointed. "Here. We'll hit land here, then hug the coast."

The captain looked up, concern etched in his weathered face. "You take a chance."

Gian set his lips. "The stakes are high. Our competition has just gained ground on us. We'll collect fresh water on shore here and crack on for Algiers." Glancing up, he saw Kate standing, back against the door, and touched his hand to his forelock in the classic sailor's salute. "Good morning." The captain headed out to the tiller, his look pensive.

"I thought you said we were faster than their larger ship," Kate whispered.

"But they are more stable in a storm," he said, "with their greater weight. And barring they did not lose a mast themselves, they would have been able to stay closer to their course." He shrugged as though he didn't care, but his eyes were serious. "They may be before us."

"In Algiers?" She chewed her lip in dread. She had no desire to meet Elyta again, ever.

"Perhaps. She'd find our destination in Amalfi. Or maybe they'll go straight to the temple. You told them I was taking the stone back there."

"But they don't have the stones to guide them."

"Maybe they don't need them." He looked away, toward the horizon. "Elyta was once a mentor to the woman called Asharti who started the whole mess in North Africa. It was Asharti who found the temple. If they were still friends then, maybe Elyta already knows where it is."

Eighteen

On the evening of the fourth day after the storm had abated, they drifted into Algiers' harbor. They had actually made good time, or so the captain said, considering. But four more days on board a tiny boat with no privacy and no chance to be alone with Gian was torture. Gian was edgy the whole time, pacing the cabin, working all night with the sailors. It was almost as if he didn't want to be with her. His answers to her questions were short if he answered at all. There was something wrong with him.

The gangplank was hardly set out when Gian appeared in coat and boots. "Gaetjens, escort Miss Sheridan to the Hôtel Africain. I have some urgent business I must attend to."

Gian registered her mulish expression. "You'll be perfectly safe."

"I'm sure I will . . ." Indeed, the sailors had all been most kind and deferential after she'd cared for the injured Jenkins.

"In case you are looking for our cargo, I've taken them with me for safekeeping."

Before she could say more, he disappeared into the crowd on the docks. She was left to gather their belongings and trail after the captain to the hotel, fuming. He might be able to keep his pockets from being picked. He'd caught her out after all. But it wasn't right to leave her without a clue as to what was next or what she was to do.

By the time she and the captain reached their destination, she was perspiring. The night was steamy. The hotel turned out to be a whitewashed affair with a tiled roof and arched windows filled with filigree iron. Inside, cool blue tiles and the luxury of indoor plants were welcome, but the French spoken by the desk clerk was even more so. Kate didn't speak Arabic. The porter deposited Gian's valise in one room and left her with the key to one adjacent.

"Thank you for all your help, mademoiselle," the captain said, bowing over her hand.

"Thank you, Captain. You have been most kind."

"Now, I must beg forgiveness, for I have a mast to see to." He grinned. "It would not do to be unready when il signore Urbano wishes to return to Amalfi."

She sincerely hoped they had a chance to make use of that new mast.

It was nearly midnight when she felt vibrations and the faint scent of cinnamon and something else wafted through the door. Could that be Gian? If so, he had gained back his scent.

The door opened and he strode in without knocking, looking strong and relaxed, ready. The circles that had hung about his eyes were gone. His face was pleasingly flushed and his eyes snapped with energy. His vibrations were faster again, almost at the edge of consciousness.

Blood. Why hadn't she guessed? She felt a fool. "I see you got what you needed."

He flushed further.

"You could have had more from me, you know."

"I couldn't risk taking from anyone on a boat that size. If they'd realized they had a vampire aboard, I'd have had them jumping overboard." He strode to the window and closed the shutters. "They're here."

"Elyta?" she gasped.

"No, Ian Rufford and his wife. They've taken a villa in the old part of town."

"You mean you weren't sure they were even in Algiers?" How like him to keep that little doubt from her.

He didn't answer, but gestured to her valise, still unpacked upon the narrow bed. "Bring your things. I'll take you to them."

"Now?"

He raised his brows. She felt silly. Midnight was not an imposition to vampires. Now he was going to try to leave her with them while he went off and . . .

But he couldn't, if Rufford didn't know where the temple was. Only she could make the stones point the way. Had he thought of that? She wouldn't break it to him yet.

She grabbed her valise. "How long will it take to get a caravan together?" That's what one did, wasn't it? She imagined a long line of camels marching into the burning sun. Sun! How would Gian travel in a caravan?

"Mrs. Rufford will know."

Mrs. Rufford?

He must have seen her look of skepticism. "She's been arranging expeditions since she was fifteen."

The villa was walled in thick sandstone brick, plastered and whitewashed. It glowed in the moonlight. Gian pounded on the thick wooden door.

"There is a bell," she pointed out.

He shot her a look of exasperation. "My fist will work just fine." He was right. The door opened and a tall man in a striped burnoose and skullcap asked them their business. Kate kept her head down to conceal her scar. The servant led them into a most remarkable room. Its floor was tiled and in the center a beautiful fountain covered with brightly glazed tiles tinkled under a square opening direct to the night sky. Banquettes lined the walls and pillows were strewn about in comfortable disarray. Lamps cast a warm light over everything.

The room was filled with the scent of cinnamon and that something else, and vibrating energy, some very high, at the edge of consciousness, and some slower, methodical almost.

A brawny man sat at a writing desk, his quill scribbling across foolscap at a furious pace. His hair was sandy brown and too long for fashion, pulled back in a ribbon at his neck. His face was bold, his chin strong. Kate would bet his coat had been made by Weston, his boots by Hoby. Matthew had trained her to look for the work of the best tailors and boot-makers.

At his feet, in the midst of piles of very old books, curled the dainty figure of one of the most striking women Kate had ever seen. Her hair was dark, coiled in intricate braids around her head. But curls escaped and framed a graceful neck. Her skin was the color of coffee with lots of cream in it. She wore native garments in a lovely pale green embroidered with gold. Her sleeves brushed her palms and a translucent wrap of the same color looped round her and fastened at the crown of her head. Meant to be drawn across her face in public, it hung open now.

As the servants announced them, Kate braced herself for the look of pity when they saw her scar. They both rose, and Kate saw that the woman's eyes were an amazing color somewhere between green and gold that put her dress to shame. She felt their glances register the scar—who could not? But there was more of curiosity than pity or shock in their eyes. Maybe it took a lot to shock a vampire. Then their gazes both moved to Gian, and their faces lit with pleasure.

"Urbano," the man said, striding forward and holding out his hand. "What the hell are you doing in these parts?"

"I am glad to find you in residence, Rufford. I have a mission most urgent."

"Well, sit down." He waved to the servant. "Tea, Abdullah, if you please."

Kate had eyes only for the woman. She had blanched, and was looking positively ill. Still she gathered herself and came forward, managing a genuine smile.

"Gian, you are a welcome sight."

Gian bent and she planted a delicate kiss on each of his cheeks. She was English too, by her accent. She didn't look English. But she didn't look like the local women Kate had seen in the streets either. As Gian let her go, she put a hand to her throat, apparently trying to catch her breath. Gian and her husband didn't seem to notice.

"Let me introduce Miss Sheridan. Miss Sheridan, Ian Rufford and Mrs. Rufford." He did not explain what Kate was doing there in his company. She could feel the two owners of this lovely house wondering. They must know him to be a notorious rake. Or maybe they only wondered why Gian Urbano was in the company of such a disfigured woman when he could have had any woman he wanted. She flushed.

Rufford bowed crisply. Mrs. Rufford took her arm. The woman was trembling. "Please, we are so far . . . from the stuffiness of, of English drawing rooms. Please call . . . call me Beth."

Kate smiled. "Thank goodness. I never liked those drawing rooms. Then you must call me Kate." Up close, those green-gold eyes were even more startling, fringed by dark lashes. She led Kate to a banquette, but in truth, Kate was half supporting her as she clung to Kate's arm. Gian was busy telling Rufford about the loss of the mast. "Are you well?" Kate whispered.

"I can't think what's come over me," the woman murmured, sinking. "I feel so strange."

"Can I ask your husband to call for something, a vinaigrette perhaps?"

She shook her head. "I'm sure it will pass." But all the color had drained from her face.

"We've come for help, Rufford," Gian said. "We're headed for the Temple of Waiting."

"Dangerous place." Rufford pulled at his loosely tied cravat as though he was too warm.

"Elyta Zaroff has acquired two stones from the fountain."

Rufford and his wife did not seem surprised. "I heard that they were out and about, or one at least. I thought when Rubius sent you after them that you were just the man for the job."

"I've got them. I'm returning them to the temple." He patted his coat pocket.

"I thought the Elders wanted them at Mirso." Rufford didn't judge. He just said it.

"Yes, well." Gian cleared his throat. "They can't fall into the wrong hands. Even if those hands are at Mirso. They're safer at the temple."

Rufford examined him, then nodded once. "If you say so, I agree. Who would not trust the man who held Algiers against all odds? And I owe you for the rescue in Casablanca."

"Which three of you had held for a month," Gian noted. Rufford waved a hand in dismissal of his own bravery. "Besides, there were many of us who came to break the siege."

"But you organized the whole," Rufford insisted. "Saved Fedeyah's and Davie Ware's hide as well as mine. And Davie's new wife too." Then he sighed. "Rough times."

Kate watched a shadow cross Gian's face. With an effort he shook off the memories she had seen haunting him from the very first time she saw him.

"Elyta wants to drive members of the government mad and take over France," he continued. "The sooner these stones are back where they belong, the better."

"Two problems," Rufford said. He got up to pace. He seemed an active man for one so brawny. "One, the temple is covered in a million tons of sand. Two, I don't think we could find the place anymore. We never knew the exact longitude and latitude. The landmarks are now obliterated. What do you think, Beth?" Rufford's brows drew together. "Beth?"

"I'm fine," the lady said, and promptly fainted.

"Beth!" Rufford threw himself down at her side, chafing her hand. "What's wrong?" he asked, his eyes wild.

Beth couldn't answer so Kate stepped into the breach. "She hasn't been feeling well since we came in."

"She's usually as strong as any five men," Rufford said, lifting her into his arms. He didn't realize, in his distraction, that his wife might not like that comparison.

"Was she well before we came in?" Gian's eyes darted about the room as he thought.

"Yes, yes." Rufford made for the door, his wife in his arms. But he stopped and turned. "I can't summon a doctor. He wouldn't know what to make of her."

Kate cleared her throat. There was one possible explanation. "Could she be . . . expecting?"

"Unlikely," Gian said shortly. "It is almost impossible for our kind to have children."

That was news, since he had a mother.

"Still," Rufford said, "I was made only five years ago, and I made her a year later. When we are young there is a better chance. It is conceivable." He didn't look unhappy that she might be pregnant. In fact he gazed down at his wife and smiled. These two were obviously in love. Somehow he had made her vampire by accident. He couldn't have meant to do it. Yet they had no air of tragic figures. Did they not consider it a tragedy?

Gian barked a laugh. "Conceivable? So to speak." Then he too grew thoughtful. "You have the blood of an Old One in you, rumors have it."

Rufford's face fell a little. "That does make it harder." Kate couldn't believe he would actually want to have children. Wouldn't they be vampire too?

Kate cast about for another explanation. "Maybe it's something about us that sickens her."

Then she and Gian looked at each other, struck.

"No," Gian said. "It's the stones. They suck a vampire's energy. Maybe if you're newly made, it affects you more. Do you feel it, Rufford?"

Rufford's gaze turned inward. "No. Or at least it is so faint as to be almost undetectable. But I do have a bit of the blood of an Old One. Beth has only my blood."

Gian's resolve showed in his face. "I'll take the stones and go." He strode to the door, almost colliding with Abdullah, on his way in with an ornate silver tea set on a tray.

"Wait." Rufford chewed his lip. "I don't want those stones out on the streets of Algiers either." He laid Beth on the banquette. Kate went to her side. "Come with me," he said to Gian. "There's a root cellar at the far end of the compound. Practically a bunker. Perhaps that will mute the effect. And it has a stout lock to keep the stones from being stolen."

"Ideal."

The two men left, leaving Abdullah staring after them. "Does Miss want tea?"

"Set it down, if you would," Kate asked. "And could you get a damp cloth?" The servant bowed and withdrew.

Beth moaned and tried to sit up. "What happened?"

"You fainted. We think it was the proximity of the jewels. To hurt Gian, he must be touched with them, but he says you are much younger."

Beth took this fantastic explanation in stride. "Oh. And

Ian has the Old One's blood, so he wouldn't be affected. I expect that was it." She laid her head on the back of the banquette.

"They've gone to lock them in some root cellar."

"I do feel better." And indeed the color was washing back into her cheeks.

"I hope waking to the sight of me didn't startle you." Kate's scar could send anyone back into a swoon. Kate managed a laugh.

Beth raised her head and looked at Kate strangely. "Actually, I thought you were very good not to stare at my eyes. People always do, you know."

Kate poured her out some tea, and handed her the cup. "They are no doubt astounded by your beauty. It's not the same thing." Abdullah returned with a cloth and Kate laid it against Beth's forehead as he withdrew discreetly.

"Not likely," Beth said, closing her eyes. "I've been called a 'brown little thing' in the drawing rooms of London. And here, I'm not Egyptian enough."

"You're one of the most beautiful women I've ever seen." Kate meant it.

Beth gave a rueful smile. "No, that would be you."

Was she making fun of Kate? She hardly seemed the type. Probably she was still a little stunned and wasn't making sense.

Gian and Rufford burst into the room. "Are you all right?" Rufford asked, striding to his wife's side. His forehead was wrinkled in worry.

"I'm much better, dear." Beth removed the compress from her forehead and looked around. "A little weak. This tea is doing wonders." She patted his hand. "I admit I could do with something a little stronger though."

Rufford was unwilling to leave his wife's side, so Gian strode to the brandy decanter on a low table. He poured Beth out a little brandy and two substantial glasses for himself and Rufford. He lifted the decanter to Kate in question, but she shook her head. Kate wondered how long Rufford and Beth had been married. The expression in their eyes whenever they looked at each other was . . . full—that was the only way she could explain it. She wanted to know everything about them. She wouldn't think why.

"Well, shall we return to the consideration of our problem?" It was Beth who prodded them back to the topic.

"I shall go with you, of course," Rufford said.

"No. You can't go, my friend." Gian looked sorry about that. He obviously trusted Rufford. "Because Mrs. Rufford can't go. Elyta may try to make contact with you for information about the Temple of Waiting if she doesn't know where it is. You wouldn't want her to find Mrs. Rufford alone and try to pry the location out of her."

Rufford swallowed. "I would not. But that leaves you in the lurch."

"No it doesn't," Kate said. "Gian knows very well that the stones tell me the direction of the temple. He'd just rather leave me behind. And now he can't." She smiled at Gian.

"But how is this?" Beth asked, sitting straighter.

"It's a long story . . ." Gian made it clear he did not want to go into it.

"No it's not." Kate turned to the others, who waited with raised brows, agog to know what she was talking about. "I see visions, sometimes." There, she'd admitted it. "And looking at the stones always brings one on. I don't go mad," she hastened to interject. "Or at least not madder than usual. And I can feel them wanting to go home. They . . . pull, for lack of a better word, in the right direction." She looked at Gian. "But only for me."

Gian sighed. "Miss Sheridan is a woman of some talents." The words escaped through gritted teeth. "That doesn't mean she should go on this expedition." The arrogant bastard really hated admitting that she was as much a part of this adventure as he was.

"I can see how you wouldn't want to put her in danger, Urbano." Rufford gave his wife one of those full looks. "But I can't see any way out of it."

"And the good thing is that I was planning to excavate the Kasbah at El Oued. I've organized a caravan to leave in two days. If we take some of their supplies and accelerate the preparations, you could leave tomorrow night."

"Excellent." Gian looked relieved.

Beth chewed her lip. "Use the pass at Blida over the Atlas Mountains. The temple is on the southeast side of the middle range. If you use every available hour of darkness—maybe eight or nine days."

"Do caravans travel at night?" Kate asked.

Beth smiled. "My caravans do."

But of course they would. What kind of a woman organized caravans and excavated Kasbahs? Kate found Beth fascinating, not only for who she was, but for the fact that she seemed at ease with what she had become.

"We'll travel both night and day, if you can tell us where to exchange animals." At the look the Ruffords gave him, Gian bristled. "I'll cover up. I'm older than you two, even though you have an Old One's blood, Rufford. I'll be fine. Kate will need to ride a camel." He glanced at her in apology. "Horses are not her strong point."

It was Kate's turn to bristle.

"If you are going to take her with you, she will need rest, as will the drivers. You can't just push them all to exhaustion, Gian," Beth scolded. "They don't have your strength."

Gian looked exasperated.

Kate wanted to distract him from the fact that she would be such a drag on his purpose. "Will you two assemble another caravan and carry on your expedition? You might as well."

Rufford laughed. "I was not included. Beth was going to explore lost civilizations on her own. Deserting me in fact. Alas, I am chained to Algiers at the moment. We are still cleaning up after our little war."

"He means they are arming the populace with knowledge of how to kill any left of the poor creatures Asharti made vampire for her army." Beth sighed.

Realization struck Kate. "That terrible plague that hit this area two years ago . . . Is that plague what you call the North African Vampire Wars?"

"That's the story we put about. And it was a plague of sorts," Rufford agreed. But then he looked at Gian. "It wasn't easy, what we did. And it wasn't clean. Innocents were hurt on both sides. But it had to be done, Urbano. You know that."

Gian, still at the sideboard, downed his glass of brandy at one gulp and poured himself another. He was upset by this "war" that the world had thought a plague. "It may have been duty, but we sullied our souls," he said. "There was no honor in it."

"That's the price for keeping the balance between vampire and human."

"The only reason you two weren't killed along with all the others who aren't born to the blood was that you destroyed Asharti," Gian said, and downed the second glass. "According to the Elders, making a vampire is an abomination. If the Elders had sentenced you and Mrs. Rufford to death too, would you still think it had to be done?"

"I would have taken Beth and run for the hills. She's my first concern. But they didn't condemn us. So I fought, as you did. Beth fought in Tripoli with Khalenberg. It's a rough world. But we play the hand we're dealt. Then we live with what we've done."

Beth smiled. "You are too hard on yourself, Gian. Yet you are so courageous. Both of you." She glanced to Kate.

"For our part, we'll deal with Elyta if she comes through Algiers."

She rose. "I'll write you out contacts for supplies and animals along your route. Use my name. You'll be treated well."

"You'll find these much more comfortable for desert travel." Beth bustled into the room with an armload of clothes, followed by two maidservants carrying boots and coats and belts and all manner of things, along with two very large carpetbags bound by complicated straps. She held up an example. Breeches. "One really can't ride a camel except in breeches or a burnoose. You seem comfortable with trousers. These will be much better than the ones you have."

Kate had been feeling lost, with everyone out making who knew what arrangements. She was going across the desert on a camel into mysterious mountains where temples were buried, carrying deadly jewels the size of apricots, with vampires on her trail. Not to mention that she was going with a vampire to do it. And speaking of that vampire, with all the preparations, he had been nowhere in evidence. He had been studying maps, and making notes, and . . . and he didn't seem to have time for her. But that was good. She didn't want to get more involved with him. Not when they might be killed.

And if they weren't killed, then what? She had no idea. In fact, there was so much puzzling about Gian, and what she wanted, and what she was afraid to want, that she couldn't even think about him.

So she welcomed the life that entered the room with Beth. The women dumped their load of clothing on the bed and the maids retreated murmuring to each other. One made the sign against the evil eye. Kate sighed.

"I'm sorry about their reaction," Beth said.

"Don't be. I'm used to it." Kate shrugged as though she didn't care.

"You are a strong person. Gian has told me all about you." Beth sorted clothes into piles.

Kate was appalled. "I don't know what he could tell you. He knows nothing about me."

Beth glanced up, smiling. "Only how you came to be involved with the stones."

"You mean that I picked the pocket of one of Elyta's vampire friends and stole the emerald?" There, that would shock her.

"He quite admires how intrepid you are. Your skills saved him from Elyta."

"He just knows my tricks. That isn't me." Kate fingered a fine pair of loose wool trousers dyed red. Dressing like this would be . . . different at least. She could put her reticule, with her tarot cards and money in the capacious pockets.

"And what do you know of him?"

The question was innocent, but Kate felt as though Beth was challenging her. "That he is arrogant. That he's used to having whatever women he wants. That he can be incredibly stubborn."

Beth sighed and smiled. "In short, a strong and attractive man. Aren't such men all like that?"

Was she dismissing those observations? Very well. "I know he values his honor and his duty to these Elders, whoever they are, more than his life." She let her tone tell Beth how stupid she thought that was. "I know he cares for his mother." She paused. "He's generous to his servants." She shrugged. "He has courage." She wouldn't say that he was also an extremely generous lover. Or that he made a thrill inside her loins even when she thought about that. That was just a measure of her weakness, not of him.

"He is all of those," Beth agreed. "They are part of what I value about him. With what he went through during the wars, I worried for him. Ian and I both did. He seemed so . . . lost afterward. Ian thought this mission to find the stone would help him find his way back."

Gian lost? That didn't seem right. "I know he hates what he did in the war, somehow."

"Yet he wants to find purpose in fulfilling a duty at incredible personal cost. That is a courageous man." She held up a sheepskin jacket. "It is cold at night in the mountains."

"He's just arrogant enough to think there's a purpose to life." Kate was thinking out loud. "And that he is the one to find it."

"And isn't there?" Beth folded clothes and put them into a valise.

"No." Kate found herself at the arched window surrounded by blue tiles, looking out over a courtyard with olive trees in it. "The only purpose is survival, and to grab what comfort or happiness you can for as long as you can hold it." She could smell the jasmine on the night air. "And that's usually short enough."

"I agree with you."

What did that mean for a woman who was vampire? What comfort and happiness could there be? But how could she ask someone about that? Desire warred with discretion in her breast. Discretion lost. "Are . . . are you sorry you're a vampire?"

"No." Beth's gaze was frank. "I find the night a comfort now. And the blood? I once worried about that. But you've no idea how sweet it is to feel the thrill of life along your veins when your Companion tastes the first copper richness of blood. In fact, the feeling of being alive and . . . more because you are two beings together is something I can't imagine being without. The senses . . ." She closed her eyes, a look of bliss passing over her face. "You can't imagine the heightened smell, the sight—even at night—and touch . . . Oh, I love the sense of touch."

Kate blinked. She knew what or whom Beth was thinking of touching.

Beth opened her eyes. "I'd wager Gian doesn't feel how special it is. He was born to it. But it's like opening a window and seeing a whole other world outside."

"Mr. Rufford made you vampire?"

"He had no choice. I'd been infected by Asharti. He had to give me his blood. Without immunity from a vampire's blood, reaction to the parasite kills you."

"So it was an accident." Beth was just making the best of a bad lot.

Beth stalked over and looked Kate right in the eyes. "Make no mistake. I would have cut his veins and infected myself if he hadn't." Her tone was fierce. "I love him. I knew he loved me. He was going to live forever. Can you imagine growing old while the one you loved did not? What kind of life would that be? Wouldn't it tear your heart out each day? No, I'm glad he made me. I'd do it for him if the situation were reversed."

Kate bit her lip. "You say that now, but . . . Forever? What guarantee is there that things won't change, and you won't end up regretting this?"

"No guarantees in life, ever. We all must live with it." Then she smiled. Her face softened. "Living without guarantees is what takes true courage." She turned to the valise and snapped it shut. "Don't worry about Elyta. My Ian can take care of her if she comes through Algiers. I'm only sorry I can't go with you. But when you come back, if you want to know more, come to me. I'll stand as your friend. And if ever Gian's attentions should be . . . distasteful to you. Just tell him. You said yourself he has honor." She grinned. "And don't let him bully you. Men will, you know, if you let them."

Beth Rufford was gone. Just like that. What had she meant by saying that Gian's attentions might be distasteful? Did she think Gian would try to make Kate vampire?

Kate shuddered. But she wasn't sure it was entirely a shudder of distaste.

Nineteen

Gian placed the boxes, one silver and one mahogany, inside his burnoose in a leather pouch slung over his bare shoulder by a broad strap. He would need them close by for Kate to take their direction. He sucked in a breath and let it out slowly, trying to relax. Taking Kate into such danger grated on him. He'd taken blood again in the city last night, but still his strength was not even enough for translocation. His vampire senses were coming back slowly. Normally he could go a fortnight without blood, but he wasn't sure he would last so long. He'd have to forage in a village. *Let me be strong enough.* He wasn't sure to whom he prayed.

He walked out onto the balcony. The night was drenched with jasmine and the faint odor of camel. Who could ever forget that smell? It was part of his memory of Algiers, along with the scent of spices in the markets, the aroma of overripe meat, the pungency of that peculiar kind of red dye being made in large vats. One fear at least had not come to pass. Algiers had not brought on the nightmares again. He'd been to the Kasbah for supplies without being paralyzed by memories. The familiar smells, the calls of the mullahs, nothing had brought on his sweating, shaking dislocations. Maybe that was because he was about to push himself and Kate into another nightmare. Or maybe it had something to do with Rufford. Just knowing that someone else shared his experience and was struggling to move on was . . . comforting.

Below him, Kate stood in the courtyard of the Ruffords' villa in the dusk under the olive trees, her hair tied up under a turban, a long flowing cotton jacket almost covering her loose trousers. She was saying her good-byes to the Ruffords. She'd pulled the end of her turban across the lower half of her face to cover her scar. She didn't have to do that. She was beautiful to him. Jupiter and Hera, but he wished he didn't have to take Kate with him. He was torn between relief that Beth Rufford's reaction to the stones held her and her husband in Algiers, out of danger, and regret that their strength and determination was lost to him. Now it was up to him alone to protect Kate, with whatever strength he had.

He should be thinking only of the success of the mission. He should be glad Kate could find the buried temple, and that Elyta had not yet found them. Should be.

But what he was thinking about was the fact that Ian Rufford had made his true love vampire. And neither was sorry about it.

Blasphemy, of course. Against every principle of the Elders. Yet the Elders dared make no complaint. And Ian and Beth Rufford could give a fig about the Elders' Rules. He watched them; Rufford's arm around his wife's shoulders, her soft looks up at him.

They felt no obligation to obey the stricture of the Elders that vampires live one to a city either. Algiers did not seem to be suffering. Gian had found Rufford by inquiring after a rich man who appeared only at night. He was surprised to be greeted not with fear, but with adulation for Rufford's work in creating schools for girls as well as boys and giving small loans to poor men who wanted to start some tiny business. Rufford had been busy. And Algiers was the better for it.

Rufford had carved a life, not only made of what he wanted, but what Beth wanted too. Gian smiled to think of Rufford daring to put up schools for boys without providing schools for Arab girls as well. There would have been hell to pay with Beth for that. And Beth traipsed off to God knew where to look for her artifacts and feed her passion for history and the Sahara. She had learned to live without the day.

He turned from the balcony and trotted through the house into the courtyard. He must let Kate say their good-byes. He daren't approach the Ruffords with the stones. The time approached. Even now he could hear the braying of the camels, the snorting of the horses, the coarse Arabic of the drivers at the end of the lane where the caravan had gathered, ready to start. The Ruffords looked his way, expectant. He touched his temple in salute.

He saw Kate gather herself. He repressed a smile. How courageous she was.

"My camel calls," she said, taking her leave of her host and hostess.

"A hot bath awaits you upon your return," Beth said, smiling. He could see the worry behind her eyes, but she would never tell them of her fears.

"We expect you back before the next full moon," Rufford growled.

Gian started for the great doors that gave onto the dusty street, herding Kate with him. "The blood is the life," he murmured in the classic farewell of vampires.

"The blood is the life," the Ruffords murmured in unison.

He and Kate walked through the doors toward the braying of the camels. They were leaving all succor behind them.

The hot bowl of the valley that held the teeming city of Algiers was long behind them. Kate shifted her sore backside on the camel's ornate saddle and pulled her sheepskin coat around her, grateful for the wool that lined the leather. The high pass through to El Djelfa had taken four nights to navigate. Gian had pressed them forward for fourteen hours a day, even into the daylight. There were perhaps twenty animals, evenly divided among horses and the camels used to pack supplies. He rode a series of the delicate-looking Arab horses, which weren't really delicate at all, but hardy creatures with great endurance. He covered himself with a burnoose when the sun was up. She knew that couldn't be comfortable for him. When they stopped, she fell to her pallet, exhausted, while he tended to the animals, made sure the men were comfortable, brought her food. She often didn't see him rest at all, since he was up before she woke.

Her animal brayed in protest as she tapped its haunch with a stick. Camels were not meant to navigate the mountain passes. It protested the small patches of snow that lined the cliffs above the narrow gorge even in June. What did a camel know of snow?

She was exhausted. Every muscle in her body ached. Her belly cramped around the dates and nuts and jerky that made their meals. She glanced to Gian, his face pale in the moonlight. He seemed a stranger to her now, implacable, remote. His duty drove the caravan and his will.

They had changed out the animals twice at villages along the way, the last at El Djelfa only a few hours ago. Beth's name opened many doors. Kate's camel was fresh, if she was not. The path began to slope down, almost imperceptibly. And then they were at a bend. The path wound down steeply below them. Gian held up a hand to stop the little caravan.

Ahead the Sahara stretched, a sea of sand, infinite, ruffled with the waves of dunes. It looked close, though she knew they would take all the night ahead or more to make it to the desert floor. The moon rode high to her left, casting cold light over a landscape that looked like she imagined the floor of the sea must look.

Gian shot her a glance. "The worst is over now." He handed her a small metal flask. "Drink this. It will warm you."

She thought about refusing. She didn't like brandy. But it was his way of taking care of her. So she took the flask and sipped. At least it was good brandy. Not like the Blue Ruin she'd been given as a six-year-old on the streets of London. That stuff had been enough to strip the skin off your throat. "Thank you." She handed it back. "But you don't know the worst is over."

He looked exasperated. She raised her brows. "True." He bit the word out, then turned again to the wild landscape below them, thinking. He touched the pouch that held the stones inside his burnoose absently. "But once we're on the desert floor we'll make our way southwest, along the cliffs until the stones tell us we've come to the right place. We must be getting close."

As far as she could tell he had no basis for that assertion. She'd looked at the map. The Atlas Mountains stretched for hundreds of miles diagonally across the hump of North Africa, dividing the Sahara from the fertile coastal strip of land. They might have to wander for weeks taking readings from the stones that led them ever farther from the pass through the mountains.

He called something in Arabic and motioned the caravan on. "There isn't a moment to lose," he said, for the fiftieth time since they'd left Algiers. Her camel groaned and strode forward with his lanky, rolling gait.

She felt like there was some string, wound through her head and her heart, that he controlled, pulling her forward toward the sea of sand below. He thought Elyta and her vampire acolytes were near, else he wouldn't rush so. Yet to her they seemed far away. The Ruffords existed in some other world. Matthew had been a part of another lifetime altogether. Here there was only biting cold and stiff joints, and a tiredness in her bones that threatened to engulf her. And ahead, an endless sea of sand out of which they would try to pluck a single spot. She had seen the place in her vision, but she hadn't seen any people there. She couldn't be sure it was Gian who delivered the stones to the place they longed to be. She couldn't be sure of anything, except that she would follow Gian anywhere.

The caravan strung out along the cliffs on the sea of sand Gian said was called the Grand Erg Occidental. The cold was left above them. The air was hot, and so dry it seemed to strip the very moisture from her flesh. They'd stopped last night in the tiny village of Laghouhat for a fresh supply of dates and goat's cheese and olives. There were no fresh animals to be had there. The village was poor, perched between the harsh mountains and the desert. They had traveled all night along the edge of the desert. Several times she'd stopped and handled the stones. They were going in the right direction. But there was no end in sight.

The sun rose. Gian pulled the hood of his burnoose up. He looked like the cowled figure of death on horseback. She could look him in the eyes since her camel was taller than his horse.

"Effendi!"

Gian turned. The caravan had stopped behind them. The drivers pointed out into the desert and talked all at once.

Kate and Gian turned to see what the fuss was about. All Kate could see was a . . . kind of a dirty smudge against the horizon. Gian scanned the way ahead, and then turned back the way they had come. She had never seen him look so grim.

"What is it?"

"Sandstorm."

Images of being buried alive in sand tumbled around in her mind. Gian shouted something in Arabic. Kate was shocked to see fear in the men's eyes. She was even more shocked when the whole group turned out into the desert floor, right toward the sandstorm. Those who rode broke into a canter, while those who led camels pulled their beasts into a run.

"What are we doing? Can't we outrun it?" she shouted to him, even as her camel broke into a rolling lope, not wanting to be left behind.

"No. We only have about thirty minutes until it's on us," he called back.

"Then why are we going directly into its path?" The man had lost his senses. They were all going to die. "At least take shelter under the cliffs."

"Look at the cliffs. See how scoured they are?"

Kate turned in her saddle. They were deeply eroded, their face a series of round pillars.

"Up against the cliffs the currents of air will boil about so no tents can stand. We'll be safer out in the open where the wind can roll over us. If we get our tents up in time."

"And what if we can't?" she shouted.

He didn't respond, probably because he knew she wouldn't like the answer. She clung to her camel. Gian raced ahead on his dapple-gray horse. He jerked to a halt and spun. "Here," he shouted. Kate hauled on her fringed reins and the camel only overshot Gian and his horse by a few yards. The men riding leaped from their horses. The camel drivers gave their charges the signal to sink to the sand. Gian strode about heaving off packs, shaking out tents. Kate's camel folded itself with the others. She clambered off. The smudge had risen up until it looked like a brown wall. The wind was rising. She couldn't see it moving toward them yet, but it must be. She didn't know what to do, how to help.

Gian glanced over to her. "Hobble the horses." He tossed her several of the short sturdy ropes. She swallowed. All right. She started with the nearest horse. The beast was snorting in dismay, but it allowed itself to be hobbled. She moved to the next. The men were working frantically to raise the tents. They pulled on ropes, while Gian drove great four-foot stakes into the ground with a single swing of a great wooden mallet. He went from one to the other as tents rose around them. One man had tied the camels together. Another tied scraps of what looked like a turban over the noses and eyes of the horses she had hobbled. The men shouted to be heard above the sirocco. The brown dust had now blotted out the sun. The air was alive with wind and sand.

Gian strode over to where Kate knelt in front of a snorting horse and pulled her up. "Time for you to retire." He pulled her to the largest tent and thrust her inside. A hefty pack came sailing in after her. He tied down the tent flap. "Pull the bottom of the tent walls to the inside and bury them in sand," he shouted.

"Aren't you coming?" she called, but it was too late. He was gone. Around her, sand shushed against the tent, and the wind howled and plucked at the canvas. The air was thick with dust, which only slowly settled, laying a fine grit over everything. The tent was dim, the sun that would normally cast a light through the canvas almost blotted out by the storm. She stood, unnerved and alone except for some muffled shouts that sounded weak against the backdrop of the wind. She pressed her lips together, frightened. The fury of the storm dwarfed their puny efforts to prepare for it. She'd always considered herself brave. But that was in the face of bad men, hunger, the disapproval of society, an uncertain future. Now the very elements that made up the earth seemed to be going mad around her. Her imagination began to cycle. What if Gian was buried in sand before he could get back to the tent? What if the wind ripped the tent and her mouth and nose and lungs were filled with sand? The shouts outside were gone, either lost in the wind, or the men who made them silenced.

But she had a job to do. The wind was fluttering swirls of sand under the edge of the tent. She threw herself to her knees, pulled the excess canvas at the bottom of the tent walls to the inside and heaved sand onto it in great, two-handed scoops. That made the tent walls sturdier. She worked with all her strength, edging around until she'd circumnavigated the tent.

Then she was done, with nothing to do but wait and listen to the wind attacking the tent. It covered her gasps in overwhelming sound. She found herself shivering, though the heat was oppressive inside the tent. She couldn't sit. She just stood there, trembling. It seemed like forever until a whoosh of sand eddied in at the tent door. Gian stumbled in, pulling a horse with him.

"Tie the flap," he shouted. Already the air in the tent was filled with swirling sand.

She didn't need to be told twice. With fumbling fingers she found the ties. Her eyes stung with sand. He was beside her, pulling the flap taut against the force of the wind. Lord, but he was strong. The eddies of sand and air died as she tied the overlapping flaps shut.

"My God, Gian, are you all right?" She pushed back the hood of his burnoose and ran her hands over his face. It was caked with sand. His hair was full of it.

He nodded, gasping, and bent over, hands on his knees. Then he straightened and went to the horse, who was sneezing and shaking his head. It was his dapple-gray. Gian took a cloth from the pack and wiped the horse's nostrils and dabbed at his eyes. "There, better?" he asked the animal, and wiped his own face and neck. He tapped the horse's knees and the beast sank to the ground. He practically filled the tent. Gian looked up at her and shrugged. "I couldn't leave him out there. He wasn't hobbled or his eyes protected. He never would have lasted."

"You don't see me objecting." She cleared her throat. "My . . . camel?" Her voice sounded small over the wind clawing at the tent. She began to shiver again.

"They're pretty hardy creatures." He didn't make any promises. His eyes narrowed as he looked at her. He bent to the pack and brought out two water sacks, some packets of food wrapped in cloth. He handed her a water sack. "Drink some of this."

The water was warm and tasted of leather as she squeezed it into her mouth. But it was heaven. "How long will the storm last?" A quiver laced her voice. Where had that come from?

"No telling." He rubbed some water over his face and wiped it with the cloth again. "This looks like a big one, though." He took the water bag over to the horse and squeezed some into the side of its mouth. Its thick tongue snaked out to lick its lips. He glanced back to her. "We should have enough water to last if we're careful." He sat. There were no bedrolls or brightly colored rugs to cover the sand. She realized how much luxury he had provided for her up to now. "Come." He patted the place next to him.

She sat and hugged her knees.

"Now, I'm going to feed you dates while you talk to me."

"Talk? What about?" How could the man want conversation when the world was going insane around them?

"Anything you like." He popped a date into his own mouth. "Take my mind off the situation, you know."

"Oh." Well, she could do that. It never occurred to her he

might need comfort, or that such an arrogant creature would ever admit it. He offered her a date. She had grown to like the sweet, chewy dried fruit. They tasted like dessert, only you could eat them all the time, but her stomach rebelled at the very thought of food. She shook her head. "I'm not going to shout," she warned.

"Settle in closer. That way I can hear you." He put his arm around her. In spite of the heat, it felt good. She had to admit that. Nothing could protect her against the force of the wind, if ever it tore its way through the tent walls. But if she had to die, she could think of worse places to do it than in Gian Urbano's arms, even if he didn't love her. Even if he was something supernatural.

"I never believed in the supernatural, you know." She had to start somewhere and it was the only thing that occurred to her.

"I find that odd." His voice was so intimate, breathing into her ear. "You who are the most supernatural creature I have ever met."

"Me!" She chuffed a laugh. "This from a vampire."

"But I think myself very natural." He made it sound reasonable.

"I suppose you wouldn't think your powers abnormal since you grew up with them."

"Leaving aside the word 'abnormal' for a moment, since I do not cede you that, perhaps that's why you don't consider yourself supernatural."

"I didn't say I wasn't supernatural. These visions I have are definitely beyond the norm. I only said it was ridiculous for a vampire to call me the most supernatural creature he'd ever met." A thought occurred to her. "Besides, I'm not sure the abnormal part is even me. I never had a vision until the stones. *They* are the supernatural force. They ruined my entire life."

"Ruined . . ." He sounded sad. Then she felt him straighten. "But you didn't have the emerald when you had the vision of Elyta torturing me. That was the first night I met you."

"Oh, dear." He was right. She *had* been possessed by visions before she stole the stone. "Maybe it's you that induces this . . . effect in me. It must be something. I'm a charlatan, remember? Really quite ordinary."

"Hardly ordinary, Kate. You are a charlatan of the first order." He chuckled. They sat there, him holding her, listening to the angry, howling wind. Kate realized she'd stopped shivering. The hard feel of his body against her side was having its usual effect. God, but the man could make her crazy for him even in the middle of a sandstorm. How long had it been since they had been intimate? Since the chapel . . .

He kissed the top of her head. "I've an idea. Tell me what you first remember."

"Why?"

"Can you just humor me for once without bickering about it?"

"I wasn't bickering." She looked up, feeling mulish, and saw the warning look in his eyes. "Oh, very well." She took a breath. She had told no one about that time before Sir found her, not the sisters, not Matthew. "The first thing I remember is waking up in a trash heap behind a tavern."

She could practically hear him thinking. "But you were what, six, you said? Most people can remember lots of things before they were six."

"Well, I can't."

"I think you're just not saying to spite me."

"I wouldn't dare spite you. Defy the great Urbano? Hardly." Still, it was hard to feel rebellious cradled in his arms. She chewed her lip, thinking.

"For most people, the first thing they remember is a face."

She wasn't most people. Still . . . "I guess I remember a face." It was just a vague outline though. She didn't even know whose face.

"Man or woman?" he murmured.

"A woman." Fear began to circle her. "She smelled like lavender." Lavender came rushing over her. Kate began to breathe hard.

"Is it a nice memory?"

Kate shook her head. She didn't want to remember this. She knew she didn't. But the smell of lavender was everywhere, and the woman's face. And she knew who the woman was and why she looked like that. She began to shake. "No. No . . . I don't want to do this."

But she couldn't help it. The memories were rushing over her now. "My God, she's shocked. I think she was shocked at . . . at me." But there was more, much more. "I remember . . . her arguing with a man. They were shouting." And then some floodgates within her burst, or perhaps it was the wind bursting through the tent walls and into her soul. "They were arguing about . . . me." Memories whirled in her head like sand. "And he said I was unnatural and he wouldn't have me around, and she . . . she said she had no one to whom she could give me. She promised him I wouldn't say anything about what I'd seen anymore. And he said she'd promised that before, and I always blurted out something and frightened everyone. And he said he was tired of being put out of their lodgings because of me. And I was just a girl, and who would they marry me off to, with what I was?" The scene replayed itself, and Kate couldn't stop it. "And then she cried and said she loved him. And that . . . she'd get rid of me . . ." Kate's voice had sunk to a whisper. Surely Gian couldn't hear her, but it was all she could manage. She felt scoured out inside. She couldn't even cry, perhaps because in those first days after the trash heap, she'd cried so much. Maybe that was why she never cried when Matthew beat her, or when Sir shut her out in the cold because she hadn't come back with anything to sell.

Gian squeezed her shoulders and leaned his cheek against the top of her head.

"They abandoned me because I was having visions even then, didn't they?"

"Yes. And you suppressed your visions because they made people you loved, and who were supposed to love and care for you, abandon you."

The roar of the storm was far away. There was enough roaring inside her. She had to master that before she could think about the storm. She realized she'd stopped breathing when her lungs heaved a breath of their own accord. "You're so lucky your mother loved you. She still loves you." She felt wrung out, exhausted.

"Yes, I am. Vampires often abandon their children. It's a perversion of the Rule that says we live one to a city. I was lucky. My mother kept me by her. When my powers came on me at sixteen, she taught me how to manage everything raging inside me. You know how sixteen-year-old males can be." He took a breath. "Young male vampires are worse. Then she sent me to Siena, only fifty miles away. She came to see me often."

"And what of your father? Did he and your mother not stay together?"

"They couldn't. Not for more than fifty years. He was human." Gian's voice was rough.

So many questions dodged about her head. "Is that why your mother could have you? I mean, you said having a child was rare . . . for your kind."

"Probably."

"So, you never knew your father at all."

"Quite the contrary. I watched him grow old and die like any human child. He taught me how to grow grapes on our estates at Montalcino. I loved him. But I've never forgiven him for breaking my mother's heart." His voice got far away now, following his thoughts back in time. "He was taken as a slave from a Barbarian army in the first century before Christ. She bought him, freed him, and married him. Sometimes I thought I'd give my canine teeth to have known them when they were courting—what it was about him that made her crazy for him. I can never imagine him being her slave. But that would have been interesting to say the least. It almost killed her to watch him age. She's never found another love to match that one with him."

In almost a thousand years. The enormity of his mother's love for his father, for him, the length of his own life, dwarfed her own pale experience. She found herself depressed. What could someone who lived but a single lifetime offer to someone who had experienced everything? And yet, his mother fell in love with a man who lived and died in a single life span. "Why didn't she just infect him with the parasite?"

"It is forbidden. If every one of us made vampires every time we fell in love, just think what would happen. People separate, then think themselves in love again. Then ones made would make others, and soon our world would be unsustainable."

Interesting problem. "Can . . . your kind drink other vampires' blood?"

"No. Very old ones can drink the blood of the newly made. But Companions of the same strength war with each other."

That was it then. No wonder it was forbidden. She felt very inconsequential. Then her usual rebellious spirit rose inside her. "Mr. Rufford is made, and he made Beth."

"And they'd be dead today at a born vampire's hands if he hadn't saved us all by killing Asharti. They are the exception that proves the Rule. And the Rules are all that stands between us and chaos." He made his voice hard. The rebellion she felt growing inside her might crash in waves against the stone behind that tone and never crack it.

Realization washed over her. "So . . . is the pain you saw your mother experience why you never keep a lover for long?" Of course it was. It didn't matter what he said. He never let himself get attached to avoid the pain he'd seen all around him growing up.

She felt him stiffen. He said nothing.

After a moment she just went on. "So why don't you find one of your own kind?"

"One to a city, remember?"

More rules.

"Sometimes we get together briefly, but it doesn't last."

"That's why Elyta hates you, isn't it?" He had abandoned Elyta, in fact, but she didn't say that. Still, it sent a chill through her. Maybe she could understand Elyta's wrath.

"Yes. But she also hates the fact that Mother cares for me. Her mother cast her off."

"Oh, that's rare." Kate snorted. "Now I have something in common with Elyta."

"No." He pulled her close. "You are strong. You didn't let it twist you. She did."

"But I am twisted, I think." Her voice was small in her own ears. Maybe the fact that she was abandoned as a child was why she was so afraid of Matthew abandoning her. She had never let herself care for him, even though he said he was her father. Could one care for Matthew? Perhaps not, but she had never tried, and right now, that seemed to be because she didn't want his inevitable abandonment to hurt more than it must.

Maybe her history was why she despised those poor weak people who were her marks too, because despising them was easier than sympathizing with them. When you sympathized with someone, it was almost like caring about them. And she held herself aloof from ever committing her emotions to anyone. That, too, might be because she was afraid they would abandon her, reject her somehow. It was all of a piece, cut from the same cloth of her past.

The realization horrified her. It meant that all the time she thought she had been in perfect control of herself and her life, above those around her, aloof—all that time her past controlled her. That one action of her mother and her father (if the man she remembered even *was* her father— she didn't really know that) casting her on a trash heap because she had visions and couldn't keep them to herself . . . that one act ruled her whole life.

In the same way Gian's mother's grief had ruined his life, when she thought about it.

She could hear the smile in his voice as he said, "You are the most straightforward person I know. And your reaction to your past has saved your life more than once, I should think."

"You mean suppressing the visions kept me from being burned at the stake as a witch." Her voice was hoarse. Even breathing seemed an effort.

"I mean that your habit of shielding your mind is why our kind can't compel you and why you can look at the stones without going mad."

"Oh."

"You see? You are quite a remarkable person. One might say . . . supernatural."

"I don't feel supernatural." She listened to the howl of the wind, and the sand shushing against the tent. "And nature feels quite overwhelming all by itself."

He chuckled again. "My dear, dear Kate." He smacked

a kiss on the crown of her head. "Now, have some cheese and some dates to keep your strength up." He reached for the pack.

Suddenly, dates and goat cheese and warm water had never sounded so good.

Twenty

Gian cradled Kate in his arms as the wind at last died down. He didn't want to wake her when she had finally relaxed enough to doze off. When he'd come in, she was obviously in shock, trembling, her skin clammy and cold to the touch. It had been all he could do to calm her. He hadn't meant to rake up her past. The last thing he wanted was to give her pain. But he had to admit that her past explained exactly why she was so cynical, so self-sufficient.

And why she would never love him. Even beyond the fact that he was a monster in her eyes, she would never let herself love. Maybe not anyone. Certainly not him. He'd heard the dismay in her voice as she asked about vampire society. The way they lived would certainly be daunting to a human. Perhaps she would let him be her friend. Perhaps she could grow used enough to him for that.

In the dark of the tent, with the wind raging outside and the heat making him sweat, all his doubts assailed him. Even if they could find the cursed temple they'd have to dig out the tons of sand that buried it. He'd taken blood in Laghouhat, but he could foresee a time when he would need to feed again. Elyta was probably safe up in the mountains right now, and if they survived, she'd be ready to swoop down on them. And Kate would never love him.

He couldn't think about all that. So he just thought about how to talk Kate out of buying a cottage in rural England. She could be the toast of Rome, or Vienna, or anywhere really. She just had to be bold enough to brazen it through. People would get used to her scar, in spite of what his mother said. If Kate let him be her friend, he'd make sure she never wanted. He'd invest her money for her, say it was doing well, supplement it if he must.

He was condemning himself to his mother's fate; watching someone he loved grow old and die. But what was the alternative? Not to see her at all? He didn't have the courage for it. If she was stubborn enough to stick to her doomed plan, he'd set himself up in England, where he could watch over her. Italy held no attraction for him now.

He felt the sun go down. His entire lower body was numb from sitting in one position so as not to wake her. But now it was time. "Kate."

She roused herself. "Did I fall asleep?"

He smiled. How could one not smile at Kate? "For a little while."

"The wind has died." She scrambled to her feet.

He rose, his limbs tingling and stiff. "You stay here." He went to untie the tent flaps.

"Nonsense. I'm going with you." She came to help him with the ties.

"I don't think you want to see what may be out there."

She swallowed. "If it's bad, you're going to need help."

She was so courageous. He had placed the door to the tent toward the mountains, yet still, when he undid the final tie and pulled the flap inward, sand poured in from a drift that almost covered the doorway. He crawled up through the small opening. "Just give me a chance to take stock," he ordered. "I promise I'll come to get you when I know it's safe."

He got to his feet. The sky was slashed with red wounds where the setting sun glinted on the high, streaked clouds. The sea of sand had engulfed the tents. Only one tent pole showed above the dunes like a miniature pyramid. Two camels brayed their protest as they struggled out of the sand. There had been six including Kate's. He could see no horses.

He strode to the surviving tent and began to dig. "Are you alive?" he called in Arabic.

"Enough alive," came the reply. He scooped sand out until they were able to open their flap. He pulled them out one by one. There were five.

Kate came up behind him with the water sacks. Could the woman never follow orders?

"Here," she offered. The men took the skin gratefully. They must not have had the foresight to grab a pack from the camels. Together the seven of them looked around. Except for the two half-buried tents, the dapple-gray horse scrambling up out of Kate and Gian's tent, and the two camels, they were alone on the rippling sand.

"That means we lost six men," Kate whispered.

"Let's just make sure." Gian staggered through the sand to approximately where he remembered pitching the other two tents and began to dig.

They didn't find anyone else alive. Gian dug up some packs they'd taken off the camels with great effort, but they left the men who'd suffocated when their tents collapsed and the animals buried under the sand. Kate imagined the bodies becoming mummies, the sand sucking the moisture from their flesh, to be found ages and ages hence when the sea of sand rippled again with wind, and their desiccated corpses were revealed.

Gian loaded packs on the camels and a smaller one on

the horse. The moon was high and cold by the time they'd finished The five men whispered together. Didn't Gian notice?

"Effendi." One Arab stepped out of the group.

Gian turned. The man slipped a long curved sword out of the scabbard at his waist and spoke again, this time an order of some kind.

Gian shrugged and opened his palms. He stepped away from the camels. But he spoke rapidly and gestured at the horse. The man shook his head and waved the sword around.

Gian's eyes went hard. Faster than she could quite comprehend, he stepped in and twisted the sword from the leader's fist. He threw it on the ground behind him. He took a handful of the man's burnoose and lifted him up, growling in Arabic. The man's eyes rolled white in fear. Gian tossed him to the ground, seemingly without effort. He landed about six feet away with a thud. Gian glared at the others, but they opened their hands, murmuring what had to be apologies.

Gian stalked over to Kate, only pausing to retrieve the sword. "Come on," he muttered. "These cowards are no use to us."

The men hurried to the camels and pulled them to their feet. Kate watched them retreat back along the cliff walls toward Laghouhat. Gian never once looked at them. But he didn't take their water or their camels either.

He unstrapped the pack from the horse, retied the straps so that he could shrug it on his own back. Kate looked out at the line of cliffs, gray in the moonlight, disappearing into the distance. What was she doing here? For a moment she couldn't think why she had come so far, and got to this place on the edge of the world where sand and wind could kill if you didn't run out of water or if vampires didn't catch you. She couldn't have stayed in Amalfi because Elyta would have found her. But she should have stayed in Algiers.

Gian rose from his knees in the sand.

Oh. Her sense of herself shuddered back into place. She was here because Gian wouldn't give up on this mission to return the stones to a place where they could do no harm. That was who he was. And he couldn't do it without her. So that had become who she was too.

He cupped his hands and bent. "You're finally going to learn to ride a horse," he said.

She didn't want to ride while he walked and carried a pack. But she also didn't want to hold them back. So for once she didn't argue with him. She put her sandal in his hands. He tossed her up on the horse's bare back. She grabbed the creature's mane. Gian picked up the horse's reins and started across the dunes back toward the cliffs.

There was no help left now. It was just Gian and the horse and Kate against a desert that could kill without reason, against Elyta and whomever she brought with her. They couldn't turn back until they found the place that was home to the jewels that drained a vampire's power, or drove men mad. They were goaded on by Gian's honor. Because he couldn't leave the job undone.

She just hoped this job wasn't their undoing.

Kate alternately rode and walked through the night and much of the day. They stopped to rest in the shade of the cliffs. Gian gave his share of water to the horse, but only after Kate had drunk. That annoyed her. If he could give up his water, so could she. She resolved to wait until he'd had his share before she sipped next time. Then he slipped the pouch from his shoulder and handed it to her so she could take a reading from the stones.

She could feel them buzzing with energy even through

the leather and their boxes. They were ramping up in power as they neared their destination. A thought occurred. She concentrated on Gian's vibrations and thought they had waned a bit. The stones were affecting him, even through their boxes. "Aren't these growing uncomfortable for you?" she asked.

"A little."

"I'll carry them from now on." He was already in pain from the light, though he kept his hands in his burnoose sleeves and pulled his hood down low over his forehead. She opened the mahogany box and took out the ruby. It gleamed like sparkling blood in the light. She relaxed her body and held it in front of her in cupped hands. She breathed in and let the air out slowly. Her hands extended almost of their own accord to the southwest and trembled. That was the strongest the stone had ever been.

"I think we're close now."

"Can you go on?"

"Perhaps, but we'll kill our trusty friend here." She didn't say that she thought Gian needed rest too. He'd been walking for twelve hours carrying a heavy pack.

He examined her and grunted. "We'll rest then."

They ate dates and dried jerky, and sipped the water carefully. She shook the water skin. There wasn't much left. Gian hugged his knees under the burnoose. She could feel his discomfort. But the moment the sun sank below the cliffs he had them moving again.

"None of these chasms looked like the one in my vision," Kate fussed, mounted again on the horse. She'd been walking for three or four hours when Gian had insisted that she ride.

"It's got to be one of these eroded wadis. The temple was cut into a chasm wall."

She thought back. "This was filled with sand. There was a huge fan of sand coming out from the cliffs."

"You mean like that one?" He pointed down the cliff face.

Kate could see nothing. "Where?"

"It's several miles away yet." His voice was excited.

"You can see that far?"

"I see well in the dark."

Of course he would. He took the horse's reins and pulled him forward. She could feel Gian's anticipation. It was more than an hour before they reached the fan of sand and scree. Was this it? Could there be two such formations? She slid from the horse's back and took the emerald from the pocket of her breeches. Holding the stone out in front of her, she closed her eyes. The emerald surged and tumbled from her hand. It rolled a little way up the incline of sand.

She hurried to pick it up. "Well, that's a first. It rolled uphill."

"You have your answer," Gian muttered. He was looking up the incline. His excitement had faded into . . . what? Apprehension?

Kate swallowed and peered up the wadi in the dark. There was a bend in the ravine. She could see nothing but the fan that seemed to gradually fill the chasm. Gian pulled the horse up the incline. It would be tough going, slogging through the loose sand.

Kate followed. What was it about this gorge that made the back of her neck prickle? "Uh, Gian, you never said what the Temple of Waiting was a temple to. I mean . . . waiting for what?" Her voice sounded small echoing back from the walls.

"It was all only a legend until Rufford confirmed it." She heard him clear his throat. The gorge was that silent. "You'll think this is crazy."

"Crazier than stones that drive you mad and want to go home?"

"I'll grant you that." His voice drifted back on the dry night air. "There was a race here before us. They weren't like us. They were tall and gaunt, with features not quite human. When men came along, they were benevolent rulers and taught us much. The Companion existed in their blood. One of them infected a spring in the Carpathian Mountains with the parasite as he wandered the world, whether by accident or on purpose no one knows. That was thousands of years ago."

"How many thousands?" she whispered.

"Ten, maybe, or eleven. Anyway, a tribe of men drank from the spring. Most died, but one did not, and his blood could help others survive infection."

"Like immunity. If you have the pox, you can't get it again." That part sounded plausible.

"Something like that." He shrugged. "Anyway, his people punished him for his lapse in infecting the spring. When it was time to go and they gathered together from all parts of the world, they accused him. Then they left him behind when they went away."

"Went away . . . where?" The skeptic in her readied itself for the reply.

"One can only guess." He looked up at the stars, cold and glittering, with speculation in his eyes. "But the legend says they left from this desert. And the one remaining built a temple in the rose-colored stone of a chasm wall, where he could wait for them to return. He supposedly built a signal so they could find him again, a pulsing fountain of . . . jewels that sent out light and energy."

Kate frowned. "And these stones are from his signal?"

"I think they are."

A signal built of jewels? Hardly. She was breathing hard from struggling through the sand that rose ever higher in the ravine. Still . . . she had seen such a fountain in her vision of the place . . . "So Rufford says this was true?" Rufford didn't seem like one to tell wild tales.

"Yes. He found the temple."

"And the mummy of the one who was left behind?" Like Egypt and the pyramids. All this was really just conjecture on Rufford's part. There was no way to know the tale.

"Oh, the Old One was still very much alive, waiting in the temple."

Kate blinked. My God—for . . . for ten thousand years? Impossible. Would Rufford lie?

"His blood is very strong. He gave Rufford a cup of it so Rufford could best Asharti."

No. She couldn't imagine Rufford lying. The unbearable sadness of being the last, left behind, waiting, struck her. "How . . . horrible." She wished Rufford's story wasn't true. Maybe he was just . . . wrong. But Rufford did not seem easily deluded either.

They turned another corner in the chasm. The walls were perhaps only twenty feet above the sand that filled it. And there, in the side of the wall, were . . . were stairs. There was no other word for them. They were cut out of solid rock, even, flat, smooth. They couldn't be natural. But they were unnatural in another way as well. The risers of these stone stairs must be more than three feet high. What kind of creature used stairs like that? A giant, or . . .

Gian stopped behind her, staring.

This changed everything.

"So . . . so what happened to this temple?" she asked.

"The Old One destroyed it. Rufford said there was some kind of vortex inside and . . . it just exploded and buried the entire place." He looked around at the sand. "Hold out a stone."

They were walking over who knew what, right this very minute. The thought made her want to shudder. She retrieved the ruby and held it tightly so it wouldn't escape. This time her arms shot out, pointing along the ravine. "Very well. We're not there yet."

They stumbled on through the deep sand again, ever upward until the walls of the chasm were no higher than their heads. The walls opened out onto a wide, sand plateau.

And there, ahead, was a striped tent, flags at each corner fluttering in the sirocco. Was it red and gold? She couldn't quite tell because the moonlight leached the color from it. One thing was not in doubt. This was the tent she had seen when she looked into the ruby. Four camels nestled in the sand to one side. Gian and Kate went still.

The tent flap opened and out stepped Elyta, followed by Illya, Federico, Sergei, and another. The air hummed with energy. They did not have red eyes, but Kate knew they could bring up their power in an instant, and that they would be too much for Gian, even if he was not still depleted from their previous cruelties.

"Welcome, Urbano, and your little scarred friend too." Elyta motioned the others forward. They positioned themselves around Gian and Kate. "I've been waiting for days."

"How did you get here before us?" The muscles in Gian's jaw bunched.

"She told me you were taking the stones home. That could only mean to the temple. You did not know its location, so you would go to Rufford in Algiers. Therefore, we sailed on west and landed at Oran. We came up northeast as you were trekking down."

She strolled forward, the aubergine of her translucent robes ruffling in the breeze. They were lined with thin gold braid, and she had gold loops in her ears and a chain laced with gold beads across her forehead. She looked every inch the Berber princess, except for her milky skin. "Now," she said to Gian, "give me the stones." She held out a long-nailed hand.

"You can have them, Elyta," Gian growled. "And me. Just let Kate go."

No, she wanted to shout. *You can't give them to her after*

all we've done to keep them from her. Maybe he was buying time. She could see he hadn't given up. His eyes flashed, not with red, but with a glint of anger.

Elyta's glance flicked to Kate. "How touching. But she has her uses too. You both do." Kate saw her eyes go red as she stared at Gian. "The stones."

Elyta would soon realize Kate had them. They were right back where they had been in the Villa Rufolo. Kate felt power hanging in the air until it pressed down on her chest and made it difficult to breathe. Was it Elyta's power? The stones, in the bag over her shoulder, trembled.

Elyta felt the stones' reaction shimmer through the power in the air. She turned her head, her eyes now carmine red. "So you have the stones," she whispered. Her hand caught at the bag.

Gian glared at her. "If you mean to take the stones away from this place, I wouldn't."

Elyta tore open the leather pouch and cupped the little boxes in her hands. She opened one. The emerald. Kate could see it winking in reflected moonlight. It trembled in the velvet lining. "Of course I mean to take them away. What good would they do me here?" Elyta snapped the box shut, grinning. "Bring these two along." She rounded on Gian. "You make any trouble, and I'll give you a session with the stones. Illya, Federico, break camp. Sergei, keep your eyes on Urbano. You can handle him easily in his condition. And confiscate that horse."

Kate wanted to shriek and just run back down the ravine. But she wouldn't leave Gian. The two took Gian's faithful dapple-gray. Elyta was muttering, half to herself. "I'll use you hard, Urbano, and maybe your little scarred friend as well. I've a taste for a woman once in a while." She opened up the mahogany box. "We'll have a lovely time all round."

Kate glanced to Gian. She could see the muscles in his

jaw working. In fact, he clenched his fists. The muscles stood out in his neck. *Just bide your time,* she wanted to say. *We'll escape her again, you'll see.* But he didn't look patient. He looked . . . furious.

Elyta chuckled in glee, standing in front of the tent as the vampires worked around her. The ruby glistened in its nest. "Oh, dear me, but you will make me powerful, probably even beyond my dreams. And I can dream a lot of power."

Indeed, power seemed to be ramping up in the air around them, even though the two vampires who were striking camp were not using theirs. The air began to vibrate. Elyta didn't seem to notice. She opened up the silver filigree box, cooing to the emerald that lay inside. She had a box in each hand now. "You're going to France, my darlings."

The wind rose up in a gust from the ravine, swirling sand around their feet. Kate couldn't take her eyes off Gian. He was staring at Elyta. And as she watched, his eyes turned red. Not the faint rose she had seen in the chapel, but carmine, deepening into burgundy. What was happening here? Had he gotten his power back? There was actually a humming sound in the air now. A gust of wind, harder this time, took the tent right out of the hands of the vampires who were folding it. Camels brayed in protest, tugging at the lead ropes that tethered them to stakes.

Elyta looked up, puzzled.

And the stones bounced out of their boxes to lie in the sand, perhaps six feet from where she stood. She gave a little cry and sprang forward.

As Kate watched, the stones simply . . . *sank* into the sand. One moment they were there, and the next moment there was just a little vortex like you would see in the top of an hourglass as it was turned and the sand leaked into the bottom half. Elyta threw herself on her hands and knees, digging at the vortex frantically. It widened.

The wind began to howl around them.

"Elyta!" Gian shouted. The sound reverberated in Kate's chest and echoed through the wind, as though the wind itself spoke through him. "Leave them! They belong here."

Elyta glanced up. The wind caught at her hair and whirled it around her face. Her eyes, too, went red. Carmine deepened into burgundy. Could Gian stand against her? He stood there, immobile. The wind shrieked. Was it another sandstorm?

"I'll get them back, Urbano, if I have to dig out this entire chasm!" Elyta would never give up, never let the stones go, or Gian and Kate either.

Gian screamed in rage and frustration. The sound was torn from his belly and carried away in the wind and the sand. Veins stood out in his neck.

Elyta's dress bloomed flame. It licked up her body and raced toward her hair. She screamed, but already her head wore a corona of fire. The wind tore at the flame and she was engulfed. The sand funnel reached Elyta's knees. The other vampires stared, transfixed. Gian slumped, breathing hard, then grabbed Kate and pulled her back, shouting something. Kate couldn't hear it in the wind that raged now around them. Elyta's features blackened. The O of her shrieking mouth was the only thing visible through the flame. Kate covered her own mouth in horror.

The sand was whirling around in the wind, but it seemed to be coming up from the vortex too. Kate could hardly see Elyta. There was only a gleam of flame in the whirl of sand. She turned to the other vampires. They were dim shapes behind the gray of a sandstorm at night.

The flames that were Elyta sank slowly into the vortex. The only shrieking Kate could hear was the wind and the sand. Gian had hold of her hand and was pulling her away. The image of Elyta's burning face twined through her mind and wouldn't let her go.

They bumped smack into something. Gian was shouting. She looked back, and there through the dim haze of sand was a vortex of black where the tent had once been, whirling up into the sky in a widening funnel. He pulled her to her knees and put his arms around her. His burnoose sheltered her from the hissing sting of the sand. The something was a warm wall against her cheek. Gian bent over her. The wind wailed.

It went on forever.

Until it stopped. Suddenly. Without warning, the wind went silent. Gian straightened. Kate looked up. The sand just fell, hissing, from the night sky, leaving a dusty haze behind it.

And that was all.

They were leaning up against the horse's shoulder. It lay with its legs tucked under it. Gian had covered its head with his left arm and the baggy burnoose had shielded the creature's eyes and nose, just as his right arm had protected her. The plateau was wiped clean, as though the tent and the vampires and the camels had never been.

She knelt there, stunned. Her senses refused to register the last—what? Moments? Millennia? Gian was blinking with an expression she imagined mirrored hers.

"What . . . what happened here?" she croaked.

"I . . . I set Elyta on fire."

His anger *did* fuel spontaneous combustion. She blinked. "You got your power back."

He blinked again. "No . . . not exactly. I used the power already in the air."

"At least she's dead."

How could he look uncertain? "Decapitation is the only way to kill us."

Her eyes widened. If Elyta wasn't dead, then she was burned and suffocating below the sand. Not something Kate wanted to think about. "What . . . what happened to the stones?"

"I . . . think . . . they went home." His voice was shattered with screaming into the wind.

"But . . . why are we still here?"

"Because we scrambled out of the way of the vortex?" He didn't sound sure.

"Or because we were the ones that brought them home, and Elyta wanted to take them away." She couldn't believe she was saying that. But she wasn't sure what to believe anymore.

The world holds vampires and spontaneous combustion, and maybe, somewhere beneath your feet, a buried temple, and one entombed alive there, waiting with a tower of coruscating jewels to signal those who left him ten thousand years ago to go to someplace . . . else.

She started to argue with herself.

Or maybe not. Maybe there was a sandstorm that created a vortex that sucked everything in sight under the sand and it was all just an accident of fate that left some alive, and some suffocated under tons of sand.

And what about Elyta being set on fire?

You can't believe that someone can set things on fire just by being angry. Stupid!

The dialogue between her two halves threatened to tear her apart. She tried to remember that girl who didn't believe anything but what she could see, who thought people didn't do anything but what was in their own best interest. Gian had been willing to sacrifice himself to his duty. As a matter of fact, he had offered to sacrifice himself to Elyta to save Kate just moments ago. She'd once thought him selfish and arrogant, but that had never been true about him, though it might well be true about her.

She looked down and saw her reticule still bulging, incongruous, in the pocket of her flowing trousers with her tarot cards, so much a part of her for so long, bulging, square, inside. These were who she was, she reminded herself. A charlatan, self-contained. The cards were only cues about what people wanted to hear, guideposts to the psyche's need to believe. One couldn't know the future.

Except that she did, and it had nothing to do with tarot cards. She didn't know what to believe right now, but the tarot cards seemed to lie when they promised her, as they always had, that anyone who believed what they couldn't see was a pigeon, ripe for the plucking.

Gian heaved himself to his feet and stretched out a hand to help her. The horse shook, spewing sand, and got his forelegs under himself. She and the horse stood together.

The sand had settled around them, leaving the small, cold moon a silver coin in the sky. The stars hadn't yet appeared out of the haze of dust. But they would. The world was wiped clean, as if Elyta and the stones had never been.

She looked at Gian. He was gazing around, disoriented, and then his eyes found hers. He blinked several times. She saw the purpose rise in them like a tide.

"Let's get you out of here," he said. His voice was startling in the new quiet.

Where? Where would she go? Her plan of living in a rural cottage seemed ludicrous. She stared around at the silent sand, not even the whisper of a sirocco to stir it. The certainty of who she was and what she wanted seemed lost forever.

The sky had gone red ahead of him. Gian's old enemy, the sun, would rise soon. There was no cover out here on the plateau. They had trudged for most of the night in the vague direction of El Djelfa. The horse couldn't go on much longer. Neither could Kate. He had only pretended to drink this night, so as to save the water for her. But there was little left. She was nodding on the horse's back, so he steadied her with a hand on her lower back. The daylight would be merciless. He wondered if he could stand another twelve hours at the equator with sunlight scraping his skin even inside the burnoose, burning his eyes no matter how he squinted. He was almost human in his weakness. He'd borrowed power from the Old One, bent on retrieving his jewels, to set Elyta on fire, but it was a loan only, and it was gone now.

But while he had had it, he had controlled the power, directed it, and shut it off when it had done its work. The vortex would have taken Elyta anyway. He knew that now. But he had made her suffer. He should be sorry for that. Maybe someday he would be.

Using that power had taken its toll. It would weaken him for the fight against the sun. He required blood. And there was no blood. Kate needed all her strength. He had to get Kate to shelter. He must prevail, even if the horse faltered. He could carry Kate. They couldn't have survived a sandstorm, Elyta, and even the wrath of the Old One just to have her die on this endless sere plateau.

Behind him, he felt the sun rise.

Twenty-one

Kate cracked open her eyes. They felt swollen. All of her felt swollen. She was in some kind of dim room. The walls were whitewashed, the shutters drawn against the heat of the day. They cast bars of horizontal light across the dirt floor. She was lying on a pallet of some kind. Her mouth felt like she had inhaled sand. An old woman was holding up her head. The crone's wrinkles rearranged themselves into an almost toothless grin.

"Drink, English," she said in that language. It was heavily accented.

Cool water poured down her throat. Kate swallowed until she gasped and choked.

"Enough. More later."

"Gian?" Kate croaked.

"The one who carried you here?"

"Yes," she whispered. She remembered sliding off the horse. She remembered the horse staggering. It had been so hot, so bright. Gian had picked her up, and dragged the horse along behind him. He must have carried her to here, wherever here was.

"He lives."

Kate didn't like the sound of that. Only just living? "Is he well?"

"He was burned as though he walked naked in the sun."

Did his burnoose not protect him? She shoved up on one elbow. "I must go to him."

The old woman pushed her back down, gently. It wasn't hard. Kate was weak as a kitten. "You rest. Later more water and food. Then go."

Kate had to find him. She remembered the bubbling of his skin with burns the night he had carried her from the lodgings in Rome. He had healed that. He could heal whatever he suffered in the desert now, couldn't he? Elyta had not weakened him that much. She couldn't have. Kate would not let it be so.

The room was swimming. Her vision blurred at the edges. She fought against the darkness that washed over her. But it was no use . . .

Gian tried to breathe. He'd heal. It was just taking longer because the stones, and using the Old One's power, had weakened him. That was all. He could bear the pain. He always had. He was naked. The thought of cloth against his skin made him nauseous. He lay on his back on a pallet of some kind. Even that was torture. An old woman came occasionally to give him water and thin gruel. She said Kate was well so he stopped trying to get up. He had not let her grease his flesh with animal fat though. That would only delay healing the burns. He'd heal faster if he had blood. But he was too weak to compel the old woman or even draw his fangs.

He had never been affected so by sunlight. It was as though he were newly made, not more than eighteen hundred years old. By the time night fell on the plateau, he had been nearly crazed with pain. The tiny village, clustered round the date palms and the pool of brackish water, had seemed a hallucination brought on by pain. It wasn't, thank the gods.

But the pain from burned flesh was not the worst. The worst stretched out ahead, in an infinite future devoid of meaning. The stones were returned. The vampire wars were over. They had receded into the past instead of being a series of ever-present nightmares that dogged his every move. Elyta was gone. The Old One had returned to waiting.

And Gian had no purpose. He could not go to the Elders at Mirso Monastery and ask to serve on other missions. There was a reason the stones had not wanted to fall into the Elders' hands, crazy as that seemed. The concerns of the Elders might be just as political as Elyta's ambitions, if to a different end. And there was the fact of his unusual powers. Had they really destroyed that other firebrand because he was uncontrolled, or because he had learned to control it, as Gian thought he had, and that made him a threat? He didn't know.

And then, when he finally healed, when he got Kate back to Algiers or Amalfi or Rome or Firenze, she was going to go to England to be unhappy in some rural backwater. He would be left, at best being allowed to exist on the fringes of her life, helping her where he could, watching her age. That was the only purpose his life could have. He twisted against the pallet and the coarse canvas cover tore at his flesh.

He dozed sometimes and dreamt, fevered dreams of Kate being harassed by village ruffians, himself unable to protect her. Sometimes he dreamed about the Ruffords, strange as that was. He didn't want to sleep. He didn't want to dream. But waking was a nightmare too. Sleeping or waking, all he felt was pain.

"How are you?" That was a stupid question. Kate carefully erased the horror from her face as Gian turned his head in her direction. She hated to think he had been healing as the old woman had promised her. Because in that case, his burns must have been even more appalling than they were now. His body was blotched with open sores weeping serous fluid. His vibrations were so low as to be almost imperceptible. She felt better after sleeping, water, and food. That seemed a betrayal.

He smiled, his blistered lips cracking. "Good," he whispered, his voice hoarse.

She wanted to burst into tears. That would never do. She couldn't burden him with her need for reassurance. She managed a tentative smile. "Liar." She knelt beside him. "Water?"

"Thank you."

She lifted his head and scooped water from the bucket next to him with a wooden ewer. He slurped the ewer dry. She laid him down carefully. Why was he not healed? It had been what—three days?

He must have read her thoughts. "It's going faster now."

"Not fast enough."

"Faster and the villagers would cast us out," he mumbled through swollen lips.

"You need blood."

His eyes registered—what? Longing? He turned his head away. "I won't die."

Kate turned and pulled the fluttering fabric that formed a door across the entrance to the hut. "But it will save you suffering. And you can't take it from a villager or they would do considerably worse than cast us out." She knelt again beside him.

"You're not strong enough."

She smiled at him. "I'm much better. If you can't draw your power, I'll get a knife."

"I won't take blood from you." This was said through gritted teeth.

"So, you can carry me across the desert, but I can't help you in return?" She raised her brows. "Arrogant, Urbano. Very arrogant." If she could provide blood, maybe his need would overcome his resistance. Getting a knife from one of the villagers might rouse suspicion though. Very well. She looked around. How did one draw enough blood to feed a vampire? She glanced around the tiny hut. She needed something sharp. A crockery bowl sat near the door. She took a breath and rose. She hit the bowl against the door-post. Shards cascaded to the packed earthen floor. *God, grant me courage.* Taking up a triangular splinter, she sat beside him, careful not to touch his ravaged flesh.

"Kate, don't do this."

"And how, pray tell, are you going to stop me?" She braced her wrist on her thigh and sliced across it as hard as she could. The shock of pain immobilized her for a moment. Then the blood welled. Gian moaned. Was it in protest or anticipation? The blood began to spurt. She'd done it. "Drink," she whispered, holding her wrist to his mouth.

He took three ragged breaths. He shook his head, convulsively. But she could feel the Companion in his veins rise a little and increase the pace of his vibrations. *Yes,* she thought, *take over for him. You know what to do.*

He fastened his blistered lips on her wrist with a growl. She smiled and closed her eyes.

Kate watched Gian sleep, fascinated. It was almost imperceptible, but his burns were healing. She had saved him pain.

She loved this man, even if he could not love her in return. She treasured his contradictions: selflessness all wrapped up in arrogance, his courage and his cowardice. And they were so alike; both allowing their past to circumscribe their future . . .

That did not mean there was any escaping who they were. There were no choices.

The sun sank below the horizon. And the pain was gone. Gian opened his eyes, and his gaze met Kate's. Her blue eyes were clear and true. She had been watching him sleep. And the feeling that he belonged with her was so strong it made his stomach clench.

"Thank you," he said. It was so inadequate. What other woman would have gouged her own wrist and let him suck her blood just to spare him pain?

She smiled. And the smile was tender. "You're welcome."

He pushed himself up, trying to ignore that smile. "We'll stay here until you are fully recovered. Then the villagers can direct us to the next oasis."

A look of tristesse passed over her face and was quickly suppressed. She smiled again, but this time it was rueful. "As you will."

The horse had survived against all odds. A few days of hay and water, and he was, if not as good as new, as good as she and Gian were. Gian had paid the villagers for their kindness with gold coins he produced from the seams of his burnoose where they had apparently been sewn.

Now the rock-strewn plateau again stretched out before them under a waning moon. That seemed fitting. The whole world seemed like it was waning to Kate. They walked. Gian led the horse. The villagers had sworn they could reach the next water hole before the dawn, and sure enough, in the distance huts rose in rectangular contrast to the rocks and the flat desert, the soft-looking fronds of date palms caressing their angles.

Kate existed in some kind of dream state. Her thoughts, hovering around her, flapped like vultures. Living in a village away from everyone suddenly seemed the last thing she wanted to do. She would miss the new cities, the excitement of duping a whole roomful of marks. No, even that was tame compared to saving the world—at the very least the whole of France. And she would miss Gian Urbano. How could she have ever guessed she would be here, with him, at the spine of the world?

The warring halves of her had stopped their debate, exhausted. She accepted that the world was not as she had always thought it. It held more things unseen than she had ever imagined. And she, who thought she was not special, was perhaps unique among humans. Were all the other things she had believed equally wrong?

The thought seemed to wind around her spine. She believed she controlled her own destiny, that she was invulnerable to the scorn of those around her, that people were inherently selfish, doing wrong at every turn either from malice or ignorance. But those things were wholly wrong. Gian did not do things from malice or ignorance. He was not selfish at all. And as for her? Her past controlled her. Her fear of being abandoned directed her every reaction. And the feeling that those around her held her in contempt, whether because of her background, or her scar, quite ruled her life. She found that contemptible.

She had never believed in love either. But that did not prevent her from loving Gian. It had happened against her will.

She was glad. He couldn't love her in return, of course. But . . . but her life was richer for having loved him. She had to tell him. She had to thank him before they parted. At least that.

"Gian." The word was out of her mouth before she could stop it.

He turned. Concern was written on his features. "Kate?"

What was she thinking? How could she expose herself to ridicule like that? He'd leave if she said it. But it was Gian. And she trusted Gian. He knew everything about her. Whatever he felt for her or didn't feel, he didn't despise or ridicule her. And he would leave anyway. So it didn't matter. He couldn't go without knowing. "I . . . I must thank you."

"It was nothing." His expression flattened itself, unreadable.

"I don't mean for carrying me across the desert. Perhaps I should mean that, but I don't."

He looked . . . wary. He should. She was about to create another barrier between them. Women had been prostrating themselves before him for centuries. He surely wouldn't want to hear protestations of love from a charlatan tramp with a scarred face. She should just motion him forward. How could she say anything anyway with the lump in her throat?

But this was something she had to do. She had to share with the person she knew best in the world her realization that what she believed about life before was wrong. "I . . . I hadn't felt . . . anything for . . . for a man, before I met you." She shook her head, disgusted with herself. Her resolve seeped away. "Women must say that to you all the time. How . . . banal of me. I shouldn't have . . ." She trailed off, unable to continue.

He had frozen. "Women wouldn't say that if they knew what I was."

What? She wagered women didn't care that he had had a thousand other women. Oh, he meant the vampire part. Probably true. She shrugged. "Nobody is perfect."

He examined her as though his life depended on it. Which it didn't. Because he lived forever. They were totally unlike, different species. He cleared his throat. "You are the only one who has ever known what I was, not only that I am vampire, but . . . but all of me. Do you . . . ?"

She frowned. Different species. There was no getting around that. "Do I what?"

"Do you think . . . you might . . . might want to spend some time with me even so?"

She realized she had been staring him straight in the face, just like she wasn't scarred. But she was. She looked down. "You don't want someone like me."

"I do." He swallowed. "I do. I love you, Kate." He was standing there, wavering in the middle of the wide, rocky plane with a waning moon arcing up from behind the stony peaks of the Middle Atlas range behind him. She was so shocked, she could say nothing. He loved her?

When she said nothing, his words began to tumble out. "I know you could never love someone you must consider a monster. I understand that completely. And it would be too much to ask to be more than . . . than an acquaintance." His gaze bounced from her, to the sand, the stars. "If you would but let me see that you are happy, perhaps allow me to visit you on occasion, I promise never to importune you for more."

He loved her? She couldn't seem to make out the meaning of the words. He couldn't love her. Not with her scar. Her fingers crept to her cheek.

He covered the distance between them in two strides. "Don't even think of that." He took her in his arms. As she was pressed against the muscles in his chest, the exotic fragrance of cinnamon and something else coursed through her. "I haven't even noticed it since the first days. I want you. Not for forever, I understand that. But . . . if you think you could bear . . . my companionship . . . for even a few years, I would be so grateful."

This was so far from the arrogant man she had come to know that she wasn't sure whether to laugh or cry. He loved her. The thump of his heart against her scarred cheek was strong and sure. And he had said that first day in the carriage that he never told women he loved them when he didn't. He prided himself on that. So, whatever emotion was really coursing through him, he at least believed it was love. That thought frightened her immensely. Because it meant she had to choose.

Her mind raced. He was saying he would leave her even now. ". . . a few years." But of course. She believed that, expected that. Hadn't she come back to Firenze to wait for him, hoping to get a month with him? No more . . . She could expect no more . . .

From out of nowhere an image of Ian Rufford and his wife Beth rose in her mind, the loving looks they saved for each other, the calm way they accepted their condition.

She blinked.

He held her away from his body, his brows creased in worry. He was expecting an answer from her. He was expecting rejection.

She looked into his clear, green eyes, and rebellion rose in her heart, anger even, at him for his expectations, at herself for hers. Damn it all to bloody hell. They were both stupid enough to let their past dictate their future. They would doom themselves to unhappiness just because they couldn't get around their history. She'd never forgive her parents for abandoning her. But if she never opened herself up to the possibility of abandonment, she'd deny herself any hope of being close to another human being. And humans needed that. *She* needed that in order to be whole. She had been half a person all her life. God, did she have the courage for this? Did he? But she couldn't control him. She could only decide what she would do. She'd always prided herself on her courage. *Then get it out and use it for something worthwhile, for once.*

She took a breath. He had her by her upper arms. The pain in his expression hurt her. She was about to give him more pain, along with an extra measure for herself, probably. They couldn't stay together. She was inviting everything she feared most.

But risking the pain of abandonment was the lesser of two evils.

She swallowed. "I love you. I never thought I could love anybody, but I love you."

His eyes widened. He searched her face even more intensely.

"It's hard for me to think you want me in spite of the scar." He started to protest, but she put a finger to his lips. "It's hard not to let my fear you'll leave me keep me from running away. But I *have* to try. You see, I don't want an acquaintance. I want a lover. I want forever." She smiled. She was fairly sure it was only a little lopsided. "I've always been greedy. Or maybe I haven't been greedy enough. It doesn't matter. I want forever, like the Ruffords have. If you can't give me that, then let us part when we reach Algiers."

He stared at her, shock making his heart thump in his chest. She loved him. So much, she wanted . . . Did she know what she was asking for? "You don't know what it's like."

"But I do." She said it calmly. "I know it all, remember?"

"Even I don't know all of it. I am what they call a firebrand, and I don't understand that."

"Then we both have parts we don't understand. I don't know why I have visions, or what to do about them." She took a breath, then had the temerity to chuckle. "After drinking human blood and compulsion, starting fires seems a little paltry."

It was the things one couldn't control that frightened one. They had that in common. "You can't make light of becoming vampire, Kate. It's irrevocable."

"I don't make light of it," she said, growing serious. "I want it. And don't you dare tell me it isn't allowed."

"The Elders—"

"I know. And the Rules." The way she said it dismissed

them as unimportant. "It's your duty to make us both unhappy by refusing to make me vampire. Haven't you done enough duty in your life? You fought those dreadful wars. You took the stones back where they belonged. A little rebellion would do you a world of good."

If my mother had made my father vampire, their love would have lasted for eternity. He knew that. His mother must know it too. She obeyed the Rules at the cost of an eternity of regret. Not to mention the fact that his father aged and died. How did she live with that? All her effort to do good in the world was really a compensation for the fact that, when her situation called for courage, she had retired from the field. All the women in his life had compared badly in his mind with his mother. Her vibrancy, her intelligence made them all pale in comparison. But Kate showed up his mother's cowardice for what it was. He didn't love his mother less. Kate had made her comprehensible. But his mother couldn't hold a candle to Kate.

And Kate wanted him. No matter that he was vampire. Enough to become vampire herself. He didn't deserve that. He should protect her from herself. He should refuse.

As he had been refusing to become involved with women all his life? His mother's pain was so frightening Gian had refused to allow the possibility of pain in his own life. Oh, he was more of a coward than his mother was. She at least had taken the plunge once.

Kate was waiting. Giving him time. Now it was up to him to give them both time. If only he could be sure what he was doing wouldn't hurt her. His eyes roved over her, looking for answers. She still had that silly silver-beaded reticule hanging from her wrist. He gave a nervous laugh. "Maybe you could reassure us both by reading our future in the cards."

She looked down, surprised, then shook her head. "They never told the future." She took the reticule from her pocket and opened it. She removed the tarot deck encrusted with gilt stars and tossed it to the hard-packed sand of the plateau. "I thought the cards were part of me. They're not."

"But you know the future," he said, trying not to sound desperate.

She smiled ruefully. "I never see my own." She grew thoughtful. "And I've never seen anything of yours beyond the time when Elyta tortured you."

They looked at each other.

He was the one to say it. "Maybe . . . maybe that's because our future is together."

She took a breath. "Or maybe not."

So. No easy answers. No guarantees. One had to just take the plunge, not knowing.

"Come on," he said, grabbing Kate's wrist in one hand, and the reins of the horse in the other. "We need shelter."

Twenty-two

Kate stood, trembling, inside the thick-walled, single-room structure that was the best the little cluster of houses around the oasis had to offer. It belonged to a family who had gladly vacated to a tent when they saw the color of Gian's gold. The floor was packed sand, the only furniture a wide bed and a table with two chairs. Gian was seeing to the horse. Kate was busy sweeping the corners of her soul to gather up any dusty speck of courage she could muster.

She was going to let him make her vampire. When he could abandon her at a moment's notice, and leave her standing on the shores of eternity. When he would *have* to tire of her, scarred as she was. When changing meant she must drink human blood, and lose the sun forever. When she would become something children had nightmares about and their parents feared.

Yes. All of that. Because she saw that there was a giant hole in the fabric of her soul. And the only way she could knit up that awful rent was to do the thing she feared most. Grab for the brass ring. Take a chance on abandonment.

The man she loved just happened to be a vampire. Well, they were alike in lots of other ways: stubborn, arrogant, sometimes angry, controlled by their pasts, determined not to be. Now they'd be alike in this one too.

He ducked in under the flap of leather that stood in for a door in the little hut. "They won't disturb us, except to leave food outside the door." He was carrying a tray filled with the ubiquitous dates, a bowl of some kind of stew, and two crude cups full of wine. It all smelled lovely. He set it down on the pallet supported by a wooden frame and rope netting which formed the bed. "Eat," he whispered. "You will need your strength."

That sounded ominous. He went around the room pulling closed the shutters, sliding the fabric or leather over the windows to keep out the rising sun.

She ate, hardly tasting the lamb stew. He did not join her, but watched from a corner, his arms folded and a closed expression on his face. Was he having second thoughts? When she pushed away the bowl, he came and knelt in front of her.

"This will not be pleasant," he said. "After you are infected, you will get sick. Then you must have more of my blood to give you immunity or you will die. There is a possibility you could die anyway, if . . . if the parasite weakens you more than I can counteract with my blood." Courage drained from his expression. He turned away. "I can't risk it."

"You can't *not* risk it, Gian Vincenzo Urbano. I want this." She was surprised at the ferocity in her own voice. "If you betray me with cowardice I will never forgive you."

He sucked in a breath, then let it out and nodded. "I'll drain the last drop in my veins to give you strength. Know that." He gathered himself. "In three days, if this works, you will recover, and you will be vampire. The instant my blood touches yours, there is no going back."

She swallowed. Why was nothing ever easy? "I understand."

He pulled her to him. "God forgive me. I'm selfish. I love you so much I can't imagine being without you. Ever."

She pulled him even closer. "And I love you so much I demand it of you."

He took a breath. "I'll try to make this as painless as possible."

"Then love me as you do it."

He blinked in surprise, and then his eyes ignited. She opened her thighs. He knelt between them and kissed her lips. He was tender, though she felt the latent power in each straining muscle in his body. She drew his head closer and deepened their kiss. His arms slid around her and he held her close. The need for him was a pain between her legs. She felt him swell against her most private parts and they ached even more.

"God, Kate," he swore softly. "I never thought you'd love me."

"Every woman who has ever seen you has loved you," she said into his mouth. He was pulling at his burnoose, even as he kissed her.

"They didn't love me. They loved the body." Then he was naked and pulling at her loose shirt and the flowing pants.

She pressed her naked breasts against his chest. Her nipples peaked. His four-day growth of beard was prickly against her lips. He was rock hard now. How she wanted him inside her! So she took his shaft in her hand and guided it to the entrance of her womb. He groaned, but it wasn't in protest. He lifted her buttocks, as easily as though she weighed nothing, and she opened to him farther so he could thrust inside her.

She threw back her head as he penetrated her. But she could not be parted from his lips for long. They collided again and again as he held her and thrust into her. She scoured his mouth with her tongue as though she was searching for something she'd never known before. How would he do it? Would he wait until the sleepy afterglow of passion? She opened her eyes, and saw his open too. They were red. She pulled back and watched in fascination as his canines lengthened. He bit his own lip. Blood welled, viscous and bright red in the dim hut. She knew now how he would do it. She threw back her head, arching her neck to invite him.

And he accepted. His kiss on her throat turned sharp, and she felt the twin stabbing pains even as he thrust into her again. This time he took only one long sucking pull on her throbbing artery and withdrew. The blood on his lips was now both hers and his own, mingled, for all time.

"Is it done?" she whispered.

He nodded. "For better or for worse."

She smiled. There would be no "poorer." Gian had seemingly limitless money. Any sickness would be fleeting. And with luck, death would never part them. "So be it," she said, and pulled him into her. He adjusted her so that his lovely cock thrust against that spot inside her that felt so wonderful. She squeezed her eyes shut in ecstasy. He was controlling the pace, and he quickened it. Her panting breaths began to have small yips of pleasure mixed in with them.

Just as she began to contract, she heard him say, "The blood is the life, my love." And then the universe shattered.

Gian held her up to drink. "Kate," he whispered. "Wake up. You need water."

Her eyes swam up to dulled awareness. It was all he could do not to cry and rock her in his arms, but he had to be strong for her. Just a little while more to watch her suffer, surely.

But his Companion was still weakened. Perhaps he wasn't giving her enough immunity. What if he had killed her? He put down the cup of water, but he still clutched her against his chest. He took the knife he had bought from one of the villagers and sliced his neck. The carotid was the strongest artery he could find, and he wanted to get the maximum amount of his blood into her before the cut sealed. He held her lips to his neck.

She sucked convulsively. The Companion had firm hold of her now and it knew what to do. He only hoped her body could withstand the fever storms. His cut closed and he laid her back onto the pallet. He wiped her naked body with the cloth dipped in water from a bucket. He had taken care of all her needs for the past three days. He had fed her blood a score of times or more. That weakened him. It didn't matter. He would live. If Kate did not, his life would be intolerable.

He sat on the packed-earth floor and leaned his back against the bed, head drooping. He hadn't slept for three days, but nightmares had been invading even his waking state in the last hours. They weren't flashes of the war, anymore. Those had no power over him. They were dreams of Kate, dead in his arms, or Kate calling to him across a dark river.

Kate opened her eyes. Something was different. The weakness, the pain in every joint, the fire in her veins; all were just . . . gone.

She felt strong. Alive. Whole. She had been a portion of who she could be all her life. And now, the thing swimming in her veins gave her a sense of . . . enlargement.

The ceiling of the hut was made of palm fronds over coarse peeled poles. She could see every frond in excruciating detail. She heard the villagers moving about in their own huts, a lamb bleating far away, even the rustle of a rat somewhere outside the hut. She could smell the dust, and the oil in the lamp and the remains of lamb stew, and . . . Gian.

Ambergris. That's what the sweet undertone of his scent was. She had smelled it once in a lady's boudoir when she was eight. How had she never recognized it as the aroma that accompanied his cinnamon?

She turned her head. He sat beside her bed, his head resting on her thigh.

"Hello."

His head jerked up. He frowned, examining her. Then his brow cleared. "Welcome. How do you feel?"

She thought about that. "Whole, I think." She sat up. He scrambled to sit beside her, supporting her back with his arm. "If you had told me how wonderful it was, I would have insisted on doing this earlier."

"Is it wonderful?"

"The only reason you don't know that is because you've never known anything else. Trust me." She looked around. Each detail of the hut stood out, even though it was dark. She felt the sun set. Startling. She turned to him. "Do you always know just where the sun is?"

He nodded, and the most tender expression came over his face. "Part of the package."

Tears welled in her eyes and spilled over her cheeks. She hadn't cried in twenty years. Surprising. He leaned in and kissed her wet cheek. It was the one with the scar. "I don't suppose the Companion healed my scar."

He shook his head. "But if you are looking to add to your collection, that won't be possible."

She sighed and shrugged. "Oh, well. That would have been too good to be true."

"I would have missed it. I know that sounds strange. It's part of who you are, though."

"But only part." It felt good to be able to say that.

"Where to?" he asked. "Do you still want a cottage in England?"

She shook her head. "Whatever made me think I could be happy there?" She thought a moment. "First we go back and make certain the contessa has recovered. Then . . . I don't know."

"I think I should like to see Italy united against their

oppressors." His tone was tentative. "The Carbonari could use some leadership, or so my mother says."

She smiled. "Ahhhh. Are you creating a new duty for yourself?"

He considered. "Duty has its place, and honor. But they aren't as important as purpose."

Like her need to get enough money to buy a cottage. That had kept her at least marginally sane for years. "Very well. I can't say I care much who rules Italy. I have no morals, you know. You shall have to provide that part."

"Agreed." His eyes were soft.

"And I need some adventure. I wonder if the Carbonari could use any spying? I'd make an excellent spy now. Especially if I can occasionally see people's future."

He looked alarmed. "Spying would be dangerous."

"Tosh. My Companion makes me strong." She crinkled her eyes at him. "I won't need you to protect me."

A wash of regret bathed his face.

"Are you sorry you changed me?" Maybe he didn't like her strength.

His expression once again dissolved in tenderness. "I suppose I am about to find out what poor Rufford has to put up with," he complained.

That gave her confidence again. After all, was she really changed? She'd always been strong-willed. And he had fallen in love with her in spite of that. "And Rufford looked like he regretted every minute of it, didn't he?"

"I suppose you need some interest as well." His grudging tone was so dear.

"What I'm interested in," she said, taking his face between her two hands and bringing him close, "is finding out what all these heightened senses can be used for."

He grinned. "Ahhhh. Let me give you the guided tour."

He kissed her. His tongue probed her mouth. And sensation flooded her, almost overwhelming, sending fire burning down her veins and into her most secret parts. She gasped.

He pulled away and grinned that devilish, boyish grin. "Did not I warn you that we have a heightened sexuality? And that was just the beginning."

She pulled him back to her. That's just what this felt like. The beginning.

Read on for an excerpt from the next book by

SUSAN SQUIRES

One with the Darkness

Coming soon from St. Martin's Paperbacks

The City-State of Firenze, Tuscany, 1821

He had more courage than she did. Didn't one always want that for one's child?

Contessa Donnatella Margherita Luchella di Poliziano looked into the startling green eyes of her handsome son and saw his father's eyes looking back at her. Children were so rare for their kind. She was incredibly lucky to have borne him. His face had a softness she had not seen there in centuries. He took her shoulders and touched his cheek to each of hers.

"I'm glad you're feeling better, Mother," he said softly.

And Gian meant it. But he didn't want to stay with her. She understood that. It was natural. So why were her eyes filling? She was being nonsensical.

"You and Kate be off. You're wasting precious darkness." The doors open to the balcony of the Palazzo Vecchio showed twilight deepening into indigo. Summer in Italy gave precious little darkness, an inconvenience to ones such as they were. In the courtyard below, the horses were snorting in anticipation, their shoes clattering on the cobblestones.

He smiled, so like his father it broke her heart, and turned away to the beautiful young woman with a scarred face who had captured his heart after he had spent over a thousand years guarding it from love. Donnatella had done that to him: made him afraid of loving a human. But he had had the courage in the end to reject her road, and now his life was richer for it. The way Kate smiled up at him and took his hand washed Donnatella with both joy for Gian and regret that she had not had his courage once, at the moment when it mattered most.

"We'll be back within a year," Gian promised. "We have much to do to bolster the fortunes of the Carbonari if we want a united Italy." A year was short in the scheme of things.

"They can wait," she said.

"Thank you, Contessa, for everything," Kate murmured, and came to hug Donnatella.

And then they were gone. Donnatella listened to the shush of Kate's slippers and the tap of Gian's boot heels on the grand staircase into the audience hall, the mutter of servants. She moved into the warm night air of the balcony as the carriage clattered away into the night below her. The scent of star jasmine hung heavy in the air. Gian and Kate had forever now. What was it the English marriage ceremony said? "'Til death do us part?" Only death never would part them, barring some bizarre accident of decapitation.

Donnatella felt tears run hot down her cheeks, surprised. She hadn't cried in centuries. She wasn't crying because her son was leaving. No. She was crying because she hadn't had the courage to do for his father what Gian had done for Kate. She hadn't made Jergan vampire because the Rules forbade it. And she had watched her love grow old and die. So short a time! Half a century only she had had with him.

And since? Lovers, yes. But not love. Not love like she had with Jergan.

She shook herself and turned inside to the softly lighted library that was part of her suite of rooms on the second floor overlooking the Piazza della Signoria. The Palazzo Vecchio had not been modernized, but that did not mean it was not luxurious. Faded tapestries lined one wall. Paintings dark with age showed their creators' genius in the human quality of their subjects' eyes and the glow of the painted skin. Turkish carpets covered the wood floors. The room smelled of the lemon oil used to polish the heavy, dark furniture. The click of the pendulum of the great clock standing in the corner marked the passing of time.

It was better to have loved and lost than never to have loved at all. Wasn't that what they said? They obviously didn't know what regret could do to one.

She sat down at her great desk, covered in ledgers and papers. She'd tried to drown herself in work. She'd pushed the world forward into enlightenment and watched it step back into darkness over and over again. She'd had such hope during the Renaissance. She had started it all right here in Firenze, only to see the Church re-institute the Inquisition in recent years. She'd always taken defeat in stride. It was always temporary.

But she was tired. Work couldn't mask the regret anymore. She picked up her pen and opened the bottle of ink. It didn't matter. What else was there but work? What else could make her life worth having lived but to leave a legacy to the world through her work? She'd started the oldest bank in Europe to finance building projects. She'd supported artists like Buonarroti and scientists like da Vinci. Though he was an artist too, of course. She, a vampire, had fought superstition and fear at every turn. That meant something.

Didn't it?

Then why couldn't she shake her regret?

Because it would have meant so much more if she and Jergan had done it together. Perhaps she could have made faster progress if she'd had his strength, his wisdom, his stubbornness to guide her. She smiled. He *was* stubborn.

If only she could take back the instant when she'd decided *not* to make Jergan vampire! He'd been wounded. It would have been the perfect time to infect him with the parasite in her blood, her Companion, who gave her all her powers, made her more alive and whole than any human was. And exacted the cost of drinking human blood. If she'd infected him and he'd survived the infection with the immunity she could give him with continued infusions of her blood . . . they would have had forever together, like Gian and Kate.

If.

Of course, if he'd died from the infection, then she'd have had no time with him at all.

And it was against the Elders' Rules. If one made a vampire every time one fell in love . . .

She threw down the pen. So they all gave up even the remote chance of happiness?

She was glad Gian had broken the Rules and made Kate vampire. And he and Kate would go on breaking the Rules, because the Rules said their kind could only live one to a city. To be constantly apart, different from everyone around you, bred loneliness. It made it easier to think of humans as lesser beings, not worth using the senses, the powers of compulsion and translocation, and all the wisdom forever gave you, on their behalf. No wonder so many vampires went mad and careened out of control.

The Elders were wrong. Gian would be stronger for having one by his side who understood him, loved him.

She would have been stronger for having Jergan.

She sighed and rubbed her temples.

What use these self-recriminations? What was done was done. She found herself staring at the painting of Triton rising from the waves. Botticelli had painted Jergan as Triton, from Donnatella's description. It was remarkably correct for the artist never having seen the man. Green eyes. Dark hair. That air of confidence. The painting was all she had left of Jergan.

The clock chimed ten. She was promised to the opera tonight, and already she had missed the first act. It would do her good to get out of the house. She pushed herself out of her chair and went into her boudoir, pulling the bellpull for Maria. The rust silk, perhaps. It made her complexion of pale olive glow. And her garnets. She took out the carved puzzle box containing her jewels from the secret compartment in the wall beside her bed and sat down at her dressing table. The bas-relief on the box was carved by Buonarroti, showing Adam and Eve in the garden. It had been a special gift from the artist after she had commissioned the statue of Gian as David that now stood in the Piazza below. Buonarroti always had a better feel for the nude male figure than the female, for obvious reasons.

She pressed open the box as she had a thousand, thousand times before, twisting just the right way. The box popped open as it had a thousand, thousand times before.

But this time a tiny drawer in the edge popped open too.

Donnatella blinked. What was this?

She pulled open the tiny drawer. A folded piece of paper lay inside. A note? But who could have put it here? Had one of her maids learned to open the box? But even Donnatella didn't know how she had sprung open this special little drawer . . .

She set the box down and unfolded the paper. Holding it to the light, she recognized Buonarroti's spidery hand. Really, how could such a brilliant artist write so badly?

"Go to the catacombs under Il Duomo. Take the corridor at the south end. Behind the end wall is something that will make you happy, Donnatella, I promise." It was signed "Michelangelo" in just the scribble one could still see on the base of the *Pieta*.

Whatever could he mean?

And why leave a note for . . . for more than three hundred years inside a puzzle box? Why, she might never have opened the little secret drawer. He'd never shown her how when he demonstrated the box back in 1501.

Maria knocked discreetly and let herself in. She bustled about opening the wardrobe. "Which dress would you like tonight, your ladyship?"

"The rust silk," Donnatella murmured, still staring at the note. *Behind the end wall is something that will make you happy.* . . . Not likely. Only one thing would make her happy, and it was eighteen hundred years too late to get it. Buonarroti hadn't even known what it was.

Still . . .

She rose so suddenly the chair toppled over. "Never mind the rust silk, Maria. Get out the dress I wore when we reorganized the wine cellar."

The maid's eyes widened. "Your ladyship is never going to wear that dress to the opera!"

"No, I am not. And find my sturdiest half-boots." She rang the bell again. It sounded as though she'd need a tool for demolition. A blacksmith's sledgehammer perhaps. Bucarro, her faithful majordomo, would know where to procure one. A footman peeped into the room.

"Get Bucarro," she ordered. This was insane. But she was going to the catacombs.

Donnatella stood alone in her rooms, the sledgehammer and a lantern concealed under her cloak. She dared not meet any late-returning revelers in the streets. So she called on the Companion in her blood. Power surged up her veins, trembling like the threat of sheet lightning in the air around her. A red film dropped over her field of vision. *Companion, more!* she thought. And that being that was the other half of her answered with a surge. A whirling blackness rose up around her, obscuring all. She pictured the Baptistery of the Duomo in her mind. Not many living knew about the catacombs beneath it anymore. But she did. The familiar pain seared through her just as the blackness overwhelmed her. She gasped.

The blackness drained away, leaving only the dim interior of the octagonal Baptistery. She did not bother with the lamp. To humans the mosaics of the dome above her would be lost in shadows, but she saw well in darkness. The place felt like the crossroads of the world. The building itself was clearly Roman, almost like the Pantheon, but the sarcophagi on display were Egyptian, the frescoes Germanic in flavor. The floor, with its Islamic inlay, stretched ahead to the baptismal font. Her boots clicked across the marble. Behind the font was a staircase. She skipped down into the darkness without hesitation. Below, the walls of the vast chamber were of plain stone, the floor above supported with round columns and arches. Marble tombs of cardinals and saints lined the edges. It smelled of damp stone and, ever so faintly, decay.

But this was not her destination. A large rectangular stone carved in an ornate medieval style lay in the middle of the floor. It was perhaps four feet across and six long, six inches thick. Setting down her sledgehammer, she stooped and lifted. *Thank the gods for vampire strength.*

She dragged the stone aside so that it only partially covered the opening. A black maw revealed rough stone stairs leading down. The smell of human dust assailed her. Rats skittered somewhere. Now she took out her flint and striker, and lit the lamp. Stepping into the darkness, she turned and lifted the stone above her once again. It dropped into place with a resounding thud, concealing the stairs. Holding the lamp high in one hand, she started down. Light flickered on the stone walls on either side of the staircase. Catacombs at night were the stuff of nightmares for most of the world. But she was not afraid. She was the stuff of nightmares too.

The stairs finally opened out on a maze of corridors,

each lined with niches to hold the bodies of the early Christian dead. Most were filled only with piles of dust now or sometimes a clutter of bones. Occasionally a skeleton hand intact still clutched a crucifix, or some shred of rotted fabric fluttered in the air that circulated from somewhere.

Before she headed into the maze, she got her bearings. She was at the north end. She must go southeast. That would take her back under the nave of the main building of the Duomo. She took a breath and started out. It took her several wrong turnings to make her way to the other edge of the maze, but she was rewarded by finding a long, straight corridor that led away from the main catacombs.

This was it. She knew it. Whatever Michelangelo Buonarroti thought would make her happy was at the end of this corridor. This was foolish. There was no doubt about that. He couldn't know what would make her happy, and if he did, he couldn't give it to her. Traipsing around in catacombs on a treasure hunt that would no doubt prove disappointing if it wasn't useless altogether was a sign of just how desperate she had become.

But she *was* desperate. She didn't know how much more she could take of the gnawing regret that had overwhelmed her in the last years. So, foolish as this was, however likely to end in disappointment, she couldn't turn and walk away. She started down the corridor.

It ended abruptly in a solid wall of plaster. She set down her lantern, her stomach fluttering no matter how she tried to tell it there was no cause for excitement. Hefting the sledgehammer, she hauled it back and slammed it into the wall with all her strength. The plaster crumbled, revealing carefully cut stone that fitted exactly together. Dust choked the air. This would take some doing. Again and again she swung at the stones until she could pry at the ruined corners. Her fingertips were bloodied. No matter. They healed even as she glanced at them. But she was going about this the wrong way. Instead of trying to heave the stone out, she pushed on it. It toppled into the darkness beyond. She pushed on the neighboring stone, and then another until she was standing in front of a large opening, coughing.

She lifted her lantern and stepped through the cloud of dust into the darkness.

And gasped.

What stood towering above her was a maze of a different kind. Giant gears and levers interlocked in some crazy pattern that was positively beautiful. The metal gleamed golden, still shiny with oil. At points in the mechanism were set what looked like jewels the size of her fist, red and green and blue and clear white. Those couldn't be diamonds, could they?

She stood dumbfounded, staring. What was this thing? A machine of some kind. But what was it for?

It was long minutes before she could tear her eyes away from the beautiful intricacy and look around the room. There was no dust, except for the puff that had wafted in from her exertions with the wall. The place must have been tightly sealed to have kept out even dust. How long had it been sealed like this? Probably since the note was written. Besides the machine the room contained only a simple metal chair, golden like the machine, and a table to match in a corner, unobtrusive. And on the table was a leather-covered book.

Emotions churned through her. Disappointment lurked at the edges of her mind. A machine could not give her back happiness, no matter what it pumped or measured. And yet, there was something almost otherworldly about this most human of creations.

She pulled out the chair, sat, and drew the book toward her. The cover had mold on it. Even a sealed room couldn't keep out mold. Carefully she opened it. The first page startled her. "For Contessa Donnatella Margherita Luchella di Poliziano, from her friend Leonardo da Vinci. I dedicate to you my greatest work."

Shivers ran down her spine. Twice in one night she had received notes from friends dead three hundred years. They must have expected her to open them long ago, since they believed she would have been dead as long as they were. Whatever they wanted her to know or do with this machine, she was very late in accomplishing.

She turned another page.

> "*When you read this, for I know you will, you will have found my machine. Magnificent, isn't it? And only I could have designed it.*"

Leonardo, the dear, always had quite an ego. Still, the man was amazing. He was probably right about the machine.

> "*I could never find enough power to test it, and yet I know it works. Or at least in one possible reality, it works. But really it is all too complicated, even for one of my intellect. I must find a way to get you here. Something you will keep by you through all the years, something valuable. A piece of art? You love the arts. Buonarroti, that dwarf, will know something. But of course, whatever I do works, because you are here, reading this, and I know you are reading this because . . .*
>
> *Or it doesn't work, and everything is changed, and I never built the machine, or wrote this explanation, and I am not who I am, and you are not who you are. . . .*
>
> *Well, never mind that. I have no choice but to fulfill my part in this epic, or this tragedy, whatever it turns out to be.*
>
> *So here is all the truth I know.*
>
> *What you see before you is a time machine.*"

Gods, do you jest? she thought, looking up at the machine filling the space. It gleamed in flickering lamplight, towering above her. The jewels sparkled as the light caught them. The possibilities flickered through her in response. What if she could go back? Undo the decision that took Jergan away from her, have the promise of happiness she had seen in Gian's and Kate's eyes this evening. This might be the one thing that *could* make her happy.

Her eyes darted back to the journal. But he said he had never tested it. . . .

> *"You are asking yourself how it works. If you care to read the journal, you will know. But if you are in haste, know this, time is not a river but a vortex, and with enough power man can jump into another part of the swirl.*
>
> *Or perhaps man can't, but you can, my dear Contessa, you who are not human. Do you think I did not notice the hum of energy about you? I measured it without your knowledge, and was astounded. The people around you feel it as vitality, a force of personality, an incredible attraction to you, but I know better. Your power is real and it is incredibly strong. It keeps you young and heals you. The you of today thinks I did not know those things about you either. But the you who you will be told me. It is the knowledge of this source of power that inspires me to build a machine worthy of its use.*
>
> *My only regret is that I will not live to see it used. But you, who started me on this quest, told me you must not find it until after I am dead. It will wait for you, who live forever, to use when the time is right.*
>
> *So, my dear Contessa, pull the lever. Use your power, think of the moment you want to be as you jump into the maelstrom. That will influence the machine. You will end up in the moment you imagine.*
>
> *But be warned: The machine will go with you but it cannot stay long in another time. To return, you must use it again before it disappears. I do not know how long it can stay. I do not know what will happen if you make it back to*

the time you are in now, or what will happen if you don't. I
give you only the means to change your destiny, or perhaps
all of our destinies. Use it if you will.

Donnatella sat there, stunned. She couldn't think. A time machine? And one that confused even the grand intellect of the one who made it. She leafed through the pages of the journal. Complicated drawings, long blotted passages containing theoretical explanations of the vortex, records of his useless attempts to find enough energy to power the machine flipped past her. She stopped and read a few. She was doing it only to delay the moment of decision.

And why? She knew what she would do here. Once she had been too timid to break the Rules and grab for the prize of true love. Now she was willing to risk everything, and determined to have the courage to do it.

Her heart thudded in her chest as she rose from the table and stared up at the great machine. Did her Companion have enough power to run it? She could just test the theory—pull back if she got some initial result. But she wouldn't. What if timidity ruined everything as it had so long ago? What if she drained herself in an experiment, making the real effort impossible?

No, it was all or nothing.

She swallowed, her eyes filling for the second time tonight.

The handle of the machine was a brass lever about three feet long and topped by a glowing jewel. She reached out for it. The great diamond fit her palm exactly.

She pulled. There was a creak, but nothing else changed.

"Companion." She called her other half out loud in the wavering lamplight. A surge of power shot up her veins. A red film fell over her field of vision. Above her, the early morning light would be filtering into the nave of Il Duomo. The priests would be moving quietly about, tending the votive candles or kneeling in prayer. The machine was still.

"Companion! More!" The whirling black vortex of translocation began to swirl around her feet. She couldn't allow that. She pushed it down, but kept the power humming in the air. There was a great grinding sound and the largest of the metal cogs in front of her began to move. Still she called the power from the parasite in her blood that was part of her, and more than her. A white glow formed a halo around her. Every detail of the cavern stood out, sharp-edged. The movement of the gears cascaded down from the great, cogged wheel to the hundred smaller ones. The jewels sparkled. Gears whirled ever faster until the eye could not follow them.

"More!" she shrieked into the hum that cycled up the scale, and lifted her arms in supplication. Her Companion was at its limit. Was that enough?

Nothing more was happening. The machine was faint behind the white glow. Her body stretched itself taut with effort. What next? She couldn't hold this level of power forever.

Ahhhh. The destination.

She thought of the moment she had almost decided to make Jergan vampire. Emotion poured through her as she stared at his wounds. She could feel the machine move even faster. It was just a blur beyond the corona of her power. And then it slowed. She saw herself from somewhere outside herself standing, glowing, in front of the great machine, as it seemed to creak almost to a halt, it moved so slowly. Had she failed? The power still poured from her body into the room. A feeling of incredible *tristesse* came over her. She would not win through. Her only hope of happiness, or of giving Jergan his own forever, faded.

She thought of the moment he came into her life. . . .

Everything snapped back to motion and she felt herself being flung like a stone in a slingshot into more and more and more speed. The jewels lit up. They magnified the power into colored beams that crisscrossed, swinging in arcs across the stone ceiling. Pain surged into every fiber of her body.

Then, blackness.